LIBRARIES
WITHDRAWN FROM STOCK

'Slick and ...
Sun

'Set in a London of East End hipsters, Tinder
hook-ups, and internships, this tongue-in-cheek
tale explores murder in the age of social media'
Sunday Mirror

'A chilling debut'
Hello

'Puts complex women and their stories front and centre'
The Pool

'Angela Clarke brings dazzling wit and a sharp sense
of contemporary life to a fast-paced serial killer
novel with serious style'
**Jane Casey, author of the
Maeve Kerrigan series**

'In *Follow Me*, Clarke creates a completely
compelling world, and a complex heroine.
Freddie is refreshing and fascinating – a credible
addition to the crime canon and a great alternative
for anyone who has grown frustrated with the male
dominated world of the whodunnit. *Follow Me*
is literally gripping – the tension levels were forcing
me to clutch the book so hard that my hands hurt!'
Daisy Buchanan, *Grazia*

'A fascinating murder mystery and a dark, ironic
commentary on modern social media'
Paul Finch, author of *Stalkers*

'Clarke turns social media into a terrifyingly dark place. You won't look at your accounts the same way again. I was hooked and couldn't stop turning the pages. With a memorable and unique protagonist, Clarke explores the phenomenon of (social media) celebrity while tapping into your fears'
Rebecca Bradley, author of *Shallow Waters*

'Pacey, gripping, and so up-to-the-minute you better read it quick!'
Claire McGowan, author of *The Fall*

TRUST ME

Angela Clarke is a bestselling author, playwright, columnist and professional speaker. The second instalment in her Social Media Murder Series, *Watch Me*, shot straight to number 15 in the UK Paperback Chart in January 2017. Her debut crime thriller *Follow Me* was named **Amazon's Rising Star Debut** of the Month January 2016, long listed for the **Crime Writer's Association Dagger in the Library 2016,** and short listed for the **Good Reader Page Turner Award 2016.** *Follow Me* has now been optioned by a TV production company. Angela's humorous memoir *Confessions of a Fashionista* is an Amazon Fashion Chart bestseller.

Angela has given talks, hosted events, and masterclasses for many, including **NoirwichCrime Writing Festival, Camp Bestival, Panic!** (in partnership with **Create,** the **Barbican, Goldsmiths University** and *The Guardian*), **Meet a Mentor** (in partnership wih the **Royal Society of Arts**), **Northwich Lit Fest, St Albans Lit Fest, BeaconLit,** and the **London College of Fashion.** She also hosted the current affairs radio show Outspoken on **Radio Verulam** in 2015, and has appeared regularly as a panel guest on **BBC 3 Counties, BBC Radio 4,** and the **BBC World service,** among others.

In 2015 Angela was awarded the **Young Stationer's Prize** for achievement and promise in writing and publishing. Angela, a sufferer of the debilitating chronic condition Ehlers Danlos III, is passionate about bringing marginalised voices into the industry. She is a Fellow of the **Royal Society of Arts**, and lives with her husband and too many books.

Also by Angela Clarke

Follow Me
Watch Me

ANGELA CLARKE

Trust Me

The Social Media Murders

This novel is entirely a work of fiction.
The names, characters and incidents portrayed in it are the work of
the author's imagination. Any resemblance to actual persons,
living or dead, events or localities is entirely coincidental.

AVON

A division of HarperCollins*Publishers*
1 London Bridge Street,
London SE1 9GF

www.harpercollins.co.uk

A Paperback Original 2017

1

Copyright © Angela Clarke 2017

Angela Clarke asserts the moral right to be identified as the author of this work

A catalogue record for this book is available from the British Library

ISBN-13: 978-0-00-817464-4

Typeset in Minion by Palimpsest Book Production Ltd, Falkirk, Stirlingshire
Printed and bound in Great Britain by Clays Ltd, St Ives plc

All rights reserved. No part of this publication may be
reproduced, stored in a retrieval system, or transmitted,
in any form or by any means, electronic, mechanical,
photocopying, recording or otherwise, without the prior
permission of the publishers.

FSC™ is a non-profit international organisation established to promote
the responsible management of the world's forests. Products carrying the
FSC label are independently certified to assure consumers that they come
from forests that are managed to meet the social, economic and ecological
needs of present and future generations, and other controlled sources.

Find out more about HarperCollins and the environment at
www.harpercollins.co.uk/green

For Claire McGowan, with thanks.

(Will people think we're at it now,
like Brontë and Thackeray?)

Only those who will risk going too far can possibly find out how far one can go.

T. S. Eliot

Amber

Hurriedly she opened her wardrobe, pulling her coat from the hanger and shoving it into her bag. She had minutes at most. Panic burnt through her body. Every fibre felt like it had been stripped raw. Tears welled up and over her eyelids, splashing onto the carpet. She tried not to snivel. There was still a chance to get away. She made it to the hallway before she remembered the photo. Her heart squeezed. She couldn't live without it. Not now. Running back into her bedroom, she reached for the frame on her bedside table.

A noise sounded behind her. A thud, and then the front door opening. She froze. Held her breath. Her hand outstretched. Shaking. Her heart hammering in her ears.

Too late.

New message:

Wanna go to a party?
Going to be bangin.
Trust me.

Kate

The table is shaking. Kate realises she's gripping it. *She* is shaking. The video on the computer screen is jerky. Handheld. Shot from a mobile. *Live*. It's a room: square and shabby. A single bulb hanging from the ceiling. Beer bottles and empty cans brimming over with cigarette ends colonise the space. She can't see any windows. But there's a closed door in the background. Is it locked? Two crude drawings – an animal and a circle – have been spray-painted in black onto the back wall. A stripped, stained duvet has been made into a hasty bed. Her brain can't – *won't* – process what she's seeing. It's like something blunt-edged is smashing into her, trying to gouge out the fear that's been buried under decades of safety, food, shelter and scatter cushions. But it's there. It's coming. An innate force within her. She recognises danger. Fight or flight. She says the words over and over in her head, until she realises it's a command: fight

3

or flight! Kate doesn't move. She doesn't make a sound. She is watching it happen.

A voice on the video shouts: 'Like up the post! Get this to one thousand likes!'

He sounds like one of the boys from her class. Young. Excitable. A child.

The girl on the screen turns to look at the camera. Her eyes focus in recognition. They look past the lens. Out. Realising. Pleading. They're looking straight at Kate. Fight or flight? The girl twists, tries to push herself up on her elbows. The man forces her down. His slim muscular back is turned toward the camera. Kate can't see his face.

'No!' The girl manages.

She said no.

The girl's speech is slurred. 'You're hurting me. *Please*. No.'

Kate reaches toward her. Her fingers futilely prod the screen. Push her laptop. She is at home. In her house. Watching this. Where is this being filmed? Somebody must hear the girl's shouts? Someone must stop this.

Comments from viewers float up over the feed:

They're so young lmao
She a slut!!
She said no. This is rape.

This is rape.

'Just one more!' the man shouts. Man? His skin is smooth, hairless, young. The girl jerks back. Claws at his face. Kicks her legs.

She said no.

He slaps the girl hard. The noise a loud crack. She's flung sideways. There's a scream. Is it the girl? Is it the man? Is it Kate? The girl scrabbles, swings up, punches him in the face. A fighter. She's a fighter.

The camera judders. Lurches up. 'Hey?' calls the voice from behind. Unsure. Young, she's convinced now.

'Skank!' The man roars, grabbing a bottle. A glass bottle. He smashes it down at the girl. Her face. Her hands. Frenzied. Slashing. There's screaming. Blood. The camera convulses. The boy's voice grows frantic. She can't make out what he's saying.

The man swipes toward the camera. 'Turn that off!' She sees his blood-splattered face. And the video feed goes dead.

Kate pushes away from her dining table, away from the computer. She stumbles, grabs the doorframe. Vomits. Liquid smacks the vinyl kitchen floor. Again. Again. She's shaking. Cold. Bile. Retching. Then she drags herself, shuddering, teeth chattering, to her phone. Pulls it down to her. Dials 999.

'Hello, emergency service operator, which service do you require? Fire, police or ambulance?' It's a woman; she sounds calm.

Kate's voice bubbles from her throat, as if someone is speaking through her. She forces the words out. 'Police. You've got to get to her. She said no. Someone needs to get there. You've got to…'

'Where are you calling from, ma'am? What is the nature of your emergency?'

Kate blinks as if her own eyelids are heavy, weighted with blood.

'I've just seen a young woman raped – stabbed. There's a lot of blood. Please: you've got to help her!'

Freddie

Oh my God. She shook her head. No way was she gonna move in with him. She was only twenty-four. Was he crazy? She had her whole life ahead of her.

'I think you've got the wrong idea.' Freddie swung her legs over the side of the bed.

'What do you mean?' he said.

She'd let him get too comfortable. She'd got too comfortable. 'This – us, like it's fun and stuff, but no.' She thought of her parents' wedding photo: her mum twenty-four years old in her lacy white dress. Each time her dad smashed the frame during a drunken rage, her mum just replaced it without mentioning it.

'No?' He sat up, the duvet falling off his naked body. 'What have the last few months been then? You've stayed the last twelve nights and you're saying this is just – what? A fling?' His eyes were wide. Stung.

Shit. She'd let her guard down. She didn't want to be a jerk. 'You know I've been sofa-surfing for months.' She grabbed yesterday's knickers from the floor, turned them inside out. 'This has just been temporary, while I find new digs.'

'You've been fucking me because it's convenient?'

It wasn't like it was all one-sided. 'You've had perks too.' He was thinking with his dick.

'Thanks a fucking lot, Freddie!' His cheeks burned red.

Anger she could deal with. She pulled her bag open. 'Where's all my stuff?'

'I gave you a drawer.' He pointed at the Ikea set under the telly and Xbox. His bottom lip shook.

'You gave me a drawer?' *No one has ever made space for you before, Freddie. That must mean something.*

'Don't you like staying here?' He reached to brush back the frizzy curtain of hair that had fallen over her face.

Yes. She couldn't breathe. She needed to get out of there. 'It's not that.'

'You don't like me then?' He let his hand fall back against the blue duvet.

'Course I like you.' She dived at the drawer. Quicker would be better. Pulled it open, started scooping her stuff into her bag.

'Then why don't you stay?' He was up now, moving toward her. His arms wrapped round her as he kissed along her naked shoulder, her neck. She felt her body give under his touch, as one hand ran over her shoulder, circled her nipple. The air in the room was hot, foetid. August was gradually turning the heat up on London. Smothering them. She would hurt him. Hurt them both. *Be strong, Freddie.*

7

'I'm sorry,' she said, pushing him away. 'I can't do this.'

His arms dropped. He stepped backwards. She didn't look. *This is for the best.*

'But…' His voice wavered. 'I think I'm falling for you.'

She froze.

'I love you, Freddie,' he said.

Freddie swept the last of her things into her bag and ran. She clattered out of the flat, pausing at the foot of the communal staircase to pull on her vest and shorts. Her heart was screaming at her to go back. *Be strong.* She heard him stumbling for his jeans, his keys, calling after her. She bolted out into the street; the sunlight wrapped itself around her in a stifling embrace. Happy bloody Monday.

Nasreen

'Thanks to Freddie, we've got a new lead,' DI Chips, too old-school to bother with new-fangled office politics, rested two meaty hands on Freddie's shoulders and gave her a grand-fatherly squeeze of pride. Nasreen doubted he'd ever been this fond of an Intelligence Analyst before. In fact, she doubted he'd ever spoken to one before.

Freddie had been recruited to the Gremlin cyber-crime team after consulting on some high-profile cases; she was internet savvy, analytical, unorthodox, outspoken, and Nasreen's old school friend. And, despite Nasreen's stellar fast-track performance at Hendon College, and her further three years of experience in the Met, it was Freddie who looked at home here. Chips was beaming at her. 'Tell us what you've got, lass?'

Freddie hiked her ripped denim shorts up as she stood.

'You could've dressed for the occasion,' DI Saunders straightened his own stiff white shirt cuffs. Not a hair out of place.

'I have,' Freddie replied. 'It's too bloody hot for anything else.'

Nasreen envied Freddie's carefree attitude, even if she didn't approve of it. The newspaper front pages blazed with the incoming heatwave, and she'd had to dry the sweat patches on her own suit under the hand drier this morning.

'I've been looking at intelligence reports of activity we know is linked to the Spice Road website.' Freddie handed round a series of reports filed by arresting officers across the force. The Spice Road was an Amazon-style website on the dark net where you could order anything at the click of a button. They could see the drugs, weapons, and sometimes people being sold and bought on the site, but couldn't see who they were coming from or going to. 'Each of those observed, questioned or charged for delivery of these drugs in these cases belong to the THM,' Freddie said.

'Tower Hamlets Massive, the Poplar gang?' DC Green's freckled skin was flushed. Despite being the newest member of the team, she'd clocked how big this was.

'We didn't know that the THM gang were linked to Spice Road.' Freddie sounded excited. Perhaps she'd been working on this when she'd blown Green and her partner's barbecue off at the weekend? Nasreen had been left talking to their gawky accountant neighbour. She had the terrible feeling they'd hoped she would see him again.

'The highest ranking THM member we've come across is a guy called Paul Robertson.' Saunders put a photo of a white

10

guy, shaven-headed and sunken-eyed, on the wall. 'Robertson served time for the manslaughter of Rhys Trap, a key member from rival gang the Dogberry Boys. An act we think was a test to prove his loyalty to those who run THM – the brothers Rodriguez.'

Nasreen knew all about the Rodriguez family. 'The brothers haven't been seen in public for over five years.'

'We suspect they're running the operation from Spain,' Chips said.

'Gotta love the Internet,' Freddie said. 'You can work from anywhere.'

'We had a trace on Robertson until a year ago when he vanished,' Chips said.

'You think he's in Spain too?' Nasreen asked.

'No sightings and nothing flagged on any of the borders.' Saunders still wasn't looking directly at her. She'd been desk-bound for the last six months, and could guess she was about to get the worst job. Again.

Saunders took another sip from his morning protein shake. 'Robertson is wanted in connection with several drug-dealing cases and an armed robbery in Bracknell. The drugs squad had a trail on him when he disappeared.'

'Someone had a bad day in the office,' said Chips. They all laughed.

The door opened and DCI Burgone entered. Nasreen's laughter turned into a cough. She stared at the ground, though she wanted nothing more than to look into his blue eyes. Freddie, Chips and Green were still laughing, but she could feel Saunders watching her.

'Sorry I'm late.' Burgone's classic Queen's English tone

instantly restored order. As he was the governing officer, Freddie would have reported her discovery to Burgone before she spoke to Saunders. 'Carry on, Pete.' Burgone took the nearest chair, the one next to her. His amber scent beckoned her closer.

Don't look. Act natural. Closing her eyes, Nasreen was back to that night: her hands in his thick dark hair, his hand cupping her chin, their lips meeting. She snapped her eyes open. It had been six months since she'd had a one-night stand with her boss. Six months since the rest of the team found out. Six months since she'd been lucky to hang on to her job.

Saunders cleared his throat. 'Paul Robertson is our best shot of getting to the Rodriguez brothers, and ultimately it's them who are running the Spice Road.' He paused to pull another photo from his file. 'Paul Robertson has a daughter, Amber Robertson, who disappeared at the same time as her father.' A chill passed over Nasreen. Saunders added the photo of a young, dark-haired girl to the board. 'She was fifteen when they went to ground.' Amber smiled up from under a fashionable floppy hat, her voluptuous curves played for maximum impact in a cropped khaki T-shirt and tight black jeans. Cases involving teen girls always got under Nasreen's skin, and she felt the familiar tightness form in her stomach.

'Pretty lass,' Chips said.

'We think she's the weakest link in the chain. Find her and we find her dad. Find him and we find the Rodriguez brothers.' Saunders tapped the board. 'Chips and Green are tied up finishing off Operation Kestrel right now, so I want you on this one, Cudmore.'

His words startled her. 'Me?' She leant forward, too eager,

12

caught the glass of water on the table in front of her. Her hand shot out to steady it. She felt the blush rising up her cheeks. Burgone was right *there*.

'Unless you've got better things to be doing with your time, Sergeant?' Saunders said.

'No, sir. Thank you, sir.' She prayed Burgone was looking at the board.

Green gave her a smile – a congrats for being back in the game.

'Get Freddie to help you with whatever she can get on Amber. I want her found.' Saunders was gathering his papers together.

'Wait, so there's a missing fifteen-year-old girl – surely someone's looking for her already?' Freddie cut over the noise of scraping chairs.

'She's been on the Missing Persons list for a year, but they're inundated.' Saunders said. 'They've done the normal checks, but until now she wasn't high priority.'

Freddie blew air through her teeth. 'Not high priority? But now we want to bang up her dad we're interested?'

'Now *I'm* interested,' Saunders said.

'I don't know how you sleep at night.' Freddie stared at him.

'Like a baby, ta.' He was always pleased to get a response.

Nasreen knew how busy Missing Persons were, and with the connections Paul Robertson had, it'd be all too easy for him and his daughter vanish. 'What about the girl's mother?'

'Died when she was three,' Saunders said. 'RTA.'

'Daughter of a dead mum and a drug-dealing dad, some kids get all the luck, don't they?' Freddie grimaced.

13

'Freddie, can I have a word – in my office?' Burgone had paused at the door.

Nasreen couldn't help but stare as Freddie left the room with him. What was that about?

Nasreen had to stop this fixation with Burgone. Superintendent Prue Lewis's disciplinary words played over in her mind: '*I forbid my officers to have relationships with their colleagues because it ruins their careers. Especially the women. People will always assume you got to where you are because of who you slept with, Nasreen. You will have to work twice as hard to prove them wrong now.*' Nasreen couldn't let her own mistakes stand in the way of doing the job she loved. She had to believe she was still of use. The tension in her stomach solidified into a hard, heavy millstone. The pretty fifteen-year-old Amber Robertson was Nasreen's shot at redemption, if she could find her.

Freddie

Fifteen years old and on the run. It'd make a good film, but it was bleak in real life. Freddie wanted to look into Amber Robertson more; no one else seemed that bothered about the missing girl. She still didn't get that about police: how could they just compartmentalise all this shit? She opened Facebook, Instagram and Snapchat on her phone. Would a fifteen-year-old really give those up as well as everything else? She herself wouldn't, and she had nearly ten years on her.

'I've just come from a meeting with the Superintendent,' Burgone was saying.

She tapped in Amber Robertson and pressed *search*. A number of profile squares appeared on Facebook. One looked familiar: same girl, same hat. Freddie clicked.

Burgone was still talking and she'd tuned out: 'And so you

can see my problem,' he finished. His face had a look of concern on it.

Her gut twisted. 'Sorry, what did you say?'

He sighed. 'I feared you might find it difficult to hear.' His sharp navy-suited arms rested authoritatively on the table. His face solemn. 'We're having to make cutbacks. I'm sorry, Freddie, but I no longer have the budget for a full time Intelligence Analyst.'

What? 'Is this a wind-up?' Burgone had offered her this role when she was broke, and she'd been surprised to discover she loved it. Putting together the pieces of the puzzle. Making a difference. She'd found the link between the Spice Road website and the Tower Hamlets Massive. She could find Amber Robertson. And now he was going to take it away from her? *Hell, no.* 'You approached *me*.'

'And you've done a brilliant job,' he said.

'Do you know how late I stayed working on that Paul Robertson lead?' She was up out of her chair now. Throwing an accusatory finger at him. Burgone's eyebrows had reacted, but he'd kept the rest of him admirably still.

'I appreciate you're upset, Freddie.'

She thought of his privilege, his entitlement. What she'd done trying to scrape together enough for a bloody rental deposit. The fallout to the L word this morning. Had that been a mistake? Now was not the time to think about that. Burgone had probably never worried about money in his life. 'I don't think you do, mate.'

'I will always be grateful for what you did for me and my family.' Burgone looked uncomfortable whenever he mentioned how they first met: a tense investigation involving his sister.

'I did what anyone would have done,' she said, cutting him off. Did he really think she would try and hold it over him? 'I don't know how you were raised, but I was brought up to help people when they're in trouble.' She thought of the embarrassment in her mum's eyes when she'd found out that her dad had pinched the money she'd been scraping together for Freddie. Gone in an optic. Literally pissed against a wall. The anger fizzled out. Burgone wasn't the enemy.

'I haven't finished yet, Freddie. I've given it a lot of thought, and there is a way I can make it work with the budget. But it will require effort on your behalf.'

She slumped back into the chair. 'I can't work any more hours.' The booze had gone months ago: too expensive, too risky. She often wondered what her dad would have been like if he'd been broke as a lad. If rent was as high as it was now. Would he have become an alcoholic sooner, or never succumbed in the first place? 'Go on then, spill?'

'I can afford to keep you on part-time as an Intelligence Analyst. But I also have funding for another different part-time role.'

'That makes no sense,' she said.

'It's down to how funding is allocated.'

'Bloody government, screwing everything up as usual,' she said.

Burgone had shifted his attention to a pile of papers on his desk, looking for the right form. 'I have budget for a Civilian Investigator. They're designed to relieve pressure on active officers, thus improving police effectiveness: it's seen as a saving in the overall budget.'

'What does it involve?' Investigator sounded promising.

She missed being out looking into leads. Not that she should ever have been meeting the public, she thought, smiling to herself, but there'd been special circumstances before.

'Your role would include interviewing victims of burglary, assault and car crime. The training programme is three weeks long, and will include briefings on interrogation techniques, how to structure an interview, and a number of aspects of the law that are relevant.' Burgone said. 'Some of it you'll know from your analytical training, and, er, previous experience.' He handed over a printed worksheet. 'And if I assign you to Detective Sergeant Cudmore for management, we may handle some of the training in-house.'

'I could go out and interview suspects?' she said.

'Perhaps not that.' He smiled. 'But certainly supporting statements from witnesses and other interesting parties. If you complete the training and probationary period, as before.'

'Will I get a business card?' She'd always wanted one of them. Was jealous of Nas's when she'd handed them over to people. It made her official. Real. She'd send one to her mum.

'Well, yes. I guess it will be useful for you to have something with your contact details on to leave with interviewees,' Burgone said.

'Okay,' Freddie said. 'I'll do it.'

'There is one more thing: this is a slightly sensitive issue,' he said.

Ah: the catch. Here it came.

'This is a fairly new scheme within the force, and not everyone is a fan. Some officers have registered concerns over the limited training and accountability of civilian investigators – this won't win you any friends, Freddie.'

She shrugged. 'No worries. I haven't got any anyway.'

He smiled. 'Then I'll make sure DS Cudmore has the relevant training criteria to cover. Hopefully you can run it alongside this Amber Robertson case. And we've had a bit of luck: another recruit has had to drop out of an existing training course, so we can get you over there today and get you started.'

'Cool.' She'd come back to the office after, to start work on finding Amber: that'd give the phone company time to get the records over.

'And it should be quite fun for you,' Burgone was saying.

Oh, yeah, I love sitting in a room being lectured to.

'It's being held at the Jubilee Station,' he said.

'What?' Her mouth fell open.

He mistook her dismay as delight. 'I know you worked with the officers there on your first case.'

Yeah, and I'd rather forget it. He handed her another printout: a list of the training details, the location, times and dates. She scanned the page for familiar names: *balls.*

'This'll be a great chance to catch up with them all. DCI Moast is leading the training – he said he couldn't wait to see you again,' Burgone said with a smile.

I bet he did. Spending time in an enclosed space with meathead Moast was not high on her to-do list. *Crap.* Now she'd have to face the music over this morning's row too. She'd wanted things to cool off for a few days. Kip at a mate's. Burgone looked as pleased as if he'd just paid off her student loan. Christ knows how many strings he'd pulled to get her onto this course so quickly. It wasn't his fault he had no idea what he'd just done. She managed a weak smile. 'Cheers.'

19

'This is a great opportunity, Freddie,' Burgone said. 'And I know you'll really make the most of it.'

She could already see the sarcastic grin on Moast's Lego head.

Standing in the hallway, the Facebook account she'd opened earlier was still visible on her phone. There were photos of Amber grinning at the camera. This was it. Her account. Freddie watched video clips of her and her friends singing on the back of a bus, Amber's eyes sparkling with mischief. There was a photo of Paul Robertson from behind, Amber holding an egg up so it was the same size as his bald head. The caption read: *When your breakfast looks like your dad! Cracking!* Freddie laughed. The sound snagged on her heart as she reached the last post. July 12 last year. The day before Amber and her father disappeared. The girl's final words.

So many special people in my life. So sorry for any hurt I cause. Love you all. Forever. xxxx

Underneath tens of Amber's friends had posted comments. Sad emojis. Broken heart photos. They started up a few weeks after the final post. As if enough time had passed that they could no longer hope for the best. Freddie scanned them quickly:

Come home soon!!!
Miss you foreva xxx
Thinking of you always xoxo

And a shiver passed over her, as she realised more than one person had posted the same message:

RIP Amber xxx

Why would they think Amber Robertson was dead?

A

He can feel the weight of her, her arms thin in his hands, her shoulders rolling, heavy. How can someone so fragile be so heavy? He had to hide her. This is his fault. He panicked. No one can know. He needs time to think. To fix this. He can still hear her screaming. He covers his ears. His heart is battering against his chest, like a dog on a chain going mental. Whoooof. Whoooof. Whoooof. Punching to get out. He feels like he's turned inside out, that everything is backwards and he can't quite grab hold of it. His hands are wet, slick. It's her. She's all over him. Blood. There is so much blood. This was supposed to be a laugh. Hot. Make him popular. This can't be happening. It's in his mouth. He can taste her. He gags. There's a hair wrapped round his fingers. A long dark hair, stuck like when one catches you in a swimming pool. Cold and dark like pondweed. No, it's cotton: a thread tying her to him. The dog in his chest is thrashing. Tearing him apart with its teeth from the inside. What has he done?

Kate

Kate hadn't been able to sit still since she'd seen the video. Her laptop, black in power-save mode, was still at its abandoned angle on her dining table. Fifty-six years old, and she couldn't bring herself to get any closer to the screen. Instead she'd focused on clearing up the mess on the kitchen floor. As she'd wiped up the sick and bile, she tried not to think of the girl's pleading eyes. She forced herself to take another gulp of sugared tea. She'd changed, and put her soiled clothes in the washing machine.

She could still smell the acid of vomit, and leant over the sink to open the kitchen window. But the familiar square of garden, in which she grew sweet peas and strawberries, twisted and turned away from her. The electric streetlight played nasty tricks with the rows of houses that stretched away over Hackney. Somewhere out there was the girl. Terrified. Hurt.

What if the boys knew she'd been watching? What if they'd made a note of her account? Could they find her? A shadow licked at the edge of her garden and she jumped. London, with its exotic blends, its languages, its music and food and dance, that dynamic that made it special, that had made it her home all her life, felt hostile. She was overlooked. An easy target. She let go of the window handle as if it had burned her. Instead she pulled the slim chain to unfurl the kitchen blind, small flecks of dust floating down onto her as she obliterated the city skyline she'd always loved.

She ran up the white-painted stairs to her bedroom, pulled the curtains up there too and fetched her perfume from the bathroom. She sprayed the scent in the kitchen, the tangerine and blackcurrant smell settling uneasily over the sour stench of sick. She would feel better when she knew they'd found the girl. Got her to hospital.

The doorbell buzzed and she jumped. It would be the police. It was a Friday night, presumably they were busy, it'd been just over an hour since she'd called 999. She slid the spyhole aside; the sight of a man made her heart rate spike. *You can see the uniform, silly woman, you know it's the police.* Still, she put the chain across before opening the door.

'Mrs Katherine Adiyiah? I'm PC Jones.' The man drew the sounds of her surname out, unsure where the vowels sat. He held up his ID. He was young, with close-cropped dark hair, and shadows under his pale eyes. She wondered how long he'd been on duty.

'Hang on,' she said, releasing the chain. 'Sorry about that.'

'Good to see people being security conscious. Better to be safe than sorry, Mrs Adiyiah,' PC Jones said.

It was an absurdly normal exchange. Words you might say about putting an extra hour on the meter for the car.

'It's Miss actually. But call me Kate. Please, come in?' She had thought there might be two of them, but there was no one else outside. The street was empty, apart from a drained vodka bottle discarded three doors down. Laughter and voices carried over from the road behind: people walking home, or on to the next venue. The gentle pulse of bass mingled with the hum of night buses, taxis, cars and takeaway delivery drivers from the surrounding roads. A man appeared round the corner, his face nothing but a dark shadow under his hood. She shut the door quickly.

PC Jones was standing in the living room, looking at the bookshelves that lined the walls. His eyes snagged on the well-loved copies that were turned out to face the room: *The Autobiography of Miss Jane Pittman*, Ngozi Adichie's *Half of a Yellow Sun*, *A Testament of Hope* by Martin Luther King. There was something about his manner that felt oddly invasive.

'Please, sit down?' She indicated the wingback that was at one end of the dining table. Her home was small: this one room served as lounge, dining room and study, leading straight into the open-plan kitchen. A two-up, two-down. Plenty big enough for her.

He hitched up his trousers to sit on the creaking chair. Kate was on good terms with the PC who worked with her at school, and would have liked to see his familiar face. Having a strange man in her home was only compounding the sense of violation she'd felt watching the video. But that wasn't PC Jones's fault. She'd witnessed a horrific crime: she had a duty to report it. She had a duty to that poor girl. He didn't look eager to get started. She forced a smile onto her face. 'Can I get you some tea, or a coffee?'

'Tea would be great, ta,' he said. 'Milk, one sugar. Any biscuits?' He rested his palms on his spread knees, like a spoilt emperor, she thought, eager and greedy.

She nodded. It was nearly 3am. She was discombobulated by it all. She busied herself with pulling the tea things down from the cupboard. She put out a cup for herself too, adding two sugars. She was still jittery. It was the shock.

'You told the call handler you believed you'd seen an assualt?' PC Jones had followed her into the kitchen unnoticed. Her body jolted in reaction. The teabag box buckled in her hand. 'Sorry, I didn't mean to make you jump,' he said, smiling.

She tried to smile back. Everything felt wrong.

She could see his distorted funhouse mirror reflection in the chrome kettle, looking at her. 'Was it out the front of the house, or from upstairs, Miss Adiyiah?'

'They didn't tell you?' The spoon was limp in her hand. 'It was online. I saw it happen online.'

'Online?' His mouth turned down at the sides and she was struck by how much he resembled a fish. 'How do you mean?'

'I was on Periscope. I was watching a live stream video, of two boys and a girl. Well, I think it was two boys, one of them was holding the camera. There could have been more, I suppose, behind the camera.' The thought horrified her. Who could sit by and watch that without intervening? She'd been unable to help. She wouldn't wish that paralysing sensation of helplessness on anyone. Though if they had deliberately chosen not to act… that was worse.

27

'Two boys and a girl?' PC Jones had produced a notebook from his back pocket.

'Yes,' she said. 'One of the boys was...' The word swelled and lodged in her throat. She coughed. 'He raped her. And when she tried to stop him he attacked her. With a bottle.'

'And you saw this online?' PC Jones said.

'Yes,' she nodded. Saying the words out loud hadn't lessened their power, but made the whole thing feel more vivid. As if she were watching it happen again. Here. In this room.

'And where was this video shot?'

'I don't know. I just clicked on a feed for London. So it must be somewhere in the city. Someone must have heard something: there was a lot of...' She wanted to say screaming, but couldn't. 'Noise.'

'I see. And what were the names of these boys and the girl?' PC Jones said.

'I don't know,' she said.

'You don't know?' His eyebrow raised on one side, and she saw the doubt in his eyes.

'I can tell you the name of the account. Here, I wrote it down.' She passed him the torn rectangle of note paper. Metronome02. It was burned on her memory, like those heart symbols floating up the screen. People had liked it; that's what she couldn't understand. Had they not understood? The policeman took the paper, his fish head nodding. She glanced at the laptop. *You must do this. You must help the girl.* 'I can show you the video.'

She walked past him before her nerve dropped. When she touched the mouse, the screen seemed to crack. The page or her eyes flickered, she couldn't tell which. The screen was no

28

longer linked to the feed; instead there was an error page: *This user no longer exists.*

'It's gone! They've deleted it.' She clicked *refresh*. The same page appeared. 'Oh God! Of course: because it's evidence.' She couldn't stem the relief at not having to watch it again, or hear it. She thought of the screams. The panicked sound of the boy behind the camera. The gurgling.

'So.' PC Jones drew out the syllables of the word, twisting it in his fish mouth. 'The video has vanished?'

'You can see for yourself.' She pointed at the screen. 'They've deleted it.'

'Right,' he looked around the room, his eyes resting on Angela Davis's *Are Prisons Obsolete?* If it had been one of her pupils she would have marched across the room and turned the book around. Made them concentrate. But as she watched him blow air out in a dramatic sigh, she felt more than just anger at his ill manners, she felt unease. 'So you're saying that you saw a video…'

'A live stream,' she corrected.

'Right,' he said. '*A live stream* during which you believe you saw a sexual assault and a stabbing take place, but you don't know where this took place, or who these people were?'

'I don't *believe* I saw it, I know I saw it,' she said.

PC Jones grimaced. 'Are you sure you couldn't have misunderstood what you saw, Mrs Adiyiah?'

'Yes.' Heat rose in her cheeks.

'Maybe it was a film, like a Hollywood one or something? They're very realistic nowadays,' he said, glancing at the vintage poster she had framed on her wall.

He was dismissing her. As if she were, what? A confused

old woman? 'I know the difference between a film and real life, thank you.'

He sniffed, taking in the perfume, and the vague sour stench that lingered in the flat. 'Can I ask if you've been out at all tonight, Mrs Adiyiah?'

'I don't see how that's relevant.' She couldn't believe he had the cheek to interrogate her.

'Have you consumed any alcoholic beverages this evening?' He looked at the glass of Shiraz next to the computer, where she'd left it.

'What does that have to do with it?' Shame bubbled inside her. How dare he judge her?

'It's late,' said PC Jones. 'Our minds can play tricks on us, especially if we've had a drink or two.' He sniffed again.

Did he think she'd drunk so much she'd been sick? 'You think I'm making this up?'

'I'm not saying that, Mrs Adiyiah.' He held his hands out to placate her. 'I'm sure you saw a very distressing video, and I'm sure you think it was real.'

'It was real.' This was preposterous. 'There was a girl. And she was attacked by the man in the video.'

'I thought you said it was a boy?' PC Jones said.

'A young man, seventeen, maybe eighteen. Not much more than a boy,' she said.

'*Right.*' PC Jones nodded.

'You should be writing this down,' she said.

'I have everything I need, Mrs Adiyiah.' He was sliding the pad into his pocket. Putting the pen away.

'You don't believe me?' The injustice of it hung in her words. He was dismissing her.

30

'I believe you've seen something that's upset you. And I believe that you think it's real. But we've had no reports of anything that would tie in with what you're claiming you saw.' He gave her a simpering, sympathetic smile. 'I suggest you have a nice cup of tea and a good night's sleep, Kate. And I'm sure you'll feel better after that.'

'I'm a teacher,' she said. As if it might make him listen, might make her real. 'And I don't appreciate your tone.'

'Very nice,' said PC Jones, heading toward the door. He was leaving. Ignoring her. She thought of the girl's eyes, staring out at her, pleading. 'You have to help her!' She thought of the blood dripping onto the duvet. 'She might not have much time.'

He gave her another placating, watery smile. 'I'll be sure to mention it in my report. Good night, Mrs Adiyiah.'

She could already guess what that report would say. She stood in shock as he closed the door behind him. He didn't believe her. A rip had appeared in the world, plunging her London into that of the poor girl's in the film. She'd ring the hospitals. Come forward as a witness. But what if she was still lying there? In that room? Not able to get help? *Think, woman, think.* Kate picked up her wine glass and downed the remains in one go. There was one more thing she could try, but it wouldn't be easy. She turned the computer towards her and started to type.

A

The water was running over his face, his clothes. He hadn't turned
the bathroom light on. Hadn't wanted anyone to wake up. But
it was never dark here. Street lamps and tower lights shone
through the bathroom window. Could they see him? He felt like
he was glowing. He crouched down, leant against the tiles. He
hugged his knees tightly. The water was red. A Lynx shower gel
bottle tumbled from the side and clattered against the floor of
the shower. He held his breath. *Please don't wake up.*

Her hair had wrapped round his arms when he'd pushed
her up. Clung to him, wanting him to stay. *Oh God.* He didn't
want to think about this. He squashed his palms against his
head. Wanted to push it all out. One minute they were
partying, and then she'd thrown the punch. If only she hadn't
done that. If only she'd just stayed quiet. Her arms had felt
small. Tiny, like his younger brothers'. He could close his whole

hand round her wrist. Easily snapped. The clothes had thrown him. The skirt had buttons and zips and everything was backwards. Mixed up. And they were softer than boys' clothes. Her top had been almost slippery. He wanted to tell Simon tomorrow. But he couldn't do that. Couldn't tell anyone. Couldn't cause any more trouble.

Water was working into his mouth now. There could be blood and hair and stuff in it. He scrubbed at his face. Spat. Spat again. Leant forwards, his head on the shower tray. He could smell the bleach down here. Water bubbling up around his nose and mouth. He was blocking the plug. He could just stay here. Let the water cover him. Drown. Forget about her.

And then he realised what he was doing. Oh God: he had to get it off him. Retching, he stood up. Fell forward, wincing, to turn the tap off. He ripped at his clothes. Until they were in a soggy pile on the floor. He was naked. Wet. *Oh God.* He pulled for a towel, scrubbed it from him. Rubbing harder, harder, as if he could scrub it off. His skin was raw. He deserved the hurt. He rubbed again. He would be grazed in the morning. Sore. Good. Then he used the towel to wipe out the shower. He kept going. Didn't know what time it was now. Wiping the floor. Wrapping his clothes up tight in the towel. Tying it in a knot. He'd have to get rid of them. His favourite jeans. How was he going to explain that? His favourite…

He froze. His teeth mid-chatter. *Her hat.* She'd been wearing a hat when she'd arrived. Evidence. That would be evidence. Where was it? He couldn't remember when he'd last seen it. When she was dancing? He had to find it. He was responsible. *I didn't mean for this to happen. I didn't mean to do it.* He crumpled to the floor. *I didn't mean to do it.*

33

Freddie

She had to show Nas the messages on Amber's Facebook page. Did the people who'd posted them know something they didn't? Could the fifteen-year-old be dead?

'Nas?'

'I've got started on Amber Robertson.' Nas cut her off, without looking up from her computer. 'I wanted to know who she stayed with when her dad was inside, given her mum's dead.'

'Right, good thinking.' Freddie nodded, aware Burgone was following her out of his office.

'Social services placed her with her grandmother – Paul's mum,' Nas continued.

That must be a good sign, she was probably worrying about nothing. Amber could be with her nan. 'So she could be there now?'

'The grandmother passed on three years ago, and there's no listing anywhere for her own mum's family. Looks like they're mostly abroad,' Nas said.

Freddie swallowed. 'I think you should see her Facebook account...'

'Guys,' Burgone interrupted them from behind.

Nas immediately turned to face him. Freddie stared at the posts on her phone: was she overreacting? They were just words. They could even be posted by trolls winding up Amber's friends?

'I've got an announcement to make.' The others looked up from their desks as Burgone cleared his throat. 'Congratulations are in order. Freddie has been promoted, and now, as well as providing intelligence analysis for the team, she will also be working as a Civilian Investigator.'

What? Promotion was pushing it somewhat. Nas looked shocked, then slightly horrified. Freddie felt her spine stiffen.

'A Civilian Investigator?' Saunders made the words sound like swears. 'That's worse than the bloody plastic PCSOs.'

She'd expected hostility from outside the team, but not from within. 'You worried about the competition?' she snapped at him.

Nas inhaled next to her.

'It was at my recommendation, Pete,' Burgone said. 'Freddie will be a great asset for interviewing. Keep you guys free to focus on managing investigations.'

He wasn't mentioning the budget cuts, or that she'd nearly lost her job.

'It's policing on the cheap.' Saunders looked past her at Burgone.

'It's happening.' Burgone's tone shifted.

'You've got to be kidding, guv?' said Saunders.

Freddie waited for Chips to back her up, but he was staring at his shoes, frowning.

'Freddie will receive proper training: she'll be attending a course at the Jubilee Station today, and Cudmore will be giving her in-house instruction during the Amber Robertson search,' Burgone said.

Nas's eyes widened. Freddie couldn't believe none of them had a good word to say about it. She'd found them the Spice Road–THM link: she knew what she was doing.

'Assuming that's okay?' Burgone added forcefully.

'Yes, sir,' Nas said, not looking at Saunders.

Freddie looked at Green, who managed a measly smile back. You could cut the atmosphere with a Post-It note. What did they think she was – just some stupid secretary banging out bloody spreadsheets?

'Well done again, Freddie.' Burgone released his Hollywood superstar smile. 'The Gremlin team are behind you one hundred per cent on this.'

Yeah, waiting to trip me up.

Burgone paused as if they might applaud. No one moved. 'Right, crack on then,' he said.

Green made a show of picking up the phone and requesting to be put through to some woman. Saunders's face was set in a scowl, and he slammed into his chair and started moving files noisily round his desk. Chips still hadn't said anything.

'Why didn't you tell me?' Nas hissed at her side.

'I only just found out myself.' She didn't feel like confessing this was all a clever ploy to keep her in full-time employment.

Burgone had gone with the promotion line: she would too. 'I'm not gonna tread on anyone's toes – don't worry.'

'Right. So you're off to the Jubilee for the rest of the day then?' Nas had her chewing-a-wasp face on.

'Actually, I was about to show you this.' Freddie thrust her phone at Nas.

'Show me on the way,' Nas turned her back on her to grab her own phone.

'You what?' She caught Green looking at them and shot her an evil. Could no one in this bloody office bring themselves to say congrats?

Nas shoved an intelligence report at her so forcefully it folded against her top. 'I was about to say before the guv came in –' Nas's voice wavered slightly over the word 'guv', and, forgetting her anger for a second, Freddie had a sudden urge to whisk her old friend out of here and away from the others. 'The last officers to speak to Paul Robertson before he went to ground: guess who? Tibbsy and Moast.'

Freddie let go of the paper. 'Shit,' she muttered, then went to catch it quickly. DCI Moast and DS Tibbsy. Nas's old team. It was like going back to the beginning: the first case that had thrown them all together. 'The gang's all back together, hey?' Freddie hoped her voice sounded jokey.

'You can go to training after we've found out if there's anything else they know about Paul Robertson.' Nas swung her handbag over her shoulder and stalked out.

'Better catch up with teacher,' Saunders said without looking up.

'What's wrong with you? Get out the wrong side of the rowing machine this morning?' she shot back.

She heard Green snort as she pegged it after Nas. She needed her to read the condolence messages on Amber's Facebook feed. She needed to start on the cellsite analysis – looking at who Paul and Amber called and texted before they disappeared. And she one hundred per cent needed Nas to not rock up at the Jubilee before Freddie could do some damage limitation post the L word bomb this morning. 'I'll meet you in the car park,' she called to Nas's back, as she neared the lift. 'I've got to grab something from the shop!'

Before her friend could turn around, Freddie bolted for the stairs. She just needed a minute to think. To send a message: contain this morning's fallout. Jesus, she hadn't even had time to change her clothes since then. In her palm, the smiling photo of Amber on her phone bounced up and down as she ran down the steps. Maybe she was overreacting, but those messages had unnerved her. She knew Nas would likely dismiss it as conjecture, or her overactive imagination, so she needed more. She needed to build up a picture of Amber Robertson's life. *Rest In Peace.* She couldn't let anything else get in the way of this investigation. They needed to find the dark-haired girl.

Freddie

Freddie walked quickly through the air-conditioned reception of the anonymous Westminster office building that housed them and the other Special Ops teams. Perhaps she could call him? And say what? *So you know you said you loved me and I ran away? Now me and Nas are headed to your station, and, well, funny story: I haven't told her about you.* She probably couldn't cover that in a two-minute call, and she probably couldn't cover it in a text either. She felt the heat of the sun as soon as the door opened: her skin prickled with the shock of going from cold to hot. Her vision quivered at the sides.

'Ms Venton, Freddie!' The voice made her jump. A tall woman in a purple sleeveless top and patterned cotton wide-legged trousers was coming down the street. 'Freddie Venton? It is you, isn't it?'

She recognised her. Beads woven into her braided bob

glinted in the sunlight. She'd interviewed her for an article she was writing about the student protests. She was a teacher – very good on the impact of rising fees on working-class kids. *What was her name?*

'Hi.' She waved and started for the other side of the road. She didn't need an audience while composing this message. Nas had already got her knickers in a twist over her new job, she didn't need more aggro for keeping her waiting.

'I don't know if you remember me?' The teacher reached her side, puffing slightly.

Freddie pasted a smile on her face. 'Student protests, right? I'm in a rush, good to see you though.'

'I've been looking for you.' The woman glanced over her shoulder as if someone might be following her.

She was clutching her handbag strap so tight her knuckles were white. She looked spooked. 'You all right?' Freddie followed her gaze; the street was empty.

'You're a policewoman now, aren't you?'

Freddie recognised the edge in her voice. *Oh, great.* She should have kept walking. 'I'm not actually a police officer, no.' Being berated for selling out to the police wasn't on her fun things to do list.

'But I saw you on the news? A few months ago, here. I found the pictures online.' She grabbed hold of Freddie's arm.

This was getting weird. Was she some kind of stalker? What would Nas do in this situation? Smile? Back away slowly? Arrest her?

Before Freddie could do anything the woman spoke again. 'There's a girl and you've got to help her.' The hairs on Freddie's neck stood up. The woman's eyes were pressing, urgent, but she didn't look nuts. Or like she was lying. She looked scared. 'Is there somewhere we can talk? Please, Ms Venton.'

Freddie's phone blared out the opening lyrics to KRS-One's 'Sound of da Police': her personalised ring tone for Nas. She sent Nas to voicemail. 'Café over there?'

'Thank you.' Relief sounded in the teacher's voice. 'You're a good person.'

'I wouldn't go that far.' Freddie's nerve endings crackled. What was this about? 'I'm sorry, but I can't remember your name?' Freddie headed to the indie greasy spoon on the corner.

The woman's voice and demeanour was still tense. 'It's Kate.'

Nasreen

She couldn't believe Burgone had just forwarded her the training manual for Freddie's new role as Civilian Investigator without another word. It was a blank email. Not even an FYI. He'd promoted Freddie while he was ignoring her. Did he feel the same as Saunders: that she was now the team member you gave the rubbish jobs to?

You're just being paranoid. You're reading too much into this. It's just a task, like any other. Look at it another way: he trusts you to train Freddie.

Or he thinks you're the only one she's likely to listen to. Perhaps taking one for the team – training Freddie – would help her get back in everyone else's good books? And where the hell had Freddie got to anyway? They could have been on the road ages ago. She tried to wind the window down more; the pool car smelt like cheesy feet. She reread the scant intelligence report DCI Moast had filed about his stop and search on Paul Robertson. It had taken place last June, a month before Robertson and his daughter had disappeared. The last official interaction between the force and Robertson.

Her mobile beeped: Freddie's name flashed up. Opening the message, Nasreen started with shock:

911. Meet me in the café on the corner.

911? Urgent? Her pulse quickened; she flung open the car door and took the stairs up to the street two at a time. Giulia's Café was on the east corner. Freddie was sat in the window, talking to a casually dressed older black woman she didn't recognise. Nasreen slowed. What was the emergency?

Freddie beckoned her in. 'Nas – over here.' She pulled over a red vinyl chair. 'This is Kate: I worked with her when I was at the *Guardian*.'

Oh, no: *press*. She didn't move towards the seat Freddie had positioned. 'We've got an appointment we need to be getting to.' How could Freddie imply this was a crisis?

Freddie lowered her voice. 'Kate needs our help.'

'I'm not talking to the media,' Nasreen hissed back. They could be with Moast and Tibbsy now, making progress on a proper case. One she needed to deliver on.

Freddie's eyebrows furrowed. 'Kate's a teacher. She's seen a violent rape.'

'What?' *A rape?* Neither of them looked like they were joking. Nasreen hung her jacket on the back of the chair, sat down and extended a hand to the woman. 'I'm DS Nasreen Cudmore.'

'Thank you for agreeing to talk to me,' Kate said.

She hadn't really been given a choice. Freddie took a swig from her bottle of water.

'Go back to the beginning,' Nasreen said. 'When was this? Where did you see it?'

'I wrote down everything.' Kate opened the black handbag that was on her lap and took out an A4 jotter. Nasreen could see paragraphs of neat blue writing. Dates. Times. Notes. And then she told them what had happened.

Nasreen studied Kate's face as she talked. She maintained eye contact. Her delivery was clear, and without hysteria. She occasionally double-checked a time and the name of the account that had hosted the feed, but it seemed as though she wanted to ensure she got everything correct, rather than that she'd forgotten any details. She didn't exhibit any of the usual tells you might see with those who were lying. When she finished, Nasreen spoke. 'And you reported this?'

'Immediately on Friday night,' she said. 'After I was sick,' she added matter-of-factly.

Two days ago. 'And what did they say?'

'A PC Jones came to my house. He thought – well, he implied – that I had been confused.'

Freddie tutted.

'I tried ringing the hospitals, but no one would tell me if the girl had been admitted. Because I'm not family,' Kate said. 'I'm a witness, aren't I? And I keep thinking what if they just left her there and no one knows?'

Nasreen let her speak.

'It was the early hours of Saturday morning by then. I'd had one glass of red wine, as I was working. That's the ironic thing: I was only looking at the feed for research. I'm compiling a paper on sexual safety and the internet among teens for a conference in the autumn term,' Kate said.

Nasreen had planned to ask why the woman had clicked onto a live stream video titled 'Live Sex'. It was an oddity – apart from the assault – in what Kate had presented so far. 'Freddie said you're a teacher?'

'Yes, I'm head of Hackney High.' She still had hold of her notebook. 'I've been there over thirty years. I was born locally, and I stayed. It's my community. My kids mean everything to me.'

'I interviewed Kate a few years back.' Freddie had remained spellbound during Kate's report, but now she was picking at the label on her bottle. 'She won a TESA award for the work she does at her school. For turning their results around. She pioneered an outreach scheme to provide positive role models for kids from broken homes.'

'I have a good relationship with a local constable, PC Scott. I tried to contact him, but he's on holiday with his family in the Algarve for a fortnight,' Kate said.

'All right for some,' Freddie said.

An award-winning head teacher who had turned around the reputation of an inner-city school. A fine upstanding member of the community who worked with the police. It lent validity to her claims about why she was watching that particular video. The Crown Prosecution would call that a good witness. There was no alteration in her voice or body posture when she spoke about either the video or her school. If she was a liar, she was a very good one. 'Do you have kids of your own?' Nasreen asked Kate.

'No, I live alone,' she answered.

Nasreen nodded again. 'And you didn't recognise either the woman or the man in the film?'

'No,' said Kate. 'There were two men. One was behind the camera. They were boys really. The one I could see may have been nineteen, the one whose voice I could hear sounded younger than that.'

'Would you be able to provide a description of the man and the woman who were visible to help make a photofit of them?'

'I don't know,' Kate faltered.

That wasn't unusual: most witnesses weren't confident they'd be able to describe suspects they'd seen, especially when put on the spot. But when questioned correctly, they often came up with the goods.

'We'll do the photofits first then?' Freddie had been typing notes into her phone as Kate was talking.

Nasreen bristled. 'Let's not get ahead of ourselves here. This isn't our case, Freddie.'

Kate's facial muscles tightened. 'You don't believe me either.'

'It's not that,' Nasreen said. 'It's just that we can't confirm that what you saw was real.' Nasreen knew what Saunders or Chips would say. There was no evidence.

'Come on, Nas,' Freddie said. 'Talk to Burgone, he'd listen to you.'

She doubted that very much. She wanted to help – this woman had obviously seen something awful – but they couldn't police the world. 'With the account deactivated, there's no way to confirm the video feed was shot locally.'

'It was London, it was tagged in London,' said Kate.

'That's easily faked,' Freddie said. 'Annoyingly.'

'It looked like local authority accommodation.'

'You recognised it?' Nasreen pushed.

'No, it just had that feel.' Kate was growing agitated. 'I've travelled, I watch a lot of world cinema, everywhere has a different light. I know that light. I've been in flats like that. It was London, I'm certain of it.'

Nasreen sighed. 'I'm really sorry, Kate, but everything you have given us is circumstantial. There's no concrete evidence that a crime has been committed here.'

'Someone must be looking for the girl?' Kate insisted.

'Yeah, people just don't disappear, do they?' Freddie said.

Well, they do actually. All the time. Nasreen tried to keep her face neutral. 'I'll run it through the Missing Persons Database: see if there's anyone who's been reported that matches the description you've given. And I'll have someone check the hospitals.' She didn't hold out much hope.

'That's all we can do?' Freddie said.

Nasreen didn't look at her friend. She didn't need her guilt-tripping her for this. A teen girl with those stab wounds would have stood out on the regular intelligence reports that were circulated among officers. She didn't doubt that what the woman had seen was real, but it probably was filmed abroad. It was likely Kate had stumbled onto a particularly nasty element of the sex trade: a trafficked girl who'd been brutalised on camera. She didn't want to make it worse by telling her that what she'd seen was probably a murder. A snuff movie. She looked at her watch. 'Freddie, we better get going.'

'That's it?' Kate said.

Nasreen felt sorry for the woman. 'How have you been

since the video? It must have been a very difficult thing to see.'

Kate's lips thinned. 'I haven't been sleeping well, but I'm a tough old girl, really. I've had to be in my job.'

Nasreen didn't doubt it. 'I can recommend a grief counsellor, if you would like?'

'I'd prefer to manage this myself.' Kate gave a small conciliatory smile. 'The doctor has given me some sleeping pills.'

Nasreen nodded. Good. She was handling this in the best way possible. Reluctantly she stood. 'It's been a pleasure meeting you, Kate,' she said, holding out her hand to shake. She wanted to make it better. 'If I can ever do anything else to help you, perhaps something to do with the school, do let me know.'

Kate clasped her hand. Kept eye contact. 'Thank you, Sergeant. I appreciate the time you've taken today.'

She felt she'd failed the woman, as they left the café. 'Ready?' she asked Freddie, trying to sound upbeat. 'Moast won't be impressed if you're late for this session.'

'We could at least try Saunders?' Freddie had a familiar stubborn look on her face.

Saunders already thought Nasreen was a waste of time, she wasn't going to gift him more ammunition. 'I can't.'

'It's not right,' Freddie said. 'It's not fair.'

'Life's not fair,' Nasreen snapped. God, she sounded like her mother. When did that happen? Six months ago she might have tried harder, but she'd been burned since then. Caring too much didn't lead you to make the best decisions. She had to be less emotional, more like Saunders. Maybe in a few years, when she'd recovered some ground, when her career was more stable, she could help the Kates of the world. But not now.

Freddie was aggressively chewing her lip, looking at her phone. Nasreen could tell she was disappointed with her. 'I need a piss.'

'Right. I'll meet you in the car park?' Freddie had to understand Nasreen couldn't do anything? She had to appreciate the difficult position she was in?

Freddie didn't reply, simply picked up pace as if she wanted to shake Nasreen off. Nasreen let her go. Turning, she could see Kate, still sat at the table by the window. Her head was bowed, as if in prayer. Her face was drawn, almost pained. A saying Freddie's gran always used came to her mind: *She looked like she carried the weight of the world on her shoulders.*

Kate

She wasn't sure how long she'd been sitting here now. She blinked away the vision of the long-haired girl lying there. Looking at her. Pleading for her help. She'd failed her. No: that couldn't happen. Did she know anyone else who might help? She wracked her brain: what was the name of PC Scott's superior? Would he listen? She was sure her cousin Yvonne used to date a cop. Or was he in the army? He was tall, neat, he had that air about him. A man in uniform. Small teeth that grimaced when he smiled. Yvonne could put them in touch. The more Kate thought about it, the more she thought perhaps it *was* the army he was in. This was hopeless. She could go in person to her local station and try to speak to someone higher up? Freddie's friend had been polite, but unable to disguise her doubt.

The video had seemed real. Sounded real. But maybe it

was staged, an elaborate practical joke? Could it be taken from a film? She'd told Sergeant Cudmore she could describe the face of the man in the film, but could she really? He was fading from her memory. He'd only looked at the camera once. His features were softened in her mind, mixing with those of her students, with other young men she knew. He could have been younger than nineteen, maybe even sixteen. She rubbed at her eyes with the heels of her palms. This was infuriating. Why didn't they believe her? Why didn't they want to help? She'd seen pity in Sergeant Cudmore's eyes at one stage. Did they think this was some attention-seeking stunt by a lonely old woman? *Come on, Kate, you're only fifty-six. Not old yet.*

Perhaps the wine had played tricks on her mind that night. It had been late. Hot. She hadn't been sleeping well. Perhaps she should do as they all kept saying: forget about it. Move on. Would someone else have given up by now? But she'd seen that girl suffer. Someone must be looking for her. Her gut twisted at the thought of her own daughter. She'd been an unexpected gift following a tryst at a teaching convention. Her father had been a kind man, funny, warm, and visiting from the States. They'd been in talks about how to make it work. He'd put in for a transfer: a swap with a teacher from a private school over here. Everything had been planned. And then Tegbee had arrived early. She'd felt the pain as she waited on the platform at Hackney Central. The hand of the woman next to her as she pointed. Blood spotting on the floor. Then her waters broke. She was three months early. Tegbee's father had got the first plane he could, but he didn't make it in time. Tegbee – *Forever* – had lived for four hours. The two of them, alone in her hospital room. She would have been at university this year, or maybe planning to go travelling. Her whole life in front of her. What if it had been Tegbee in that video? The thought was unbearable. That was someone's daughter. Someone's child.

The phone vibrating in her handbag jolted her back to the present. It was a number she didn't recognise. She cleared her throat, aware tears were calling to her.

'Hello, Kate Adiyiah speaking.'

'Kate, this is Freddie Venton.'

'Freddie?' She looked up, confused: she couldn't have been long back inside the building.

'I've only got a second.' She heard something that sounded like a flushing toilet in the background. 'I believe you,' Freddie said, 'and I've got a plan. You got a pen handy?'

Nigel

Miranda had been very clear, there were to be no more indiscretions. In return, she'd promised she would try harder. But she'd been quick to forget that. It wasn't on. There were two people in this marriage, and she wasn't pulling her weight. She had use of the house in London, though she preferred the estate in Chipping Campden. Her attention was always with the harridans she called friends, attending endless expensive lunches where no one ate anything. All the women had the same stretched faces, stringy bodies and fingers sharp with rings from past and present husbands. It was bad enough having to touch their cold hands at work, pressing the flesh, their rings jabbing like sharp teeth. They made him work for every single penny. All the jovial smiles and hours spent listening to their inane charity chatter.

Once, he'd thought of Miranda as different. When they'd

been at university she'd seemed fresh and fun, she'd worn her hair loose past her shoulders, and laughed at his jokes. Here was someone who was as passionate as he was about his purpose, his career. Now he felt cheated. As if she'd been a mirage to lure him in, a siren, her own desires the rocks on which he crashed. She'd driven him into this intolerable position.

Young party members always looked up to him; he was used to that. Occasionally an upstart would try to win his spurs by picking an argument, but there would be no using him as a stepping stone. As if the prime minister would be able to cope without him! That's what people failed to appreciate. If they attacked him, they attacked the cabinet. They were primed to protect Nigel, not that he couldn't dispense with the whippersnappers himself. They always had such flimsy arguments based on nonsensical anecdotes. Too used to letting their phones and their computers think for them. Jade had been different.

He loved how her fat breasts and bottom shook when he made her laugh. She'd taught him that LOL meant 'laugh out loud' and not 'lots of love'. It had been natural to progress things. Tempting. She was there every day in the campaign office, touching his arm, fluttering her eyelashes at him. But he hadn't succumbed. He'd done the decent thing. That's what Miranda failed to grasp. He had never, in person, acted in an ungentlemanly manner. They had merely exchanged words. Some naughty little messages. It was all a bit of harmless fun. But Miranda would not be reasoned with. It was she who'd put him in this ludicrous situation. How was he supposed to do his job if he wasn't allowed online? Not everyone sent handwritten note cards like her cronies. Many of his constituents reached him via Twitter. Support for policy announcements was more easily achieved with a click. Besides, it was damning to suddenly disappear. One couldn't simply close one's accounts unnoticed. People would assume, wrongly, that he had something to hide. The vultures would be on him within seconds. So he'd elected to do what was best for them as a couple. Miranda's comprehension of these things was weak at best. He'd requested Quentin change all the passwords in front of her. Told Miranda it was a direct order from Number 10. She'd believed it was a security issue, and those accounts would only be used for work from now on.

Switching service providers was straightforward. The internet really did make everything much more readily available. He was shrewd, he stayed away from anything too obviously titled; he didn't want any stray hacks getting hold of his cookies and whatnot. Besides, it was easy enough to find what he wanted on more mainstream applications. The promise had been there tonight, but it wasn't at all what he'd hoped for. Utterly repulsive viewing. People actually enjoyed this filth? He had suggested to himself that he had imagined it; it had, in truth, been a long day. It was now the early hours of the morning, and he was onto his third scotch. But his mind couldn't conjure something as repugnant as that. Boys at the club joked about a bit of slap and tickle, but this went far beyond a touch of the whip. He felt quite sickened that someone would even make a film like that. And it was certainly film. Wasn't it? Staged. Special effects and all that. He'd stumbled into some nightmare vision of a sick man's imagination. Because if you were going to attack someone, it made no sense to do it on camera. He took another sip of scotch, the ice dripping away slowly into nothing. It *had* been strikingly real. He poured himself another two fingers. Unnerving in its brutality. But it couldn't *actually* be real. Because that would be unimaginable.

Nasreen

'I made some calls while I was waiting,' Nasreen said. She had the engine running as Freddie slid into the car. She wanted to forget about Kate and the film she had seen. And she didn't want to row with Freddie about it.

'I found Amber's Facebook account – she hasn't posted since the night before they disappeared. It looks like a goodbye – she says she's sorry and loves them all,' Freddie said, a pen tucked behind her ear.

Could Amber have known they were running away? 'I spoke to the head teacher at her school,' Nasreen said. 'He confirmed she didn't show up the day her dad disappeared, and they received no telephone call or letter in relation to her absence.' Amber's former teacher had obviously run through this before, and had given an emotion-free, inclusive account of what had happened. 'They tried to contact both

Paul Robertson and Amber, but both phones had been switched off, as we know.'

'There's a load of comments under her last post – the friends on here didn't look like they knew it was coming,' Freddie said, lowering her window as they drove through Westminster.

Nasreen wanted to look at the posts, but she knew she'd feel sick in the car. 'All the statements taken from her friends at the time suggest they were surprised.'

'They could be lying – you know what teens are like,' Freddie said.

Nasreen didn't like to think about lying teens; it reminded her of what she and Freddie had done when they were that age. The lasting pain they'd caused. Nasreen indicated and pulled onto Lower Thames Street. The river twinkled next to them in the sunshine, the pavements clogged with groups of lacklustre tourists licking ice-creams.

Freddie shifted in her seat. 'Some of them have written RIP under her message.'

Rest in peace – why would they do that? 'Probably just a teen thing.'

'You don't think they know something we don't?' Freddie said.

'Make a list of everyone on there – see if we can find out who they are, and if they were close to Amber. Could just be randoms,' she said.

'Or trolls.' Freddie leant back and rested her flip-flopped feet on the glove compartment.

'Feet down, please. This is police property.'

'You need to chill out, Nas.' Freddie left her feet where they were.

Was this about not being able to help her friend Kate? 'You okay?'

Freddie kept her eyes fixed on the road. 'Why didn't you say congrats about my promotion?'

Oh God: she'd been so preoccupied with what it meant that Burgone had promoted Freddie whilst dumping her training on her that she hadn't thought about Freddie at all. She winced. 'I'm sure I did.'

'You agree with Saunders then?' Freddie shifted in her seat so she was facing her accusingly, all bare legs and arms.

What had Saunders said? 'Of course not,' she said, flustered.

'Well, you don't sound thrilled about it. Only Green's said anything nice.' Freddie was developing a sulk.

Despite her bolshie attitude, Freddie's ego was fairly fragile. She'd worked hard since she'd started with the team, harder than Nasreen had thought she would, if she was honest. And she'd turned up some pretty good results: making the link between the Spice Road and Paul Robertson was impressive. She deserved this accolade.

'I'm happy for you,' Nasreen said. And she was. Wasn't she? She just had this irrational jealousy that somehow Burgone thought Freddie was a stronger asset to the team than her. That he'd written her off because of what had happened in the past. She was acting crazy: she knew it. She had to shake off this stupid analysis of everything Burgone did and said. Otherwise it was going to sabotage her work.

She realised Freddie was staring at her. How long had she left her hanging?

'Convincing,' Freddie said drily.

'Congratulations,' Nasreen said.

'Cheers,' Freddie said sarcastically.

Well, that went well. The flat-fronted textile shops and redbrick office blocks of Whitechapel Road bordered them. The minaret-style sculpted silver tower at the side of the Brick Lane Mosque glinted sunlight across the windscreen. Nasreen cleared her throat. 'Still looks the same round here.' When she'd started at the Jubilee after her fast-track training, she'd hoped joining the flagship East End force would springboard her career. She would never have guessed it would catapult her straight to the top: to Special Ops. Perhaps it was too fast? Perhaps she should have stayed here. But then she'd never have met Burgone at all. And despite everything that it had cost her, that would have been worse.

'They closed down The Grapes,' Freddie said.

'The station's local? No. How do you know that?' Had she missed a get-together with the old team? Had they frozen her out as well?

'Night out a few months ago. Seeing uni mates.' Freddie looked up from her phone. 'We're here.'

The Jubilee Station, the ageing 1970s jewel in the Tower Hamlets policing borough, loomed before them. All concrete and white-metal-framed windows.

'It's such a clusterfuck,' Freddie said as Nasreen signalled and turned into the place it had all started.

Freddie

She'd nearly blown it then. Practically told Nas she'd been back here, because she was focusing on Amber. She was just a normal kid. Did she know what her dad was up to? Did it matter? Paul Robertson was part of THM. The Rodriguez Brothers didn't limit their empire to drugs, they were linked to people trafficking. After working through intelligence reports in the last few months, Freddie understood more about what these gangs did than she ever had before. Women and girls forced into the sex trade. Abuse. The territory wars. People were tortured, killed. She thought of those she knew in journalism, who insisted everything they owned or ate was fair trade, who boycotted Starbucks and Apple because they disagreed with their aggressive retail strategies, or because they used sweatshop workers to make their shiny products, but who had no problem shoving coke up their noses. Drugs were linked to abuse and death. She didn't think she'd ever be able to smoke hash again.

On Amber's Facebook she was beginning to see a pattern. 'I think I've got something.'

Nas pulled into a space in the square concrete carpark out the back of the Jubilee Station and cut the engine. A wave of heat rolled over the car. 'What is it?'

'This Corey Banks guy appears, and then reappears. He's all over her feed by the end. In December 2015 it states they're in a relationship. She had a boyfriend.'

'Maybe she still does. Find him and we might find her.' Nas took the phone from her. Her face turned pale. 'Oh God.'

'What? What is it – do you recognise him?'

'Yes. And his name's not Corey Banks.'

'Freddie Venton!' A shout from outside made them both jump, as DCI Moast's hand slammed onto the top of the car. Nas dropped her phone. 'And Cudmore.' He squatted down next to her open window, so his Lego head was on a level with hers. His leering face had lost none of its charm.

'Sir,' Nas said, scrabbling for the phone.

'Just had a call to make my day,' he said, grinning at Freddie. 'I hear you're going to be in my class this arvo.'

'It was sprung on me.' She reached for her phone, taking in the little shake of Nas's head about the guy calling himself Corey Banks: *don't mention it.* This whole police practice of only saying stuff on a need-to-know basis was balls. Surely if they all knew what was going on, they'd stand more chance of figuring stuff out? For all they knew, Moast had relevant information. 'I'd rather stay out here with the bins, to be honest.'

'Venton, Venton, Venton,' Moast said, opening her door and standing back. 'Don't be like that.' She sighed and swung her legs out. Timing, as ever, was not Moast's strong point. 'Besides –' he grabbed her arm and put his face right up against her ear '– now you officially work for the Met I'm your superior. You've got to do what I say.'

'Get off.' She shook her arm free.

Nas slammed the car door behind them. Moast turned and grinned at her with his marble tombstone teeth. 'And if it isn't the Met's finest rising star. Hope you tell all the adoring top brass that it was me who taught you everything you know, Cudmore.'

Moast had clearly not heard about Nas's slip-up a few months back. Nas walked over and held her hand out. 'Good to see you, sir. How are you?'

'Same shit, different day, Cudmore,' he said, aggressively pumping her hand. Still a posturing asshole. This afternoon was going to be torturous. 'You just dropping your kid off at nursery, or have you come to learn something they can't teach you over at Special Ops?'

'I've come to pick your brains, if you've got five minutes? It's regarding a stop-and-search you and Tibbsy carried out last June.' Nas had her game face on: sucking up.

'Sure thing. We'll get Venton here to make us all a nice drink and we'll have a chat,' he said as they walked towards the propped-open fire exit of the station.

'I'm not a sodding barista,' Freddie said. She wanted to know why Nas had looked so freaked out.

'Ah, yes, but you were.' Moast stood back to let Nas enter the building before him. Then he stopped, turning to block her way. 'And you always will be to me.'

Great.

'You nearly cost me my job back then,' he said menacingly.

'And your management of the case nearly lost me my life.' She pointed at the scar on her forehead: the permanent chewed reminder of just how badly he'd screwed up on the Apollyon case.

He laughed. 'I'd watch your mouth if I were you. You've got to pass this afternoon's session to get your new job, and guess who gives the marks?'

'Father Christmas?'

He tutted and shook his head. 'Still not learnt any respect, I see, *Freddie.*'

'Guv?' a voice from behind them called. She turned to see the rangy frame of Tibbsy lumbering through the car park carrying an M&S sandwich. Maybe she and Nas could lose these guys and talk in the Ladies?

Moast swung an arm over her shoulder. 'Look what the gods have gifted us, Tibbs. We're going to have some fun this afternoon!'

Who was the guy calling himself Corey Banks, and why had Nas looked so scared when she'd seen his photo? As they trooped inside, sweat prickled on Freddie's brow. Ignoring the chatter around her, she focused on the hard, sharp question that was cutting through the noise: and what did that mean for Amber?

Nasreen

'I don't want to keep you,' Nasreen said. Tibbsy had joined Moast and Freddie in the Jubilee's polystyrene-ceiling-tiled hallway. She needed to get back to the office and confirm her suspicions about what she'd seen on Amber's Facebook. This could potentially change the whole direction of their investigation.

'Still sprinting ahead, hey, Nas?' Tibbsy enveloped her in a hug, pressing her face into his white shirt. She could feel his collar bone against her cheek. He smelt vaguely of shower gel and sun cream. 'You back to stay?'

She laughed. It had been such a long time since anyone had seemed so pleased to see her. Again she wondered if she'd made a mistake in leaving. Tibbsy was a good partner.

''Fraid not. This is a flying visit. Wanted to ask you and the guv about a stop-and-search you did last June. Paul Robertson – the Rodriguezes' drug runner?'

'Ha! I remember that.' Moast signalled for them to duck into his office.

Tibbsy's face had flushed pink. 'Not my finest hour.'

'Why's that then?' Freddie asked, as they squeezed into the room. The plant in the corner had died since she'd left. Nasreen wondered if anyone else had watered it. Or even noticed the brown leaves.

'Bit of a cock-up, wasn't it, Tibbs?' Moast grinned.

'Yeah, well, I didn't know who he was, did I?' Tibbsy rubbed his hand across the back of his neck, and looked at the floor.

'He got a right royal bollocking from the Drugs lads: they had surveillance on Robertson, when this lunk walked right up and started asking questions. I'd only popped into the office to get some gum. Can't leave him unattended: he's like a bloody big kid.'

'Why did you talk to him if you didn't know who he was?' Nasreen said. Freddie was stood in the doorway, her arms folded over her chest. It wasn't like her to sit on the sidelines.

Tibbsy glanced up quickly before looking back down at his shoes. 'He just seemed like trouble.'

'Don't give me that,' Moast said. 'He was doing his whole knight-in-shining-armour bit.'

'He was shouting at some girl,' Tibbsy said nervously. 'I just didn't like the way he was going off at her.'

'What did she look like?' Freddie asked.

Tibbsy shrugged. 'I dunno.'

'Liar. He only noticed 'cause she was fit,' Moast said with a laugh. 'So he wades in with his badge out, breaking up a fight between one of London's most notorious gangsters and his missus. Lucky he wasn't packing heat.'

'You know that for sure?' Nasreen said. There were rumours Paul Robertson had been involved in the fatal shooting of an officer twenty years ago, but nothing had ever been proved.

'He backed right down. Said he was sorry for the fuss,' Tibbsy said, turning pale. He'd obviously since learnt of Paul's reputation.

'What colour hair did she have?' Freddie said.

Tibbsy shrugged again.

'Long and dark,' said Moast. 'She was a right stunner. Shut her mouth as soon as this one walked up to her. You've got that effect on women, don't ya, lad?' Moast was enjoying Tibbsy's embarrassment.

'What were they arguing about?' Nasreen asked.

'How old was she?' Freddie said.

'I dunno. Young. Twenty. They were just going at each other in the street.'

'She had some balls on her,' Moast said. 'Not many people would speak to Robertson like that. I thought I was going to have to radio for backup when I saw Tibbs striding over there. Left my debit card in the shop and everything.'

'What happened?' said Nasreen. Freddie was frowning, pulling her phone out of her pocket.

'He said he didn't want no trouble. She said she was fine and we left it at that,' Moast said. 'Didn't really want to push Robertson without backup. And I'd seen his name on intelligence reports: I knew we probably weren't alone.'

'Did she look like this?' Freddie held out her phone.

Moast took it. 'Yeah – that's her. You know who she is?'

Freddie nodded at Nasreen. 'Oh, yeah: we know all right. That's his daughter Amber.'

67

'But they're a different colour!' Tibbsy said disbelievingly.

Freddie rolled her eyes. 'So's Nas's dad: it's not like it's a bloody miracle, you tool.'

Tibbsy blushed again. 'Sorry,' he said to her.

'Don't worry about it.' Nasreen shook it off. 'So he was arguing with his daughter in the street twelve days before they both disappeared.'

'Yeah, and on the same day she posted on her Facebook page that she was feeling down and "everything sucked",' Freddie read from her phone. Nasreen was starting to piece together a picture in her mind.

'That's his daughter.' Moast let a whistle out his teeth. 'She looks like a goer.'

'She's fifteen in that photo.' Freddie minimised the page.

'No wonder he was doing his nut!' Moast laughed. Tibbsy made a half-hearted attempt to join in, before a look from Freddie silenced him.

Now Nasreen wanted to get back to the office more than ever. 'That's been really helpful.'

'Has it?' Freddie sounded surprised.

'Thanks for your time, sir,' Nasreen said, holding out her hand for Moast to shake again.

He gripped it and grinned at her, wrapping his other hand over hers. 'Always a pleasure, Cudmore. Stop by whenever you like. But next time leave Venton in the car, yeah?'

She smiled and nodded, keen to get out of there. If she was right about the man calling himself Corey Banks then this could be explosive. They could have been looking at this all wrong. She was halfway down the corridor back to the car when she heard the slap of Tibbsy's feet on the linoleum behind her.

'Hey, Nas,' he called.

'Hey, Tibbs – remembered something else?'

'What?' His eyebrows knitted briefly together. 'Oh: no. Sorry. I just wanted to say I was sorry again. For what I said in there. You know me: big mouth – big feet to put in it.' He looked sheepish.

'Seriously, forget about it. I have,' she said.

'You promise? Because you and me have always been cool, haven't we?'

'Yeah, sure,' she said growing uneasy. Did he want something? Perhaps he was on the lookout to progress from the Jubilee himself?

'Cool,' he said. 'That's cool then. Brilliant.' He took a step back, his long arms flapping at his side. Half a wave. 'Right. I'll be seeing you then.'

'Right,' she said, smiling.

'Stop by whenever you want.'

'Okay,' she said, stepping backwards herself.

'Okay – so I'll see you.'

'Bye,' she said, sensing this could go on for ages. Tibbsy might want to drag his heels today, but she had things to do. Increasingly pressing things. She glanced at her watch. She could be back at the office in twenty with a bit of luck. Not that it was likely to make a difference now. Not after so long. She could be mistaken, obviously. Could have misread the situation. Briefly she closed her eyes and prayed that that was the case. Because if she was right, if what she suspected were true, then the consequences for Amber could be very bleak indeed.

Kate

That night she'd taken down the box from its shelf. It wasn't pretty, like she really deserved, but it was waterproof and fireproof. A safe box. A safe place for her to be. She slipped off the chain she wore under her shirt and pushed the small gold key into the padlock. It was silly keeping it locked, really. No one else lived here, no one else would begrudge her this, but she preferred to keep it personal. It was a secret between her and her girl.

Gently she opened the lid. Her senses greedy for it, she reached in, pulled out the small knitted blanket and held it to her nose. She could smell her: her baby. She closed her eyes. She was back in the hospital room again.

So happy and so sad, all at once. Light seemed to pour from Tegbee, her big brown eyes staring up at her. Her eyelashes were so long, and she had a dusting of hair that curled round her scalp like silk. *She was the prettiest, most beautiful baby she'd ever seen. And she was hers. She'd made this little miracle. She stroked her full cheeks as the girl blinked. She didn't even cry. Only grizzled once, but she stopped when Kate started to sing to her. Hush little baby, don't say a word, mama's going to buy you a mocking bird. And if that mocking bird don't sing, mama's going to buy you a diamond ring. The doctors must have made a mistake. There couldn't be anything wrong with a child who was so perfect.*

Kate opened her eyes: *don't think of that bit.* Don't think of the pain. Not tonight, not now. Carefully, she laid the blanket on the table. She hadn't had a drink since the night she'd seen the video, but today was a special occasion. Regardless of everything else going on, she would still celebrate. As if she were here. The bottle was chilling in the fridge, still wrapped in its blue tissue paper from the deli. *Only the best for my girl.* She opened the cupboard where she kept her best china and took down one of the crystal flutes her sixth formers had presented her with on their graduation.

'That was the year we lost three boys,' she said out loud. 'One to leukaemia, and two to juvenile detention.' She unfurled the tissue paper and loosened the safety cap of the bottle. 'But it was also the first year that one of our students made it into Oxford.' She held the cork, twisting the bottle. 'His name was Dwayne Haden. You would have liked him.' The cork popped and a stream of bubbles frothed out of the bottle. She laughed as she caught the fizz in her glass. Then she poured one more and took them both back to the table.

Under the blanket was the onesie Tegbee had worn on that first day. She'd buried her in the christening dress that had belonged to Kate's mother. They'd had to take Kate's womb out when Tegbee had arrived; she knew there'd be no more children. She lifted out the photos. Her and her baby smiling. You could she had her father's eyes. But Tegbee's lips were from her mum. Sometimes she couldn't help imagining what she would look like now. She'd be so beautiful. Tall like her dad. Would she love the same books as her? She'd planned on sharing her favourite films with her little girl, curling up on the sofa with her in her arms. Reading to her at night. When she was older they would have spent summers in Ghana and the States; she was going to teach her all about her heritage. The bubbles rose in the glass and popped. Kate lowered her flute and clinked it against the one on the table.

'Happy nineteenth, baby girl.'

A

Her body is warm, soft. His duvet barely covering her naked ass. Her leg pressed against his, the rhythmic push of her hip. He starts to gasp. Her hand softly works its way down under the covers, down his chest, round his nipple, down his stomach, tracing the line of hair that's started to grow there. He gulps. Tries to control himself. And then he's stroking her beautiful face, feels the flesh turn cold and come away in his hands. Chunks of meat fall from her. He tries to push it back, hold her together. He starts as her bone fingers close over his dick. Her beautiful dark eyes fall onto swivelling nerves. Her lips laugh and fall away from her skull, biting into his face, and scurry across his body, hungrily drawing blood. Her flesh peels back and she's sinew and muscle and then skeleton. He tries to get away, but laughing she mounts him. Pushes him back. She claws at his chest, plunges her fingers into him, grabs his heart. Pulls it out.

He can see it beating as she squeezes, and her hip bones snap closed over his cock.

He has screamed himself awake too many times. So he won't sleep. Nights are the hardest. He sits in the corner, on the floor. The bed is too soft. He tries to count to stay awake. Recites what he knows about the solar system. *The solar system was formed 4.6 billion years ago.* Tries to keep moving. Paces his room. *There are eight planets that orbit the sun.* Mum thinks he's sick. It started off as a lie; maybe it's not any more. *In decreasing order of size the planets in the solar system are Jupiter, Saturn, Uranus, Neptune, Earth, Venus, Mars, Mercury.* He doesn't speak to anyone. Shuts his brothers out of his room. *You need a degree in engineering, biological science, physical science and mathematics to be an astronaut. You must have 20/20 vision. You must be between 62 and 75 inches tall.* His phone beeps. The number is unknown, but he knows who it is. Hands shaking, he opens it.

Blood is thicker than water.

Blood. He keeps his phone by his side all the time. *You must have at least 1,000 hours minimum flying time in a jet.* Turns his music up to try to block out his breathing. The sounds of her. Headphones don't work. *You must have 20/20 vision.* His books are unopened. His laptop closed.

The sun sets again. Light pours through the curtains. *You must have 20/20 vision.* He watches it shrink down the wall. *You must have 20/20 vision.* He walks to the window. His mum is on night shift and the flat is quiet. His brothers are sleeping.

Fam. Blood. *You must have 20/20 vision.* He didn't close his eyes all night. He didn't go to sleep. It's dark outside, and in his reflected face he sees hers. Blood. They will be looking for her. *You must have 20/20 vision.* He has decided. There is only one way out. Only one thing he can do. He watches himself mouth the words:

'I'm going to kill you.'

Kate

Her eyelids fluttered. Her neck felt stiff. Her wine glass was still in her hand. She must have fallen asleep on her chair. She'd taken a sleeping pill and she probably shouldn't have had alcohol. She was groggy. Thirsty. She shifted in her seat and then stopped. There was someone else here. Someone in the room with her. Had the man from the film found her? Kate opened her eyes a fraction. It was still dark outside. Night time. It felt cooler. It was the early hours of the morning. Should she pretend to still be asleep? Cry out? Years of teaching had taught her that a strong stance was best: no weakness. She sat up quickly. Her eyes open. 'Can I help you?'

A tall black woman was standing in the corner of the room. She didn't flinch or move when Kate spoke. Instead she smiled, her white teeth beautiful in the dark. Something caught at Kate. She didn't feel scared. She felt calmer than she had for a while. It was the tablets, she told herself. The woman stepped forward into the strip of yellow streetlight that shone through the window. A silver charm bracelet jingled around her wrist. Kate had seen one like that before. Many years ago. She must be hallucinating: the pills.

'Tegbee?'

When the young woman spoke, her voice was as familiar as her own. The voice she'd carried in her head every day for nineteen years. 'Hello, mama.'

Kate held her breath, not wanting the mirage to fade.

'I've missed you.' Tegbee smiled and stepped towards her. Her baby girl. All grown up. Perfect. So perfect. She smiled at her, tears forming in the corners of her eyes.

Answer your
phone. We need
to talk.

I can explain.
Just pick up.

You can't
hide from me.

Pick. Up.

Don't do anything
stupid. Anything
you'd regret.

…
…
…

This isn't over.

Nasreen

Nasreen felt the familiar pull of tension in her stomach as she neared the office. But it looked like only Chips was in. She'd spent the evening poring over all the files she could find. This was not looking good. At some point she must have fallen asleep; she'd missed a call from Freddie, but it was gone 1am by the time she woke up. Too late to call back.

Chips looked up from the teetering barricade of folders on his desk. 'You get me one of those, lass?' A soft puffy finger pointed at the Espress-oh's bag she was carrying.

'Skinny mocha it is.'

He beamed. After forty-odd years of drinking black coffee with a dash of milk, Chips had been converted to the sickly drink by Freddie. He was a man of routine, his physical bulk a metaphor of his immovability, and yet within two weeks of working with him Freddie had changed the habit of a lifetime. She had that effect.

'Is DI Saunders in?' She tried to sound casual.

'He's in a meeting with the boss.' Chips sipped from his drink. 'This really is cracking.'

Freddie's voice carried from the corridor. 'Hey, Milena, it's me. Just to say cheers for letting me crash last night. I left the key under the bin outside. Hope the night shift wasn't balls. Catch ya soon.' The door to the office opened and Freddie appeared, her hair piled haphazardly on top of her head. The same cutoffs on as yesterday, but with a shapeless T-shirt. She pointed straight at Nasreen. 'You and me need to talk. I called you.'

Nasreen replaced the lid on her own reusable coffee cup. 'I was working on the case.' She pulled the files she'd had at home from her bag. 'The guy calling himself Corey Banks on Amber's page is better known as Alexander Riley, or Lex Riley as he's known on the street.' She passed Freddie the printout of Lex she'd made from the Police National Computer.

Freddie read it and blew air out through her lips. 'He's a known gang member?' She dropped her own rucksack behind her.

'Yes. The Dogberry Boys.' Just thinking about it made her feel a bit sick. Amber was fifteen when they were talking online. When she described him as her boyfriend.

'Didn't Paul Robertson go down for killing one of their members?' Freddie asked.

'Yes. They're rivals.' She watched the colour drain from Freddie's face. 'They've been in an escalating turf war for the last few years.' It didn't bear thinking about. But they had to.

80

'Why'd he change his name?'

'Presumably because Amber or her father would have recognised it,' Nasreen said.

'But he was dating the daughter of one of the Rodriguezes' head guys… Shit.' Freddie shook her head in disbelief. 'So, what, he was trying to get into her life undercover?'

Nasreen nodded. 'What if we weren't the first ones to think that Amber was a good way to get to Paul Robertson?'

Freddie sat down heavily. She was staring at the printout in her hand, her face echoing Nasreen's yesterday when she'd recognised him. A look of shock. Lex Riley's sneering mugshot leered from the top corner. 'He made first contact,' Freddie said. 'I've seen the message on her Facebook page. He approached her.' It all fitted. 'He set her up? Catfished her?'

Nasreen's stomach tightened. A fifteen-year-old child. 'It looks like it.'

'We could have this all wrong: she might not be on the run with her dad. You think Lex Riley could've got to her?' Freddie looked at her imploringly.

She wished she could dismiss her fears, but sleeping on it hadn't helped. Lex Riley wouldn't waste his time stringing Amber Robertson along for a laugh. He was the cousin of Jay Trap, the head of the family that had dominated the Dogberry Boys for the last two decades. He wasn't some bit-part player. He'd been implicated in a stabbing on the Dogberry estate. The case had collapsed before it made it to court, when the key witness backed out of testifying. Nasreen had read that the witness's pet dog had been found skinned outside her house. Alive, just. There'd been a note pinned to the poor animal: *your children are next.* You didn't mess with these people. Lex could have only been interested in Amber for one reason: because of her father. This was a gender-flipped honey trap. 'We need to find out everything we can about Lex Riley. Can you look at any intelligence reports we have on him?'

Freddie nodded. 'I should get Amber's telephone records today with a bit of luck – I'll see if I can trace contact between the two of them.' Grimacing, she took the papers back to her desk.

What had happened to Amber? Images of a skinned dog formed in Nasreen's mind. She picked up a cold half-drunk tea someone had abandoned on her desk. Clear desk, clear mind. She was halfway between the office and the staff room when she heard Saunders's voice behind her.

'Skiving off already, Cudmore?'

His petty mind games were particularly pathetic when contrasted to her growing fears about Amber. But she didn't have enough to bring it to his attention yet: it was just a theory. They needed to compile more evidence. She smiled, determined not to let him get to her. 'Just tidying up.'

'That's my mug,' he said with a grin. 'Ta for cleaning it for me.'

'I'm just taking it to the kitchen.' Being a skivvy for her Inspector wasn't part of her job description.

'Won't take you long to run it under the tap.' He turned into the office, calling: 'Make sure you get all the tea stains off. And I'll have a fresh one while you're there, Sergeant.'

Blooming cheek! She crossly shook the cup upside down over the sink in the slender kitchen and flicked the kettle on. *And yet you're still doing it, Nasreen? Get a grip*. As a small rebellion, she didn't rinse the cup before she dropped in a fresh bag on top of the cold tea. Saunders was training to swim the channel, and his nutrition plan didn't allow sugar, so she added three teaspoons. The water boiled like her resentment.

She marched out of the kitchen in a rage, and slammed straight into Burgone. She swerved, trying to save his tailored suit from the hot tea. He jumped backwards.

'Whoa!'

Boiling liquid sloshed over her thumb. 'Ow!' She swapped hands, shook it off and stuck her thumb in her mouth.

'Are you all right?' Burgone's blue eyes looked at her with concern. He stepped towards her and reached for the hand that she was still sucking. Suddenly she felt absurdly sexual, and she let her fingers drop. He caught hold of them and gently turned her hand over in his. Running his piano-player touch lightly over the damaged skin. Every cell in her body felt primed. She daren't speak. 'We need to get this under the cold tap.'

She nodded dumbly as he took Saunders's mug from her and led her to the sink. He turned on the tap, before tenderly holding her hand towards the water. The shock of the cold brought her to her senses.

'It's fine,' she said, shaking him off, wincing as the water splashed onto his shirt, turning the white fabric transparent. It clung to his toned abs. She tried not to stare. 'Sorry. I'm being stupidly clumsy.' She tried to laugh.

'Do we need to get the first-aid box?' he asked, inspecting the burn. She wished he'd look away. Leave. She was surprised the water didn't hiss into steam when it touched her skin: she felt hot with shame.

'No, no, it's fine. Honestly,' she said.

He picked up the mug again and gave it a quizzical glance. 'I thought you only drank herbal tea?'

He remembered! Get a grip, Nasreen. 'It's for DI Saunders.'

'He's got you making tea for him?'

She panicked. She didn't want to seem like a grass. Or a whinger. 'I was going to the kitchen anyway.' *To take back his cup.*

His face relaxed into a glorious smile. 'I'm so pleased you two are starting to bond.'

Was he? Had she been wrong? Did he really care what had happened to her since their one-night stand? 'I wouldn't say we're bonding, exactly. More that he's acknowledging my existence.' She was being inappropriate, but Burgone smiled.

'He's a good cop, you can learn a lot from him.'

She nodded: Saunders's record spoke for itself. Though Lex Riley's potential involvement with Amber might derail her chance to prove herself to him. If Lex Riley had got to Amber – got to Paul – then finding the girl might not lead to Robertson after all.

Burgone straightened off the kitchen ledge. 'Right. Keep up the good work, Cudmore,' he said, his voice suddenly authoritative.

She looked up, confused, as he strode out. It was only then that she saw Freddie leaning against the kitchen doorframe, watching them, arms crossed, her eyebrows raised questioningly.

Nasreen cleared her throat. 'Have you found something?'

Freddie was holding papers in her right hand, but she didn't move. 'Don't you think it's time you got back out there, Nas? Join Tinder or something.'

Nasreen turned the tap off, keeping her back to her friend. 'I'm a cop, I can't go on Tinder.'

'It'd do you good: sex is a great stress relief.'

Nasreen felt her ears burn hot. 'We're not all sex mad, Freddie,' she said. Her mate's track record of one-night stands was something she wasn't comfortable with.

'Sex is natural,' Freddie said. 'Make you less uptight, won't it?'

She wouldn't take the bait. 'I take it you didn't come in here to discuss my personal life?'

'Or lack of it,' Freddie said. 'Nah. I came to show you this.' She held out the printouts. Nasreen dried her hand on the tea towel and started to flick through them. 'About twelve months ago, Lex Riley went to ground,' Freddie continued. She had highlighted the mentions of Lex Riley in surveillance reports and intelligence the force had gathered and posted on the PNC. His name appeared frequently until July last year. The last mention of him was at a meeting with Jay Trap on 12 July. The two men had been observed meeting at Trap's club, the known HQ for their operation.

'The last known sighting was the day before Amber and Paul Robertson disappeared?' she said. That couldn't be a coincidence.

'I think he's lying low,' Freddie said. 'Waiting for the heat to die off.'

If she was right, it'd mean Lex was involved in the father's and daughter's disappearance. Her stomach fell away as she thought of the laughing teen girl from the photo.

'There's more,' Freddie said. 'It's not good.'

Nasreen took the printout Freddie passed her.

'Lex also had his own Facebook page – under his real name,' Freddie pointed at the paper. 'That went quiet shortly after he started messaging Amber as Corey Banks. But look at the status he posted minutes after he contacted Amber that first time.'

As if confirming all her fears, Nasreen's mouth went dry as she read:

If you cross me I will come for the people you love. I will destroy them. I will take you apart piece by piece.

Nasreen

The printout buckled in Nasreen's hands. 'He was trying to get to Paul through Amber.'

Freddie nodded.

The girl could be in very real danger. She could be dead. This was looking more complex than she had originally anticipated. Saunders wouldn't be pleased, but she didn't care. Amber was an innocent in this. Checking no one else was listening, Nasreen spoke quickly. 'We're changing our focus. We need to find Lex Riley.'

She needed to speak to someone at Drugs and ask if they had any theories about where Lex Riley might be hiding. Someone who wouldn't blab to Saunders. In the office, Green had arrived and was eating granola at her desk, watching the news. She knew the DC had done a stint at the National Crime Agency; perhaps Green had a mate there she could ask for

Nasreen? She put Saunders's tea on his desk – he didn't bother to look up. If she could move fast enough she could start asking questions before Saunders got wind of it.

A face on the news report Green was watching jabbed Nasreen like a paper aeroplane. 'Can you turn the sound up?' she said

'This is an office, Cudmore, not a youth club,' Saunders snapped from behind her. 'Urgh! What the hell have you put in this tea?'

She didn't turn around; her eyes were fixed on Green's screen. 'Sorry, sir, but I recognise her.' *Oh, no. Freddie, what have you done?* The woman on the screen was sat in the studio. Her suit jacket neat. She looked nervous, a little too stiff, as she answered the newsreader's questions. The beads in her hair were still.

'Another schoolfriend like getting her face on the telly, does she?' Saunders glared at her and Freddie in turn. She hated the press. They caused nothing but trouble. She looked at Freddie, who quickly looked away.

Green turned the sound up. The newsreader's voice filled the room. 'I'm here with Kate Adiyiah, a teacher from East London, who claims she witnessed a rape on the live streaming app Periscope. Kate can you describe what happened that night?'

Nasreen rounded on Freddie. 'You did this!'

'I didn't!' Freddie put her hands up in mock surrender. 'I promise.'

'What's going on?' said Chips, still clutching his mocha.

How had Freddie done it? Is that why she was calling her last night? 'We know her. Freddie knows her. She came to see us.'

'She reported a rape and you didn't think to mention it?' Saunders said.

'… Somewhere out there, someone is looking for the girl in the film. She could need help.' Kate's voice rung out through the office.

Would you really have listened if I had come to you, Sir? She realised then there was no trust between her and Saunders. She was already plotting to go to Drugs behind his back. No trust means no relationship. That could be fatal in their line of work. 'The hospitals haven't received anyone who matches the girl's description. No one's been reported missing. There's no evidence that a crime has been committed, at least not locally,' she said.

'Reports of this horrifying video have grown on the internet, after police failed to respond to Miss Adiyiah's reports of the crime,' said the newsreader. 'Who did you speak to, Miss Adiyiah?'

Nasreen's heart missed a beat.

'My local station, and I reached out to a policewoman I know, but no one has been able to help.' Kate looked unsure. Her eyes flicked to the side, off camera.

'Can you confirm that two of the officers you spoke to were Freddie Venton and Detective Sergeant Nasreen Cudmore? Two specialists in e-crime, from the Gremlin Taskforce? Viewers may remember them as the same two young women who worked on the infamous Hashtag Murderer case, and the high-profile kidnapping of Instagram star Lottie Londoner last year.'

Kate looked wrong-footed. Nasreen couldn't hear her response as it was buried by Saunders bellowing next to her. 'What the bloody hell?'

'Ah,' said Freddie.

Chips had a vaguely amused smile on his lips. Green blew air out through her teeth.

'Reports of this alleged crime have spread across social media after Buzzfeed interviewed Miss Adiyiah about the incident, as part of their ongoing campaign against internet misogyny.'

Nasreen turned to stare at Freddie.

'Okay, to be fair, that one was me,' Freddie said.

The phones started to ring in the office. 'That'll be the superintendent wanting to know what the fuck's going on!' Saunders said.

'You wrote an article about it?' She couldn't believe Freddie would do this.

'Course not,' Freddie snapped. 'I just put her in touch with a contact of mine. I didn't even know if they'd run it.'

The phones were still ringing. Nasreen snatched up the nearest and barked, 'Yes?'

Burgone's voice cut through her and she felt her temperature rise. 'Nasreen. I've just had a call from the press office. I think we'd better have a little chat. Bring Freddie.' The mark on her hand burned.

He'd think she'd done this deliberately. That she'd betrayed him to the press. 'Sir...' She started to try and explain, but he'd already hung up. And he'd just been nice to her. They were just starting to make progress. She replaced the phone. Cleared her throat, aware they were all watching her. 'Freddie, the boss wants a word.' Green caught her eye and raised an eyebrow. She willed the red to leave her face.

'Righto.' Freddie grabbed her phone from her desk.

'You didn't think to mention this at all? Nice one, Cudmore,' Saunders sneered as she walked past. Then turned to Green, shouting. 'Turn that crap off. That's enough distraction for one day.' Chips was chuckling.

'What the hell were you thinking?' she hissed at Freddie as they approached Burgone's office. Thankfully his door was closed. Could she make a break for it?

'You said you couldn't help,' Freddie said with a shrug. 'What did you expect me to do? Just forget about the girl she saw attacked?'

'She could be making it up!' This was a reckless way to behave. And Freddie had dragged her into it. How the hell was she going to explain this to Burgone? Instinctively she covered the mark on her hand.

'How was I to know she'd get on the bloody news?' Freddie snapped.

'For God's sake, Freddie, you know how *those people* work,' she said.

'What do you mean by "*those people*"?' Freddie stopped in the corridor.

'Press, journalists, they don't care about Kate or the girl!' She rounded on her.

'People like me. I used to be a journalist, before I got dragged into this hellhole. What is the point of doing this job if we can't help people? We were gonna use Amber to try and find her drug-dealer dad; we're as bad as Lex Riley. And we weren't going to help find the girl Kate saw attacked? It's not fucking right!'

'I don't make the rules, Freddie...' She was cut off as Burgone's office door flew open.

91

He stormed out, his face red with anger. 'The whole building can hear you going at it! Will you shut up and get in here now!'

Nasreen wanted to die. She wanted to fall through the floor beneath her feet. She thought she might cry. But Freddie, lit up like a firework, hadn't burnt out yet. She went storming into Burgone's office.

'We should be helping Kate, not leaving it to bloody Buzzfeed,' she shouted.

Christ. Nasreen ran after her.

Burgone was turned away from them. Hands on hips, looking up as if asking for strength. 'You finished?' he said to Freddie.

Freddie exhaled. 'It's not right, that's all I'm saying.' She flopped onto the seat opposite the DCI's desk. Nasreen remained standing. Even at her most misguided Freddie couldn't really have thought this was a good move. She felt ambushed. Freddie had dragged her name into this, and now she had to stand here while Burgone acted like her boss, disciplined her after the moment they'd just shared in the kitchen. She didn't know if she could bear it.

'I've just had a call from the Superintendent,' Burgone said. He was still turned away. His suit jacket hanging on the back of his chair. For a second she caught the scent of amber. His smell. 'She just got off the phone with the Chief Super, who wants to know why his rest day fry up was interrupted by your names coming up on screen.' He paused. Nasreen gritted her teeth and straightened her back. 'Why *our name* was mentioned as part of the breakfast news?'

'My bad,' said Freddie.

He turned towards them and rested his palms on the desk. Nasreen couldn't meet his eye. She looked at his forehead, his hairline a dark wave she'd once washed her hands in.

'Do you know this woman – Kate Adiyiah?'

'No,' she answered. At the same time as Freddie said, 'Yes.'

'Ah,' said Burgone. 'This is beginning to make more sense. I didn't think going to the press was your style, Cudmore.' The use of her surname stung. She longed for him to call her Nasreen. She focused on the spot on his forehead, watched it undulate as he talked. She knew every part of him by heart. How long his eyelashes were. The faint freckle by his ear.

'Who is she?' he asked Freddie.

'A teacher.' Freddie's voice still had an edge to it. She didn't like being interrogated. She didn't like being answerable. She didn't like being here.

'Yes, I gathered that. Who is she to you?' Burgone said.

'I don't see how that's any of your business,' Freddie said.

Nasreen held her breath. Burgone smiled. 'It became my business when she mentioned my team on national television.'

'Wasn't my fault,' Freddie said, shrugging. 'I'm not the boss of her.'

Why couldn't she see what she'd done?

'Let's try this another way,' Burgone said. 'Is what she's saying correct – that she witnessed a rape being live streamed?' He looked at Nasreen.

She didn't react in time. His eyes locked onto hers and she involuntarily took a sharp breath in. 'I… there's no evidence to support her claims, sir,' she managed.

'Yes, but do you believe her? I presume Freddie does, or

else Kate Adiyiah wouldn't have ended up splashed all over the news.'

'I didn't have anything to do with the television thing. I told you,' Freddie said. 'Everyone knows TV is dead anyway.'

'Nasreen?' Burgone looked at her. Nasreen could hear the clock ticking on the wall. She thought of Kate Adiyiah sat in the café. Her neatly written notes. Her hands, calm on the table in front of them. The steadiness of her voice. Her breathing. She hadn't touched her ears. Her face. Hadn't looked around the room. Or away. And until the end, when Nasreen said they couldn't help her, her voice hadn't altered.

'Yes, sir, I believe her.'

A

He hears the key in the door. The shout of welcome. As if
nothing has happened. He stares at his phone. *Need to talk.*
He knew B'd come. There is a knock at his bedroom door. It
opens without an answer. He stays on his bed. Doesn't look
up. Doesn't want to see his face. He just has to say the words.
Not looking would be easier.

'All right?'

He nods. *Just say it.* Swallows.

B strolls around the room, his hands in his pockets, bending
to look at the newest sky map on the wall. 'Still shooting for
the stars, hey?'

He could be a stranger. Alien. Unknown. But he's not. He
knows his every move. His every breath. A very familiar
stranger. *You know him. You trust him. You have to end this.*
His foot taps the beat of his heart against the floor. Fast.

95

Doof, doof, doof, doof, doof. A drum and bass rhythm to his madness. His mouth is so dry. His throat so dry. Dry. Dry. Die.

'Cat got your tongue?' B leans against the desk. Arms folded. Face set. Trouble.

You called him here. You wanted to talk, so talk. Say it. Say the words. This is the solution. You know it. This is the way out.
'I…' His throat clogs. Full. Don't be sick. Not now. Not in front of B. The phone turns in his hand: faster and faster, keeping time with his foot. His heart. His mind.

B looks bored. Pushes off the desk. *He's going to leave before you can say it. Say it. Say the words. Do it.*

'Thank you for coming,' he manages.

'"Thank you for coming" – what do you think this is? A tea party?' B's laughter cracks like thunder.

He's happy. Relaxed. Better than you. He's not guilty. Because this is your fault. Do it. Do it now. 'I'm going to go to the police.'

B raises his eyebrows. Lets them fall. Shakes his head. 'You need to think about this.' He looks at his star chart sadly. 'You don't wanna go to college any more?'

It hurts. Of course he wants to go to uni. To study. Become an astronaut. That's always been the dream. The goal. He feels himself floating away from it, weightless, as if he's been cut free. B, his room, Earth, getting smaller. Until it's only a speck. The human body can't survive in space. You'd have fifteen seconds until you lost consciousness. Your skin would swell up to twice its size. Skin. Swelling. Floating.

B is looking at him. Waiting.

Tell him you can't sleep. Tell him you can't live with the

96

screams. *Tell him you can't do this any more.* 'I'll tell them it was an accident. That I... I...' *You can't even say it, you coward.*

'But your mum?' B's voice is almost a whisper.

He flinches at the mention of her. 'I have to do this.'

B shakes his head. 'You can't do that to her, bruv.'

But I can't live like this.

'Think about your brothers. Me. What's gonna happen if you go to the five-oh? Hey?'

He can't form the words. His brothers. He hasn't thought about them.

'You gonna miss seeing them grow up? Keeping them on the straight? And for what?' B shakes his head again, as if he's being unreasonable. As if it's lunacy. Is it? Is he? He exhales: 78.04 per cent nitrogen, 13.6 per cent oxygen, 5.3 per cent carbon dioxide, 1 per cent argon. B sits next to him on the bed. Puts an arm over his shoulders. Warm. Heavy.

He swallows. His skin grows damp where B's arm rests. 'I gotta do this.' The weight increases.

'It's done, bruv.' B squeezes him. 'You can't give up on all this because of one mistake.' He sweeps his other hand round the room.

It's small but it's his. Only his. In prison he'd have to share. It's violent, he knows that. Knows the stories. 'Can you teach me some moves, B? To fight?'

B laughs. His face freezes as he realises he's serious. Shakes his head. 'You're no fighter. You're a thinker, mate.' He taps his finger against his forehead.

It's impossible for a healthy person to voluntarily stop breathing. Hold your breath and you pass out: your body naturally breathes for itself. Survival.

B's hand tightens on his shoulder. His fingers push into his muscles. He winces. 'You're not built for inside.'

'But she… her…' He tries to force the words out. Fails. Floats away.

'This ain't just 'bout you. I was there. I'll go down as well…'

'No. I'll tell them it was nothing to do with you.'

'But I helped after… My fingerprints and stuff, it'll be on her. And I won't be going to no playschool juvie,' B said.

He shakes his head. 'That's not what I want. Not what I meant to happen.'

'This is bigger than just you. They'll put me in with THM. Just you watch. I won't have no protection then. They'll jump me, and then it'll be…' He runs his finger over his neck.

DNA. He hasn't thought of that: *stupid. Stupid. Stupid.* He can see blood. Springing up. It's coming through the carpet, pushing into his room, sucking at his feet. He blinks. Breathes. *It's not real. It's not real.* 'I just…' He doesn't want to cause any more pain.

B walks over to his desk, picks up his fossil. Found it on a school trip to the Jurassic Coast. They weren't supposed to take souvenirs, but he couldn't help himself. The lines of the mollusc in the stone. Like a beautiful carving. Was that the start of it? His first bad act. Thou shalt not steal. But he had. He'd taken it because he wanted it.

'This your favourite rock?'

'It's a perisphinctes tizian.'

B weighs it in his hand. 'They'd kill you with this inside. Put it in a sock and then… smash!' He swings his arm towards him.

Duck!

98

B laughs. Shakes his head. 'Afraid of an itty bitty stone.'

Fear squeezes his chest. He can feel the thuds of the rock pummelling into him. Dents. *You deserve that. You got it coming. Be brave. Be a man.*

B is still looking at the fossil. 'I can't protect your mum if I go down.'

The thought of his mum… The dark corners… Shapes moving towards her. Men moving towards her. He shakes his head.

'I'm glad we had this chat.' B bends to look into the telescope, hands in his pockets. He taps the side of it. 'This ain't working. It's broken.'

'The cap's on.'

'Ain't it always the way.' He straightens. 'Remember what we said, yeah.' B pulls the door behind him, the air stream blowing papers from his desk.

He rights the telescope. Cold in his hands. He picks up his notes. Straightens them on the table. Tears threaten his eyes. *You gotta be brave. Do the right thing.* He can hear his mum singing as she moves about the flat. Snippets of lyrics then humming. She does that when she's happy. *Do the right thing. You gotta do the right thing.* He lifts his Apollo star chart, which is hanging black and sad, half snagged down the wall. He pushes the corner into the Blu-tack. It gives under his thumb, spreading, pressing into the cracks into the wall. This is him now. Shape-shifting. Squashed, hidden, hiding his darkest secret. Disappearing into the background. *Do the right thing.*

Nasreen

A knock on Burgone's door broke the silence.

'Come!' he said, finally looking away from Nasreen. She looked at Freddie, who raised her eyebrows at her.

'Sorry to interrupt, guv.' Green poked her head nervously into the room. 'There's a telephone call.'

'Take a message, constable,' Burgone said.

'Well, the thing is, sir –' Green looked nervously from Nasreen and back to the DCI.

'I'm in a meeting,' Burgone said.

'They asked to speak to Freddie Venton or DS Cudmore, sir.' Green's fingernails were white against the doorframe.

Why would someone ask to speak to her or Freddie... unless?

'Who is it?' Burgone's brow furrowed.

'Some lady. She said she was watching the breakfast news

when she saw about the live streamed video thing, and anyway, she thinks her kid watched the same film as that woman did.' Green exhaled the words quickly, as though pleased to be rid of them.

Nasreen's chest tightened. Kate hadn't made it up. Someone else had seen the girl attacked too.

Burgone pushed air out of his cheeks and rocked back on his chair. Freddie was grinning from ear to ear. 'You know what that is?' she said, looking between Nasreen and Burgone. She didn't give them time to respond. 'That is another witness.'

And suddenly Nasreen understood. 'That's why you tipped the press off?' she said.

Freddie nodded. 'Yup.'

'You knew there wasn't enough evidence based on what Kate had said alone, but if other people had seen the video, if other people came forward, there would be more witnesses.'

'More people are harder to ignore,' Freddie said.

Nasreen shook her head; it was a bold move. Risky. Very Freddie.

Burgone got up, moved his office chair out from under his desk and sat down again. 'I'm trying to work out if you have breached the Official Secrets Act,' he said, looking at Freddie.

She didn't falter. 'It's not our case – I can't have broken the Official Secrets Act by talking about something we weren't even working on.' She looked insanely pleased with herself.

Nasreen's mind was already flying forward through possible ramifications. Their names being quoted on national television wasn't great, but they could argue they weren't to blame for that. Or, at least, she wasn't to blame for that. But what about Kate? It could be a crackpot who'd rung in. A timewaster who wanted a bit of the action and a bit of attention. 'It could be a hoaxer?'

Burgone scratched at the invisible stubble on his cheek. He did that when he was thinking. 'I don't approve of your actions, Freddie. But now this team is linked to the incident within the public's mind, I think the best way to exercise damage limitation is to take control of the situation.'

'You're letting us take the case?' Freddie leant forward.

'We don't know for sure that there is a case yet,' he said.

'But we can investigate it, yeah?' Freddie pushed.

Nasreen bristled.

'You cannot investigate anything, you are an analyst and a partially trained interviewer. Though I'm sure I don't need to remind you of that.' His voice took on a slight warning tone. 'You cannot continue to behave in this irresponsible manner if you want to make a go of this job, Freddie.'

Freddie's lips pursed.

He turned to look at Nasreen. This time she was ready. Green was still hovering in the doorway, unsure if she should stay or go, or what to do about the woman on the phone. 'Cudmore, I want you to take the lead on this, as your name has already been released.'

The hairs on her arms stood up. 'You do want us to investigate it?'

'I want you to talk to this alleged witness and any others you can find. I want the interviews correctly recorded, in case we receive any awkward questions from the press. It's August, silly season, they like something they can get their teeth into at this time of year. We don't need them whipping the public up into a paranoia over this. I want to know if the video was real. If it was shot in this country. And if it wasn't, I want the public to be reassured that people aren't going around raping women on film. Okay?'

'In addition to working on the Paul Robertson case?' Nasreen asked. They still needed to see if they could find Lex Riley. Find out if he had anything to do with Amber and her father's disappearance.

'Is that a problem?' Burgone said.

'No. Not at all. I can do that.' He was letting her lead the investigation. An investigation that could be a load of twaddle. Could lead nowhere. An investigation where they had one, possibly two witnesses, and no victim. She swallowed.

Burgone seemed to catch the moment. 'Don't worry, Cudmore. I'll ask DI Saunders to provide guidance where necessary. Make sure you're not alone on this one.'

Oh, no. That wasn't what she wanted. She went to open her mouth, to say she'd rather not work with Saunders at all, but Freddie and Green were here. She wouldn't be that unprofessional. 'Yes, sir.'

'Green?' Burgone said. 'Go tell the caller DS Cudmore is coming.'

Freddie jumped up. 'We need to find this girl.'

Nasreen turned and followed her out of the office in a daze. How was she going to manage both this and the Amber Robertson case? Pull yourself together, woman. This is your chance. Do a good job on this and you prove yourself not only to the team but to Burgone. Possibly even the Super. She swallowed. She needed to tell Freddie her fears about the girl in the video. That this might not have a happy ending.

Back in the office Freddie made a beeline for her desk.

Green was already at hers. Phone in hand. 'She's on line two, Sarg,' she called.

Without looking at Saunders, Nasreen picked up the receiver, took a breath and connected the call. 'DS Nasreen Cudmore speaking.'

Paul

He rubbed his hands together, feeling specks of sweat, dirt and skin roll from his palms and settle between his fingers. He wiped them against his jeans. He felt dirty. That's what it was. Grubby. *Shameful.* He looked over his shoulder. Ridiculous. There was no one there. It was just him in his shitty room, in his shitty flat. He closed his eyes, as if that might help. But then all he could hear was the noise from outside. The angry hum of the city, a thousand bees at the window. And his own breath. That was worse. It caught in his throat. Like it caught in hers. He gasped. The room rushed back. He grappled for the fake leather of the sofa, trying to get a handful. He's here. Above the chicken shop. Next to the Nelson pub. Alone.

The anger hit him hard, right in the solar plexus, radiating along his nerves. Hissing and spitting like water droplets on a hot pan. He welcomed it. Felt it. The heat. The burn. Warning him. Teaching him. This was what he needed to survive.

He won't go back. He can't. He's sacrificed too much already. He'd given everything to get here. Here to this shitty hovel. He covered his ears, his nose, screwed his eyes shut, as if he could force it out. Keep it away from him. The photo tucked into the mirror looked at him. Unblinking. Smiling. He turned away.

He needed to calm down. He needed to think. This was not the first time he'd seen something he ought not to have. He laughed. It was funny. This was supposed to be a laugh. He never even thought twice. It was fucked up. Royally. He kicked himself. *How long have you been in this game, bruv?* You can't let your guard down. Ever. No one could know what he saw. Could they? He looked at his tablet: was it a threat? He clicked through: it was gone. Not just the vid, but the account. Ghosted. *Good idea.* He moved fast: deleting his own account, deleting them all, wiping everything. All gone.

How will she find you now? The voice was small, insistent, it sounded like her. It stung. He didn't ask for this. He didn't ask for any of this. He stood quickly, the tablet squeaking against the sofa. He hated this fucking sofa. He kicked at the empty pizza boxes, the seeping silver tins. He hated them. He picked one up. Hurled it with all his might. Yelling now. Shouting. Noodles slid like wet hair down the wall. He swung at the coffee table with the base of his foot. Tore at the sofa, clawed the cushions from the back. Pulled. Ripped. Foam burst from the fake shitty leather like a zit. He roared at the unfairness of it all. He pulled down the telly with a satisfying crash. His hands strong on the wooden chair. *Why was it even*

106

here? There was no fucking dining table. He brought it down on the tablet. Smashed. Smashed. Smashed. Then he turned on the rest of the room, pulled, punched, round-housed the ghosts. His mum passed out on the floor. The shadow of his stepdad at his bedroom door. The men. The money that changed hands. The filthy fucking perverts. The kid with the knife in the back alley. The lads with the baseball bats. The showers inside, that first time. He punched wildly, madly, fists and feet, destroyed every one of them. Glass, fibres, paper whirled around him. He caught the mirror and it cracked. The photo fluttered away and he grabbed for it. It shouldn't touch any of this. He had to catch it. Keep it clean.

He fell to his knees. *He can't go back.* He held the photo in both hands, at the edges. Afraid his touch would contaminate it. Afraid he'd destroyed this too. The girl smiled out at him, as if she knew. He gently cleared a space among the guts of the sofa, the debris, smoothed away the mess and laid the photo face down on the floor. *Please forgive me.* And then he rested his head in his hands, because it didn't matter what he did. What he broke. Who he hurt. Where he ran to.

He knew who the girl in the video was.

Freddie

The mum who'd called in following Kate's appearance on telly must hold the key. Freddie had combed through the growing number of articles that had featured interviews with Kate, and watched the TV footage back: at no point did Kate describe the girl or the two assailants in the video, apart from noting they were men. If the mum's kid described the attackers and victim in the same way as Kate did, they had to be talking about the same thing.

The mum – Mrs Nicolson – was on her way in with her twelve-year-old son. As was his twelve-year-old pal, with his dad, Mr Brook. Freddie could just imagine how that conversation went down. She knew why twelve-year-old boys would click on a video stream entitled 'live sex' but she didn't know how Mrs Nicolson had found out. The plan was to interview them before bringing in and separately interviewing Kate

108

tomorrow, then compare and contrast. Burgone and the others would have to take the case seriously then.

But Freddie hadn't forgotten about missing Amber. She laid her paperwork over her desk and started to scan it. A pattern started to form in front of her eyes; a pattern that had to mean something. She needed to speak to Nas before she disappeared into the interview with the twelve-year-olds. Nas didn't want Saunders to know they were going after Lex Riley, so, checking no one else in the office was looking, she texted her:

Meet me in kitchen. Code amber.

She waited till Nas's phone beeped, and then she left the office. Burgone's door was closed. Good. They didn't need eavesdroppers.

Nas joined her in the staff room about a minute later.

'What you got?' Nas sounded efficient. If she was still pissed about the whole Kate-on-the news thing, she'd obviously decided there wasn't time to show it. Freddie could work with that.

Freddie spread the pages on the kitchen worktop, her hands moving fast in her excitement. 'I've found another link between Lex Riley and Amber and Paul Robertson.'

'Where?' Nas glanced behind her like Saunders might be lurking.

'I got hold of Amber's phone records. She repeatedly communicates with this number – which we believe is Paul Robertson's pay-as-you-go phone. She also regularly communicates with this number, also associated with pay-as-you-go. The messages and calls start on 27 October 2015, which correlates to when we see increased communication between Amber and Lex on Facebook.' Freddie showed her a spidergram-style chart of the cell site analysis she'd done. 'The last message is sent from Lex's phone on 13 July this year.'

'Same as the last messages sent from Amber and Paul's phone,' Nasreen said.

'Exactly.' Freddie nodded. 'Can't be a coincidence, can it?'

'Chips would say he doesn't believe in coincidence.' Nas frowned.

There had to be a link between all three disappearing at once.

'There's more: the phone I believe is Lex Riley's makes two calls to Paul Robertson. One straight after the other.'

'What? Why would they be talking?' Nas ran her finger over the chart.

This was her clincher. It was all stacking up. 'Wait till you hear what date the calls were made on: July 1.'

'That's the day Tibbsy and Moast saw Paul and Amber arguing in the street,' Nas nodded.

Lex Riley could be linked to the argument between Robertson and Amber that Moast and Tibbsy had witnessed. 'Maybe Robertson found out about Lex,' she said.

'But then why would Lex Riley call him?' Nas asked. Something didn't add up.

'I don't know. But I've done some more digging. And I think I've found Lex Riley.'

Green's voice from behind made them both jump. 'Sarg, there you are. I've been looking for you: the first kid has arrived,' she said, leaning into the kitchen.

Crap. Freddie grouped all the paperwork together fast. They didn't want this getting out. Amber and Lex Riley would have to wait; the hunt for the girl in the video was about to begin.

Freddie

'Anything for me, Venton?' Saunders made her jump. He enjoyed creeping up on people.

Her work on Lex Riley was right next to her on her desk. She had to get him away from here before he spotted it. She handed over her notes on Kate and the video. He would be interviewing one kid with Green, while Nas talked to the other with Chips. She'd have to watch on the screens outside. 'Can't I come in with you?' she tried.

'Don't push your luck,' he said, turning back to his own desk, and Freddie slid her Lex Riley notes into her drawer. Saunders ran his fingers through his hair, and checked his teeth in the mirrored frame of the photo he kept of him and his boyfriend. It featured another guy, all three of them in triathlon Lycra, post-race with medals round their necks. 'This joke of a case is already taking me away from proper work.'

The kids had only come forward because of her: this was a *proper* lead. Two more potential witnesses. And still he wasn't taking it seriously. 'Why'd you never bring your bae to the pub after work?'

'Bae? What are you – twelve?' Saunders put the frame back on his desk, in exactly the same spot, at a forty-five-degree angle towards his chair. *Anal.*

'Just getting you in character for your interview – you're going to scare them witless being so ancient.' He had ten years on her, which meant he had twenty-two years on the poor kid in the room.

'With age comes experience, something you and Cudmore don't seem to get. I proved my stripes. I get to interview the alleged witnesses. You're a former café worker, you get to make tea.'

Not this old thing again. 'And after I found you a new case and everything!' Freddie rolled her eyes.

Saunders tried not to smile.

Got ya.

Chips and Nas were standing outside the interview rooms: meeting-room offices that had been requisitioned as 'child friendly'. Freddie was pretty sure that if the kids were old enough to click on a 'live sex' video they were old enough to deal with a less plush room, but whatever.

'Did you get anything on Master Leo Nicolson?' Saunders looked at the printout she'd given him. 'What kind of name is Leo? What is he, a lion?'

'Very popular nowadays,' Freddie said. 'These kids are from Highgate, you're lucky they're not called Gabriel and Apple.'

'If I have kids they'll get good solid names.' Saunders wrinkled his nose.

'If you have kids they'll need therapy. Or taking into care,' Freddie said.

'Speak for yourself,' Saunders said.

'My generation will never be able to afford to have kids: you're looking at the pinnacle of humanity right here,' Freddie said.

'God help us.' Saunders rolled his eyes.

Nas cleared her throat as they drew level. 'Both Leo and his mum and Dylan and his dad are already waiting.' Freddie knew she meant for them to keep it down, but Saunders seemed to be deliberately ignoring it.

'Great, let's crack on with talking to the little perverts then!' The top of Nas's ears flushed.

'Sure I can't go in with Nas or something?' she said. Last shot.

'I think it'd be better if you watched for inconsistencies within the two stories,' Nas said quietly. Did she think they were hoaxers as well?

'You take Leo the lion, and we'll take Dylan –' Saunders ran his finger over his notes '– Brooks. Sounds like a bloody river,' he muttered under his breath.

'You happy with that, lass?' Chips smiled at Nas. 'This is your show.'

'More like a circus.' Saunders slapped the notes on Leo Nicolson into Nas's chest so she had to scrabble for them.

'Yes. Thank you, sir.' She smiled at Chips.

'The more you let him bully you, the more he's going to do it,' Freddie said as Chips opened the door for Nas. 'You gotta give as good as you get.'

113

Nas shot her an evil. 'I've got this, thank you.'

Freddie ran back into the office and logged into the two cameras that were recording in each room, running the feeds next to each other. Kate was telling the truth – were these lads?

114

Kate

Her phone hadn't stopped ringing. She hadn't expected the intensity of the questions. Hadn't known they would ask about Freddie and the nice policewoman. She'd done this because she'd wanted to help, but the news anchor had switched when they'd gone on air. Kate felt stupid. She should have seen it coming; he'd been too polite off camera. Too friendly. The doorbell went again, but Kate had learnt to ignore it. Newspapers, television shows, they all wanted interviews. The spotlight was on her. She felt hot, exposed, uncomfortable. She pressed *play* on her answerphone messages.

'This is a message for Kate Aday-yuuur. This is Sandra from *The Family Paper*. We'd like to talk to you about the alleged sexual assault you witnessed being live streamed.' Alleged – that meant they didn't believe her. 'I've left a couple of messages already. And I'd like to ask you about some information we've been given – regarding the breakdown you had in 1997? Some people have alleged –' that word again '– that you might be making this up? That this could be another episode? It'd be best if you gave your side of the story, Kate. Call me anytime on –'

Kate silenced the phone, her hands shaking. Another *episode?* She'd never imagined they would drag that up. How did they know about back then? About when she'd lost Tegbee. If they did start printing things, what would it mean for her school? She'd been younger when it had happened, her head teacher sympathetic. It had been easier to hide the small classroom incident. And after she'd been signed off and had counselling she'd been better. She'd returned, and very few people had asked questions. But now she was the head. She was the school. They needed their Outstanding Ofsted rating. She and her staff had fought hard for that. What would the governors say? This couldn't threaten it. It couldn't be allowed to impact on her pupils. But she had a duty of care to the girl in the video too. She loosened the collar of her shirt.

The sleeping tablets were where she'd left them on the side. The half-drunk bottle next to the packet. Her heart ached. No, that was silliness. She was just craving some comfort. Last night had been a dream, a lovely wonderful gift of a dream: nothing more. She should call someone. Talk it through. Someone she trusted. Ama, her closest friend, was out of town. And she always switched her phone off when she was abroad. What hotel did she say she was staying at in Bali? Which resort? She couldn't remember. Her phone started ringing again. *Unknown number.* She just needed to talk to someone she trusted. Be with someone who loved her. Was it so wrong to want solace? She rejected the call.

Kate walked to the sideboard. Picked a clean glass from the draining board, and poured in the flat warm wine. She knew it wasn't real. Knew it couldn't really be Tegbee. It was just a trick of the tablets. A hallucination brought on by the alcohol. But it felt real. There was respite in it. A calm she couldn't get elsewhere. And a greed. She knew that. It had been an awful day. An awful week. Why should she be denied her child, when others had theirs? What harm would one more vision do? She unscrewed the bottle, took two pills, put them in her mouth and swallowed them down with a mouthful of wine.

Nasreen

'I knew something was wrong! I knew it!' Heather Nicolson, a tall slender woman in skinny jeans and an expensive-looking fine knit, was shaking her honey blow-dried hair with such ferocity Nasreen was worried she'd dislocate something.

'Muuuum! You're so embarrassing.' Leo, rangy and fair like his mum, but not yet comfortable in his own skin, had sunk further than seemed possible into his hoodie jumper. Nasreen felt for him. Mrs Nicolson was going full pelt.

'No boy of twelve starts wetting the bed!'

'Mum!' he cried.

'I should never have let him play with that Dylan boy. Who doesn't have parental controls on their computer? Leo is not allowed his laptop in his room without the door open. We have rules about these things.' With each word Heather smacked the back of one tanned hand into the palm of the other.

Chips looked somewhere between bewildered and amused. They needed to calm her down if they were going to get anywhere. 'Can I get you a cup of tea or some water, Mrs Nicolson? I understand that you've had quite a shock.' She tried to move her towards the sofa, to get her to sit with her son.

Mrs Nicolson acquiesced, her vivid face collapsing into well-worn lines of exhaustion and worry. It was now four days since Kate said she'd watched the video; if this boy had been living with the aftershocks for that long, so had his family. What had Mrs Nicolson thought was wrong when her son started screaming himself awake at night and wetting the bed? What horrors had she imagined? And was the truth worse than what she'd feared? Gently Nasreen guided her to the sofa.

'Do you have herbal tea?' Mrs Nicolson asked meekly. 'I've never been in a police station before.'

Nasreen felt sorry for her. Though the plush surroundings of their office block were hardly your normal police station. God knows what she'd have made of the battered Jubilee. 'What about a nice camomile?' She nodded. 'And what about you, Leo, would you like something?'

He shook his head.

'Say "no, thank you,"' Mrs Nicolson snapped, out of habit. 'I'll just be a moment.'

When she came back Leo was sat in silence and Chips was doing his best to engage Mrs Nicolson in small talk. 'Difficult coping with this heat, isn't it? We could do with a bit of rain, hey, lass?' he said as she passed the mug to Mrs Nicolson.

'I wonder if there's a storm coming? The pressure is intense.'

119

The woman managed to heave her face into half a smile, before lifting the hot cup to her lips and blowing. It was better now she had something occupying her hands.

'Aye, probably,' Chips said. 'What do you think, lad? Think it's going to rain?'

Leo shrugged his shoulders, his blue eyes still staring at the ground. But she could feel his discomfort. He was putting on a show for them, but the freckles that still dusted his nose highlighted the fact that he was still just a kid. One who'd potentially seen something very disturbing. She settled herself back in the chair opposite them, matching Chips's relaxed posture. Leo clearly hadn't encountered police before. His eyes kept flicking up and around the room, as if it might suddenly change into a cell. 'I want to reassure you, Leo, you are not in any trouble,' Nasreen said.

'He is with me and his father,' Mrs Nicolson snapped. Leo winced.

'Please.' Chips gave her a warm smile. 'Let the lad talk.'

'I knew something was wrong! Knew it!' Mrs Nicolson's voice shot up an octave. 'It wasn't until it came on the news and he –'

'Mum!' Leo begged. Nasreen guessed he'd reacted in some way: been sick possibly? Or cried? Both would fit with trauma.

Mrs Nicolson seemed to deflate. She reached out and took hold of her son's hand. 'He was so upset. So distant. I just didn't know what to do.' Leo hung his head but he let his mum keep hold of his hand. 'Do you have kids, detective?' She looked at Chips, and Nasreen wished she had a few more years under her own belt. Something to help her reach this woman.

'Aye, two girls. They're married now, kids of their own, but they never stop being your babies.' Chips's puffy face crinkled into a sympathetic smile. He patted one of his hands against his suit jacket. Nasreen knew he kept photos of his grandkids in his wallet.

Nasreen tried for her best smile. Chips had Mrs Nicolson, it was her job to reach Leo. 'So you saw the video at your friend Dylan's house, is that right, Leo?'

Mrs Nicolson contained her reaction to a small tutting sound. Leo pulled his hand from her, ignoring the hurt on his mother's face. 'Yeah.'

'And you were staying over, were you?'

'Yeah.' He didn't look up.

She was going to have to get him to relax before he would open up. One-word answers weren't going to help them. She wished they'd found an independent appropriate adult; what twelve-year-old boy wanted to talk about looking for porn in front of his mother? She tried a different tack. 'How long have you been friends with Dylan for?'

'Too long,' Mrs Nicolson started to say, but Chips shot her a friendly but warning look. *Let the lad talk.*

'Leo?' Nasreen prompted.

He glanced at his mum and then back at her. 'Dunno. Couple of years probably.'

'How often have you stayed at his?' She was trying to avoid questions that could just be answered with one word.

Leo shrugged and worked one white trainer against the other, deeply uncomfortable. 'Dylan's parents are more chill.'

Mrs Nicolson looked hurt, but managed to stay quiet.

'Do you often look for… intimate videos online?'

121

His eyebrows and face creased into a look of disgust. 'No, man. We're not freaks. We were bored. Seeing who was live. We just clicked for a laugh.'

'And do you remember the name of the account you clicked on?' he said.

'Nah.' He shook his head, the bluster going out of him. 'I wish we hadn't,' he added quietly. 'I wish I'd never seen it.'

A shell-shocked look had crept into his eyes, and she no longer wondered if this was a hoax. Whatever this kid had seen, it had freaked him out. 'Can you tell me who was in the video, Leo?'

He swallowed. Nodded. 'There was a man. Black. He didn't have a shirt on. And he was… he was…' Mrs Nicolson went to take his hand, but Chips gently pulled her back.

'Like, I knew something was wrong. She wasn't, like, responding, you know?' Leo said.

'The female in the video?'

'Yes.' He swallowed again. His young forehead tense. He was leaning forward now, his elbows on his knees, twisting his fingers together.

'Can you tell me about her?'

'She was out of it. Drunk, I guess.' He shook his head.

Nasreen could just imagine what Freddie would say now. That even if she had been drunk, then the girl didn't deserve this. 'And what was the man doing?'

'He was having sex with her,' he said. The words absurdly mature in his mouth.

'And she was out of it?' He was raping her.

'Yeah, to begin with,' he said. 'Then, like, she spoke. Like, she told them to stop.'

Her heart was beating fast now. 'Them?'

'Yeah, there was a kid behind the camera. Like, doing the filming. You could hear him talking.'

This was sounding more and more like what Kate had seen. If only he could remember the name of the account, then she could be sure. Perhaps Dylan would? 'Did you see the other male at all?'

'No.' He shook his head. His eyes were unblinking pools of regret.

'How old would you say the man in the video was? And the man who you only heard talk?'

'The talking one was younger. Like maybe my age?'

Nasreen felt her blood run cold. Seeing this twelve-year-old boy in front of her, thinking of another child his age witnessing that, being part of that, was devastating. 'And the other?'

'I dunno. Older. Maybe sixth form, maybe like uni age?' he said.

She nodded her encouragement, bringing the conversation back round to the hardest part. 'And what about the woman? How would you describe her?'

'She had long black hair. And she was, like, dark – like Jessica,' he said to his mother.

Mrs Nicolson, who looked like she was trying very hard not to cry, managed to say, 'Jessica's mum is black and her dad is white. Very pretty girl.'

Long dark hair. Mixed race. The hairs on Nasreen's arms stood up. 'How old do you think the woman was?'

'I dunno, like, a few years older than me, I guess,' Leo said. *Sixteen maybe?* 'And there were no names used in the film?'

'No.' He shook his head.

'Any other identifying features of either the man or the woman?' she pushed.

'No.' He shook his head again. 'Sorry.' He tried to clear his throat. A tear fell across his cheek. He swiped at it with the back of his hand. 'I'm sorry.'

'Oh, darling.' Mrs Nicolson pulled him to her, and he crumpled into her. 'It's okay.'

'I'm sorry, Mum.' He wept into her shoulder. Tears fell from Mrs Nicolson's eyes as she stroked the back of his head.

'It's okay, shush, shush, it's okay.' She gently rocked him.

Chips was pursing his lips glumly. She nodded at him and signalled at the door. They couldn't continue today. Even if Mrs Nicolson allowed it, which she didn't think for one second she would. 'We'll give you guys some space,' she said quietly and they got up and left the boy crying in his mother's arms.

Outside Chips puffed air out. 'Poor lad.'

She wanted to know what Dylan had to say. But her mind was ticking over, matching up possibilities. 'I didn't get to ask about the location. I should have started with that.' That was a mistake. Perhaps Leo had recognised where the video had been shot. Dammit.

'He needs a break,' Chips said.

'I know. I'll give them five minutes and make sure they get a car home.'

'No wonder he's been having nightmares if he saw that wee girl raped and stabbed.' Chips shook his head. 'You can't even keep your kids safe inside their own bedrooms.'

She nodded, suddenly thankful that her own parents had been so strict about internet access when she was a teen. But the tech had already changed since then. Though Mrs

Nicolson had been adamant about her own parental controls, she was quite confident most twelve-year-olds could circumvent them with ease. She thought of how easily Freddie had got round her mum's password-protected internet when they were twelve, so they could watch an eighteen-rated film. The worst she'd suffered was a sleepless night, when her imagination had got the better of her. And Freddie had been there to read to her till she finally fell asleep. Suddenly she wished she was back there with her childhood best friend. Poor Leo. Four days ago the horrific adult world had brutally battered into his conscience. No matter how much his mum loved him, they couldn't get that back. 'I'm going to ask if he can talk to a photofit artist about both the victim and the suspect,' she said.

Chips nodded. Could she show him a photo? In his current state it might be too risky. She didn't want to trigger a post-traumatic stress episode: they needed Leo to be calm enough to talk. If they could find a suspect, they'd need him to be strong enough to potentially give evidence in court.

'Messy one this,' Chips said, as if he were reading her mind.

'Yes.' She chewed on the side of her cheek.

'What you thinking, lass?'

It was something that Freddie said. About how no women matching the description Kate had given had been treated at hospital. How no one matching that description had been reported missing. What if that was because they were already reported missing a year ago? What if they'd been missing all this time? *Her mum is black, her dad is white.* Leo could have been describing Amber Robertson. Lex Riley was potentially involved in her disappearance, and he was part of a gang that had links to sex trafficking and video nasties. Had Amber been sold into the trade? And ended up in a snuff movie? Would anyone have survived the attack Kate described? The thought of the smiling girl whose photo was pinned on the board next door meeting her end like that was sickening. Was her imagination playing tricks?

Nasreen hated saying it, but she couldn't ignore it any longer. 'I think we might be looking for a body.'

126

Freddie

'There are no sightings or reports of Lex Riley after the disappearance of Paul and Amber. But I searched for Corey Banks, on the off chance he was using that name. Again, nothing. But then I had a look through all his known associates. Two weeks ago, surveillance reports that Jay Trap, Lex Riley's cousin and head of The Dogberry Boys, went to Sydenham.' Freddie spread her paperwork over the sink unit in the Ladies.

Nas had texted her as soon as she was out of the interview with Leo. Saunders was accompanying Dylan and his dad downstairs; they only had minutes. Both Dylan and Leo had confirmed the same story. They'd clicked on a live streamed video link titled 'Live Sex'. Dylan had even been able to confirm the name of the account: Metronome02, the same account Kate had independently given. They corroborated her report.

'Sydenham is a bit off Jay Trap's patch,' Nas said.

'Yeah, and he met a tall, shaven-headed guy with a dragon tattoo on his arm, in a local café called May's Place. Trap called his associate Cory. The surveillance dude spelt it with no e – see.' Freddie showed her the report.

'The dragon tattoo? That's the tag of the Dogberrys – according to his file Lex has one on his left arm,' Nasreen said.

Freddie had found that out too. 'Better than that, the surveillance dude noted that "Cory" left the café first, and entered the building opposite. It's flats. The basement is registered to a Korey, with a K this time. Korey Banks. He hasn't even bothered to change alias.' That was where he was living. She'd found him.

'Brilliant,' said Nas.

Freddie beamed. She loved impressing her. 'So now what?'

Nas looked at her watch. It was already six o'clock. 'We debrief with Saunders about Dylan and Leo's statements about Kate's video. She's coming in tomorrow for her interview, but I think it's fair to say they've watched the same thing.'

This had to make Saunders and the others take note. 'You can't ignore three witnesses.'

Nas nodded. 'Did you hear how Leo described the girl in the video?'

'Yeah, mixed race, long dark hair.' Freddie froze as she gathered the papers about Lex together. 'Oh my God: he could have been describing Amber. You don't think it's her, do you?' Her stomach lurched.

Nas grimaced. 'The Dogberry Boys have been linked to people trafficking and the illegal sex trade in the past. It would be a big coincidence, but we have a missing girl who on paper matches the description of Amber.'

'We have to show Kate and the kids the photo of Amber,' Freddie said. The thought of Amber, the funny, bright girl she'd got to know through her social media, being raped on film was too much.

'We can't.' Nas shook her head. 'It'd be meaningless without the link between Lex Riley and Amber, and the moment we reveal we're after Riley, Saunders will have us off this case. He's not interested in finding Amber unless it leads to Paul Robertson. And going after Lex Riley will be stamping all over the Drugs lads' territory – he definitely doesn't want that.'

This was nuts. 'So we do – what – nothing?'

Nas shrugged. 'I don't want to give up on Amber any more than you do, Freddie. But the best way to keep working on this is to keep quiet about any possible links between the two cases right now. I shouldn't have mentioned anything. I've no evidence. It was just a thought.'

A thought that had lodged itself in Freddie's chest.

'Let's hope my suspicions are wrong,' Nas said.

Freddie's gut tightened. They couldn't just ignore this. 'We need to see the photofit from Leo, Dylan and Kate.' To see if it looked like Amber. Freddie ran through everything they knew and everything they didn't know. 'What about the room?'

'What?' Nas said.

'The room the filming took place in. Kate said it felt like council accommodation. Don't they bulk-buy for that kind of thing? What if we did a photofit of the room to see if anyone recognised it? If it's local authority they might.'

Nas blinked. 'Okay. I don't know if the artist does that – I can ask.'

It was something. If they could find the location then they

had a chance of helping the girl. They couldn't just sit here and wait.

'And in the meantime we go after Lex?'

Nas nodded. 'I'll meet you downstairs in the car park after we've spoken to Saunders.'

Freddie nodded. She gave Nas a two-minute head start back to the office. Being seen coming out of the Ladies together was too risky. She lifted up her T-shirt and stuffed the paperwork about Lex into the waistband of her shorts. If it was Amber in the film Kate had seen, she wanted to get her hands on Lex Riley as soon as possible.

Freddie

They'd made it out of the office without anyone seeing them. The windows of the pool car were wide open as they reached the airless streets of Sydenham. 'It hasn't cooled off at all,' Freddie said. It was gone 7pm.

'Going to be hotter tomorrow,' Nas said.

They were both anxious about talking to Lex Riley. Both making stupid small talk. 'You seen my new business cards?' Freddie held one out for Nas. 'Freddie Venton, Civilian Investigator, pretty cool, huh?'

Nas smiled. 'Pretty cool.' The car crawled past dingy shop fronts, which gave way to gentrified coffee shops and cock-tail bars with upended crates as stools to suit the nappy clappers.

'He's gone up in the world then?' Freddie said. 'I couldn't afford to live round here.' She couldn't afford to live anywhere.

Nas signalled to pull right. 'Perhaps he got a promotion for his trouble.'

She didn't like this. The way Lex had catfished a fifteen-year-old girl, it was screwed up. She caught herself before she got cross at Amber for not being smarter. Freddie had been fooled herself online. Lex could have used Amber as bait to get to Paul. And when he was done with her what further use would he have for the girl?

'This is the street,' Nas said.

Grand Victorian houses stood shoulder to shoulder down the road. What had Freddie's Romanian Uber driver called them? 'Sticky' houses: houses that were stuck together, terraced. It felt fitting in this heat. Nas parked up, and Freddie followed her out.

'It's this one.' Nas pointed at the stone steps, flanked by pots of red flowers, leading down to the basement of a brightly painted white house.

'He's gone underground,' Freddie said.

'I thought you could lead this one. We can call it fieldwork – part of your training.'

Despite everything, Freddie couldn't help but grin. Maybe Nas had warmed to her new role. 'Do I get to play bad cop?'

'Only if you want this job to be short-lived,' Nas said. 'You're gathering intelligence. Information that could be useful for officers. Stick to the guidelines I gave you – you have read them, haven't you?'

When would she have had time for that? Besides, she'd watched enough interviews to get the gist. How hard could it be? 'What do you take me for?'

'This is a great responsibility, Freddie.' Nas said. 'Your work could really make a difference. It could lead an officer to an important breakthrough in a case.'

Trust Nas to make it sound lame. 'You mean I do all the work, and you guys get all the credit?'

Nas frowned. She loved all this rules and training nonsense. 'Do you want to do it or not?'

Freddie's sandals flopped down the stairs and she pressed the black-painted doorbell. This didn't look like a gangster's home. Not that she'd ever been to one before. 'Come on then.'

Nas walked past her and along the slim paved strip that ran in front of the window. Shielding her eyes from the sunlight with her hand, she peered in. A blind had been pulled down on the other side. 'Can't see anything.'

There was movement through the mosaic glass panels of the front door. A shape. Dark. Large. Looming. Freddie wanted to say someone was coming, but her mouth had gone dry. The sound of a bolt, and then another, broke the illusion. This was excessive security for what looked like a fairly salubrious road. Who double-locked themselves in the house when it was still light? Someone who was worried about who was coming for them. Or someone who didn't want someone to get out? The final lock clicked, and the door opened. Lex Riley stood in front of them: tall, broad-shouldered and wearing a low, loose weightlifting vest top, a towel slung round his shoulders to catch the sweat. They'd found him. A dragon tattoo, the sign of the Dogberrys, curled round his bicep and hissed smoke at them. His arms were as wide as her legs, and Freddie instinctively stepped backwards. She felt Nas's hand in the small of her back, steadying her. Stopping her from retreating. Lex Riley scowled as he took in Nas in her smart white shirt and black trousers. Eau de cop.

'What you lot want?' he said.

Freddie knew this was her cue. She was to lead the interview. She opened her mouth. Nothing came out.

'Lex Riley?' Nas said.

'Whatever it is, I had nothing to do with it.' He started to close the door. Lightning fast, Nas was past her, ramming her black workboot in the way. His steak-slab hands pushed back. 'Move it, pig.'

'There's no need to be unfriendly, Lex,' Nas said. 'I'm DS Cudmore and this is Civilian Investigator Ms Venton.' Nas pulled her ID card from her belt. 'We just want a quick word.'

Lex lowered his face so it was millimetres away from Nas's. 'Fuck off.'

Nas didn't flinch. Freddie held her breath.

There was a noise from above. Water rained down onto them. Freddie let out a yelp and looked up. A small, white-haired lady was watering the flower-filled window boxes that hung on the railing. 'Oh! I am sorry! I didn't see you there!' she cried.

Lex's demeanour immediately changed. He stepped away from Nas, smiling and waving up at the little old lady. 'How are you today, Mrs Koo?' he called.

What the hell? Freddie felt her shock register on her face.

'Oh, you've got guests – I am sorry!' Mrs Koo said. Freddie saw the woman's eyes flick over Nas and take in the ID she was putting back into her pocket. She tilted her little bird head slightly, her smile slightly strained. 'Is everything okay, Korey?'

Nas raised an eyebrow.

'Huh!' Lex gave a fake laugh. 'All fine. All fine. Friend of my… err, my sister.' He turned, his warm smile instantly crumbling and said under his breath: 'Get inside.'

Nas strode past him, and Freddie followed, giving Mrs Koo a goodbye wave. They walked straight into the kitchen, a large wooden table dominating the space. Past that, Freddie could see a bedroom, the edge of the bed, and a weights bench opened out in front of double glass doors. Through that was a small garden. Lex Riley was four years younger than her. No one her age could afford a garden in London. Legally.

He shut the door and turned to face them. 'This is harassment.'

'Why are you using a different name, Lex?' Nas said.

'No law against that.' He crossed his arms. Freddie frowned. What was all that about outside? All that good-boy act?

Nas was walking around the kitchen, stopping to look at a spice rack and a small row of cookbooks. A slight breeze from the open back doors made the tan-coloured curtains flap. Nas had paused at a two-pint milk carton and open tub of protein powder on the counter. She picked up the half-drunk glass next to it and sniffed.

'Put that down.' Lex was across the kitchen in two strides, and snatched the glass from Nas.

Nas smiled at him.

'Sorry to interrupt your workout,' Freddie said.

'What do you want, cop?'

'I'm not a cop,' she said. 'I just work for them.'

'Same boss, ain't it,' he said.

'And how's your boss doing?' Nas said. 'Are you expanding the Dogberry Boys round here?'

'Don't know what you're talking about.' He downed the rest of his shake. His shoulder muscles rippled.

He had a jagged scar that wound down one side of his ribs, like a shark had taken a bite out of him, 'Why did you move away from the estate?' Freddie asked.

'I've left all that behind,' he said.

'You've left the gang?' Freddie raised her eyebrows. She didn't think that was possible.

Nas glared at her: too direct.

'Yeah, you lot keep trying to pin stuff on me,' he said, his mouth twisting into a half-smile that turned into a sneer.

She had to get this back on track. This cocky twerp was distracting her.

'We have a witness who saw you meeting Jay Trap,' Nas said.

Lex shrugged and picked up the carton from the counter. 'So?'

'He's still head of the gang, Lex,' said Nas. 'You're still involved.'

'He's fam. No law says I can't see him.' He opened the fridge and shoved the milk carton next to a bottle of orange juice and some Alpro.

Freddie was still trying to place her questions in order. Nas should've given her more warning to prep.

Nas pulled a photo out of her back pocket. 'This is Amber Robertson. Do you recognise her?'

Lex's eyes flicked over the photo. The muscles in his jaw tensed. 'Never seen her before.'

This Freddie could do. She found her tongue. 'We know you were talking to her on Facebook.'

'Do you now?' He leant back against the fridge, his arms crossed, relaxed. Don't lose your cool, Freddie, pay attention to your gut. You're good at this. You're good at spotting things. 'I don't have no Facebook,' Lex said with a laidback smile.

'It's under the name Corey Banks. Same name this flat is registered under. Bit of a coincidence, don't you think?' she pushed.

'Like I said, I've got no Facebook – you can check my phone if you want.'

'The account has been dormant since last July,' Freddie said. 'But it's got your photo on it.'

'You guys should get onto that. Sounds like identity theft.' He smiled. She stared at him.

Nas was still holding out the photo of Amber. She stepped towards him. 'Amber was fifteen when this was taken. She's been missing for a year. She'd be sixteen now. Just an innocent kid.'

'We all got our troubles,' said Lex, shrugging.

'How are you affording to pay for this place, Lex?' Nas said.

'Driving a cab, ain't I,' he said.

'You've got the knowledge?' Freddie was dubious.

'Nah, I've got satnav. I'm with Uber.'

'Right.' Freddie used Uber – who had she been in a cab with? Also, a taxi was a great cover for driving round London and stopping at different addresses. An Uber XXX delivery of drugs. 'You're not working now?'

He shrugged again. 'I'm a night owl, what can I say?'

Under cover of darkness, Freddie thought. 'Where were you on the thirteenth of July last year?' Freddie pushed.

His eyes glinted. Was that recognition? 'I dunno. Where were you?'

To be fair she had no idea. 'It was a nice day. Were you at the pub? A barbecue?'

'Like I said, I don't know.'

'Do you know a Paul Robertson?' Nas said.

'Nope.' He pushed himself off the fridge. Rising up like a bear on its hind legs. 'I'm bored of this shit now. I don't have to answer your questions.'

'Amber is Paul Robertson's daughter,' Nas said.

He walked past and opened the front door, holding it for them. 'Out.'

Nas kept holding the photo out. Lex's gaze rested on it a second too long.

'You sure you don't know her?' Freddie said.

'This is an abuse of my human rights.' Lex's lip curled and he flicked his eyes onto Freddie. She felt her windpipe constrict in response to his stare.

'Thank you for your time, Lex,' Nas said, putting the photo back into her pocket.

'Whatever. Don't come back again without a warrant.' Lex closed the door after them.

They walked back up the steps in silence. The water droplets spilt by Mrs Koo had already evaporated. Nas unlocked the car and they propped the doors open. 'What do you think?' she said.

Freddie wasn't sure. 'I don't trust him. He was quick to get us out of there as soon as we mentioned Amber and Paul.'

'Yeah, I thought that,' Nas said.

'And did you see the way he looked at her photo?'

'It's not enough for a warrant. Or for us to flag it with Saunders,' Nas said.

Freddie turned back to look at the basement flat. Did it hold a clue to what had happened to Amber? They were no closer to knowing. And despite the interview with the twelve-year-old boys this afternoon, they were no closer to identifying either the victim or the assailants in the live streamed attack either. The thought that the two cases could be linked, that she was standing so close to Lex Riley, who might have caused harm to Amber, made her shudder. 'We need to know more.'

Amber

A thin slither of sunlight cracked into the room. Her eyes blinked grit, scraping noisily across her aching head. It was hot. Her throat felt full of sawdust. She needed water but she daren't move. How many days had it been now? Two, four, five? She'd lost count. She needed a doctor. A chemist. She was so tired. She rolled herself with effort, her limbs heavy and sore. Nausea quivered over her. She clutched her stomach. Oh god, she was so scared. She wanted her mum. She wouldn't cry.

She heard his trainers pounding against the steps. He was back. Sweat prickled over her skin. It was time. She had to find the words. Had to convince him. Had to believe he would help her. That he would do the right thing. She wouldn't cry. Wouldn't.

Kate

'I'm not sure I can do this. I'm not strong enough,' Kate said.

'Of course you are. You're my mum: you're the strongest woman I know!' Tegbee stroked her hair. Kate closed her eyes and savoured the touch of her daughter's hand.

'They'll say I'm having a breakdown again.'

'And you'll prove them wrong,' Tegbee said.

Kate sat up, and looked at her daughter's beautiful face. She still had her dad's eyes. 'They'll take you from me,' she said.

Tegbee raised an eyebrow. 'Let them try!'

Kate laughed despite herself, picking up her glass from beside her on the floor and putting it on top of the table.

'Are you feeling tired?' Tegbee said. Such a caring girl.

She nodded. So very tired. For a long time now. And this. 'I can't stop thinking about that poor girl. What if it had been you?'

'You need to rest,' Tegbee said. 'You push yourself too hard, mama.'

'You sound like your Auntie Ama.' She smiled at her daughter.

'That's because Auntie Ama knows what she's talking about!'

She laughed again. It was so good to talk, so good to laugh with Tegbee. When had she last felt like this? She waited for Tegbee to say something, to laugh too. But she was gone.

Her heart felt empty in her chest. She screwed her eyes shut and shook her head. *Oh, Kate, what are you doing? You're cracking up, girl.* She had to go to bed. She had to sleep; tomorrow she was going to see Freddie and Sergeant Cudmore. She was going to give her statement. She thought of the voicemail message she'd deleted from her phone. When they saw the papers, would they still believe her? When they knew her secret? Her old secret. She looked at the bottle of pills on the side. She had a new one now. Wearily and with effort she ignored its siren call and carried her tired body upstairs. The curtains were already drawn in her bedroom, the open sash window creating the meekest of breezes. She folded her dress and laid it on the chair, then slipped off her sandals and lay on top of the covers. The temperature had dropped a couple of degrees. That would help. At least for a few hours. She closed her eyes, hearing Tegbee's voice in her head, again and again: *'You're the strongest woman I know.'*

Nigel

Nigel was flossing when the phone rang. He was in the main bathroom. Miranda preferred the en suite. Less far for her to be bothered to walk. It was Quentin calling, his campaign manager. With all the upset recently in the cabinet, perhaps another of his erstwhile colleagues had been let go? He could be about to be offered a more senior position.

'Quentin, my good man, what can I do for you at this late hour – or shall I guess?' He couldn't keep the delight from his voice. After all his hard work, he was about to receive his payoff. What suit would be best for the press conference? The lean-lined navy one looked best if he was standing. Save that for entering number ten.

'Nigel, there's been a bit of an issue.' Quentin's voice carried more than its usual insipid whine.

'An issue?' Perhaps they'd want to do a joint announcement,

143

him standing shoulder to shoulder with the prime minister. A united front.

'Yes, err, well, the thing is…'

'Spit it out man.' He'd have to cajole Miranda into ironing his pink shirt.

'It's Simone.'

He took a moment to place the name. Simone. Oh yes, the delightful girl he'd met at the party conference. Magnificent breasts. 'What about her?'

'She's gone to the press.'

He dropped the plastic floss packet and it bounced off the sink. 'She's what? What do you mean?' *Magnificent breasts.*

'She's alleging that you sent her inappropriate messages.'

'Nonsense.' The cheap little strumpet was just trying to get her face in the papers.

'She has screenshots, Nigel.'

'I don't care what she's got: she's lying.'

Quentin sighed. 'Screenshots are pictures. She has pictures of the messages you sent.'

Nigel sat down heavily on the toilet. 'You can do that? What does she want?'

'More than we could find. The *Sun* have been on the phone. They've got the exclusive. They've paid a pretty penny for it.'

'The money-grabbing bitch.' Those magnificent breasts had been an elaborate trap.

'What were you thinking, Nigel?' Quentin was now at full whine.

'I was thinking that she was a nice young woman. The conniving cow. The paper set me up – don't they have history of doing this?'

144

'She's only seventeen.'

'She told me she was at university! Christ. Can we stop them? How much do they want?'

'It's not a question of money, Nigel. They're going with the story. They have… err… pictures.'

He closed his eyes as a wave of nausea crashed over him. Oh God. 'She told me to do that. She tricked me!'

'You're sixty-two years old, Nigel. I don't think that's going to wash,' Quentin said.

'What are we going to do? Miranda will go spare.' He jumped up. Grabbed a can of shaving foam and wielded it like a sword. 'We need a plan of action. Come on, Quentin – this is what I pay you for!' He wouldn't let this little strumpet destroy everything he'd worked for. He wouldn't let her take his money away.

'Does she have anything else, Nigel? How many messages did you send her? Any other photos?'

'Christ knows, I didn't keep notes,' he snapped.

'Right. Well, we'll need to counter the claims.'

'The prime minister's going to haul me over the coals. That greedy little bitch.' He slammed the can into the side of the wash-basin. If he got his hands on her…

'As there's no deniability, I think we'll have to go for contrition. Can you do that? Can you look sorry?' Quentin said.

'I'm sorry I ever met the little slut. This was a setup. She's the one who should be investigated.' How dare she do this to him? How dare she?

'We don't have long before the first editions are out. You made the front page. They're going with the headline "Member of Parliament" to match the, err, photo.'

145

'Oh God.' He flopped onto the rim of the bath and put his head in his hands. The phone fell to the floor.

He could hear Quentin's tinny little voice. 'They've pixelated it, which is something. I'd expect more reporters. The paparazzi will be out. Only let them get a photo of you and Miranda. None of you on your own.'

Rage ripped through him. It wasn't fair. He didn't deserve this. He snatched the phone back up. 'What am I going to do?'

'Were you drinking? We could go with the alcoholic line, book you into The Priory? Position this as your breaking point.'

Ridiculous. 'I'm not giving up my whisky, Quentin. No man could take that.'

'Okay... narcotics are more serious. It'll be harder to gain sympathy from the voters for that. We need something that will make them empathise. Something that will show them you're sorry. That you and Miranda are moving forward. Together. That this is an isolated incident.'

Thoughts whirred through his mind. Faces. That peachy bottom of the intern. Jade's laughing bosom. The maid at the conference hotel. The dogs started to bark and scrabble downstairs. The doorbell rang. Insistent. Continuous. He heard movement coming from the bedroom.

'Who on earth is that at this time?' Miranda called. 'Nigel, are you in there?'

He flung open the bathroom door. She was wrapping the belt of her towelling bathrobe around her. Cold cream had gathered in the creases in her face. 'Do not answer the door!'

'What is it? Whatever's the matter?' she said. 'Who are you talking to?'

'Quentin, I'll call you back.'

'Nigel, we can't hide from this! Nigel!' He hung up on the gibbering voice on the phone.

This was her fault. She'd driven him to it. Denied him. He looked at his wife with hatred. 'Do not go to the door, Miranda.'

'You do not tell me what I can and can't do, Nigel.' Miranda swept past him.

He grabbed for her wrist. 'Can't you listen to me for once in your life, woman?' Her skin was cold, papery in his grip, nothing to soften the brittle bone.

'Get your hands off of me,' she said, her eyes like lumps of coal. He dropped her wrist. The doorbell buzzed again. The dogs were howling incessantly. Scratching at the door.

'Mr Smitherson!' A voice came from downstairs, shouting through the letterbox. They were vermin. 'Mr Smitherson! I'm from *The Family Paper* – do you have any comment in response to the allegations?'

Miranda's eyes hardened, became two bright diamonds slicing through his skin. 'What have you done, you stupid man?'

A

He saw her on the news. A stranger. But someone who saw him. There was no hiding now. She knows. She knows. He could see it in her face. Twisted. The damage he's done. *What will your mum say?* He tries not to imagine his mum making that face. Twisted. He has to make it better. He'd been to see her. One last time. He runs his finger over the petals of the flower. A head in his hands. Soft, silky, like a mane. He thinks of the film he always watched at his gran's. *The Wizard of Oz.* The mane of the lion. A cowardly lion. But he has no heart too. Can't have. It's been ripped, pulled from him. He did that. He started this. Tin man.

The air is colder up here. Scurrying along the top of the tower block, carrying dust. Where does dust come from? Human skin cells. Ashes to ashes. Dust to dust. Other people must have been up here. Other people's skin. He walks to the

148

edge before he falters. His breathing is fast. Don't panic. Look out, not down. The street calls to him. But he keeps his gaze forward. At the lights stretching away. Blinking to warn low-flying aircraft. He wants to be an astronaut but he doesn't like heights. Something else to work on. Warming up. First the climbing frame at school. Then the garages round the back. Then his window, open wide. Closer, closer. And here. Finally. There is no safety rail. *You shouldn't be up here.* The caretaker used to tell them off, but he left years ago. Never replaced. The lock on the door never replaced. He used to stand in the middle, imagine helicopters landing. Taking him away to America. Waving, waving goodbye. The blades would blow the dust. The human skin cells.

The petals tickle his fingers, dance in his palm as he walks to the edge. He steps up onto it. A box covering pipes maybe? Don't think about that. Look forward, never down. He holds his arms wide, as if he is trying to hug the sky. Pull London into him. This is the only way. He must pay for what he's done. An eye for an eye. A life for a life. He closes his eyes. He's always wanted to fly. To soar above everyone.

He hears the door open behind him. The steps aren't hurried. Trainers on the roof. The squeak and crunch. He knows the rhythm. They could fly together.

B sounds calm. It's a command. An order. He's been sent to save him. 'Get down.'

He lets his arms fall slack at his side. Opens his eyes as he lets the flower go, the pink petals tumbling through the air until the black swallows them up.

149

Freddie

'Your pal's a nut bar.' Saunders slammed a copy of an open newspaper onto her desk, jogging her morning Berocca.

She pushed the newspaper and its 'Live Stream Sex Teacher Breakdown Hell' headline away. 'She had depression nearly twenty years ago, so?' The article had been requoted and recycled over news sites this morning. She'd already read two think pieces on stress and mental health issues in teaching. Poor Kate, it was shitty to be pawed over like this by the press. She knew: she'd been there herself.

Nas, who was beginning to look a little wilted round the edges from the heat, appeared in the doorway. She or Saunders were always in first. Sooner or later someone was going to ask why Freddie had suddenly caught the early-morning bug. She pushed against the bottom drawer of her desk, making sure it was closed over the sleeping bag. 'All right, Nas?'

'Cudmore.' Saunders whirled round to greet her, his shirt-sleeved arms open wide. 'Just in time. Can you explain to your little mate here why your pal hitting the news as a head case is such a bloody mess?'

'What?' Nas looked stricken. She deposited her jacket and Frappuccino on the nearest table. Saunders swept the paper toward her and she caught it and scanned the print. 'Oh, no.'

They were all getting in a twist over nothing. 'I thought you were cooler than this, Nas,' said Freddie. This was all Kate needed now. More judgement. 'You lot need some Mind training or something.'

'It's not that,' Nas said. 'This'll discredit her as a witness.'

'What? A bit of depression?' Freddie had managed about four hours sleep last night, by the time she'd got back here after interviewing Lex and made sure security had finished doing their rounds. She'd cricked her neck from sitting head down, hiding in the Ladies. She was too tired for this.

'Defence team'll use this to rubbish her in the eyes of the jury.' Saunders smacked the paper Nas was still reading with the back of his hand, so that it crinkled and puffed up into her face. 'Says here your mate Kate even started to hallucinate. She's useless. They'll tear her to shreds.'

Freddie realised he wasn't taking pleasure in this; he looked genuinely pissed off. This wasn't a wind-up. 'Crap,' she said. She didn't know things like that could be used against you in court.

'So we've got one witness who's crackers, and two child witnesses who are notoriously unreliable,' Saunders said.

'It's hard to get juries to believe children: they often present too many inconsistencies,' Nas said with a sigh. 'Dammit.'

'They both said they saw the same thing. A girl being attacked by a lad. They described them in the same way.' Surely any jury would see that?

'Not quite,' Nas said, looking uncomfortable. She folded the newspaper and handed it to Saunders, who promptly slammed it back onto Freddie's desk. Nas ignored this tantrum and picked up her drink and jacket. 'Leo described the girl as mixed race, Dylan said she was tanned. He thought she might have been Italian, or maybe even Arabic.'

They could still be talking about the same girl. Freddie thought how Tibbsy couldn't get his head round Amber's mixed parentage. They could still be talking about Amber.

'Who knows what they'd say under cross-examination? Reasonable doubt, that's all it takes.' Saunders held his arms out. 'Congratulations, ladies, you've got yourself three duds.' He took a bow.

Freddie slumped back in her seat. They'd gone from confirming Kate's story to destroying it. *Shit.* 'Now what?'

'We get Kate, Leo and Dylan to speak to the photofit artist as planned. Release them to the press.' Nas sounded efficient. Refocused after her distress a few minutes ago. She was steadfastly ignoring Saunders who was making irritating laughing sounds after each suggestion she made.

'Can you shut up?' Freddie snapped at him.

'I'm technically your superior, Venton,' he said, dropping his voice so it was a low warning rumble.

Really? He was doing this now? She stared back. 'Fine. Can you shut up, sir?' she said.

The air crackled between them. 'Then we'll see if we can find anyone who matches the description,' Nas continued.

'Capitalise on the press interest in this case. See if anyone calls Crimestoppers. If anyone recognises either the victim or the suspect.'

Freddie reluctantly looked away first. 'That's it?'

'Unless you've got any other bright ideas?' Nas's voice had an edge of tiredness.

Freddie looked at Kate's photo in the newspaper, as all the ground they'd made crumbled. No matter how fast she reacted, she felt the truth about the girl in the video slipping away from them.

Freddie

'Sarg, you're going to want to see this.' Green came running into the office holding up her phone. Freddie pushed the newspaper with Kate's face on it out of the way.

'What is it?' She was waving it too fast for Freddie to see.

'The news,' Green said, running past them to her desk, waking up her monitor and typing in bbc.co.uk. She turned it towards them, with the sound up. It was a press conference; the Tory MP Nigel Smitherson was in front of a microphone-covered stand, with a pinch-faced woman in an expensive skirt suit next to him.

'Hey, he's on the front page,' Saunders said.

'Caught with his dick in his hand. On camera phone,' Freddie said.

'Shush,' Green said. 'Listen.'

On screen flashbulbs could be seen going off, and Nigel Smitherson cleared his throat to speak.

'I have made a grave error. I have let down not only my constituents and myself, but also my loyal and dear wife, Miranda.' Smitherson took the woman next to him's hand.

'She looks thrilled,' Saunders said.

Smitherson's pompous nasal voice continued. 'I am but a weak man. I have succumbed to an addiction. Corrupted by the ample technology we have at our fingertips.'

'That's not all he's had at his fingertips,' Freddie said.

'Shush,' said Nas.

'Today I shall be entering rehab for sex addiction,' Smitherson said.

Freddie laughed out loud. 'The only thing he's addicted to is getting what he wants.'

'I have chosen to make my affliction publicly known, because this is no longer about only me. I have a duty to my constituents, the prime minister and the general public. I have a duty to justice. I'm not proud of it, but five nights ago I watched a live streamed video that has subsequently come to the attention of respected members of the press.'

No way.

'At the time, I mistakenly believed it to be a distasteful mock-up. I have now come to realise I witnessed the savage and brutal attack of a young woman.' He paused, wiping under his eye as if a tear had appeared. Miranda smiled at him adoringly, though it didn't quite reach her eyes. 'I am understandably distressed by what I have seen, and how far my illness has taken me down the wrong path. I therefore will, despite personal cost or embarrassment to myself, be cooperating fully with the Metropolitan Police Gremlin Taskforce to aid their investigation.'

They all looked at each other, stunned.

Nigel was reaching his rousing finish. 'Regardless of how I came to stand before you this morning…'

'You got caught with your pants down!' Freddie couldn't believe this.

'Our main focus must now be to find the perpetrator of this heinous crime and bring them to justice. I have every faith in the fine, upstanding men and women of the British Police Force and have no doubt this poor girl will soon be found, and the culprits brought to justice.'

Freddie could not believe what she was seeing. Was he really using the rape of a woman, possibly Amber, as a 'get out of jail free' card for his infidelity? 'I have no doubt he's a five-star cock.'

'Has he spoken to you?' Saunders asked.

'No, sir,' Nas said.

'I got the heads-up from a contact at the Beeb,' Green said. And they stared at the screen as Nigel Smitherson smiled and posed, looking contrite with his wife next to him while the flashbulbs went crazy.

Kate

'Where we going, mama?' Tegbee was sat next to her in the back of the police car.

Beads of sweat formed on Kate's brow. She must have drunk too much last night. Or taken too many pills. How many did she have? One, two, three? Oh, Lord, please forgive me. The policewoman driving hadn't turned around. She obviously hadn't heard Tegbee. She couldn't see her sat next to her, her long legs crossed at the knee. A simple black dress in this heat. She screwed her eyes shut. Took a couple of deep breaths. Opened them.

'Why are you ignoring me?' Tegbee's big eyes were questioning, bordering on hurt.

'I'm not,' she said under her breath.

'Sorry, Mrs Adiyiah, what did you say?' The detective looked in her mirror. She was young, thirties maybe. Open features. Introduced herself as DC Green.

Kate's voice sounded high. 'Nothing important – I just said it's hot!'

Green smiled over her shoulder. 'It needs to break.' *Break*. The word echoed through her. 'The pressure's giving me a headache.'

Kate managed a smile. A nod. Say something? 'Yes. So hot.' She couldn't do this. They were going to ask her to go over it again. They must have seen the papers. Read the accusations. They would think she was mad. And maybe she was?

'Sorry the air con isn't really working – police cuts, ha!' Green laughed. 'Least the traffic's moving. Get some air into the car.'

'Yes,' Kate managed.

'She seems nice,' Tegbee said.

Oh God. Was this punishment for wishing her daughter back? For wanting just to spend a few precious moments with her? She'd broken the natural order. Transgressed. Gone against God's will. *Let the wicked forsake his way and the unrighteous man his thoughts: and let him return unto the Lord, and He will have mercy on him; and to our God, for He will abundantly pardon.*

Lord Jesus, please forgive me. I only wanted to help the girl. I didn't know this would happen. And I can't, I can't wish her away again. She closed her eyes. Swallowed the barb that was lodged in her throat.

'Almost there,' Green called.

Kate opened her eyes. Nodded. Slowly she turned to her side. Tegbee was looking out the window at the big glass office block where Freddie and Sergeant Nasreen worked. *For God so loved the world, that he gave his only begotten Son, that whosoever believeth in him should not perish, but have everlasting life.*

Smiling Tegbee turned back to her. 'Don't worry, mama. I'm going to help you.'

Nasreen

On the whiteboard was a photo of each of the witnesses: Dylan and Leo looking small against the comfortable office backdrop, Kate Adiyiah looking nervous, and Nigel Smitherson staring confidently into the lens. Linking from these were three question marks. Under two were written 'suspect A' and 'suspect B', and under another was written 'victim'. Under each of these was a list of what they knew, or thought they did, about each person so far. Suspect A: black male, possibly late teens, close-cropped dark hair, slender but muscular, between five foot nine and six foot two, though none of the witnesses had seen him stand up. They'd said he'd been wearing dark blue jeans and black fitted boxers, but again, none could be sure. Why had none of them not thought to take a screen shot? Or a photo with their camera? That was unfair: Nasreen knew they'd have been in shock. Even Nigel

160

Smitherson, who'd arrived with his press secretary and an official photographer who'd been stopped at the door, had seem genuinely spooked once he started talking about the video itself.

Nasreen sighed; this felt like it was impossible. Keep going, she told herself. Right. Suspect B: male, of unknown ethnicity, possibly younger based on voice? It wasn't really anything to go on. They couldn't even tell anything about the phone the video had been shot from. They just knew he had a smartphone, one with a camera. There were hundreds of thousands, probably millions, of smartphones in London. And that's if they were sure they were definitely looking at a crime that had been committed here. All but Dylan had confirmed they had clicked on the London area, before selecting the 'Live Sex' titled piece. Dylan couldn't remember: they'd been playing PlayStation at the same time.

Nasreen had spoken to a colleague at the CPS. Witnesses who'd seen crimes through CCTV, which had subsequently been lost or destroyed, had been called to court before. There was a legal precedent for this. They could work with what they had if they had a suspect to charge. Suspect A and Suspect B had yet to be identified. And then there was the small matter of there being no victim. Everything was backwards. Not for the first time, she cursed the technology that had led them here.

And then there was Lex Riley and the missing Amber and Paul Robertson. She tended to agree with Freddie: Riley had reacted to Amber's photograph. He definitely knew who she was. The sketch artist had come back with his approximations based on what Leo, Dylan, Nigel Smitherson and Kate had said about the two who were visible in the live stream feed.

161

Their representations of the girl all looked different. There were possible similarities to Amber, if she'd lost weight. And if she'd been trafficked that was a reasonable assumption. Again their descriptions of the man in the film had produced four separate drawings, though all four had shown two lines shaved from the guy's left eyebrow. Like a little diagonal train track. God knows what the sketch artist would make of their descriptions of the crime scene; they were yet to come.

'You're working late.' Burgone's voice made her jump.

He was stood in the doorway, his jacket slung over his arm as if he were on his way home. Automatically Nasreen went to smooth her ponytail, then felt herself blush. They hadn't spoken since he'd yelled at her and Freddie for Kate's surprise TV appearance. Not privately anyway.

She realised she hadn't said anything. 'Oh... I... the case.' She waved her hand around as if that would indicate something, then giggled nervously. She felt her blush grow.

'How you doing?' he said, stepping into the office.

'The team are working really hard. We are confident that all four witnesses saw the same film, the same assault, and the addition of Nigel Smitherson as a witness will strengthen the case for the CPS...'

Burgone walked towards her quickly, dropping his jacket on a nearby desk. Her voice trailed off as he stopped centimetres from her, his eyes holding her. She could smell his scent. She thought he was going to reach out and touch her face. Instead he spoke softly. 'I meant how are you? How are you coping with all this?'

'I... I'm up to the job. I'm confident I can find Amber, and Paul Robertson. That I can find the victim and the perp in

162

the video too.' She kept looking at his lips, imagining kissing them. Tried to regulate her breathing.

'I never doubted it for a second. But are you okay?' Burgone took her hand, and Nasreen felt like the whole world tilted. 'How's your burn?' He ran his fingers softly over the mark. 'This is a distressing case, emotionally hard – you know you can come to me if you need anything.' He looked back up at her eyes, a sweep of dark hair falling over his own.

If only she could go to him for what she needed. There was a noise behind him. Burgone let go of her hand, stepped back from her. They turned to see Freddie, who was standing in a loose baggy T-shirt in the door.

'Ah. Didn't mean to interrupt,' Freddie said backing out of the room.

Nasreen felt her face blush again.

'Not at all,' said Burgone clearing his throat. 'Sergeant Cudmore and I were catching up about the cases. All done now.' He strode to the desk and collected his jacket. 'I'll say goodnight then. Freddie, Sergeant,' he said, nodding. He was out of the room fast.

Freddie pulled a grimace. 'Sorry!' she whispered to Nasreen. She was holding a toothbrush and toothpaste in her hand.

Nasreen tried to recover her composure. 'Just talking about work… you know. I… What are you doing here so late?'

'Bit awks,' said Freddie. 'I'm prepping for a date.'

'Nothing awkward about that,' Nasreen said.

Freddie glanced toward the empty door. 'Maybe you should try it?'

'I'm too busy for dating,' she said, busying herself with the sketches on her desk.

'That wasn't what I meant,' Freddie said.

Nasreen wanted to stop this conversation. She couldn't talk to Freddie about it. She couldn't talk to anyone. There was no situation. She'd just been talking to her boss. That was perfectly reasonable: millions of people did it every day. Just a discussion between a boss and his employee. Oh God. She looked at Freddie, whose hair had been brushed flat against her head. 'You look more like you're getting ready for bed.'

'I'm hoping he's a goer.' Freddie walked to her desk and shoved her things into her drawer. 'Anyway, isn't this late, even for your goodie-two-shoes act?'

Maybe it would be good to have a second pair of eyes. Someone to bounce this off. 'I needed time to process everything we know. The heat's giving me a headache.'

'That Nigel Smitherson's creepy isn't he?' Freddie replied. 'You see him leching over the receptionist downstairs?' Nasreen nodded; he wasn't an appealing person. Freddie picked up a file from her desk and sat next to her. 'And the way he described the victim: "cheap looking". What a bastard. He was the one who was wanking off to her being raped.'

Nasreen shuddered. 'He asked if me and Saunders would pose with him for a photo for the press,' she said. 'I thought Saunders was going to punch him.'

Freddie laughed. A moment of silence fell between them. Freddie cleared her throat. 'Now I don't want you to freak out, Nas, but I need to tell you something.'

Panic pulsed through her. Was Freddie going to try and talk about Burgone again? She had history with going rogue on things. She wouldn't put it past her to have signed her up to one of those Date My Friend websites. 'Why?'

'I know you said we couldn't show Amber's photo to any of the witnesses…'

Nasreen felt a fleeting sense of relief before the words hit her. 'What have you done?'

'Look, there's no need to panic.' Freddie held both hands out like she was trying to calm her.

'No need to panic?' Burgone trusted her with these cases. She needed to win Saunders over. She needed to find Amber, and suspect A and suspect B. And she had to do it all swiftly. 'What do you mean, no need to panic?'

'I spoke to Kate when she was here,' Freddie said.

'You did what? Freddie, what were you thinking? You could have compromised the case! Saunders could take us off this – off both of these!'

'I know, I know, but I trust Kate. She's sound.'

Just when she thought she had Freddie under control, when she thought she understood, she did something like this. 'Did anyone see you?'

'No, it was in the Ladies,' Freddie said.

'Well, that's certainly off record!' Nasreen slumped back onto the desk. Took a deep breath. 'And what did she say?'

'That she couldn't be sure,' Freddie said.

'What does that mean?' Nasreen said.

'That there were similarities. I mean, if the girl on the video is Amber, she'd look different to how she did a year ago, right? If they'd trafficked her – starved her, given her drugs.' Freddie's voice was angry, not sad.

Nasreen didn't want to admit she'd thought the same thing. 'Kate only saw her for a few minutes maximum. Her hair was in front of her face. She was partially obscured by the duvet on the floor and the suspect attacking her. Both they and the camera were moving. It's not enough to go to Saunders with.' Nasreen didn't know if it would be better if they just accepted it was Amber. The Dogberry Boys weren't known for holding back when it came to meting out their own justice. If Amber had become a pawn in their turf war, anything could have happened.

Freddie's phone started ringing. 'Dammit.' Freddie went back to her desk, looked at it, frowned and cut the sound. 'Probably PPI.'

In Nasreen's back pocket, her own phone vibrated. Perhaps it was the same person. Saunders calling to bollock them? She recognised the caller. 'It's Moast.'

'What does he want?' Freddie said.

Nasreen held the phone to her ear. 'Hello, sir, what can I do for you?'

'Sorry to bother you when you're at home, Cudmore.' Moast sounded vaguely echoic.

'No worries, I'm still in the office.'

'Good,' he said. 'Look, I wasn't sure whether to call you or not, but you need to know this.' There was the sound of a ringing phone in the background, and she realised the DCI must still be at the Jubilee Station. She'd worked with him long enough to recognise his business voice. She jumped off the table and went back to her own desk, grabbing a pen, ready. Freddie hovered around her, trying to hear what was going on.

'What is it, sir?'

Nasreen was not expecting what he said. She had to ask him to repeat himself twice. It made no sense.

'So you'll get here as soon as you can?' Moast was saying.

'Yes,' she answered, aware she was nodding, even though he couldn't see her. 'I'll bring Freddie.'

'Oh, goodie,' Moast said.

Freddie looked at her quizzically. 'You'll bring me where?'

Nasreen gathered together her files, her notes; she didn't want to forget anything. 'You need to blow your date off.'

'Says who?' Freddie reached out for her. 'Nas, hold still: what is it? What's happened?'

Nasreen stared at her friend. They'd have to talk to Saunders now. 'We're going to the Jubilee Station.'

Freddie's face went pale. 'Why?'

Nasreen couldn't believe she was saying this. 'Paul Robertson just handed himself in.'

'What?' Freddie's mouth fell open. 'When? Why?'

'About half an hour ago. He said he saw the video. He saw the live stream video.'

'What the hell?' Freddie said.

'The same one as the others.'

'No way. It's a trick. Some kind of con?' Freddie was following her around while she gathered up her stuff.

'I don't think so. Said he won't speak to anyone but us. Saw us on the news.'

'We get the best fans,' Freddie said. 'We weren't even on the news.'

'Yes, but our names were. Freddie, you need to get your things,' she said, nodding at her desk. 'We'll have to call Saunders on the way. He's going to want to be there. And we'll need to let Narcotics know.'

'Jesus, Robertson's been on the run for like a year – why would he do this?'

Nasreen swallowed. Let her eyes drop to the ground. Took a deep breath. 'He said one more thing.'

'What?' Freddie said.

She tried to form the words in her throat. Looked at her notes for guidance, something that made sense of all this. 'He said he recognised the girl in the film.'

'Holy shit,' said Freddie. And they both turned to look at the photo of Amber Robertson.

Kate

'Why did you say you couldn't be sure if it was the girl in the photo?' Tegbee appeared as soon as she'd stepped back into her house. She was in cut-offs and a crumpled linen shirt, as if she'd just come in from the garden.

Kate locked the door behind her. There were no photographers outside today; at least that was something. The light on her answerphone was flashing and she pressed *play*. The machine beeped once.

'Hello, Kate, this is Michelle.' Head of the PTA, a friend, she'd known her for years – she could hear the tightness in her voice. 'I'm sorry not to catch hold of you – I've tried a few times. I've seen the news and I wanted to check you were okay. And… There's no easy way to say this. We've had a number of calls from parents.' Michelle gave a loud sigh, and she could imagine her friend taking her glasses off and rubbing at the bridge of her nose. 'They're worried, Kate – they've seen the reports of your health problem.' There was another pause. Another sigh, quieter this time. 'Some of them are asking questions about your suitability to lead the school. I know you are probably fine. That there is an innocent explanation for all this. If I could just speak to you. Give me a call when you get this. Okay?' Kate pressed *delete* on the machine.

'We don't need her,' Tegbee said.

'We do,' Kate replied. What was she doing? Talking to herself? No, worse. She turned away from her daughter.

'It could have been me in that room,' Tegbee said. 'Me in that film.'

'I can't do this any more. I'm sorry.' She closed her eyes. *Please forgive me, Jesus.* 'You are not real. You are not here. You are dead.' The words echoed round her dining room, bounced off the kitchen cupboards. Kate opened her eyes. There was no one there. She was alone. All alone.

Freddie

'He's not answering. I've texted him.' Freddie hung up her phone. First on the list of things to do if she ever sorted out a place to stay would be to take driving lessons. Nas always got to drive.

'Try his landline – the number's in my phone.' Nas shoved it at her.

'You've got Saunders's home number, you know that's weird, right?' She opened Nas's phone. You'd think as a cop she'd have a passcode activated. 'And this is extremely hack-able!' She waved it in the air.

'He's my boss. I have everyone's contact numbers – that's standard, Freddie.' They were both sniping at each other, both nervous of what they were about to find out.

She couldn't get her head round Paul Robertson just handing himself in. All the time they'd spent tracking him and he just showed up. She had to focus on that. Couldn't think of Amber, of her being the girl in the video. About where she was now?

The phone picked up and a man answered. 'Hello?' Not Saunders.

'Oh, hi, is Sound— Is Peter there, please?' This must be his partner. The man in the photo on his desk. What was he like – the guy who loved Saunders? Was Saunders just as OCD at home? What was their place like? She couldn't imagine him living in the shitholes she'd been viewing lately.

'Who's calling, please?' the guy said. She could hear music in the background: sounded like Wild Beasts' *Big Cat*. Were they one of those couples who danced round the kitchen while they cooked together? Last week she'd been doing that, though it was a cut-price ready meal from M&S in the micro-wave, and she and L-bomb had been singing into beer bottles like microphones.

'I'm calling from his work… I'm a…' Saying she was an analyst sounded lame.

'Say you're calling on my behalf,' Nas interrupted.

'Look, just tell him it's Venton, yeah?'

'Freddie.' The guy sounded like he was smiling. 'He's mentioned you.' Weird. 'He's just laying the table – hang on.' Domestic Saunders was too much for her brain to cope with. She heard the man's hand muffle the phone as he called for him, 'Pete – phone. It's Freddie from work.'

There was movement, rustling, as presumably the phone was handed over. The music was muted.

'Saunders.' Saunders's voice was just as it ever was. He could have been in the office. She should have asked his boyfriend's name while she had the chance. Had a little Google. How could a guy as cold as him have a happy long-term relationship when she couldn't? *You could if you wanted to. Shut up.*

'It's Freddie,' she said.

'So we established,' Saunders said. 'I'm assuming you're not calling for a friendly chat?'

'If you'd picked up your texts I wouldn't have had to call,' she said. Bloody phones, why did anyone still use them to talk on any more?

'For God's sake,' Nas snapped. She grabbed the phone from her hand.

'Hey!' She was driving!

'Sir, it's Paul Robertson. He's handed himself in at the Jubilee. We're on our way there now.' Nas paused. She hadn't taken her eyes off the road. It was dark now, London traffic was still slow. 'He says he has information pertaining to the identity of the woman in the alleged video.' She fell silent. A tiny flinch of her cheek. Then held the phone out for Freddie to take.

'Hello?' She held it to her ear.

'He's gone. He said he'd meet us there. Then he hung up,' Nas said.

'Charming,' Freddie said.

Nas bit her lip. Two hands back on the wheel. 'We're going to have to tell him that we've found Lex Riley. That we think there's a chance it's Amber in the live streamed video,' she said.

'More than a chance – her dad's just handed himself in!' Would they take them off the case now? 'We could have winged it – not called him,' Freddie said.

173

'No, we couldn't,' Nas replied. She didn't smile.

Freddie stared out as they passed Aldgate Underground Station. People thronged outside the pubs, laughing and smoking, clutching pints, handbags between their feet. It was still hot. Stupidly hot. She had her shorts on and her night shirt. Well, the T-shirt she wore when she was sleeping in the office. She pulled the fabric into a knot at her waist, trying to disguise it. Wished she had her bra on. 'Maybe it's not him. Maybe it's someone just saying they're Robertson.'

'Moast and Tibbsy have both met Robertson before. It's him,' Nas said.

Nas parked the car round the back of the station. Freddie tried to identify the other cars, but they all looked the same. Her phone started ringing. She recognised the number as Saunders. 'Seriously, what is up with you people and bloody talking on the phone?' She held it to her ear. 'Yeah?'

'I'm here, where are you?' Saunders snapped. She had to give Paul Robertson props for timing. He couldn't have rocked up at 9am, could he?

'Coming in now.' She realised she didn't actually know where Saunders lived. She'd been imagining a soulless new-build place, but he must be based somewhere not far from here. Could she see him in a characterful converted house around Shoreditch, Brick Lane, Stokey? The thought that she'd been this close to him over these last few months, that she could have bumped into him and his beau in the street, freaked her out. Before he had time to reply, she hung up.

Inside, she scanned the hallway. Phones buzzed. They passed busy offices. Further away she could hear shouts. She was alert for a familiar voice, a familiar movement. She hated being here; it reminded her of what had happened back then. Of how she'd got her scar. And now it would remind her of Amber.

'Cudmore!' Moast appeared at the top of the corridor in front of them. He was in his favoured outfit of a tight T-shirt and jeans. And right behind him was Saunders, who was also, bizarrely, in jeans and a T-shirt, though his were a bit more trendy. Freddie had never seen Saunders out of a suit before. It softened him. It was disturbing. 'I was just getting to know your superior here.' Moast clapped Saunders, who was broader and more muscly than him, across the back.

Nas, who also seemed wrong-footed by casual Saunders, faltered. 'Sir. Sir.'

'It's like some terrible police casual wear catalogue shoot,' Freddie said as they walked towards them.

Moast laughed. Saunders scowled and she saw him look at his watch. For someone who spent long hours in the office, he was absurdly tanned. Did he do that at the gym too?

'Shall we step into my office?' Moast said. 'It won't be as fancy as yours, I'm afraid, Saunders.'

'Not a problem, sir.' Saunders smiled. Of course! In the maddening police hierarchy Moast was higher up the food chain than Saunders. Freddie grinned: two alphas, two bosses of Nas; this could get interesting. 'Thank you for letting us interview our suspect.'

'Nice to see the mighty Gremlin Taskforce in action.' Moast opened the door off the corridor. They filed into the small space, Saunders's nose wrinkling at the half-empty coffee cups and folders that were piled across the desk. Moast strode past them, a grin on his stupid square head, and sat down in his chair.

There was just one chair this side of the desk. Nas glanced out of the corner of her eye at it, but Saunders didn't let his eyes drop from the DCI.

'Well this is all very *X Factor*, but if nobody minds I'm gonna sit down.' Freddie pushed past Nas and flopped into the chair. Let them get tired legs while they did their Alpha-off or whatever this was.

'A stint in Special Ops hasn't given you any manners then.' Moast raised an eyebrow at her.

Freddie rolled her eyes. 'Can we get on with this? You may not have anywhere else to be at this time of night, but I have a life.' *Yeah, sleeping in the office. Ironic, Freddie.* She just wanted to get out of this place as fast as possible. It was making her skin itch being here.

Both Saunders and Nas started talking at once.

'Sorry, sir, after you,' said Nas, while Moast laughed.

'As I was saying,' Saunders said. 'You believe you have Paul Robertson in custody?'

'I don't believe, I know,' Moast said. 'He's obviously one of those who's had his head turned by the *Special* ones. He says he'll only talk to Venton and Cudmore.'

'Out of the question,' Saunders said. 'This is a high-level ongoing investigation. As supervising officer I shall be interviewing the suspect. If it is indeed the suspect.'

'Why can't Nas and I talk to him?' Saunders and Moast were still eyeballing each other. She wanted to know what he knew. If he'd seen his daughter… She shivered.

'I think it's fine if DI Saunders and I conduct the interview, Freddie,' Nas said.

'Stop being so gay, Cudmore. I taught you to have back-

176

bone,' Moast sneered. Freddie watched Saunders's face; he didn't visibly register the insult.

Saunders glared at Nas. Wrong-footed, and struggling to make sense of the power play, Nas tried to push on. 'If it is indeed Robertson.'

But Moast had years of being an arse on the younger Saunders. He was marking his territory with devastating effect. 'Don't you start that too,' Moast said. 'You're not insinuating I can't make a simple ID of a wanted crim?'

Implying, you mean implying, you tool.

'No, sir,' Nas said. Freddie could see her hands behind her back: she was digging her nails into her palm.

And they hadn't confessed to finding Lex Riley yet. They were like bloody children. She needn't have come here, needn't have put herself through this. 'You're just going to cut me out?'

'My suspect has asked for Cudmore and Venton,' Moast said.

Saunders swallowed. 'With all due respect, sir, he is not your suspect.'

'Funny – he's in my nick,' Moast said. 'Besides, I thought I might like a crack at him myself. Get myself a few brownie points from the Kremlin. I'll take Cudmore in, soften him up. Sure I can get him to talk.'

Screw this. Freddie stood up. 'I'll get on then. Leave you all to swing your dicks around.' Fucking waste of time. Coming to this PTSD-pit, in this heat, to watch these gorilla throwbacks go at it. Nas with her simpering sirs was encouraging them! She could read the transcript of the interview tomorrow.

'You can't go,' Saunders said.

177

'It's after six o'clock. And you ain't the boss of me,' she said, shoving past him. He had his mouth open. Best not to look at Nas. Irritation powered her out through the door.

'*Bye, Miss Venton!*' Moast called. Jackass; he'd done this deliberately.

She couldn't bear the thought of hearing Robertson describe the brutal assault of his daughter. No one, no matter what they'd done, deserved to go through that. And she didn't need it. She was better off sticking to the bloody numbers. Least cell site charts didn't have massive bloody egos.

There was the noise of a door opening further up the hallway. Something inside told her not to look, but her neck was turning her head, her eyes recognised the shape immediately. Like she knew his aura before she could fully see him. *Get a grip, Freddie.* He stared at her. Her stomach contracted. He didn't look like he'd slept. His hands hung limp at his side, like a little boy's. He pursed his lips, half smile, half grimace.

He didn't look surprised. He knew she was here. Was he waiting in case she came out the room? Had he been stood there, listening? For a horrifying moment she thought she was going to blush. She let the anger harden her, protect her.

'Hey,' she said.

'Hey you.'

Nasreen

'I really think we should just get on with this.' The words were out before she could stop them. Both Moast and Saunders stared at her. A trickle of sweat dribbled between her shoulder blades. The Jubilee Station budget did not run to air con. She braced herself for the shouting. They'd already lost Freddie; what if Robertson really wouldn't talk unless they were both here? 'If you both want to do the interview, that's fine. But we do have a missing vic, and two suspects out there.'

'Don't get your knickers in a twist, Cudmore,' Moast said. 'Course you and golden boy here can have a crack at Robertson. Just a bit of bants, innit?'

Saunders didn't smile, but his shoulders did drop by half a centimetre. Right. She had to focus on the task at hand. Stop sweating. They needed to know what Robertson had to say for himself. Freddie had already checked that there

179

were no known links between him and any of the other witnesses. She didn't think there would be, but you never knew. Robertson had grown up in Poplar; he and Amber had lived in the tower he'd lived in since the sixties. It wasn't a million miles from Hackney High, so potentially Kate Adiyiah could have taught Amber, but that wasn't the case. He really was just another one of the two thousand people they estimated had seen the stream that night (based on the number of likes the others had remembered). 'Which interview room can we use?'

'I've got him in one already. Follow me.' Moast swung past them.

She tried to give a sympathetic smile to Saunders, but he was having none of it. 'Sir, I need to tell you something that might be pertinent to this interview.' He was going to kill her.

Saunders stopped, and turned his eyes to her.

Nasreen swallowed and pushed on. 'Amber Robertson had a boyfriend called Corey Banks. Corey Banks was a fake name being used by Lex Riley, who is a known member of the Dogberry Boys.'

Saunders's eyebrows were rising.

'And Narcotics sort of lost him a year ago – the same day as Amber and Paul Robertson disappeared. And we found him.' She thought his eyebrows would disappear off the top of his forehead.

'You found him?'

She kept going, desperate to get it all out. 'Yes, and we spoke to him. And we think he could be linked to the disappearance of Amber. That perhaps he trafficked her.' Saunders's face paled. 'That she might be the girl in the video.'

Saunders's face switched from pasty to puce. 'And you're only just telling me now?'

She felt the case crash down around her. 'It's circumstantial…'

Moast leant back into the room and slapped his hand against the wall. 'You coming?'

Saunders gave him a smile. 'Of course.' Nasreen's heart was racing. 'We will discuss this matter later, Sergeant,' he added sternly.

Nasreen wanted to explain, but there wasn't time. She had to get through this interview. Deal with the fallout later. 'I've got Freddie's compilation of the other witnesses' interviews, sir,' she said, passing him the notes as they walked down the hallway. One of the recessed ceiling lights still flickered. There was still a scuff on the rubber floor. It was strangely comforting.

'How do you think we should play this?' Saunders flicked through the notes.

You just asked my opinion? She was stunned. Maybe Moast's little stunt had corrected some balance. 'I… I want to know why he turned himself in. He said he recognised the girl in the video. If it was Amber, then I don't want him to clam up or get so emotional he can't speak. If he recognised her, maybe he recognised the men as well?'

Saunders nodded. 'I agree.'

Really? Okay, keep going. 'I think it'd be best if we take it back to the beginning. Don't go straight in about the video, see what we can get from him first before that.'

Saunders sniffed thoughtfully. Moast slowed at the interview room in front of them. A young PC she didn't recognise was stationed on the door.

'He asked for anything?' Moast said.

'Just a Coke, guv,' the PC said.

'All right,' Moast said. 'You need anything, I'll be watching on the camera, so just give us a wave.' He signalled at the observation room across the corridor.

'Thank you,' Saunders said.

'Let's see what you got then,' Moast said with a wink.

Nasreen felt her stomach tighten. She didn't like the notion of instinct; she thought it was an excuse for some cops to be lazy. But still, there came a point in each investigation where, if you were lucky, you could feel the wind change direction. She felt that now. That this was the moment the case would open up. That Robertson could give them some answers.

'I'll start,' said Saunders, shoving the notes back to her and opening the door. No time to take a couple of calming breaths. This was it.

She followed him into the small interview room, head held high. No fear.

Paul Robertson looked up from the small table he sat at. His eyes hooded, dark, full of hate. Despite the heat, he was wearing a hoodie, his bald head shrunk down into it. He looked like a threatening turtle, if that was possible.

Saunders, used to the setup, flicked on the tape recorder and announced, 'Interview with Paul Robertson commencing. Officers present DI Saunders and DS Cudmore.' He casually pulled out the chair opposite Robertson. Nasreen followed and took the chair to his left.

Robertson was looking at her; his eyes had an intensity she found uncomfortable. Like he was seeing past her facade. She felt stripped, but not in a sexual way.

'You're DS Cudmore?' His voice was gruff, sanded by booze and fags. His hands still inside his pockets.

'You all right with that Coke?' Saunders said. 'You want another? Something else?'

'You don't look like a Cudmore,' Paul said.

She couldn't look at Saunders to check her response was okay, because it would appear weak, and she had the very real sensation that that wouldn't work with this man. 'It's my father's name. My first name is Nasreen. After my mother's mother.'

He nodded, thoughtful. 'What about the other one they mentioned? You ain't Venton?' He jutted his chin at Saunders.

'Venton wasn't available. It's late,' the DI said.

Robertson's thick lips vibrated with a snort. He wasn't like a turtle, he was like a horse. A wild horse.

'Why'd you turn yourself in?' Saunders was keeping his tone light, casual.

Robertson had been in this situation before. He'd survived in the THM gang and made it quite high up for a reason. He wasn't going to fall for any tricks. 'Yous lot were never gonna find me, was you?'

'It seems you beat us to it,' Saunders said.

'Seems I did,' Robertson said. Despite having come here of his own free will, he was still fighting with the situation.

Nasreen's hope that he'd simply talk was ebbing away. Was this something else? Some kind of trick? 'We've been looking for you for over a year,' she said. Robertson leant back in his chair. Looked at her again with those eyes. 'Since the four-teenth of July, to be precise.'

She watched the date hit. The tightening around his jaw. 'Yeah?' he said.

183

'Yes,' she said. 'Where have you been?'

'I ain't telling you that. I ain't here for that.'

'Then why are you here, Paul?' Saunders said.

'You don't get to use my name, rozzer.' Robertson's bald head seemed to be sucking the light from the room.

Saunders was calm. 'You're not really in a position to play the hard man, boy. How 'bout we just charge you and send you on your way. Bet you're looking forward to your stay at Her Majesty's pleasure.'

Robertson bared his teeth. Saunders made to push his chair back.

'You don't want a lawyer?' she said.

'I told you, I ain't talking 'bout that. I'm here about that flick.' For the first time his voice shifted away from confrontational.

He didn't seem upset, or at least not on the verge of tears. 'Tell me about it?' Nasreen suggested.

Saunders sat himself back down and rested one arm on the table as if he were down the local, waiting for a pint.

'I seen it. I know the bird in it,' he said. Discomfort licked at the edge of his face.

'How do we know you saw the video?' Saunders said. 'I'm struggling to see why you're here. What you're getting out of this.'

'Because I ain't no nonce,' he said, angry. 'What's wrong with you? You fucked up in the head, rozzer?' His hand was out of his pocket, his fingers a gun bouncing off his own temple. Nasreen's whole body ached to respond. To jump. To move. She stayed still. 'That's someone's daughter, boy!'

Someone's? They let silence descend onto the room.

184

Robertson was now looking at the table, his fingernails scratching at a crack in the vinyl. She wanted to blurt it out. *You said someone's? But not yours? Not Amber?* But he was volatile, distrustful. Why was he even here?

Saunders drummed a finger against the table. 'The duty sergeant tells me you didn't have a phone on you when you came in. No wallet. No keys. Nothing.' *What? That made no sense.* She gritted her own teeth, realising Saunders hadn't bothered to impart this nugget to her. Then again, neither had Moast, though she thought it was at least possible that he didn't know. It was like Saunders to do his homework. Even if he only had seconds. 'You want to tell me why that is?' Saunders said.

'No comment,' Robertson replied.

Damn.

'Are you being set up, Paul?' Saunders said.

'No comment.'

He was clamming up. Resorting to old tricks.

Saunders drummed another finger. 'Has someone got something over you?'

'No comment.' Robertson had turned monotone. All eye contact gone. They were losing him.

'Where's Amber?' she said.

Robertson's arm shot out. Too fast, he had her by the wrist. Hard. Forcing her arm, and her torso down onto the table. Her heart shot into her mouth. She tried to pull back as Saunders jumped up and lunged across the table

'Let her go.'

'No.' She held out her right arm to stop Saunders. Robertson was staring at her. But not like before. There was something

185

else in his eyes, something embedded behind the anger and the hate. Fear. He was frightened.

'Let DS Cudmore go.' Saunders' voice was calm, as if he were just asking him to pass a pen.

Robertson didn't let go. Her eyes were locked on his. She could feel her pulse beating against his fingers. Or was it his pulse beating into her? She knew Moast would be at the door outside. She knew he and the PC would be in here in a second. That they were all poised. Robertson was a violent man. A skilled violent man. How much could he hurt her in that second? She swallowed. 'You don't know where Amber is, do you?' she said quietly.

'That is someone's daughter on that fucked-up film,' he said. 'That could have been my baby.'

'We want to find the people responsible for what happened to that young woman.' She daren't look away. She could feel the seal forming between her and Robertson's skin. *Don't think about it.*

Suddenly he let go. Flopped back in his chair. She pulled her wrist towards her, rubbed it with the other hand.

'I don't know her name. She lives at one of my customers' houses. Some posh knob in Islington. She looks after his kids,' he said. He looked dejected. Crumpled. He'd come in to tell them that. Because of the girl. Because he didn't know where Amber was. She felt a strange mix of relief and sadness. It wasn't Amber. But this girl, this nanny, she'd found herself on this horrific live stream. How? And why hadn't she reported it?

'It's not your customer – the posh knob – in the film assaulting her?' she said.

'Nah,' he said.

'And you don't know her name?'

'I said I don't.' He didn't look up. 'She's young, only a few years older than Amber would be.'

Would be? Past tense. 'And the name of the customer?' She circled her wrist, moving the blood back round.

'I don't know,' he said. 'But I can give you the address.'

She already had her pen ready, writing as he spoke. They'd run it through the PNC, see who was registered there. Find out who this girl was. 'And you're sure it's the same girl?'

'She ain't the first person I seen die.'

A shiver ran down her spine. All the witnesses had said the feed cut out with the girl still struggling. This was her worst fear. 'What makes you think she's dead?'

He looked at her. 'I know about arteries. About blood. She's dead.'

Dead. Whether he'd made a mistake about who was in the film or not, Nasreen believed him. He'd just sacrificed his own freedom for a dead girl he didn't even know the name of. 'And you really don't know where your daughter Amber is?'

He shook his head. Amber wasn't the girl in the live stream. That wasn't the fear. She saw it now, seeping from his every pore, felt it bruising round her wrist: Paul Robertson thought his daughter was dead too. Something had happened to make him think that. A man like him wasn't prone to hysteria. He knew the streets. He'd told them himself. This was not the first person he'd seen die. How many of those had he thrust the knife in or pulled the trigger on himself? It was as if

Amber was being pulled away into the darkness. He felt responsible. This was the act of a guilty man.

Saunders leant forward, placing both hands on the table so it creaked under his weight. 'Don't you ever lay a finger on a member of my team again.'

Nasreen

Immediately after his revelation, Paul Robertson had clammed up and demanded his lawyer. Moast was waiting for them outside the room, concern written across his face.

'You shouldn't have let him touch her, muppet!' He rounded on Saunders as the PC closed the door behind them.

'She's a grown-up,' Saunders said without stopping.

'Where'd you think you're going?' Moast said. 'This is my station, and we do things by my rules. And we protect our women.'

She cringed at the words. She was also standing right here. 'It's fine, guv, honest. Nothing to worry about.'

Moast was still scowling.

'Can we get this checked on your system?' Saunders had the address Robertson had given. 'I'd like to know who the mystery girl in this film is.'

'I'd like to know why you didn't once ask him about the Rodriguez Brothers, pal?' Moast stepped toward him, squaring his shoulders.

Jesus. Not again. Saunders stared at him, impassive.

'Look,' she said, stepping between her old boss and her current one, feeling like a referee. 'It's late. Why don't we grab a cuppa first? Rehydrate? Yeah?' She was desperate to know who lived at that address, who the woman was, but she knew Saunders wouldn't sanction a door knock at this time of night. Not on the word of Robertson. It could be a wind-up. Better to go in the morning, which meant the best they could do now was verify their facts. And they could do that after a breather.

'Good idea, Cudmore,' Saunders said, making an effort at a friendly smile. Moast might be senior, but she knew Saunders could run rings round him. 'Where's your canteen, sir?'

'Canteen!' Moast scoffed. 'They closed that months ago. We don't have the same budget as you lot at the Kremlin.'

'You still using the stationery cupboard?' she said hastily.

'Stationery cupboard?' Saunders raised a questioning eyebrow at her.

'It's what they call the room they use as a mess,' she said.

'We got all your mod cons – tea, coffee, milk, even a little microwave.' Moast swung his arm over Saunders's shoulders and began to lead him down the corridor.

She kept time beside them. *Please don't ask if they have rooibos.*

'You're gonna love it.' Moast gripped the handle of the mess door and pulled it open with a flourish.

'Fucking hell!' The words flew out her mouth. Inside, naked from her T-shirt down, her legs wrapped round Tibbsy's waist, was Freddie.

'Fuck!' Tibbsy grabbed for his own suit trousers, which were currently round his ankles. The movement released Freddie, who lurched backwards into the small side unit, knocking into the jars of coffee and boxes of teabags.

'What the fuck?' Saunders said.

'Tibbs!' Moast cried.

Oh, my God! Freddie and Tibbsy. Here! In the bloody station!

'Will you shut the fucking door.' Freddie reached for the handle, flashing them all a thick triangle of hair before wrenching it shut.

'Get the fuck out here now!' Moast roared.

Doors were opening up and down the corridor, as questioning faces peered out to see what all the fuss was about.

Even Saunders looked shocked. Nasreen had clasped her hand to her mouth.

'One second, guv!' Tibbsy called from within the cupboard.

What the hell had Freddie been thinking? She'd thought she'd left! Gone for at least… did that mean they'd been… all this time? Nasreen felt her ears flush. She didn't know what the hell to do. Moast stepped towards the door like he was about to open it again. Saunders's eyebrows were still sky-high. She looked at the floor.

'What's going on, guv?' called a guy from down the hall.

'Get back to work!' Moast roared. This was no wind-up now. He'd properly blown his top. She opened her mouth. Tried to think of something to say. Anything. *Christ, Freddie, what the hell have you done this time?* Tibbsy was presumably on duty; this was gross misconduct. *Gross.*

The door opened and Freddie was stood there, arms folded over her chest, glaring at them. 'Get a good eyeful?'

How could she even begin to speak like this?

Tibbsy straightened his tie and shoved his shirt into his waistband. He reached out and pulled Freddie back by the arm. Nasreen waited for her friend to turn on him. But something more shocking happened. Freddie let him. She remembered how weird Tibbsy had been the other day. All that desperate checking that she wasn't offended. How reluctant Freddie had been to come here. How she'd kept looking at her phone. Freddie and Tibbs. Tibbs and Freddie. Christ.

Freddie

'Sergeant, get the hell into my office!' Oh, crap, Freddie had seen Moast turn this colour before. Tibbsy went to step over a box of PG Tips. Saunders was looking like a goldfish. This was not good.

'Cudmore, get this *thing* out of my station!' Moast screamed at her.

Tibbsy stopped. Turned around, unfurled his full rangy height. Squared up to his beloved Moast. 'That wasn't cool.' She loved him a bit then. Then realised what she'd thought.

'If you don't want your arse served to you for breakfast, you will shut the fuck up and get in my office!' Moast roared.

How dare he speak to Tibbsy like that? 'What does that even mean?' She stepped towards him. He'd always been a bully. Nas's hand shot out and grabbed hold of her arm. 'Ow!' She tried to shake her off.

Nas dug her fingers in and pulled. Moast glared at her, before frogmarching Tibbsy toward his office. Tibbsy turned at the door, doing those stupid puppy-dog eyes he did. She'd been just about to come as well.

'What the hell do you think you're doing?' Nas screeched at her.

Saunders was still stood in front of the cupboard. Moast's door slammed. The light fittings shook. She tried to shake Nas off. The indecipherable roar of Moast's voice was coming from behind them like a fireball.

'How could you be so stupid?' Nas was saying. 'It's reckless! Irresponsible! Immature!' She dragged her through the open door, Freddie just managing to stay upright as they stepped into the car park out back. This was bad. Real bad. Would Moast get her sacked? She wasn't sure Burgone would back her on this one.

Saunders was right behind them. 'That was brilliant!'

'What?' Nas stopped. Freddie ploughed into her.

Saunders started to laugh. They both stared at him, open-mouthed. His face, usually taut with tension, crumpled like a dropped sock. Nas looked flabbergasted. Saunders gripped his stomach, bent forward. She felt it start like a tickle. Then the laughter came. Pushing up out of her body.

'Your face!' she managed. 'When that door opened I thought you were gonna faint!'

'Moast's voice – *wha' the fu' is goin' on?*' He could do a blinding impression of him, she'd give him that.

'Oh my God! Stop! Stop!' Freddie clutched herself. The ridiculousness of the last few days. The weeks. The months. And now this. She couldn't stop.

'And when your –' Saunders bashed his palm against his knee. Freddie was crying with laughter now. Big gulps of warm air shaking her insides. They started to slow.

'Have you two finished?' Nas, arms folded, tapped her foot like Sonic the Hedgehog glaring at them. The car keys in her hand.

Saunders reached for her, pointing with his other hand at the furious Nas. Giggling like he was high. That set her off again. She'd flashed them all!

'Dirty fuckers!' she managed.

'For God's sake.' Nas turned and unlocked the car. Freddie fell against Saunders. What a night. Caught shagging in a police station! She wished she still wrote her blog. This was gold. Gold!

They managed to get into the car. Saunders in the front – 'Shotgun, I'm the boss!' Her in the back. Windows down. Nas's stony silence. She'd calmed down. Just a few aftershocks of laughter now. The reality setting in. She was in trouble. Big trouble.

She could see Nas's ears were still red. 'I don't know what to say to you, Freddie.'

'You sound like my mum,' she said.

'You do,' said Saunders.

Nas ignored him. 'You do realise you've probably cost Tibbsy his job?' She was gripping the steering wheel so tight it was a surprise it didn't break.

That would be awful. She tried to brazen it out: convince herself. 'He'll be fine. He's Moast's lapdog. He loves him. He ain't going to do anything.'

'I don't know how you can be so cavalier! After you did

that! In front of!' Nas voice was rising. 'This is the worst thing you've ever – ever – done!'

All remaining mirth drained away. Freddie put her head in her hands. *Shit.*

'Least she didn't shag her own boss,' Saunders said from the front seat. Though it lacked his usual malice.

Nas made a squeaking noise.

Freddie peered out between her fingers. Did he really just say that?

Nas had gone pink now. 'I … we… I am not discussing this with either of you.'

'You need to relax, Cudmore,' Saunders said. 'Maybe if you shagged him in our stationery cupboard it'd make you feel better?' His face creased into laughter again.

'Sir, I find that inappropriate,' Nas said.

'Burgone's hot – I would!' Saunders collapsed into full-blown hysterics again.

Crap. Now he was having a pop at Nas. Freddie rubbed her hand over her face. She needed to do some kind of damage limitation. Could she get Nas to speak to Burgone? Maybe Moast wouldn't dob her in. Maybe he'd think Saunders had it covered? Once Saunders was back in his police suit, would he still think it was funny? She looked at her phone. No messages from Tibbsy. The Thames was a black sequinned silk scarf next to them, reminding her of the photos on Amber's Instagram. 'What did Robertson say?'

Saunders snapped back into work mode, his voice hardening. 'Oh, yes, we need to have a little chat about Lex Riley. He's on the Drugs Squad watch list and I don't want them complaining we've been trampling all over their investigation.'

'They couldn't even find him!' Freddie cut in.

'I want a full report on my desk by morning, Cudmore. I'll relay what you've found over to Narcotics and they can take it from there.'

'But it's relevant to the Spice Road site. That's a bloody drugs site,' Freddie said. 'Why do they get Riley?'

'Because he works for a rival gang. He has nothing to do with our case,' Saunders said.

'But he could be responsible for Amber being in that video,' Freddie said. This was ridiculous.

'Amber's not the girl in the video,' Saunders snapped.

What?

'Robertson doesn't know where Amber is,' Nas said. 'He handed himself in because he didn't want another parent to be in the same position as him: he recognised the girl as a nanny at one of his clients' house. I think he felt guilty about Amber being missing. We know Lex Riley called him before they all vanished. Maybe he already had Amber, maybe he was taunting him. I think he felt turning himself in was some kind of penance.'

She tried to process what they were saying. So Amber wasn't the girl in the video, but she was still missing. 'Do we know the name of the girl in the video?'

'No,' Nas said sadly. 'And Freddie, you should know… I've been thinking it for a while. And what Robertson said supports my fears. I don't think the girl in the video can have survived the attack. I think we're looking for a body.'

It was as if the car filled with water, rushing into her ears and eyes and mouth. They couldn't know that. Freddie tried to speak.

'Cudmore and I will run the address he gave us through the PNC. See who's registered. Then we'll pay them a visit tomorrow,' Saunders said.

The girl in the video was dead? But there was still a chance Amber was alive. And they were closer to knowing who the girl in the video was. Who suspects A and B were. Closer to bringing them to justice. 'What about me?' Freddie asked.

'After your performance tonight, we'll have to wait to see if you've still got a job come morning,' Saunders said breezily. And Freddie felt the bottom fall out of her world.

Freddie

She was up and dressed before his alarm went off. The sun was already white with heat, even under the film of trapped smog that sat over London like a duvet. She shuddered at the accidental emotional memory from Kate's statement: the white, bloodstained duvet on the floor. Tibbsy was lying on his back, naked apart from a pale blue sheet. One arm was resting over his forehead, his hand taut. The other was across his waist, fingers pointing down. It made it look like he was Vogue-ing in his sleep. She smiled. He slept in the weirdest positions. He stirred, and she straightened, pulling her bag onto her shoulder. His hand twitched, then rubbed his eyes.

'You all right?'

'Yeah, early start: need to make a good impression,' she said. Last night she'd begged – actually begged – Saunders not to report her to Burgone. He'd agreed, on the condition that she owed him one. Not a great position to be in, but at least she still had her job, if Tibbsy could get Moast to keep his mouth shut.

'Cool.' He propped himself up onto his elbows. His hair sloping up away from his scalp. He was such a dork. How had this happened?

'You okay?' she said.

'Sure,' he said, nodding.

'I mean, you did get caught with your dick in a *thing*,' she said.

'He didn't mean it like that.' He ran his tongue around his mouth.

She smiled. 'He did.'

'Nah. It was the shock. And the whole shagging at work thing.' He gave her a sheepish grin. 'He calmed down after I bought him a double brandy.' That sounded promising. 'How was Nas?' They hadn't talked last night when she'd arrived back from the office to find him already in bed. Picked up where they'd left off, then she'd fallen asleep in his arms.

'She'll get over it,' she said.

He looked at her. 'What happens now, Freddie? Are you gonna stay?'

She tightened her hand on the strap of her bag. Her stomach tensed. 'This case is taking up all my headspace. I need to just focus on this for now.'

He nodded, lips pressed together, looking resigned rather than sad. 'I'll still be here when you're done.'

'Good luck with Moast.' She fumbled for the door handle. The room felt airless.

Outside was worse. The humidity was building. The heatwave was here in full force. Nas and Saunders were going straight to North London. She was going to put together what she could about the couple that lived there. William and Elizabeth Gardner. Two kids. Home in Islington. It sounded so innocuous. But there was one other person listed at the address. A temporary resident from Italy. An au pair named Calinda Gallo. Eighteen years old. She hoped Nas was wrong. That Calinda would open the door. That for some reason she hadn't come forwards till now. With Robertson having handed himself in they now had five witnesses. It was time to finally find out what had happened to the girl in the film.

Kate

She was asleep when the phone rang. She must have slept late; groggily, she reached for her mobile. 'Hello?'

'Kate, it's Freddie.' She shook her head, trying to clear it. What time had she finally drifted off? She looked about the room. No tablets last night. No drink. There was no one here.

'Freddie, hi.' She felt her chest tighten.

'Are you at home?'

She didn't want to say she'd only just woken up. 'Yes,' she answered. Looked at her face in the mirror. It was dented on one side, kissed by the pillow. She rubbed at the spot over her eyebrow.

'Good. I've sent you a photo.' The bedroom grew very still. 'We think we have a possible name for the girl in the film.'

'You've found her?' Her heart squeezed. She'd sent a photo. Oh God, she couldn't look at this. Couldn't do this.

'No, not yet,' Freddie said. 'But we have a name: Calinda Gallo. She's an eighteen-year-old au pair from Italy. I've got a photo from her agency. We're talking to the family she works for now.'

She knew it. They were going to find her. They were going to catch him. This would soon be over. 'And you think that's her?'

'It might be,' Freddie said. 'I've emailed it over.'

Life pulsed through her body. 'Hang on – my laptop's downstairs.' She ran out of her bedroom, hurried down into the living room. The computer was still on the table.

'We're speaking to the others too, seeing what they think, but I wanted to let you know first.'

'Thank you,' she said, willing her computer to load faster. She typed in her password. Waited for the bar to light all the way across. *Come on. Come on.* 'Just logging in now.' She waited for her inbox to load. There is was. An email from Freddie Venton. She clicked on it. The photo auto-opened, filling her screen.

She drew a sharp intake of breath. Sat down with a bump on the chair. Her hand clasped over her mouth.

'Kate? Are you still there?'

She nodded.

'Kate? Did you get it? Did it come through? Hello?'

'I'm still here,' she managed. The girl was beautiful. Bright brown eyes. Big smile, lovely teeth. And long dark hair.

'Do you recognise her?'

She stretched out a hand and stroked the screen. Nodded. 'It's her.' Her parents. In Italy. Oh, it was awful. A tear fell from her eye, rolled and plopped onto her breast.

'You're sure?' Freddie asked.

'Yes. I'm sure. It's her.' Calinda Gallo. Calinda, you poor child.

'Thank you, Kate. I'll give you a call later, yeah? Don't speak to anyone else about this, okay? No press or anything like that.'

She was still stroking the photo. 'Of course.' Eighteen years old.

After Freddie had gone she didn't know how long she sat staring at Calinda Gallo's photo. Touching the girl's face as if she could feel her soft skin, as if she were tucking the hair behind her ear. She knew those eyes. She knew every one of those eyelashes.

'We did it, baby girl. We found her.'

Nasreen

They had to find the Gardners. Nasreen lifted the metal knocker, a ring in a lion's mouth, suitably expensive and threatening, and swung it again against the wooden door. The sound reverberated through the hallway. There was no movement inside.

Saunders was standing between the two clipped balls of hedge that framed the bay window. 'Can't see anyone in there.'

Nasreen bent down, opened the letter box, called into it. 'Hello? Mr Gardner? Mrs Gardner? It's Detective Sergeant Cudmore, we'd like a word.' *We'd like to know if you're involved in the possible death of an eighteen-year-old girl.*

Saunders stepped back, thrust his hands in his pockets and sniffed. 'This is a waste of time.'

Nasreen's palms were damp from the heat. 'You think they're involved and they've done a bunk? They haven't reported Calinda Gallo missing. If it is her in the film.' She hadn't been able to sleep last night thinking of the look in Paul Robertson's eyes when he'd mentioned Amber. More three-storey Victorian villas stretched away from them down the street. 'You want to see if we can get round the back?' She couldn't see any side passages.

'I want to get an iced tea. And a car like that.' Saunders nodded at a silver Porsche that was parked two doors down. 'But we don't always get what we want.' He looked up at the bedroom windows. 'Unless you're Freddie. She seems to get everything she wants,' he added with a laugh.

'Can we not talk about it, sir,' she said. Even by Freddie's standards she couldn't believe her friend had been so stupid. If word of her little performance with Tibbsy got back to Burgone she'd be sacked, and then what would Nasreen do? Freddie was the only one who took Nasreen's work seriously. They worked well together. No, more than that: they were partners. They had each other's back. How could Freddie risk that?

'Don't tell me you're one of those?' Saunders said.

'One of what?' He was still punishing her for not telling him about Lex Riley.

'One of those boring millennials who don't do sex,' he said.

She ignored him, focused instead on looking for the car that was registered to the Gardners. A black Range Rover.

'You don't do booze, you don't smoke and you don't do sex. What do you do in your spare time, Cudmore?' Saunders was enjoying himself.

Fantasise about you being fired. He was playing games. He knew very well why she didn't drink. It had hardly won her friends in the past. 'I prefer to focus on the job in hand.'

'Ah! Got you – a bit of self-love, hey. Nothing wrong with

206

that. Good for getting rid of tension. I've spent many a happy night with my hand.'

Her nose wrinkled in disgust. 'I don't want that mental image, thank you very much.' Why couldn't he just get over it?

'You need something in the wank bank, Cudmore? Not getting any action?'

She thought of Burgone and how she'd reacted to him being so close last night. And blushed. She took a few steps down the street, making a show of looking at the cars. Tried to move the conversation on. 'Can't see their car here.'

'I'm glad I'm not in your generation,' Saunders said. There were only ten years between them, but he liked to use any opportunity he could to add distance, to remind her she was younger. 'Loved my twenties. You kids make everything so boring now.'

The heat was making her more irritated. She could hear Freddie in her mind. See her looking at her pointedly. *Stand up for yourself.* 'Says the guy who measures three parts almond milk with one part water for his breakfast oats.'

When Saunders didn't reply, she tentatively glanced back to check he wasn't about to shout at her. But he wasn't looking at her at all.

'See that?' Saunders pointed at the identical pristine white house next door.

'What?' She shielded her eyes again. The windows glinted like blinking eyes in the sunlight.

'That is a Neighbourhood Watch sticker.' He vaulted the small dividing railing between the Gardners' house and the next.

How had she missed that? She was letting him distract her. Or the heat was getting to her.

'And we all know that means nosy neighbours.' Saunders leant on the doorbell of the next house, humming the *Neighbours* theme tune.

Hurrying, she reached his side, as a tall woman with silver hair swept into a chignon opened the door.

'Yes?' the woman said.

'Your bell's got stuck.' Saunders prodded the doorbell again, the chimes ringing out through the black-and-white-tiled cavernous hallway that stretched behind them. Nasreen caught a puff of cooler air from inside. 'That's it.' He prodded it again. 'Fixed it. This is DS Cudmore, and I'm DI Saunders.'

The woman clutched a veiny hand to the neck of the white blouse she was wearing. 'Is everything okay?'

'Oh, yes, nothing to worry about, Mrs… sorry, I didn't get your name?' he said.

'Mathers. Pamela Mathers,' she said.

'Sorry to bother you, Mrs Mathers, but we're looking for your neighbours – William and Elizabeth Gardner.'

'Lizzie and Will are away,' she said. 'Is anything wrong?'

'You don't happen to know where they've gone, do you?' Saunders smiled warmly.

'They're at their house in Cornwall,' she said. 'They spend the summer there. Much healthier for the children. Young people don't get enough fresh air nowadays.'

'Do you know if their au pair went with them?' Saunders asked. Nasreen was detailing the hallway. Neat. Smelling of lemons and floor polish. A shiny dark wood chest of drawers the only furniture visible. A mirror above it.

'The Italian girl?' Mrs Mathers' face wrinkled slightly. 'I presumed she had because I haven't seen her since they left.'

'And I don't suppose you have a contact number for the Gardners?' Saunders said.

'I have both Will and Lizzie's mobile telephone numbers, in case of emergency,' she said. 'Can I ask what this is regarding?'

No, you can't. 'Would you mind, please, giving me those numbers?' Saunders said. He smiled reassuringly. 'We would very much like to get hold of them.'

'And nothing is wrong?' she tried again.

'You got a pencil ready, Cudmore?' Saunders said. She pulled her pad and pen from her back pocket.

Mrs Mathers wasn't used to being ignored. She looked at Nasreen, a slight distaste at the corner of her mouth. 'You know she smokes in the garden, that girl? When Will and Lizzie are out.' Cigarette butts could provide vital DNA evidence; Nasreen stored the thought away. Mrs Mathers was still looking at her. Nasreen knew the type. *We don't like suspicious-looking strangers.* And by suspicious they meant anyone who didn't look like exactly like them. She smiled sweetly at the woman.

'The number, Mrs Mathers,' Saunders pushed with a smile. 'If you don't mind.'

'Hold on a moment.' She headed to the chest of drawers. 'I'd invite you in, but Matilda's just been, and she gets so upset if people walk over her clean floors.'

Or you do, Nasreen thought.

Pamela Mathers opened the top drawer and lifted out a black leather-bound book. Gold lettering sparkled in the cool hallway. Nasreen longed to step into the cool air. It was an address book. Old-school. The woman took her time, licked her finger, turned to the right page. 'Here we are.' She read the numbers out.

'And I don't suppose you have a contact number for the Italian girl?' Saunders added.

Nasreen had been thinking the same. If the au pair, Calinda Gallo, was the girl in the video then they could trace her phone. Find out where she'd been. Possibly where she was now.

Mrs Mathers looked surprised and then suspicious. 'Why do you want to speak to her?'

'Police business.' Saunders smiled. 'Do you have a contact number for her?'

'Of course not,' Mrs Mathers said.

Nasreen felt the balloon of hope in her stomach deflate.

'Thank you for all your help, Mrs Mathers,' Saunders said.

'If that girl is in trouble I have a right to know. I've been living next door to her,' Pamela said.

If she paid this much attention, she must have seen Robertson if he came here as regularly as he said.

'Mrs Mathers.' Nasreen pulled her phone from her pocket. Scrolled through her photos. 'Can I ask if you've ever seen this man visiting the Gardners?'

The woman's mouth contracted into a cat's bottom. 'Yes. I spoke to Will about him, actually. Horrid-looking man. Turned up all times of the day and night.' *Did he now?* The Gardners had a healthy habit, by the sounds of it. 'He has a motorbike. I told Lizzie the noise was very disturbing.'

'Do you know what he was doing here?' Saunders said.

'He's a delivery driver. For Will's firm. Brings over computer disks and files. He works so hard, that man, and all his wife does is go to yoga. Running around in those legging things. I don't see why they need an au pair.'

A delivery driver. Well, that was a truth, of sorts. It supported what Robertson had claimed.

'Thank you again, Mrs Mathers,' Saunders said. Nasreen tucked her phone and pad back into her pockets.

'What has he done? The delivery driver?' Mrs Mathers' desperation to be involved hung about her like perfume. The hint of scandal. *And the police came to my door. The shock of it all.* 'Should I call someone if I see him?'

That was highly unlikely, as he was currently banged up in the Jubilee.

'No need for that. Thank you for your time, Mrs Mathers. DS Cudmore will give you her card – and if you ever want to contact us you can call her.'

Nasreen shot him an evil look. This was all she needed. A nosey neighbour with a hotline to her. Reluctantly she handed over her card. Mrs Mathers didn't look thrilled with the prospect either. Clearly she wanted to keep in touch with the DI himself. She didn't say thank you.

They walked swiftly back to the car.

'Want me to call the Gardners?' Nas asked.

Saunders was chewing his lip. 'And risk them doing a bunk? Not likely.'

For a blissful second she imagined they could go down to Cornwall. She could almost feel the breeze from the sea. The beach. Compared to dry, dirty, hot London, it sparkled like paradise in her mind. 'Shall I call the local force then?'

'I've got a pal who lives down there,' Saunders said. 'We were at Hendon together. I'll ask him to go have a chat with *Will and Lizzie.*'

'Could Calinda be with them? Robertson could be lying,

or confused.' Robertson hadn't looked like he partook in his own product, but you couldn't always tell.

Saunders reached the car and unlocked it with his fob. 'Try not to sweat on the seats,' he said as he opened the driver's side.

Scowling, she settled into the passenger side. It smelt of his aftershave. She went to open the window. 'Don't do that. The air con will kick in in a second,' he said fussily.

Hot air blew into her face. She already felt queasy and they hadn't set off yet.

Saunders's beloved dance music started up. Something she didn't recognise, not that she ever did. She thought about what he'd said about his twenties. Imagined him out clubbing till the early hours. It was too personal an image. She'd learnt to keep everyone in their correct boxes. Saunders existed at work, nowhere else. How could Freddie blur those lines, after she knew what had happened to her? In her head, Burgone smiled. Stepped out the edge of his box.

Saunders was tapping his fingers against the steering wheel in time to the track. 'I need to refuel. We'll stop off for lunch. I'll give Crofty a call – get him to pay them a visit. Check how far Bodmin to Rock is,' he said, waving his hand at her. She couldn't look at her phone in the car: she'd be ill. Saliva pooled in her mouth. 'If Calinda isn't on her jolly holidays in Cornwall, I want to know where she is. And why the hell *Will and Lizzie* haven't reported her missing.' Saunders slammed on the brakes, hammering on the horn at the black cab that had stopped in front. 'Use your bloody mirrors!'

The sickness rose in Nasreen.

Freddie

Freddie nervously looked up each time someone moved in the hall. Where were Saunders and Nas? They must have spoken to the Gardners by now. She jumped up when she saw Green approaching. 'You seen all the witnesses? What did they say?' she asked Green.

Green opened the folder she was carrying. 'I took the teacher and the politician. Khan took the kids. He could only get hold of one. The one who coughed up to his mum,' she said, sliding out a photo of Calinda Gallo.

It was the same headshot Freddie had got from the agency, selected and styled, she guessed, to appeal to prospective parents. In it, Calinda wore a smart shirt buttoned all the way to her neck, which looked comically old-fashioned. No cleavage to tempt wayward fathers and frighten off nervous mothers, she assumed. Her face was bare of make-up, clean,

213

her hair neat and brushed so it fell behind her shoulders. Her smile was warm and open, one front tooth slightly crooked, lending her an endearing quality. A touch of goofiness. 'The Nicolson lad?'

'Yeah,' Green said. 'Poor kid. Khan said he cried when he saw the photo.'

He recognised Calinda then. Kate had too. 'What about the politician?'

'He kept me waiting for bloody ages.' Green scooped the photo back into her folder. Headed for her desk. The air conditioning hadn't taken the pink out of her face yet. 'You know the type: too busy to talk to plebs like us.'

Chips made a grunt of recognition.

'Yeah, but what did he say?' Having a positive ID on the girl in the film must be a good thing. That must bring them one step closer to finding her. To finding suspect A and suspect B.

'His office is twice as big as this room.' Green dropped the file on her desk and lifted up a glass. 'And he's got three secretaries.' She shook the glass as if liquid might be hiding in it.

'Wish I had three secretaries,' Chips said. 'Would make my life a lot easier.' He slapped one of the piles of paperwork that filled his desk.

'You've got Venton,' Green said.

'Ha ha.' Freddie shot her a look. So far Saunders had kept his word: neither Chips nor Green seemed to know about last night. Nas didn't seem to be talking to her at all. She was getting the silent treatment. 'Can we cut to the chase? Did he or did he not recognise Calinda?'

'Oh, he recognised her all right. Went quite a funny shade when I showed him the pic,' Green said. 'Then one of the secretaries – I think they were all called Sophie – asked if there was going to be a press release, and could they proofread it first!' She laughed.

'Bloody cheek!' Chips said.

'Like we're his private PR firm or something!' Green said.

Robertson, Kate, the politician, one of the kids. That was four people who'd individually confirmed it was Calinda on the tape. So where was she?

For a girl who was living abroad, Calinda updated her Facebook page frustratingly infrequently. There were some photos of her at a music festival a few weeks ago, her hair wavy and relaxed, eyes heavy with mascara, wearing a cotton T-shirt and jean shorts. Gripping a plastic cup of beer and standing with friends. Freddie had noted all their names. Started to build the picture.

'Where do these people come from?' Chips said.

There was a pause and she looked up. They were both looking at her: waiting for her to join the chorus against the idiot politician. 'Yeah, he's a wanker,' she said.

Chips and Green laughed. 'Totally,' said Green.

Freddie had already changed screens. Refreshed her email. Nothing more from the telephone company yet. Calinda had registered a mobile phone nine months ago, when she'd arrived in the UK. Chips had said the agency woman had seemed unbothered. They weren't interested in 'keeping tabs' on their staff, once they were settled with families. She'd made the point that these were adults. Freddie had listened while Chips, ever the father figure, had pointed out that at eighteen

Calinda was only just an adult, and living in a foreign country. And their responsibility. The woman had huffed and accused him of being pro-Brexit. Which left the Gardners. Freddie checked the time. There'd still been no word from Nas. Perhaps they had already arrested the Gardners and she just hadn't bothered to tell her. She looked at her phone. No text. No WhatsApp. Nothing. She had a feeling that if she tried to call her she'd get voicemail. Nas was obviously still sulking about last night.

The phones rang, but Green got there first. 'Cudmore, any news?' she said into the receiver.

Dammit. Freddie tried to work out what Nas was saying, but Green was mostly saying yes, and taking notes.

Freddie clicked back onto Calinda's Facebook page and clicked onto 'photos of Calinda'. There were images of her in Italy, giving piggybacks to what she guessed were younger siblings. They were all laughing. She was a natural. It was obvious why she'd been drawn to becoming an au pair. There was no sign of her on Twitter or Instagram. Snapchat came up with nothing. Then she thought of it. Stupid not to have checked before. Freddie clicked into Periscope, the live streaming site Kate and the others had seen the video on. She searched for Calinda Gallo. Nothing. Could the account have been hers? Deleted by the others after? Perhaps. Or perhaps she hadn't been on the site at all. Had they asked to film her? Had she consented without knowing what she was committing to? No, Kate had said she'd been out of it. Gone in the eyes. Taken something. Did the Gardners share their stash with Calinda? She thought of Calinda's buttoned-up shirt, and the cropped denim shorts. Could

William Gardner be the man in the film? Did he drug Calinda to sleep with her?

'*Great*,' said Green sarcastically into the phone. What was going on? Green grimaced as she hung up. 'Saunders and Cudmore are on their way back. The Gardners are away in Cornwall.'

'Is Calinda with them?' Freddie couldn't believe this.

'No,' Green said.

Then where was she? 'The live stream was six days ago – have they been away all that time?' Freddie asked.

Green shrugged. 'We'll know more when they get back, I guess.'

This was taking too long. They needed to find the crime scene. They needed to find Calinda. And then there was still the question of Amber. Nas had promised Saunders she would leave the Lex Riley lead alone, but Freddie hadn't. If she could find out what happened to Amber maybe they could trade information with Paul Robertson. Saunders wouldn't care what she'd done regarding Amber, if she could get him nearer to closing down the Spice Road website. 'So they're just gonna wait till the Gardners get back?'

Green blew the hair away from her face. 'Nas said they'd been on to the local lads. They're sending someone over to see what they can find out.'

'How far away are they?' Freddie was pacing between Green and her desk.

'I don't know – Chips, do you know how many forces there are in Cornwall?' Green said.

'Thinking of asking for a transfer?' he said.

'I mean, how long before Nas and Saunders are back?' She

wanted to crack on with what they had. The heat had ground everyone down, slowed them; it was like they were all treading water until the lifeboat arrived. If it ever did.

Green shrugged. 'I fancy an ice-cream – you want one, guv? Venton?'

'No.' Freddie was beginning to suspect she was the only one with any sense of urgency on this. She wasn't about to presume Calinda was dead like Nas. It didn't make sense. 'Why haven't there been any suspicious smells called in?'

'I'll have a Cornetto, lass.' Chips rummaged in his pocket for change. 'What smells?'

'The body – Calinda,' she said. She hated speaking about her like this. 'If she was killed in the video and someone's stashed the body, then it would smell in this heat, surely? Someone would get wind of it?' Decomposing. Her stomach flipped.

Green's forehead wrinkled. 'You're putting me off the idea now.'

'Good question, lass.' Chips turned his chair to face her. 'A body would be ripe by now.'

All trace of pink drained from Green's face. Freddie pushed on. 'So she can't be dead,' she said.

'Or the body is hidden very well, or placed somewhere that reeks already,' Chips said. 'There used to be a gang, back in the day, who used to hide bodies near a sewage works on the edge of the city. Everyone assumed it was the waste smelling.'

'Minging,' Green said.

None of the witnesses could be one hundred per cent certain the girl was dead. It's not like they could have checked her pulse. The video was cut quickly after she was attacked.

'I think it's still possible she's alive. That she's being held captive somewhere.'

Trapped for six days. Desperate for help. But was it better than being dead? Freddie sat down defeatedly. Maybe Nas and Saunders would know more. Would have something of use. So far the questions were mounting up, and the answers were diminishing. Things were running the wrong way. If Calinda was alive then where was she being held? They didn't even know where she was attacked. Green chewed her lip, lost in her own thoughts, passing Freddie on the way to get an ice-cream. It was such a frivolous, summery thing to do: eat ice-cream in the office. Freddie wasn't sure she'd ever get used to the way cops could do this: pop everything in a box. Stash it away. Laying the terrors into coffins, screwing the lids down, burying them. She thought of Tibbsy. Nothing stayed hidden for ever.

Nasreen

'She's supposed to be inter-railing.' Saunders was at the office door already, his frustration clear in his voice and pace.

Chips crunched the end of an ice-cream cone into his mouth. Green was licking a Solero. Nasreen didn't look at Freddie; first she hadn't told her about her promotion, and now she'd neglected to mention she was in a relationship with Tibbsy. And they were supposed to be friends.

'Calinda was meant to be inter-railing?' Freddie asked, heading for Saunders, who was settling into his squeaky chair.

'That's what I said,' Saunders said.

'That's what the Gardners said?' Freddie asked. 'And you believe them?'

Saunders was clicking at his desktop, his face closed.

'The family left for Cornwall on Friday morning.' Nasreen

started to fill in the gaps. Careful to aim her words at Chips, as if Freddie wasn't really there. Saunders had been like this since they'd got off the phone to his Cornish contact. Angry at the Gardners' apparent lack of concern. Angry at the fact that an eighteen-year-old had ended up missing and no one had noticed. 'Calinda stayed to attend her night school.'

'They were making her take English lessons!' Saunders interjected. Despite not meeting them himself, he'd taken strongly against the Gardners. Casting them as spoilt and reckless, when really they knew very little about them. Nasreen didn't think it was the family's fault if the girl had been taken. They'd given her the summer off, and her plan had been to go back to Italy over the next couple of weeks, doing some travelling on the way. This should have been the beginning of an adventure for her, but something had gone wrong.

'Which night school?' Freddie said. 'Did she go?'

'Highbury Tech.' Nasreen had made the call while they drove back. 'She's marked off on the register. I'm getting a list of contacts for the teacher and the other students who were there that night sent over.'

'It was someone at the school, then?' Freddie pushed.

She wished Chips would pipe up. She didn't know how much longer she could avoid looking at Freddie. 'We have no way of knowing that.' She reached her own desk. There was an A4 envelope waiting for her; she picked it up.

'The last message sent from her phone was that night,' Freddie said. 'There's a cell site hit on a mast in East London. Could have been when she was at school? You're sure you believe them, the Gardners?'

'I'm getting a search warrant for their house,' Saunders said.

'They're driving back up this afternoon. They want to be there while we search the place.' Nasreen opened the envelope. Inside was a brief note from the sketch artist – *As promised, I've done what I can with the witness statements.* As Freddie had suggested, he'd drawn the room from the video. It was rectangular. No windows visible, as the witnesses had said. Across the back wall he'd painted two small graffitied pictures of what looked like an animal and a blob. A blue door was closed in the background. A bare bulb hanging from the ceiling. The ceiling itself not too high, so not a period property? The ceiling had been detailed in Artex swirls. The uniformity of it reminded Nasreen of Freddie's gran's council flat. The proportions. That cheap mass-market door handle. It was a council property. That fitted with what Kate had said, but there must be thousands of council properties in London. And they weren't one hundred per cent sure that it was in London. Calinda had been at Highbury Tech until 8pm on Friday, the live stream video was seen at 1.30am on Saturday. That meant this location could be anywhere that was five and a half hours from North London. What had happened in those missing hours? There were still too many unknowns. Too many questions.

'I'm not waiting for the Gardners to get back and destroy any evidence,' Saunders was saying. 'We need Calinda's computer. Her stuff. I want that place combed from top to bottom for signs of assault. And I want them arrested for possession as soon as they get back.'

'You think the video could have been shot in their house?' Freddie pointed at the papers in Nasreen's hands.

'Her passport's not been used – I checked.' Nasreen looked at the room sketch; it didn't look like it would be inside the polished Victorian house they'd stood outside of. The ceiling was too low. It was run down. Not at all like the front room had looked. Could it be a room out the back, maybe a garage?

'Cudmore?' Saunders held out his hand. She handed the papers to him. 'These the sketches from the photofit?'

Freddie peered over his shoulder. 'Looks like a local authority place to me – don't you think?'

She'd thought the same, but couldn't bring herself to agree with Freddie.

'I want to know if Calinda left for her inter-railing trip or not,' Saunders said, looking at the papers. 'Green, get on it.'

'Yes, sir,' Green said.

'Give Freddie the numbers when they come in,' Saunders said. 'See if there was any communication between her and her classmates. What do you think, Chips?' He handed the sketch over.

'Where're my glasses? Chips started patting his empty pockets.

'You need contacts,' Freddie said.

'It's only for reading. This is what happens when you get to my age, lass. The windows get a bit clogged up.'

Freddie started looking through the piles of paper and newspapers that covered Chips's desk. Nasreen glanced around, in case he'd left them on the edge of someone else's table. She'd found them in the kitchen last week, next to the kettle.

Saunders was still issuing orders. 'I want interviews set up with everyone who was in that class that night. I want to know where Calinda went after. Who she hung out with. Anything we've got.'

'What about her parents?' Nasreen asked. It was looking increasingly likely that Calinda was their girl.

Saunders sucked air through his teeth.

'She might have been in contact with them – any of those messages or calls to Italy, Freddie?'

'Not since Friday afternoon,' Freddie said from under the desk. 'Got them!'

'Must have knocked them off,' Chips said, taking the glasses.

'How do you want to play it?' she said to Saunders. They didn't have a body, but they had increasing evidence that Calinda had been attacked, even though most of it was circumstantial. Her parents had a right to know.

Saunders's face was stern. Nasreen felt sick; she wouldn't want to make this call. 'Let's get into her room. Her computer,' Saunders said. 'See what more we can find out before we go to them.'

'They might know she's missing,' she replied.

'Then why haven't they come forward?' he countered.

'Maybe they have. Who knows which police station they would have contacted, but it wouldn't be us, would it? They'd have had to Google a local police station, probably one near the Gardners.'

'What about Kate being on the news?' Saunders said.

'She's been on UK news. Even if they had seen that, there was no description of the girl in the video, no reason to think it might be their daughter. No one ever thinks things like this happen to them,' she said. 'I think they should at least be made aware of the situation now.'

'We don't know what the situation is,' Saunders said. 'We go to them when we have something concrete.'

'We've got witnesses,' Freddie said.

'You want to tell them some strangers, people who've never met their daughter, reckon they've seen her in a video?' Saunders said, shaking his head 'We go to them when we have more.'

'Looks like the Dogberry estate,' Chips said suddenly, staring at the sketches, his bottom lip stuck out in concentration.

'You recognise it?' Freddie asked.

'From that?' Saunders said.

'I've done a fair few jobs on that estate over the years. All the flats are the same. Or they were 'til people started buying them off the council and doing them up,' Chips said. 'Plus that looks like their tag.'

'The graffiti?' Nasreen stared at the sketch.

'It's not a very good one, I'll give you that, lass, but don't you think that looks like a dog and a berry?' Chips pointed a puffy finger at the spray-painted shapes on the wall. They had had a clue to where the location was all along and none of them had realised it.

'Where the Dogberry Boys are based?' Nasreen said. Where Lex Riley used to live. That couldn't be a coincidence.

'You're sure?' Saunders said.

Freddie was back at her desk, on Google. 'Shit. You're right. Look.' She turned the screen toward them. On it was a photo

225

of a room that did look like the one in the sketch. 'I knew it was a council place!'

'It does look very similar,' Nasreen conceded.

'And look: here's some of their tag.' Freddie clicked onto photos of graffiti images that matched the shapes on the back wall of the room.

'What was Calinda doing on the Dogberry estate?' Saunders was saying. 'How'd she get there from college?'

'Email me that photo, Freddie. I'll see whether it looks right to our witnesses,' Nas said.

Freddie was scrabbling through her notes. 'The last cell site hit on her phone was off a mast in Poplar: that fits.'

'I want to know who she was with,' Saunders said.

'We can find her then? She must be on the estate. We can find the crime scene.' Freddie's voice was urgent. Excited. She could smell the scent of the trail.

'Dogberry's huge, lass,' Chips said. 'There must be at least ten towers.'

'We can search them though?' Freddie said. 'Go flat to flat?'

'We can't get inside without warrants. And we won't get warrants to search the whole place,' Nasreen said. Never mind the manpower involved.

Freddie was tapping at her keyboard. She stopped. 'Shit. It says here: The Dogberry estate consists of four blocks, each of which consists of three towers. Each tower is thirty-one storeys high, and contains two hundred and seventeen flats. How many's that?'

'Too many,' Saunders said.

'Two thousand, six hundred and four,' Freddie said.

226

They needed more information to reduce the search area. 'And isn't the Dogberry the one with the tunnels?' Nasreen asked.

'What tunnels?' Freddie's face had coasted back into desperation.

'Aye,' Chips said. 'They built it in the seventies, with all these tunnels underneath – I think they were supposed to be for utilities and mail transport or something – but they ran out of money before they finished.'

'So they just left them?' Green said.

'Yup,' Chips said. 'But they've been put to good use by the Dogberry Boys. Intelligence know they run drugs, communications, guns, people, the lot through them.'

'Christ,' said Green.

'Their own escape routes?' Freddie said.

'It's like a bloody rabbit warren,' Chips said. 'I know many an officer who's been hot on the tail of a target only for the bugger to effectively vanish.'

'They go to ground,' Freddie said. 'Literally.'

'Do they run between all of the towers?' Nasreen asked. It was like doubling the search zone. Where would they even start? They had to comb it all. They had to find the crime scene. They had to bring whoever did this to justice.

'Aye, and then some. If I remember right they go for about a mile or so, and pop up in some industrial estate. That's where they were supposed to take the mail and stuff in from, originally, I guess.'

'Meaning you could take something, like a body, say, and get it away with no one seeing?' Nasreen's mind was spinning.

'Shit,' said Freddie.

'We won't get budget for searching that lot, no matter how many poncy MPs are involved,' Saunders said.

She could go to Burgone, see if she could persuade him? No that was madness. He'd be accused of favouritism.

'We need more info to shrink our zone.' Saunders was pacing. 'Some graffiti doesn't mean it's definitely the Dogberry we're looking at. It's not like councils don't bulk-buy paint and all that crap; it could be another estate. We need more.'

Nasreen pulled up the details of the witnesses. First she'd check the image with them, see if they recognised it. Then start working through those who were in Calinda's class. If she had ended up on the Dogberry perhaps she'd gone with someone from there. There were fifteen names on the list, eleven who'd been in attendance that night. No one's listed address was on the Dogberry. There was a missing chunk of time yet to be accounted for.

Freddie was still reading the Wiki entry for Dogberry Towers, muttering to herself. 'Two thousand, six hundred and four,' she said. 'Five miles of underground tunnels. Fuck.'

Calinda could have been anywhere. Could *be* anywhere. Instead of making it easier to trace her, the photofit sketch had opened up a whole new set of possibilities to them.

Freddie clicked onto a photo and a diagrammatic drawing of the towers opened on her screen, not quite an official blueprint, but detailed enough to show a dozen tunnels criss-crossing beneath them. Stacks of flats, piled on top of each other, and rings of carved-out walkways below them. It reminded Nasreen of something she'd seen before, but she couldn't put her finger on it. Freddie had obviously been thinking the same thing, because the next words that came out of her mouth sent a zing of recognition through Nasreen. She swallowed. Freddie blew out air, talking to herself, repeating the words again, as if it might change their meaning. It didn't. They fell hard and heavy into Nasreen's mind.

'Dante's circles of hell.'

Nasreen

'She's dead, isn't she?'

Hana Richter was a slender but athletic girl. At twenty-four, she was the same age as Nasreen, but she seemed somehow younger. Though that could just be the impression given by her racer back vest and tanned limbs. A runner, Nasreen would have guessed, and over here to work at a large mobile company.

'I'm a software engineer,' she'd explained. 'I took the class to get better at casual terms. I can do business English.' She'd been at the college that night with Calinda, and had been released from work to come answer their questions. But now, what had been a relaxed and smiling face had grown taut. She looked anxiously between Nasreen and Saunders.

'Why do you say that?' Saunders asked. Nasreen felt it was unnecessary; the girl wasn't daft, she'd been asked to attend a police interview urgently, and they were asking questions about her friend. It wouldn't take much to work out that Calinda was in trouble, or really, really in trouble.

'I should have gone with her,' she said. 'But I had a big meeting the next day. I needed rest.' She shook her head, as if to undo what had been done.

'Go with her where?' Nasreen asked.

'Sorry. I start from the beginning,' she said, correcting her posture, as if she were straightening her story out. 'Some of us went for a drink after class. Calinda, Sven and some of the others, they were going home for the summer, so it was like a goodbye.'

Nasreen was careful to use the present tense. 'Are you good friends with Calinda?'

'Not so much,' Hana said. 'She's a nice girl, but a child, you know?'

'Would you say she was immature?' Saunders asked. 'Naive, possibly?'

'No,' Hana said. 'She just wants to have fun, you know? She's young, yes, but not stupid.' She looked away for a second and her face clouded. 'Please, has something happened?'

'We're simply trying to build up a picture of Calinda and her movements after last week's class,' Saunders said. 'What happened at the pub?'

'Why can you not ask her?' Hana's eyes looked from Saunders to Nasreen. She'd obviously decided Saunders wasn't going to break.

Nasreen felt bad for the girl, but they didn't want anyone jumping to conclusions, not when they couldn't be sure what

231

they were dealing with. They didn't need panic spreading. 'Hana, it would be helpful if you could answer the questions,' she said softly.

'Okay.' Hana nodded. 'We were having a drink…'

'Where?' Saunders asked.

'The Nelson, it is behind the college.'

'And who else was there?' Saunders was writing this down. Nasreen studied Hana's face as she answered, listing the names of her fellow students.

She counted the names off on her fingers, meticulous. She was observant, keen to get it right. Which helped them. 'Yabani stayed only for the one, because he has a new baby.'

'And what time did you stay there until?' Saunders said.

'I think 'til just after ten. Wait: I can check.' Hana took her phone from her back pocket, a shiny slab in her hand. 'I took an Uber. Yes. It arrived at 10.22.'

'Did you leave alone?' Nasreen said.

'Yes, it was a nice night. We had our drinks outside the pub. Sidney saw someone he knew, and they joined us. Three of them. One man, two girls. It was getting too busy for me. All fun, but I had to get home.'

'And Calinda was still with them at that point, when you left?' Nasreen said. They would need to speak to Sidney's friends.

'Yes, they were talking about going on. Someone knew of a party,' Hana said.

'Where?' Saunders asked.

Hana looked pained. 'I can't remember. I wasn't interested – I was going home. They were all – how do you say – excitable?'

Nasreen nodded. Were they just on the booze at this point,

or had one of the group brought drugs? Calinda had been on something in the film.

'Can you remember anything about where they were going?' Saunders asked. They'd left messages for Sidney, whose name was on the class register, but his phone had rung with an international tone.

'It was something funny,' Hana said.

'Do you know the names of Sidney's friends – the ones who'd joined you?' Nasreen asked. If they could trace them, they might find out where they'd been headed that night.

Hana shook her head. 'Jason was his name, I think. I don't remember the girls,' she said. 'I work with a Jason – that is why I remember his.'

'No surnames?' Saunders said.

'No, sorry,' she said.

'And what did they look like?' Nasreen pushed. Perhaps someone else at the pub would recognise them.

'One of the girls was like you,' she pointed at Nasreen. 'With the long black hair. And the man, he was African-American.'

'He was American?' Saunders asked.

'No, I don't think so,' Hana said.

Saunders looked confused. Nasreen guessed that Hana had learnt a lot of her English from movies and TV shows. 'You mean he was black?'

'Yes, and tall,' she said. 'He had no hair.' She ran her hand over her head to indicate a cropped cut.

'Do you know how Sidney knew them?' Saunders asked.

233

'I think he knew the other girl – she was loud, and with hair all on top of her head,' Hana said. 'I think they used to work together.'

Nasreen knew how nights like that worked, the ebb and flow of youth, drawn to each other in bars and clubs. She had friends who always wanted to keep going. Who were always looking for somewhere that would still serve, or that still had music, somewhere to keep the night alive. Friends like Freddie, she thought. Nasreen would have left like Hana. Calinda was young though, eighteen, abroad on her own. The Gardners had already left, so there'd be no kids to look after in the morning. She could have been caught in the moment, pulled into the party, one more big night out before she left.

'Can you remember where they were going to?' Saunders said. 'Which area? Were they talking about walking? Getting the tube?'

Hana took a big breath, focused on a spot on the table. 'I think they were going by bus? I know they said the name. It was funny. A word I've not heard before…' She tapped at the table with her fingers, as if the wood might crack open and reveal the secret.

'Do you remember which way it was?' Saunders prompted.

She shook her head. 'I thought it was a club to start,' she said. 'But it was a party, I think, at someone's house. Someone was messaging the girl, the one who looked like you.'

It was almost imperceptible, but she knew Saunders's interest was piqued too. A party. Was that where they'd headed?

Hana clicked her fingers. 'It was like a strawberry, or a

blueberry. But with… yes… Dog. Berry. They were going to a place called Dog Berry, I remember now. You know it?'

Oh, yes, Nasreen thought, we know it.

Freddie

'You don't want to interview any of the college kids, lass?' Chips was carrying a Diet Coke in from the kitchen. Freddie dumped her bag on the floor. He wasn't wearing his jacket, and his sleeves were already turned up. Were it not from the tide marks around the edge of his face, the dampness of his hair from outside, you would have thought he'd been here for hours. She could see some files regarding the Spice Road website open on his desk.

'I can't cope with this fucking heat much more.' She'd successfully avoided talking to Tibbsy again last night; he'd worked late, coming in after she'd already crawled into bed. And this morning she'd waited until he'd gone for a pee and then she'd been up and out of there in minutes, giving his bleary-eyed, confused face a peck on the way. She'd squeezed his bum for good measure. She did want to kip there again tonight, after all.

'Drink?' Chips waved the Coke at her.

'Shit. I forgot.' She'd been so busy running through what they knew so far in her mind, she'd forgotten about coffee.

'Ach, never mind, Janie's always on at me about cutting down on caffeine anyway.' Chips manoeuvred himself into his chair.

'You know that has caffeine in it, right?' She looked at the can.

'Aye, but she doesn't.' He grinned.

'Nas and Saunders at it already?'

They'd spent all of the previous afternoon interviewing those who'd been at Calinda's class. There were still a few they were struggling to get hold of, but they were beginning to build a picture of what had happened. After class, Calinda, and several others from the group had gone to a local bar. From there one of the group, a guy called Sidney whom they had yet to track down, saw some friends. Those friends joined Calinda and the others, and Calinda and Sidney had left with them to go to a party that they'd been invited to on the Dogberry estate. It didn't seem to be either Sidney's or his friend's party; the invite appeared to have come from someone else via message. Freddie had listened in to several of the interviews, and all of the recordings; she knew, with the exception of the elusive Sidney, that everyone else they had to question had left the pub earlier. Let Nas and Saunders dot all the i's and cross all the t's, it sounded like a waste of time to her. They knew there was a party on the Dogberry estate that evening, and that someone had been inviting people via social media. She wanted to search Twitter, Facebook and Instagram to see if she could find anything referencing the event.

'They've still no sign of the lad who went with Calinda to the party,' Chips said.

They'd obtained a photo of Sidney from his student ID at the college. He was a small Chinese guy. He couldn't be the one attacking Calinda in the film. But Kate and the others might have made a mistake about the voice they heard off screen, the voice of the person filming it. The German college student had said Sidney was softly spoken and quite quiet. Perhaps Kate and the others hadn't heard a younger voice, but a quieter voice? He'd given the address of a youth hostel on his college form, but they confirmed he'd moved out six weeks ago. There were no Sidney Chens on the police database.

'Green says his student visa's expired,' Freddie said. If he'd gone back to China, they had no other contact details for him. 'He might know whose party it was. Where it was. He could be involved.'

Chips frowned. 'None of the witnesses reported a Chinese accent in the live stream, lass,' he said.

Freddie chewed on her cheek. 'I know. It just feels like another dead end.'

Chips gave her shoulder a squeeze. 'It happens. Try not to lose heart.'

Frustration formed in a lump in Freddie's throat. She swallowed. That wasn't good enough. She would worry at this until she had an answer. Until she knew what had happened. She was better at it here than she would be in some room going through the motions with a confused kid.

She clicked onto her computer and began to type. She tried #Dogberry first of all. Photos of the towers she recognised from her wiki search appeared on Instagram. She scrolled through: a photo of a burnt-out car, a group of lads making gang signs at the camera, one with a gun pointed toward the lens. Was that a real gun? And why pose with it if it was? Didn't they know the police could see it? Then she remembered she was the police. She made a note of the account name, in case she was ever asked. There were several groups of people posing together, with their faces partially covered by scarves. Could they be part of the Dogberry Boys gang? She searched for that hashtag, and was amazed when an actual account name called Dogberry Boys appeared. 'Chips, I reckon the Dogberry Boys have got their own Instagram page. She tapped it in again. 'And a Facebook one!'

'You sure?' Chips said.

More photos appeared on the Facebook page. Lots of masculine posturing, some of graffiti tags; one image showed a line of bats, baseball, cricket and what she thought was rounders, lined out in height order. 'This can't be them, right? No criminal gang would advertise themselves like this.' It was absurd. Everything was tagged with the same hashtag. 'It's a brand. They're creating a brand.'

Chips raised his eyebrows. 'I've been out of the game for too long – but might be worth sending these over to the Trident lads,' he said.

'They must know they're posting these.' She looked at a photo of two guys who were leaning against an expensive-looking sports car.

'Guess it makes it easy to know who you're looking for,' Chips said.

'And what you're looking for.' She pointed at another image that was a close-up of a Rolex watch on some guy's wrist.

There was a photo of a police incident board with a load of laughing face emojis underneath. 'Christ,' she muttered under her breath.

'If they don't know about it over at Trident, they're going to love you,' Chips said.

But Freddie wasn't listening. She'd scrolled down, a video automatically starting to play as she did. Thumping grime music played. A party. It was dark. Flashes of light clipped across the moving bodies, the faces of those singing along, the bump of hips. The crowd parted slightly, and the camera turned to watch a young woman who was winding up and down as she danced. The lighting switched to strobe and the image looked like it was animated, or from an old-fashioned black and white movie. Long dark hair whipped across the lights, her face flashed toward the camera, just once, just for a second, before the pulsating noise and lights swallowed it up. But it was enough. 'That's Calinda! That's her!'

'Where?' Chips was at her side. 'Where did you find this?'

'Wait, look.' She rewound the video. Played it again. 'This has been posted on the Dogberry Boys' Facebook page.' She waited, counting down the seconds to the strobe, the flick of the music, how everything went black and white just as the girl's face turned towards the camera.

'Fuck,' said Chips.

Frozen, blurred at the edges from dancing, the face was unmistakably that of the girl in the agency photo. Calinda Gallo.

240

A

'Police have confirmed they have a suspected victim in the so called Live Streamed Rape case. The high-profile case, involving the alleged live streaming of an assault of a young woman on the social media platform Periscope, saw disgraced MP Nigel Smitherson reveal he had been one of the viewers of the film. Police believe the woman in question may be Calinda Gallo, an Italian foreign exchange student, who was working as an au pair in North London. Calinda was reportedly last seen on Friday, August 4, at an English language course at a college in Highbury, North London. It is thought that Calinda visited a local pub, The Lord Nelson, with friends. Police have reason to believe that she then attended a party at the Dogberry council estate in East London. If you saw Calinda at any point that evening, or since then, or if you have any further information regarding this case, you can contact Crime Stoppers on –'

'Hey!' his brother squeals. 'I was watching that!' He snatches the remote from his hand, bounces over him and into his twin. They roll together, shouting about Minecraft.

He manages to stand. Puts one foot in front of the other. One foot.

One.

Foot.

Calinda. He hadn't known her name. Calinda Gallo. Calinda. One foot. Breathe. Keep going. Calinda. She was Italian. He'd known that. He thinks. Or maybe Greek. One foot. Breathe. One foot.

He reaches his bedroom. Panting from the exertion of not screaming her name out loud. He could whisper it. *No.* One foot. One foot in his hand, her foot. Her skin soft, cold. And he'd let her go.

If you have any further information regarding this case…

He's going to get caught. He's going to go to prison. Oh God. Mum. He's going to die. He thinks of fists pounding into flesh. Smashing into bone. A PlayStation controller in a sock. A razor blade melted into a toothbrush. He'd Googled it, knew how they did it. How they got to you. A life for a life. He crumples against his wall, slides down. Shaking. No tears. A life for a life. End it now. If dropped from this height he would shatter. One quick step and it would be done. Smash into bone. Splinter. Split. Burst.

Coward.

Coward, you won't do it.

He screws his eyes shut. Slowly he parts his lips and like air he says the words. So quiet even his heart strains to hear.

'Calinda Gallo.'

Freddie

'So far no one has come forward with concrete information about the location of the party, which we believe took place on the Dogberry estate.'

Saunders stood in front of the twenty or so officers packed into the room. On the wall was printed the still of Calinda taken from the video Freddie had found. It hurt to look at her being so vibrant, so alive. Freddie tried not to let it show: welling up in a room of cops wasn't recommended.

'This video evidence was found on a Facebook site that seems to be run by the Dogberry Boys,' Saunders said. 'Leading us to believe that they, or one of them at least, may have organised the party.'

'No one's gonna come forward then,' snorted ratty DC Morris.

'There are no known links between Calinda and the Dogberry Boys, and we believe she may have ended up at this party by chance.' Nas was doing her best commanding officer routine to the assembled group. They were going to start a major door-to-door campaign on the Dogberry estate. See if they could find someone who had seen something and was willing to talk.

'We're not very popular on the estate,' Saunders was saying.

'Waste of bloody time,' Morris said.

'So we need to handle this carefully. A lot of people are frightened of the Dogberrys,' Saunders said. 'But if they've branched out into video nasties I want to know about it and get it shut down.'

Freddie frowned. That didn't sit right with her. Surely a porn video, if intended for distribution, would have been exactly that: distributed. Kate and the MP had both used the word 'escalated'. And if it was a business venture then why put it on a free-to-view channel?

'I don't reckon this is about money,' she said. Faces turned to look at her.

'Says the secretary!' quipped Morris. There was a burst of laughter. Saunders glared at her as if it were her fault.

'The Dogberrys will protect one of their own,' Nas said. 'We have to consider that this was premeditated. Calinda could well have been in the wrong place at the wrong time, but we still can't discount the idea that the gang are involved. We need to tread carefully.'

'The Trident lads have the Dogberry estate under surveillance,' Saunders said. 'So we're keeping this as clean as possible. We're asking if anyone saw Calinda on Friday the fourth of August and the early hours of Saturday the fifth, or if they'd seen her there before.'

Lex Riley had infiltrated Amber Robertson's life through Facebook. Pretended to be someone else. Targeted her like a mark. Had the same thing happened to Calinda? She had a Facebook account. She was online. Freddie would go back and double-check her interactions – those in English. Look for boys, men, people who might be Lex. Those who might be a predator. She couldn't help but feel the two cases were linked.

'Get into people's apartments if you can. Keep your eyes open. Make sure you're familiar with the artist sketch of the suspected crime scene,' Saunders said. It was frustrating knowing it must be somewhere in those two thousand flats. 'And see if we can find out where this party was. I want to know who was there. I want names, people.' He tapped the wall six times, to punctuate each word. Underlining them. 'We. Need. To. Find. A. Body.'

This is what it had come to. Find a body and you get forensics. Clues. Something for the parents to mourn. Nas still hadn't spoken to her about anything other than the case. She looked tired. She'd had to arrange a translator to reach Calinda's parents, before they released the name to the press. Calinda called them every week on Thursday at 9pm Italian time. Today was Thursday. They didn't know she'd been missing. They thought she had started travelling back, was enjoying herself in France. But Calinda had never left London.

245

Her parents were flying over now. There would be another press conference. Saunders hoped the sight of crying parents might prompt someone to talk.

Freddie thought she ought to call her own mum. She hadn't spoken to her for a while; didn't want her mum asking questions about her love life. No matter how many times she told her she was focused on her career, she never believed her. *Probably because you're lying, Freddie.*

'Cudmore will assign pairs and towers,' Saunders said. Morris huffed. 'We want a solid day on this. Every resident spoken to. If someone's out – go back later.'

The room shuffled and scraped into standing; the cops, a lot of them in uniform, had been drafted in. This was the big manpower push.

Freddie walked over to Nas, who was handing sheets of addresses to cops. 'Am I with you, Nas?'

'You're taking South Tower F,' Nas said, handing a sheet to Green.

'What about us?'

Nas didn't meet her eyes; instead she passed the next list to the short PC behind Green. Green looked at Freddie and nodded her head toward Nas, raising her eyebrows in a 'what's that all about?' way. Freddie shrugged. She'd stood by Nas when she'd copped off with Burgone; she could do with some of that support back, not judgement.

'In the way again.' Morris shoved into her. Freddie tripped, banging into the table.

'Watch it!' She rubbed her leg.

'What are you even doing here?' he said. 'Shouldn't you be

making coffee, or are stationery cupboards more your thing nowadays?'

Shit. How did he know about Tibbsy?

'Good one!' snorted the short PC.

Did they all know? Panic fuelled her tongue. 'Jealous you've never had it at work, Morris, or jealous that you've never had it at all?' She wiggled her little finger in his face.

'Least I ain't easy,' he sneered.

Someone had blabbed. 'Oh, yeah, poor, bad me for having sex. Jesus, get a life or a bottle of lube, you creep.' She went to walk away. Nas was silent, looking at her stupid lists. Not even attempting to have her back. It wasn't Nas who'd told him about her and Tibbsy, was it?

'Slut,' Morris hissed.

Freddie stopped. Rage detonated within her. 'That all you got? *Slag, slut, whore*?' Freddie felt the words roar out of her. How could Nas betray her like this? The whole room was watching now. 'One-syllable micro insults. At least try, Morris. Come on: show a bit of creativity. Call me a narcissist, sanctimonious! I get worse in ten seconds online than your tiny reductive binary bullshit brain can even think of.'

'That's enough!' Saunders voice cut across the hushed room.

'He started it,' Freddie spat. 'He just couldn't finish. Story of his life, I bet.'

Someone whooped from the back, and the room burst into laughter. Saunders silenced them with a stare. Freddie looked at Nas, who just shook her head and looked away.

'Cudmore, if you can't keep control of the team in here, how are you going to do it in the field?' Saunders said.

'How is this my fault?' Nas's ears tinted red.

'It's worse than having children.' Saunders snatched the papers from her hands. 'Who else needs to know where they're going?'

'They're all assigned,' Nas said.

'What about me?' She couldn't believe Nas was still holding out.

'No one's available to babysit you through this.' Nas didn't look at her. 'We'll be too busy with the search.'

'*Burn*,' hissed the short PC.

Saunders let his eyes rest on her. Nodded. 'This is proper policing – get your butt to your desk and get on with your job. We need names of those who were in that party video.'

'You're going to leave me here?' She couldn't believe this.

'I still need your help on the Spice Road case, lass,' Chips said. 'Use some of those analyst modelling skills, hey?'

She knew he was trying to help her. Give her a lifeline in this silent room, while half the team watched her being humiliated. 'Sure.' *Seriously, Nas – nothing?*

'Right. Cudmore, you're with me.' Saunders clapped his hands. 'Let's get going, people. It's going to be a long hot afternoon and I'm gonna make you sweat.'

He was like a demented aerobics teacher. Freddie was pissed off at him too. He loved being in charge just a little too much. Bloody megalomaniac.

'I was going to partner with Green, sir?' Nas said as they all started for the door.

Freddie allowed herself a little smile.

'You don't get to make that call,' Saunders said. 'If you can't even get the team out the door without a bloody mothers' meeting.'

Nas turned to glare at Freddie. This time she was ready. Armed. She stared back. This wasn't over.

As the last of them left, Chips gave her a nod. 'All right, lass?'

'Yeah.' She dropped onto her chair. Clicked open her computer. 'Let's find these fuckers before they do.'

Nas had sided with bloody Morris, the man who always spelt her name wrong because he 'didn't like no foreign names'. She must be really pissed off.

Spelling. That gave her an idea. She tapped into Insta and put in #Dogbery. People mistyped when they were drunk. Or autocorrect messed with you. Two images opened. One similar to the group of youths, posing on Facebook, and one more. A chill ran over her skin. A selfie of two people. She could make out the blurred background of the party from the video. It had been posted minutes before the video had been put on Facebook. A close-up of their faces; there was no mistaking it. Calinda smiling up into the phone, her glassy pupils wide, and a guy grinning next to her. Black, young, probably late teens. You could see his shoulders, his arm, strong but lean, cropped hair. Her heart started to beat faster. She clicked on the photo. It had been posted by a Donovan Grant. She wrote the name down, clicked onto the PNC and typed it in. His driving licence stated he was eighteen years old. Her mouth was dry; she reached for the leftover glass of Berocca from yesterday without taking her eyes off the screen. She could hear her breathing quicken.

'Chips, we need to call Nas and Saunders,' she said.

'What you got, lass?' He looked up from his screen.

'Donovan Grant. Eighteen years old, no priors, registered as living at flat 109, Tower A, Dogberry.' She turned the screen towards him to show him the photo of Calinda and Donovan. 'I reckon he's the one we're looking for.'

A

They were all over the building; he'd seen them pull up in their cars. Police. He's counted twenty-four of them. Two cars and a van. They'd piled out the back like soldiers going into enemy territory. He can see others watching from the windows. Phones up. The place is buzzing. The Boys will have gone to ground, scurried away like rats. But the police aren't here for them. This isn't a drugs bust, not with this many of them. This is bigger. This is a manhunt. They're coming. Coming for him.

He squeezes his palms against his head as if the idea might pop out. The cerebrum contains 86 billion neurones. Billions of dendrites and axons. Neurones are connected by trillions of synapses. All telling his body to run. Run. Hide. Jump.

He hears the doorbell ring. The thump on the door. Too late. You've left it too late. They know.

They know.

Nasreen

Nasreen rapped her knuckles against the door of flat 109 again. They'd come straight here as soon as Saunders had received the call from Freddie. There was no time to be disappointed that Freddie hadn't chosen to call her. You'd think she'd want to make it up. Prove she could be trusted after her little outburst in the office. She spoke quickly, under her breath, aware doors were being opened a crack up and down the dim, pockmarked corridor of Tower A. 'You sure you don't want to bring him in?'

Saunders was jiggling beside her, barely suppressing his eagerness to get inside. 'Nah, let's not let on what we know yet. I want to talk to him here.'

Taking Donovan back to be interviewed would take him away from the crime scene. The crime scene that could be behind this door.

They heard movement inside the flat. She planted one foot back in case he decided to make a break for it. They heard a chain being taken off and the door opened. The young man, the one who'd been wide-eyed in the photo Freddie had sent, was stood there, his T-shirt and jeans dishevelled as if he'd been asleep in them.

His eyes took in their suits. She saw the fact they were cops register on his face. A slight flicker. Alarm?

'Yeah?' he said. He cleared his throat, and rubbed at his eyes. He'd clearly been asleep.

'Donovan Grant?' Saunders said. Nasreen looked around Grant into the flat. Through the magnolia-painted hallway behind him, she could see a peach-coloured lounge and the edge of some tan leather sofas. This wasn't the stripped-bare, run-down and graffitied room on the video.

'Who wants to know?' Grant had hold of the door handle. Though his voice was thick with sleep, he couldn't hide the wariness that lay underneath.

'I'm Detective Inspector Saunders and this is DS Cudmore,' Saunders said. 'Mind if we come in for a chat?' Saunders stepped forward, shouldering the door from Grant's hand, as if it were an accident.

Grant looked stunned and stepped back. 'What's this about?'

Nasreen stepped into the hallway, quickly closing the door behind her, so the three of them were bunched together in the landing of the flat. She counted three doors in addition to the one to the lounge. 'Anyone else here?'

'My mum's at work,' Grant said, looking between her and Saunders. The whites of his eyes were wide, confused. 'You can't just barge in here…'

Saunders, still with his hands in his pockets as if strolling through the park, walked into the lounge and turned to check the doorway off to the kitchen. 'Nice colour – you pick this?'

Nasreen stayed where she was. Move and Grant would have a clear line of escape run at the door. And though she couldn't hear anyone else, it didn't mean there wasn't someone behind one of these doors.

'Do I look like I like pink?' Grant's confusion was fast being replaced by bluster.

'Prefer something a bit more masculine, hey,' Saunders said. 'Bit more manly. That your style, is it?' Saunders was moving round, checking there was no one else here.

'What's he on about?' Grant said to her. Nasreen folded her arms. Didn't let her face shift.

'Shall we sit down, Donovan, have a little chat?' Saunders stretched out his arm, inviting him into the lounge.

Grant looked like he was about to object, but thought better of it and followed Saunders in. The room was homely: neat rows of photos of Donovan, and of what looked like two younger brothers, lined the sill of the big window that spanned one wall. The dimensions of this room matched the crime scene sketch, though they were the mirror image. An even-numbered flat perhaps? She realised she was sitting on a sofa in the spot Calinda had been attacked in that room. She tried not to shudder.

Grant was looking between them nervously. He didn't know how to deal with them, and that made her think he wasn't part of the Dogberry Boys gang. Most gang members knew their 'rights' from a young age. Grant was showing signs of stress, not bravado.

255

Saunders leaned back so the leather sofa creaked. Gave her a nod.

'Donovan, can you tell me where you were on Friday, the fourth of August, between the times of 10pm and 1.30am the next morning?' she asked.

His eyes darted from Saunders to hers. Thrown that she was asking him questions. She could almost see his thought pattern – which one of them was he supposed to talk to? 'Err... I dunno,' he said.

Saunders gave an elaborate sigh. 'Shall I jog your memory? We know you were at a party here on the estate,' he said.

'Might have been.' He looked at the floor.

'We have photographic evidence that places you at the party that night.' Nasreen took her phone out. 'With this girl.'

Grant looked up, a faint flicker of a smile kissing his lips. 'So what if I was? Nothing wrong with a party, is there?'

'Do you recognise this woman?' she prodded.

'Yeah, she was well fit. Well up for it,' he said.

'Well high, from her diluted pupils,' Saunders said wryly.

'I don't know anything about that,' Grant said. 'I don't do that shit.'

'You didn't slip her a little something to liven her up?' Saunders said.

'God, no. Is that what she's saying? 'Cause she's got the wrong brother. I'm not into all that. No judgement on those that are. But it's not my scene.'

Saunders and Nasreen stared at him, letting the silence grow so big it was almost suffocating. Letting him talk.

'Seriously, like, she's got confused. Ask her. I didn't give her anything. Ask her!' he said, more urgently this time.

'That's going to be a little hard, as we believe she's dead,' Saunders said.

Nasreen saw the shock hit. A detonation on his face, just under his eyes. And knew.

'Dead?' Grant said. 'Whoa, hold on – this is serious. Dead? Christ. I mean I didn't know her, only met her that night, but dead?'

'And yet you posted a photo of her online. This girl who meant nothing.' Saunders raised an eyebrow at him.

The second wave washed over Donovan: realisation. 'You think I had something to do with this? No. No. I didn't even know the girl. She was just some girl at a party. We had a dance. We had a laugh. She was fine so I took a snap. That's it. I promise. I was out of there at one. Work in the morning, wanted to get to the gym before that.' Panic was flaring through him, loosening his tongue.

'So you don't know what happened to her?'

'No, I swear,' he said.

'Did you see her dancing with anyone else, notice who she was with?'

'No, it was packed. Dark, man,' he said.

'And which flat was this in?' Saunders asked.

Grant's face paled. Another realisation. 'I don't know.' His eyes suddenly fell to the floor.

He was lying. 'You don't know?' Saunders said. 'You were at a party but you don't know where it was?'

'Err… I've, like, never been great with directions,' he said.

His eyes were glancing around. To the sides. Up at the door. Something had spooked him. Had he lied? Had he taken something that night? Nasreen thought of the silence in

257

response to the press appeal. The cracked doors. The eyes watching. He was scared of the gang. 'Are you familiar with the Dogberry Boys?' she asked.

'I'm not into that. I just want to keep myself to myself,' he said. 'Honestly, ask my mum. She'll tell you.'

'But you went to a Dogberry Boys party?' Saunders said. They weren't wholly sure the gang had organised the event, but Grant's reluctance to talk supported the theory. He was scared.

'I don't know,' he said.

'You don't know if you went to the party or you don't know if it was a Dogberry Boys party?' Saunders said.

Donovan looked up. His eyes pleading, darting between them. 'Please,' he said. 'I gotta live here. I gotta think of my mum. I'm sorry, but I don't know where it was, okay.'

The Dogberry Boys ruled this estate. Even inside this safe family home, their influence was felt. What had it been like growing up here? What had he seen? Cars torched. People beaten. Knife wounds. Gun shots. There'd been a drive-by from a rival gang not that long ago. Three dead, one a small child who'd been in the scrub playground between three of the towers. Four years old when a war had come to his home.

'Did you take any other photos or videos that night?' Nasreen asked.

'No, you can look.' He held out his phone. The image of him and Calinda was framed either side by an image of blue sky over the Thames and a photo of a stack of pizza boxes. 'Day job,' he said by way of explanation.

She nodded. Saunders lent forward. 'We can offer you protection, help, if you could just tell us where the party took place. We know it was on the estate, we just need to know which tower, which flat.'

'I don't know,' he said. His eyes and voice steady now. Resigned.

'A girl was murdered, Donovan, an eighteen-year-old, just like you, starting out in her life,' Saunders said.

'I'm sorry for her, for her folks and that, but I can't help you,' he said.

Nasreen felt Saunders bristle next to her. 'What do you think, Sergeant, you reckon he's lying? Reckon he was dancing with the *fine* girl and wanted to take things further, hey? Fancied a bit of fun? What happened, she not so willing? And after you'd given her some stuff as well? I mean, that's not on, is it?' Saunders switched tactics and applied pressure. *See how the suspect reacts.*

Donovan jerked back. Horrified. 'No. Seriously. I had nothing to do with this. I left. I left at eleven, you can ask Josh, the kid next door, he was there. I saw him videoing it and shit. Like, you must be able to prove it from his phone and stuff, yeah?'

'He was videoing the party or videoing the girl?' Nasreen said.

'Both. The girl. She could move. He was into it. He was dancing with her when I left. They were tight. He can tell you. Check his camera. That'd prove I left, right? That I was gone by, like, eleven? Shit – she really dead?'

Nasreen took out her pad and paper. 'What's Josh's full name and address?'

'Josh,' Grant said. 'Joshua, I think. I don't know him that much. He lives next door with his mum. Josh Chapman.'

'Thank you,' she said.

259

'And you'll check with him, right?' Donovan said. 'He'll tell you that I left?'

'We're going to need to take this in.' Saunders took Grant's phone from next to Nasreen on the sofa, switched it off and pulled a plastic bag from his pocket. 'Double-check you haven't deleted anything we might find interesting.'

Grant looked pale. Stunned. 'When can I have it back?'

'Give DS Cudmore your contact details and we'll be in touch,' Saunders stood up. 'And don't think about skipping town, okay? I've still got my eye on you.'

Nasreen

A woman in a nurse's uniform answered the door to flat 107. Her face was shiny, a radio and the television blared in the background, and they could make out the gunfire of a computer game. 'Yes?' she said.

'Mrs Chapman? I'm DS Nasreen Cudmore and this is DI Peter Saunders. I wondered if your son Josh was in, and if we could have a quick word with him?'

Nasreen had had Chips run him through the computer. Twelve. No previous priors. His mother and twin brothers were also registered at this address.

Mrs Chapman was drying her hands on a tea towel. She glanced down the corridor. 'You'd better come in.'

Nasreen tried to keep her smile unthreatening. They needed to check Donovan's phone. They needed to get hold of Josh's. This could be another wild goose chase, but she kept playing

Donovan's words over in her head: *He was into it.* Josh could be suspect B who was filming behind the camera.

'What's this regarding?' Mrs Chapman looked at her watch. 'I have to leave for work soon.'

The hallway was identical to the one next door, but it was painted in a warm orange tone, and hooks on the wall held a clutch of coats, scarves and triangular PE bags. Children's shoes were lined up underneath. 'We believe Josh may have been present at a party where a missing girl was last seen,' Nasreen said.

Her face clouded. 'A party? Tsk. He's only twelve. He shouldn't have been to any kind of party. Melanie's supposed to watch him when I'm on nights. You sure you got the right boy?'

Melanie must be her older daughter: nineteen years old and registered at this address.

'It was on Friday, the fourth of August.' Nasreen showed her a photo of Calinda. 'Mrs Chapman, do you recognise this girl at all?'

'No, I don't think so. But there are so many kids coming and going round here, I could be wrong.' The hallway was steamy from the kitchen, and the smell of onions frying made Nasreen's stomach growl.

'Joshua!' Mrs Chapman called. 'There are some people here to talk to you.' She turned back to them. 'Always got his head in his books. I know I should be pleased, but sometimes I wish he got some fresh air, you know? Especially when the weather's so nice.'

'You work nights, then?' Saunders said.

'Means I can be here to get the kids to and from school, make sure they eat properly,' she said.

'Tiring though – we do nights too,' he said jovially. 'Were you on last week? It was still hot at three am!' Saunders made the question sound light and inconsequential, but Nasreen knew he was working out if anyone could vouch for Josh's whereabouts last Friday. Mrs Chapman might not have recognised Calinda, but her son had been seen dancing with her. He might know where she'd ended up.

'Monday to Friday', she said. 'And no air con at the hospital!'

'Ooof,' Saunders said. 'In that regard we're lucky.'

She led them into the lounge. Two boys, aged about seven years old, were sprawled over cushions on the floor, attached to the telly by the umbilical cords of games consoles. The screen glowed and exploded in bright colours.

'What's all this mess?' Mrs Chapman grabbed some of the red cushions and returned them to the sofa.

The boys sat up, without taking their eyes from the screen.

Saunders was taking in the rest of the room, where a neat row of books filled a small bookshelf. 'You run a tight ship,' he said. 'My house isn't anywhere near as tidy as this, and I haven't got any little people.' If Saunders's desk was anything to go by, Nasreen would expect his home to be immaculate, but she knew he was establishing himself with Mrs Chapman. Ingratiating himself. He'd been worried by what Donovan had said as well.

Mrs Chapman beamed at the compliment. 'They're good kids.'

'How many do you have?' Nasreen asked.

'Four: Melinda's the oldest, then Josh, then the twins, they're eight,' she said.

'And do you have a partner?' Nasreen wanted to know

263

where everyone was. Who everyone was. If Josh had been involved, then someone could have helped him hide the body.

'He cleared out seven years ago,' she said with a smile. 'We do fine without him. I keep my kids away from trouble. They go to church every Sunday, work hard at school. Melinda's at college now – doing her NVQs.'

'They look like they're doing just great,' Saunders said. He was looking at a carving on the wall. 'Is that Armenian?'

'Why, yes!' Mrs Chapman said. 'How on earth did you know that?'

'I went travelling round there when I was a student,' Saunders said. 'Have you been?'

'No, it was a present from my sister's husband. His family are from there originally. I always say we'll go one day. Josh and his cousin are close. They'd love it.'

A loud blast came from the television screen and the twins exploded into giggles. Nasreen smiled; they reminded her of her sisters when they were younger – they always seemed to have hold of each other, pushing, pulling, tapping, like acrobats that raced and tumbled round in constant contact.

'Hello, lads,' Saunders said to the twins. 'What's this then?'

'Lego Star Wars,' answered one of the boys.

'Right, you two, that's enough for today,' Mrs Chapman said. 'I need to speak to these nice police officers.'

At the mention of police one kid looked up, his mouth open, staring at them. The other didn't take his eyes from the screen. Mrs Chapman marched across the room and switched the console off. The screen plunged into black, and the boy let out a howl of frustration. 'Muuuuuuuuum! I was on level nine!'

'Shut up.' His brother elbowed him in the ribs. 'It's the Feds,' he hissed.

'For real?' The kid turned his big eyes on them, a mixture of awe and fear on his face. 'You're police?'

'Go wash your hands before dinner.' Mrs Chapman took the hand consoles away and tucked them into a drawer under the television.

'What are you doing here?' One of the children asked Nasreen.

She'd always found her sisters easier once they'd got past eleven and could hold a better conversation. 'Erm... I'm here with DI Saunders.'

Saunders rolled his eyes at her.

'Have you got a gun?' the other child asked. 'My friend Marlon says that all cops have guns, and if they see you out of school they shoot you dead, and he's ten.'

'Andre!' Mrs Chapman said. 'Don't be so cheeky.'

'I don't have a gun and I'm not going to shoot anyone, I promise,' Saunders said.

Andre looked unconvinced. 'Can I see your badge?'

'Andre! That's enough!'

Nasreen waited for Saunders to lose his temper, but instead he dropped down so he was crouching in front of the boy. 'American cops have badges, over here we have warrant cards – you want to see?'

'Cool!' said Andre's twin.

Saunders took out his ID and handed it to the boys, who passed it reverently between them.

'Okay, that's enough now,' Mrs Chapman said. 'Detective Saunders is a very busy man. Give him that back, and go wash your hands for dinner. Tell Josh to come here. He usually has his headphones on,' she said to them, by way of explanation. They watched the two boys excitedly bowl out of the room. 'Thank you, that was very kind,' she said to Saunders, handing his warrant card back.

'We're to present it if anyone asks to see it. Just following procedure,' he said, smiling.

Nasreen was still reeling from seeing this side of the detective. Perhaps he wanted kids himself?

The door from the hallway creaked open and Josh appeared. The air caught in Nasreen's throat. He looked like the photofit sketch of suspect A. She could see bits from all of the witnesses' descriptions in him. And the one thing they'd all remembered: two lines were shaved from Josh's left eyebrow. Like a little diagonal train track. He was tall for his age. Gangly. Strong. His hair shaved close to his head. His eyes widened in alarm when he saw them, before looking at his mother. Saunders clocked it too.

'Josh, these officers want to ask you about a party you went to?' Mrs Chapman said. 'I'm not happy about this, young man, you're too young to be out. Especially round here.' She turned back to Saunders. 'I don't want him mixing with the wrong sort.'

Saunders nodded, but she knew he was thinking the same thing: what if Josh was the one who was the wrong sort?

A roomy basketball shirt hung over Josh's broad shoulders, extenuating his frame, like he might suddenly spurt another few inches up and across to fill it completely. But his face was smooth and soft still, catching him between being a child and a man.

'I didn't go to no party,' he said.

'We have a photo of you there, son,' Saunders lied. She knew he'd clocked the boy's nerves too. 'We just want to ask you a few questions.'

He hadn't moved from the doorway, and Nasreen felt her leg muscles flex. Her body sensing he might run. 'Shall we sit down? Perhaps have a drink, if that would be okay, Mrs Chapman?'

'Yes, of course,' Mrs Chapman said. 'We're not a hot drink family, but I think I've got some teabags somewhere.'

Josh voice rang out clearly. He sounded alarmed. 'No!'

'Whatever's the matter, Josh?' Mrs Chapman said.

'You'll be late for work,' he said. 'We've got coke and juice and stuff.' Was he trying to get rid of them? His right leg was jiggling, and he kept glancing at the kitchen. 'I'll go.' Josh turned towards the kitchen.

Saunders tilted his head slightly and Nas took the signal. 'It really is a lovely carving,' she exclaimed, using the movement to step in front of the hallway door. Block the boy's exit.

'I'd quite like a tea if it's not too much bother, Mrs Chapman,' Saunders said.

'Of course not. Josh, I don't know what's got into you,' Mrs Chapman said. 'You've forgotten your manners.'

He was anxious that they were here.

'What about you, dear? Would you like one?' Mrs Chapman smiled at her.

'Just a glass of tap water is fine for me, thanks,' Nasreen answered.

'It's not good,' Josh said. His eyes were frantic. His breathing heightened. 'You can't have it. I told you, Mum – I got bottled for you and the twins.'

'Josh, what's the matter? What are you talking about?' Mrs Chapman looked embarrassed. 'He watched some documentary on the internet and has this idea that the tap water isn't okay to drink,' she smiled apologetically.

Josh was halfway to the kitchen now. 'You haven't used the tap water, have you?'

'Josh, you're being silly. Bottled is so expensive.'

'Mum, tell me you haven't! You promised!' He was sounding angry now, his eyes bulging.

'I think you need to calm down, son,' Saunders said.

'I'm not using bottled for the vegetables, Josh, that's just silly,' Mrs Chapman said.

The effect on the boy was instant. His face was drained of colour. He steadied himself against the wall.

'Josh, what is it?' Mrs Chapman reached for him.

Her son stumbled backwards. 'Oh my God,' he said.

He turned fast, ran at her, caught Nasreen on the shoulder. The impact a slap. Her leg clipped the edge of the sofa and she lost her balance. Her elbow slammed into the wall next to the wood carving as he raced past. She made a grab for him, but missed.

'Josh!' Mrs Chapman screamed.

'Don't run, lad!' Saunders bellowed.

Nasreen launched herself off the wall and started after him, Saunders a second behind. He was going for the door. She grabbed her radio from her belt. But before he reached the threshold Josh swerved and flung himself into the bathroom. Refracted sunlight from the opaque window filled the hallway.

The twins shouted, and then they all heard him vomit.

Nasreen's boots squeaked on the laminate floor as she

brought herself to a halt as the twins bundled out of the bathroom, screaming, 'Gross!'

He'd been sick? Now what? She looked at Saunders. What was happening? Her heart was thumping. Her elbow throbbed. Mrs Chapman was clutching the front of her tunic. She looked from Nasreen to Saunders.

Saunders very calmly said: 'Mrs Chapman, I'm sorry but we're going to need to get some of my colleagues to search your flat.'

'My son!' Mrs Chapman said.

'Cudmore, get onto Chips. I want the water supply of this tower switched off. We need to get the residents outside.'

And then she got it. Oh God. The plans she'd seen on Freddie's computer. The designs of Dogberry Towers. Calinda's body hadn't been taken out in one of the underground tunnels. It was here all along. Nasreen clicked her radio on. 'This is DS Nasreen Cudmore, to all officers in the vicinity of Dogberry estate Tower A: we need to execute a full and swift evacuation of Tower A. Repeat...'

'What is it? What's happened? What's he done?' Mrs Chapman was saying.

Saunders gently moved her away from Nasreen and the sound of her crackling radio and her twelve-year-old son retching in the bathroom. 'One of my officers will be here in a minute to wait with you. I'm afraid I can't let any of you leave for the time being.'

'But I'll be late for work!'

Nasreen called Green with her other hand. 'I need you to report to flat 107, Tower A,' she said as soon as she answered.

'You need to tell them you can't come in,' Saunders was

saying to Mrs Chapman. 'You're going to need to be strong for Josh right now.'

'I can't miss work! Why won't you tell me what this is about? Is it about that girl? The one in the photo?' Mrs Chapman's voice had shifted to pleading. Nasreen turned away. Green, hearing raised voices in the background, acknowledged she was on her way.

'Get the twins into their room,' Saunders said as the two young boys stared at their distressed mother. 'And don't use any of the tap water.'

'I don't understand.' The woman clutched at Saunders, as if she might shake the truth out of his shirt. But she didn't want the truth. Nasreen looked at the little shoes under the coats. The truth was going to destroy this family.

A

The toilet swims with bile. Yesterday's carrots wink at him. *How could she use the water? How could she? She'd promised.* Oh God. The twins are squealing behind him. He forces the door shut. The police are on the other side: the young one, the pretty one – he didn't think cops were pretty like that. And the man: sucking up to Mum. He'd seen that before. Seen that off before. He needs to think. He's got minutes. Seconds. He checks the window. Only the top opens in here. He could smash it? Use the soap dish? Jump? But he can't.

Coward. Face the music.

His mum sounds funny. He can hear her. Her voice high. Not like it is at work with her patients. Or at home with them. Like it was before. When Dad left. He probably sounded like that. Do they know? Of course they know. He reeks of it. Guilt. Face the music.

271

All he can think of is the splash. The splash she'd made when she went into the water. It should have been good. He'd wanted to clean the blood off her. To wash her clean. To make her look perfect again. But not like that. It was dark and cold. She'd be alone in the dark. He slumps back against the wall. Think. *Think.*

He wants to rinse his mouth. Banish the biting acid from his throat. But the twins have the bottle of water he'd left in here. The thought of running the tap makes him retch again. Like that horror movie. Where these people go to this club, not knowing it's full of vampires. And when the music starts, the sprinkler system kicks off. But it's not water, it's blood. Spraying down on the screaming clubbers. That's what he thought would happen. That her blood would trickle down, run through the building, covering them all. Covering his twin brothers. Oh God. What has he done?

He should've gone when he heard them next door. That was his shot and he didn't take it. It's all so mixed up. He's in trouble. Serious trouble. They have him. But maybe that's okay? Maybe it's better? He's wanted to turn himself in, he's wished for this, hasn't he? It should be a relief, shouldn't it? But it's not just about him. *I can't protect your mum if I go down.* He owes B. He pulls his phone from his pocket. Taps fast, furious on WhatsApp:

Feds. Run.

The reply comes through straightaway. He blinks at the message. *No.* Must be a mistake. Autocorrect. Josh's heart hammers in his ears. He needs water. He needs to drink. He can't do this. He reads the reply again. B can't mean that? Panic floods through him, bursting from the toilet, submerging the whole room. He is under water. He is drowning. He doesn't know what to do. The message jars in him, but before he can act, before he can try to stop it, someone is hammering on the door. A voice booms from the other side.

'Josh, this is DS Cudmore. Open up. Now.'

And, terrified, he does.

Nasreen

The doorbell sounded. Green was leaning on it, her uniformed partner PC Millman next to her, his full high cheeks pink from exertion. He was in his late forties, and Nasreen was relieved to see someone with a bit of gravitas. She didn't know how well Green would cope with this. How well *she* would cope with this.

'Everything all right?' Green glanced past them into the hallway. Mrs Chapman was settling the twins into their bedroom, their wariness at her distress apparently softened by the treat of being allowed to play Minecraft. They'd have to get hold of Melanie, the oldest daughter – Nasreen didn't want to get social services to watch the twins when they took Josh in.

Nasreen shook her head. Everything was not all right. Josh would need to be questioned. And, judging by his behaviour, it was looking like he'd be charged as well.

Saunders poked his head back round from the lounge. 'Green, constable,' he said. 'You need to stay with Mrs Chapman. She has three children here – the twins are in there with her.' He pointed at the bedroom. 'And Josh is twelve – he's in here. Don't let him out of your sight.'

Twelve. She still couldn't get over it. Her first possible child killer case. They were the stuff of legend. Grim, distasteful stories swapped in Hendon's training college canteen. Not real. Not happening right now.

'Sorry, ma'am.' Millman crossed behind her. She wanted to tell him not to call her that. It sounded ridiculous.

'Me and Cudmore are going on a little expedition,' Saunders said. 'And don't touch the water.' He pointed at Green.

'Why – what's in it?' she said.

'You don't want to know,' he muttered as they headed out into the hallway.

They could hear the voices of residents below, the bellow of an officer guiding them down. At the end of the corridor a uniformed officer was remonstrating with a woman holding a cat.

'I'm not leaving without Percy,' she was saying. She had an old-fashioned pinny over her dress, like Nasreen's nan used to wear.

'This way.' Saunders jogged off in the other direction. The hallway was hot and smelled of cabbage. They reached the stairway and started their climb, the building echoing all around them. Squeezing its residents out like icing. Nasreen could picture them pouring out onto the concrete square below. It wouldn't be long before the press arrived. The estate was close enough to the money of Canary Wharf to warrant a bit of a scandal. A bit of judgement for the poor souls who live here.

'I'm sorry I missed him back there, when he ran,' Nasreen said to Saunders. She could kick herself.

'Not the ideal moment to take a tumble,' he said.

'I didn't fall, he caught me and then I...'

'Hurt yourself?' Saunders didn't stop.

'Just my pride,' she admitted. Though she thought she'd have a bruise on her arm where it hit the wall.

'Good, no forms to fill out for that.'

The stairs stopped at the final floor of flats. Saunders walked briskly along the corridor, neither of them having anything left to say. Or the words to say it with. They were focused on the task at hand now. This was her job. The worst, most awful part of her job. Least she wasn't usually the first on the scene. She longed for the strange comfort of the crime scene tape, the rustle of SOCO suits. 'Should we not wear protection?'

'You worried?' Saunders said.

'So we don't mess up the forensics,' she said.

'I'm not radioing in a team until we're sure. That'll go down like a lead balloon. Put your gloves on, and try not to trip over anything again,' he said as they reached a door marked Maintenance. Sweat stuck his shirt to his back. 'Ready?'

She nodded. Saunders turned the handle and gave the sticking door a shove.

'Doesn't look like maintenance have been here recently,' she said.

'Budget cuts.' He tried the light. 'Bulb's gone.'

She took her torch out. Clicked it on to show a small narrow metal staircase leading up to what she assumed was the attic.

'Ladies first,' Saunders said.

Great. She wasn't about to decline after his comments about her falling over. She bit her lip and placed a foot on the first step. The sole of her boot clanged against the metal, echoing up and away from them.

'Sounds big,' he said.

She carried on walking. Wanting to cling onto the small handrail, but knowing it'd be better for the SOCOs if she didn't. It smelt damp. And under that there was something sour. The room opened up and along the breadth of the tower. The ceiling was low, almost touching the three water tanks, which were as big as children's swimming pools. It was hot up here. She wondered why people always thought hell was below, when heat rose? Something scurried in the corner. 'Was that a mouse?'

'Hope so,' Saunders said. 'Where there's mice there's no rats.'

She didn't want to question it if that was true. Sweeping the torch around, she could see marks in the dust. 'Looks like footprints.'

'Stick to the edge, don't touch anything,' he said.

She could hear the flap of pigeons. Outside? Inside? She flicked the light up but saw nothing but dark tendrils of dust hanging from the flat ceiling. Gingerly they made their way along the edge of the room.

'Looks like the service hatch is open on that one.' Saunders shone his torch up onto the top of the first huge tank, high-lighting the door that stuck up like a metal fin. Signs of disturbance. Unlike the rest of the room, it seemed to radiate cold. 'You want me to go first?' He indicated at the ladder that mounted the side.

Yes. 'No, I'm fine. Hold this.' She gave him the torch. The metal rungs were bubbled rusty twists under her plastic gloves, and reminded her of burnt bones. She tested the ladder with one foot, not sure if it would take her weight. When it did without a creak, there was nowhere to go but up. It didn't take long to reach the top. The hatch loomed open in front of her. She could sense the expanse of water beneath.

'Pass me the torch.' She leant back and reached down. It was lucky they were both tall. Feeling its reassuring weight in her hand, she leant into the hatch and shone the beam over the water. Breaking the still, black sheen of this manmade lake was the curve of a pale hand. Long hair floated in the water. Face down. She felt the ladder waver under her feet. Clung on tight with both hands, clanging her torch against the ceiling of the tank as she tried to steady herself.

'What is it?' Saunders called. 'What can you see?'

'We've got a body, sir,' she said, needing the comfort of rank. Wishing she had let him go first.

She heard Saunders sigh behind her in the dark. 'Poor girl.'

Freddie

Freddie couldn't concentrate on anything. Chips had given her some cell site research for the Spice Road case, but that just made her think of Paul Robertson and what had happened to Amber. She still felt like she was missing something from their interview with Lex Riley. But thinking about Riley made her think of the Dogberry Boys, which made her think about what was going on on the Dogberry estate right now. It had been thirty minutes since Nas had called in, spoken to Chips and said that they didn't think Donovan Grant was their man. Then ten minutes ago Green had called in to say they'd evacuated one of the towers and Saunders would call Chips in a minute. What was going on? No one was telling her anything. She'd tried a cheeky text to Nas, but got no response. This is where her part of the job wasn't fair. She was supposed to be able to get out and interview people now, do some work on the ground, but, as usual, when the 'real police work' started they froze her out. She was nothing more than a glorified secretary.

Chips's mobile rang and he picked it up with his usual 'Chips'.

Freddie knocked a pen off her desk, so she had an excuse to get up and go closer.

'Right. Yup.' Chips was making notes. All she could hear of the other voice was a tinny squeak – sounded like a female. Probably Nas, eager to tell him what was happening while she kept her in the dark. It wasn't fair. She'd led them to Donovan Grant, who'd apparently led them to a new lead. If they knew something they should share it. She hated that the police service worked on a need-to-know basis. She didn't understand how you could see the whole picture if you weren't allowed to see all the parts of the puzzle. 'You want me to set up here?' said Chips.

Set what up?

'Righto, lass,' Chips said.

Definitely Nas. Dammit. This was getting petty now. Stupid. She was right behind Chips when he hung up and turned round, looking surprised to see her there.

'Don't sneak up on someone who's been trained in arm-to-arm combat, lass,' he said. 'You nearly gave me a heart attack.'

'What did she say? Was that Nas? What's happening?'

'They've found a body,' he said, all humour gone from his voice. 'It looks like our lass. She was stashed in one of the water tanks in the towers. The pathologist is on the way now.'

Freddie felt her stomach lurch. 'It's Calinda?'

280

'Aye, looks like it.'

All hope was gone. She was killed in that video. Killed and then her body was dumped. Images of Calinda writhing in the party video flooded her mind, mixed with images of Calinda struggling in the water. She blinked them away, suddenly not so sure she really did want to be there. 'Have they got him, suspect A?'

Chips nodded. 'Nas says he's only twelve, but old-looking for his age.'

'He's a kid!' she said. Her skin crawled at the implication. How could a child do that? Was it hormones out of control? Was he born evil? Kate had said things had escalated. For a horrible moment she thought about how this might not have happened. 'Are we going over there?'

'Nope.' Chips shifted in his seat. 'They're bringing him in. Nas asked that I keep everyone out of the hallways.'

'What?' She couldn't believe she was hearing this.

'She doesn't want the lad to get freaked out,' he said.

'He's a killer. She doesn't want me to have anything to do with her victory!' This was ridiculous.

'Now come on, lass, you know you're not a cop,' he said.

'As you keep reminding me. All the bloody time.'

'Maybe an early lunch is a good idea,' he said. 'Cool off.'

She snorted. This stupid office politics was beneath Nas. She was just jealous because Freddie was with Tibbsy, when Nas couldn't be with Burgone. That Freddie was happy with someone. The thought struck her: am I happy with Tibbsy? Is that why Nasreen's angry at me? Not because of the shagging, but because I could have something she can't? What would it be like if she and Tibbsy were forbidden to date?

The thought made her feel hollow, as if something important was being scooped out of her.

'You all right, lass?' Chips was at her side. 'You've gone pale.'

'Yeah. I'm gonna go for a fag. Cool off a bit.' She shook her head. Not wanting to believe herself.

'Want me to call if we hear anything else on Calinda?'

'No. I won't be long.'

Freddie pressed the button agitatedly for the lift. Tapping her cigarette against the packet already. How long would it take Nas and Saunders to get back from Dogberry? She didn't want to get busted in the wrong place. Couldn't be doing with the aggro. Her head was already swimming as it was. *Tibbsy makes you happy. Does that mean that you...* The lift stopped at the next floor down, and two guys got in. Both in shirt sleeves and tie, in the middle of a mindless conversation. The tinny beat of music came from the taller one's discarded headphones, which were dangling round his neck.

'You coming to the game on Sunday?'

'No, we've got lunch with mates.'

'*We've*? Ha! You've changed, mate.' One of the guys laughed, revealing coffee-stained teeth and a couple of fillings.

The tinny beat of music continued. Suddenly the song that had been playing in Lex Riley's kitchen popped into her head. The lyrics and the bass rolling through her mind. 'Best I Ever Had' by Drake. Something about his fridge tugged at her memory. Did it have something to do with Paul Robertson? With the Spice Road drugs website? She was trying to keep too much in her mind, when she needed to tackle one thing at a time. *Best I ever had*. The thought of not being able to see Tibbsy, of not curling into his arms at night, hurt. Shit, Freddie. You haven't got time for a relationship. And you definitely don't want one with a cop, you have enough of them at work. But the more she thought of Tibbsy's goofy grin, the more she smiled. *We.* She had to stop thinking like this.

The heat rose up and swallowed her whole as she stepped outside. Instant sweat. Nice. She checked her phone: still nothing from Nas. Being kept in the dark was rubbish. She thought again of Calinda. Lowered herself slowly into the sadness. Around her people flitted for early lunch breaks or off to meetings. A taxi or two trundled past. Everyone just getting on with it, as if nothing had happened, but somewhere people's lives were being ripped apart by the discovery of the body. Calinda's parents – would they have landed yet? Would they know? She didn't want to think about the pain that would cause.

Lighting her cigarette, she raised her hand as if lifting a glass in memory of Calinda: the girl who'd fought back. And she thought of Kate, how she'd kept fighting despite everything. How without her it was a very real possibility Calinda wouldn't have been named or possibly ever found. Her parents would never have known what happened to their child. This was Kate's victory. It was her strength and tenacity that had brought them here. She deserved to know. Nas wanted her to keep her head down, and no one would care if she popped out for a bit. Freddie fired a text off to Chips. Stubbing her cigarette into the road, she checked her back pocket for her wallet and Oyster card, then set off for Westminster tube station.

Nasreen

The rising humidity hadn't dissuaded the residents who were stood on the other side of the cordoned-off Dogberry Tower A, whispering to each other with their phones held up. They'd have seen the CSIs go in. These things always got out. There were too many people here: officers, SOCOs, someone was bound to say something. Let it slip. There would be no dignity for the poor girl. Nasreen felt tense with the weight of it. People drank that water. Bathed in it.

Burgone would know by now. She wished he were here to hold her. What had Freddie said? Five witnesses, no body. Well, they'd found the body. But it didn't feel like a victory. This never got easier.

Saunders hung up the phone and walked back towards her. 'Green's accompanied Josh and his mother back to the office. Chips has got the recording equipment set.'

'Those poor twins.' Nasreen had contacted Mrs Chapman's sister. Josh's mum had brought the two boys out to her while the SOCOs started on their home. The kids had been excited at all the commotion. Not understanding that their brother was being taken away for questioning because he'd hidden the body of a dead girl. Because he was suspected of raping and murdering the same girl. 'The water tank room can't be our kill site.' Nasreen tried to focus on what they had to do next. 'It doesn't match what any of the witnesses described.'

'We need to organise a line-up to see if any of them confirm him as suspect A,' Saunders said. 'But I want a crack at him first.'

Nasreen swallowed. 'I can't believe he's only twelve.'

'I've seen enough in my time to know that anyone can be capable of horrific things, if the right pressures are applied,' Saunders said gruffly.

Typical for Saunders to position himself as some all-seeing guru. She'd seen things. Knew things. They all felt old the day they joined.

'Inspector!' The round shoulders of Mike Snow, senior crime scene manager, appeared out from the tower. There was a ripple from the crowd as they saw the SOCO suited figure.

'How we looking, Mikey?' Saunders asked.

Snow's usually genial face remained thin-lipped. 'We've got her out. We'll need to drain and sift the water, save everything we can for analysis. I've got a service engineer up there so we can extract the filter.'

They nodded. 'Is it Calinda?' she asked.

Mike looked at her with mild disapproval. 'Obviously the

285

body has yet to be formally identified. But it's a female, late teens or early twenties, long dark hair, slim figure, based on the clothes. Multiple abrasions and stab wounds to her face, arms and torso.'

She nodded. Needed to regain ground. That had been a stupid thing to say. No crime scene manager would commit to a premature ID. But so much of this investigation had been off whack. 'How long would you say she's been in there for? Roughly.'

'The water's cold, so it's probably slowed the rate of decomposition. But from the bloating, and livor mortis, the dark blue discolouration of her skin across her abdomen, chest, arms and legs, I would say you're looking at about a week, give or take a day,' he said.

Her stomach turned. 'Was she alive when she went in the water? How far did they move her?'

'We won't know for sure until the pathologist has filed his report,' Mike said. 'But given the extent of the injuries, she would have lost a lot of blood prior to going into the water. There's not that much blood up there. Suggesting she was attacked at a different site.'

The attack must have happened in Tower A, before they'd carried her upstairs to the tank. 'I don't understand how no one saw them move her,' Nas said.

'That's for you guys to figure out,' Snow said. 'It looks like there's a broken glass bottle caught in the filter, so we could be looking at your murder weapon as well.'

'Chances of getting DNA off it?' she said. None of the witnesses could remember clearly whether the assailant was wearing gloves.

'Any DNA left would likely have been contaminated with that level of water passing over it, but we'll recover it and test for fingerprints,' Mike said. 'It's a good thing really,' he added, looking at the crowd the other side of the tape.

'What is?' Nasreen shielded her eyes from the sun.

'Those tanks empty out and refill throughout the day, gallons and gallons of water,' he said. 'That would have watered down all of the blood and fluids the body released post-mortem. No one would have noticed it at all.'

Nasreen felt her stomach fall away, and bile lick the back of her tongue.

'Can we have a look at her?' Saunders began walking them back towards the tower.

We. She didn't want to show her reaction on her face. She knew what bodies looked like if they'd been submerged in water. Knew, but had never seen one up close before. Mike nodded and they followed him up through the eerily quiet tower.

Full of bustling and rustling CSIs and with its dark dusty corners illuminated, the attic of Tower A felt less spooky. As she and Saunders picked their way through the room, there were whispers, and silence gradually fell over the working forensics. They knew what she and Saunders had come to see. The body of a girl laid out on a plastic sheet on the floor.

'Who brought those in?' Nasreen pointed at the bunch of magenta chrysanthemums resting against the bottom of the water tank. Had they let a member of the public in? Or had someone brought them up from the growing crowd outside?

287

No one answered. No one wanted to take the blame for an act of remembrance, an act that might have compromised the forensics here. She was such a young girl.

Water had pooled around Calinda, as if it was coming from inside her. It probably was. Her denim mini skirt, once grey, was soaked a darker colour, almost black. A hoodie clung to her slim body. The dye in her black ankle boots had started to run. They weren't meant to be submerged. Neither was the human body. Nasreen had been carefully avoiding looking at the girl's skin. Though she could see her hoodie was slashed, jagged, like an animal had taken chunks out of it.

'Your friend Kate was right then.' Burgone's voice came from behind, and she thought she'd imagined him, willed him here by her side. To hold her hand in this awful moment.

'All right, guv?' Saunders stood up from where he'd been squatting next to the girl.

She risked looking at Burgone. His face was set; grim and professional.

'What a waste.' He shook his head.

She wanted to go to him, to feel him wrap his arms round her. Heal her. This was awful. Instead she forced herself to look back at the body. 'Her watch stopped at just after 1.45,' Nasreen said. It was a traditional analogue watch, with a now fraying leather strap. The kind you might receive as a gift. Did her parents buy it for her? Perhaps for her eighteenth.

Burgone's smart brogues creaked as he walked across the room. Crouching next to her, he rested his hands on his knees and bent to look. 'The watch face isn't smashed, so presumably it stopped in the water.'

'Donovan Grant said he left the party at 1am, and at that

point Josh Chapman was dancing with Calinda,' Nasreen said.

'So we're potentially looking at a forty-five-minute window, during which she was raped, murdered and transported up here,' he said.

'The pathologist report will tell us more,' Saunders added. His hands were in his pockets, his usual insouciance back. 'You want in on the interview with the suspect?'

Burgone pushed himself back up. Nasreen stood too. Suddenly aware she'd be effectively kneeling next to him otherwise. Everyone in the room was watching them. No, not them, *him*, Burgone. Jack the Lad. One of the Met's finest. This was a big case. He'd come to see the body; he was about to take over. Saunders would be his partner, he was the next officer. Annoyance prickled through her. They were here because of her. Because of her work. It showed in Saunders's face too. The big boss coming in now that they'd found the body.

'No,' Burgone said. Nasreen caught Saunders's eyebrows rise before he brought his face back into line. 'You and Cudmore should continue. I trust you. Both.' He looked at her. She felt her face flush, nodded, wished her hair was down so that she could hide behind it.

'Righto,' said Saunders. 'We'll get back to the office then.'

'I will brief the press, though,' Burgone said.

Nasreen saw Saunders's jaw tense. 'Do you not think I'm better placed to do that, Jack?' She'd never heard him talk back to Burgone before. Suddenly she wished they were back in the office, away from prying eyes.

'It's not a reflection on you, Pete. You're the right person to lead this investigation,' Burgone said. Even though it was she who'd instigated things? She tried not to get riled.

'So why aren't I giving the press briefing?' Saunders wanted the acclaim, clearly.

'Do you know how many journalists are out there already?' Burgone said. Nasreen imagined them all snapping away when they saw the DCI arrive. But this point seemed to animate Saunders more. He was hungry for the fame. She'd rather stay away from all that. Public speaking wasn't a strength of hers, and besides, you could get more done undercover. With fame came responsibility, responsibility she now saw etched on Burgone's face.

'You don't think I can handle it?' Saunders said.

'The Super wants me to liaise with the press from now on. This is a good thing, Pete. It'll give you more time to focus on bringing charges against the suspect.'

Saunders grunted. Thrust his hands in his pockets and walked to the other side of the room.

'Sorry about that, sir,' she stammered.

He looked at her. 'You aren't responsible for DI Saunders,' he said.

But she did feel affronted on Saunders's behalf. She and Saunders had found the body. It was their police work that had led them here. And this felt like it was being taken from them. As if they couldn't fully be trusted. But she didn't say that. Instead she attempted a joke. 'Thank God.'

Burgone smiled. Nodded with pursed lips. 'Keep up the good work.' Then he turned. Repeated it again, so everyone could hear. It was a team pep message. Not meant for her.

As soon as he'd left, Nasreen saw Saunders bolt from the

room. Hurrying she caught up with him in the corridor, pressing the button for the lift. 'You okay, sir?'

He looked startled, as if he'd only just clocked she was there. Then cross. 'We haven't got time to muck around, Cudmore.'

'You just ran off!'

'I want to know what Josh has to say for himself.'

Why did Josh bring Calinda here? Panic? Fear? Not for the first time, Nas felt a tug of worry, that there was something they weren't seeing.

'Why is this taking so long?' Saunders slammed his hand against the wall. Turned and started down the stairs.

Nas hurried after him, passing a SOCO on the way, trying to keep up. The woman was crouched down, looking closely at the stairs, muttering to herself. A word caught Nasreen's ear as she passed. She stopped. 'Sorry, what did you say?'

'I'm not waiting for you, Cudmore,' Saunders voice barrelled up from below.

'I'm coming, sir,' she called. The SOCO pulled back, looking startled. She was a woman in her forties, with dark hair and a few white wisps.

'Sorry.' Nasreen put a hand on the SOCO's arm. 'I don't mean to interrupt, but did you just say something?'

'Thinking out loud,' the officer said.

'Cudmore!' Saunders voice was further away, but still a roar.

Get to the point. 'I thought I heard you say something about blood?'

'There isn't any,' the SOCO said.

'You mean on this step.' Nas pointed under her feet.

291

'Nowhere. There's none on any of the stairs,' the woman replied.

'Cudmore!' Saunders screeched from below.

Nas turned. Ran down the stairs. Not doubting Saunders would leave her here. 'Thank you!' she called behind her to the puzzled-looking SOCO. With each step, the same question shook through her. *Why was there no blood?*

Kate

Kate's phone pulsed in her hand. A message from Freddie:

I'm in your area. Stopping by.
Need to talk.

That sounded ominous.

'I'm so tired, baby girl.' The words echoed around the empty space. She'd thrown the tablets out. A moment of strength because she knew she was feeling weak. It felt like losing her daughter all over again. Fresh waves of grief constantly welling up inside her and threatening to overpower her. Would there be more questions? More doubt? Now that they know the name of the girl – Calinda – Kate had thought it would be over. But it was never going to be over.

Ama had been on the phone. Brisk in her need to help,

she'd found her a lawyer. A lawyer! As if she was the one on trial. She was apparently to help prep her for court. If it got that far. Kate was a fifty-three-year-old woman, a head teacher, and now they were coaching her on how to be heard. She knew Ama was trying to help. She'd explained that the defence would try to undermine her credibility as a witness. She must prepare to be questioned. Prepare to be doubted. She thought of Jesus alone in the desert, forty days and forty nights. We must all undergo trials. Her stomach contracted at the thought. The tablets had left a soreness, a bruise on the inside. They would call her a liar, she knew that. Already her words had been dissected, spread about, turned over. She felt the weight of each thing that came out of her mouth now. One wrong word, one wrong turn of phrase, and they would destroy her. Because that was how it worked. To defend a killer, you must discredit a witness. It was still her word against his. Perhaps it would be easier if the killer wasn't found? The idea reared up and frightened her. *How could you even think that?*

She must normalise this. Practice saying her name.

'Would you have liked Tegbee, Calinda?' The words sounded strange, unreal. She must practice. 'Calinda.' She would have to say it in court. In front of her parents. In front of their pain. The bruise inside throbbed. 'I won't fail you, baby girl. I promise.'

The doorbell jolted her from her thoughts, and the image of the girl, blood dripping from her eyelashes, whipped away with relief. One day she hoped to picture her whole, smiling, like in the photo Freddie sent her. She flicked the kettle on, and grabbed a tea towel to dry her hands as she hurried to the door.

She opened it and the world slowed. Shifted into black and white. It wasn't Freddie. It wasn't the police. It was him. The man from the film. The one who'd killed Calinda Gallo. He was tall in real life, towering, blocking out the sun. Two lines shaved into his left eyebrow. Like a diagonal train track. He went to smile and speak and say whatever lie he was going to open with, but then he saw it too: she recognised him straightaway. There was no need to bother with pretence. The tea towel fell from her hand. The curve of his skull, his sharp cheekbones, his hands. It was *those* hands. Strong, sinewy, for someone so young. His eyes hardened and before she could cry out he had a hand over her mouth, and the other on her arm. He was squeezing her, pushing her, and they half fell backwards into the house. She struggled, but he was too strong for her. He kicked the door closed behind him.

Nasreen

They'd watched them through the live feed camera. Josh looked tiny in the interview room, his mother crying next to him. They'd asked if he wanted a lawyer, if Mrs Chapman had wanted a lawyer, but the woman had shaken her head. Every now and then his mother looked up and said: 'What did you do, Josh? What did you do?'

The first time she did it Saunders had rushed to the door as if to interrupt: if he answered without getting it on tape, if he said anything but then clammed up, they were screwed. But the boy hadn't said anything. He looked shocked. Traumatised.

'I think we should ask for a different guardian,' Saunders suggested.

Chips sniffed. Rubbed his wrist under his watch, as if the skin was itching. None of them were happy about this kid being here. Nas had arrested kids, angry kids spewing bile and rage and swagger before. Back when she was at the Jubilee it was too regular an occurrence. Nicked them for stealing, drug running, stabbings, caught in the cross hairs of society, she'd see them at eleven for nicking bikes, at twelve they'd be lookouts for the gangs, the small and nimble ones fed through open windows to wriggle out with laptops and flat-screen TVs. They were happy to come into the station for a hot drink and a biscuit. To have a bit of attention. Comfortable in the knowledge they knew their rights, that after a few hours they'd be out again. It was a badge of honour to be questioned. The shock when they turned fourteen, got detained, charged and carted off to prison was visceral. Too late and in too deep. Juvie was more violent than the main prisons; it was a raging hierarchy. She'd seen kids like that since she'd first been on the job; felt, in a strange way, that she'd grown up with them. Which was why she knew. They all knew. Josh wasn't like that. There was no history of involvement with the police, no record of him being mixed up in anything at all; he didn't have any swagger, or even any seeming idea of what was happening. He was just a scared little boy. But he wasn't little really. It was a trick of the mind. He was a good five foot eleven. Strong. They had their man. This boy was their man.

'He's not going to talk with his mum so upset,' Saunders said.

'He's scared,' Nasreen said.

'Hmmmm. I don't think you should go in for this one, Pete,' Chips said.

Saunders made a clicking sound. 'I'm in with the mum.'

'Yes, but we're not interviewing her. The lad's already distressed,' Chips said.

'It'll take time for us to get an alternative guardian, and I'm not sure she'll agree anyway,' she added. This was shaping up to be tricky for multiple reasons. Apply the wrong pressure and Josh could break completely: lock his secrets in for good. There was something slightly mechanical about him. As if he were processing it all: like a computer. And the computer was overheating.

'I think Cudmore should lead,' Chips said. 'I'll sit in. Give her support. You've already aligned yourself with his mum – let's save that in case we need it.'

Nasreen waited for the angry rebuff, but it didn't come.

'I've not met the lad yet,' Chips continued. 'But he's going to see me as your average cop: a threat. Cudmore's younger, softer. When she wants to be.'

'I'm not soft.'

Chips ignored her. 'She's the way to go.'

Saunders's shoulders were hunched forward. He was still sulking about Burgone talking to the press. They paused for a moment. All staring at the screen. The only sound Mrs Chapman's snivelling. Saunders blew air through his teeth. 'Okay.'

Okay. Soft it was. He was only a twelve-year-old boy, she told herself. You can do this. She wondered where Burgone was now. Organising the press conference? About to walk through and see her performance on the camera? For a moment she was reminded of how this had started. With five people, probably more, watching a young girl being raped and murdered on a live streamed video. They were watching the suspect now on a live video stream. It had gone full circle.

Josh looked up with alarm as they opened the door, instantly eyeing Chips warily, as predicted.

'Is Detective Saunders not coming?' Mrs Chapman sounded panicked.

'I'm DI McCain.' Chips held a puffy hand out for her to shake. His voice soft and warm. 'Myself and Sergeant Cudmore are going to be interviewing Josh today. All right, laddie?'

Josh's eyes grew wider. Nasreen flicked on the tape recorder, stated the name and date, and all who were present.

'How you doing, Josh, do you want anything to drink? A Pepsi or anything?' she started. She had to try and get him to relax. She could feel Saunders's eyes on her, studying every movement, every word, every reaction. Would Burgone be there too?

Josh shook his head.

'For the benefit of the tape, Josh is shaking his head.'

He looked with alarm at the tape recorder.

Keep going. Act like it's normal. Start easy. 'Josh, can you tell me how old you are?'

He nodded, his voice small and cracked. 'Twelve.'

'Thank you,' she said, smiling. 'You're doing great. And can you tell me where you were on the night of Friday, the fourth of August, 2016?'

Without moving his head he glanced at his mum. Took a breath. Nasreen held hers. 'At a party.'

Mrs Chapman snivelled again.

'It's okay.' Chips gave her hand a squeeze. 'He's doing well.'

She could hear him breathing. A quick, hard rasp, his eyes fixed on a spot on the floor between them. The room pressing in on him, curling his shoulders, curling him into himself. 'And where was this party?' Nasreen asked.

Another pause. A wait. An exhalation. 'Dogberry.'

If they could find the crime scene they'd be able to send the SOCOs in. Pull as much forensic evidence as they could: corroborate their witnesses' stories. 'Where on the estate?'

His right leg started to jig. 'Some of the flats are empty.' He swallowed. Didn't look up. 'We heard people were getting together.'

We? 'Did you go with someone else, Josh?'

His leg stopped. His lips clamped shut. He shook his head.

'It's just that you said "we"?' Was this the other person behind the camera?

'People, you know. On the estate.'

Not convincing. She tried a different tack. 'Do you know who organised the party?'

A small shake of his head, more like a tremor.

'And did you recognise anyone else at this party?'

He twisted the hem of his T-shirt tight round his fingers so they turned white with pressure. 'No.'

'Okay,' she said. 'Do you remember this girl being there?' She lay the smiling photo of Calinda on the table.

His reaction was instant. He jolted back away from the photo. His fingers flung away from his tangling fabric as if he'd been burned. Then he held his arm there, partially raised, like a string puppet, staring at the photo. He didn't move his eyes.

'You want a closer look?' She said, moving it towards him. His hand floated forward a fraction. 'Take it if you want.'

He took the photo and cupped it softly in his hands. Nasreen felt a chill run over her skin. Something wasn't right here. He stared deep into it. Mrs Chapman made to move, perhaps take it from him, but Chips held up a palm to still her.

They were all staring at the snap now. 'Her name is Calinda,' she said. 'But I think you already know that.'

He nodded, and, almost like a breath out, said: 'Yes.'

'Did you see Calinda at the party that night?'

There was a silence. 'It's my fault,' he said. His voice was thick.

Nasreen tensed. A tear rolled down Josh's face. He held the photo away so it wouldn't get wet. 'She was dancing.' He smiled sadly. 'Laughing. And, and I thought it was a laugh.' She found herself nodding with him. Aware he needed encouragement to keep going. Reassurance that this behaviour was normal. That they would all have done it. 'She was dancing for the camera. Kept blowing kisses. I wasn't the only one filming.'

'Who else was filming her, Josh?'

He shook his head. The tears came faster. 'My likes were going mental. They were loving her!' He sped up, his words crackling like fireworks across the table. 'So many comments. We found an empty room and we were mucking around. She was into it, she was…' His voice broke. Caught. Stumbled over itself. Shuddered into a sob. He pushed on.

Keep going, Josh. Keep going.

'And… and… like, all these people were cheering. They were sending all these comments. They were saying she loved it. They were saying it was well hot! And there was so many likes. We were racing up the charts. And I just kept thinking, wait till they hear about this at school. And…' His words faltered. He heaved with another sob. Snot bubbled out of his nose.

'What happened, Josh?' she asked.

'Then she was freaking out. And I said to stop. But she hit him. Really fucking hard and… and…'

Nasreen felt her blood run cold. They'd got this wrong. This wasn't suspect A. Josh was *behind* the camera. Josh was Teen B. But how could he match the photofit? 'Who hit Calinda, Josh? Who was with her in the video?'

'It was my fault!' he shouted. 'He'd never have done it if I hadn't been egging him on. They said do her harder. That she liked it. Don't you see? If I hadn't have been whooping… Then she wouldn't have freaked out, and if I hadn't have screamed… If I hadn't have scared him… I made him do that. It's my fault. My fault!' His body shook with the effort. His mum gripped his hand tightly.

Borderline hyperventilation. If he got worse they'd have to stop. A decent lawyer would argue he was under duress. They were so close. 'Who did it, Josh? Who was the other person in the video?'

'B – Benedict,' he managed.

Mrs Chapman made a mewling, desperate cry.

'My cousin.'

Freddie

Freddie came off the tube dripping with sweat, and it wasn't even that busy. The bottle she'd brought with her had been drained in minutes, even the condensation licked from it. The street Kate lived on seemed to quiver around her feet. Like wavy mirages in the country and western movies her dad used to watch. There was no refreshing pool of water in Hackney though. Maybe she should forget this? She didn't have to tell Kate anything in person. A telephone call would do. She could get a Frappuccino and sit in some air-conditioned Starbucks. Nah, she'd a right to know they'd found Calinda. That her drive had led them here.

She tugged at the T-shirt that was now stuck to her back, a fleeting relief of air passing between fabric and skin. Her body craved open grassland. There was a nice park near Tibbsy's. Thinking about Nas and Burgone, how her friend couldn't have the man she loved, had made her think. She'd been frightened of how she felt. Of what was happening to her. She'd seen her dad hurt her mum over and over again. The wounds never quite having enough time to heal before they were split open once more. His mistress, otherwise known as the bottle. It wasn't Tibbsy's fault she came from a fucked-up family. But it wasn't hers either. She'd get strawberries on the way home, maybe a bottle of Cava, and they could have a celebratory picnic under the shady trees. She'd tell him how she felt then. You're adulting, Freddie, she smiled to herself. She could just imagine his goofy face now.

The even numbers were on the left-hand side of the street, and she counted down till she reached Kate's door. It was a whole house, and for a moment she was wistful for the luxury of space. At Tibbsy's, they'd still be sharing one bedroom, in a shared two-bed flat. But least it was a start. Kate's door knocker reverberated through the building. She took a step back and waited. A black cab hummed past, swinging into and out of the road. She bet this was a rat run for the cabbies.

She checked the time. Perhaps Kate was upstairs? She tried the knocker again, this time easing it back and cracking it down against the door twice. She could hear movement, feet hurrying down the stairs toward her. The door flew open, and there was a man, gorgeous, tall, his smooth muscles curving out of his faded t-shirt, jeans hung down over his Nikes. He was panting lightly.

'Sorry, I was looking for Kate? Kate Adiyiah?' She looked at the next door down – did she have the wrong house?

'She's out.' The guy had his hand on the door handle as if he were about to pull it closed.

304

'I texted her to say I was coming – it's important. She's been helping us with a case and I have some news for her.'

'You're the police?' He opened the door a fraction more, curious.

'Nah, not me: I just work with them,' she said.

'Oh, right, sorry, yeah. She said you'd be coming. I'm her nephew.'

'Freddie, nice to meet you.'

'You best come in then.' He stepped back so she could come inside. The corridor smelt of bread, as if Kate had been baking. It opened up straight into a dining room with a couple of chairs and bookcases. Beautiful books lined the shelves, and she immediately wanted to stroke them. Colourful posters hung on the wall. He closed the door behind her. It was cooler in here. Shady.

'What did you say your name was?' She smiled as she turned back to him.

Oh my God. Her brain blinked. Refocused. Air snagged in her throat.

'I didn't,' the man said. He was pointing a gun straight at her.

Nasreen

Of course they looked similar if they were cousins – more than one person could shave their eyebrow! Dammit, they'd been so taken in by Josh's panic over the water, his apparent guilty actions and the discovery of the body, that they'd immediately thought he was suspect A. It was like he believed it too. Nasreen needed to get Josh to grasp the enormity of what had happened. It was as though by watching it unfold through the filter of his phone, he'd been detached from the reality. 'You understand Benedict was raping Calinda, Josh?'

He looked startled. 'No. B wouldn't do that. She liked him: they danced together.'

'That's not consent, lad,' Chips said quietly.

He shook his head. 'If I hadn't have panicked, if I hadn't screamed… then none of this would have happened.' He was still shaking his head.

He'd watched things escalate from dancing to assault, one eye on the number of likes he was getting. Nasreen's throat contracted. He was a kid caught up on the drug of endorsement; those who'd liked the video at home were culpable too as far as she was concerned. 'Several people who saw the video suspected Calinda might have been drugged,' Nasreen said.

He stared at her. 'No.' He sounded upset again. 'They're wrong.'

'I'll read you an extract from one of the statements: "The girl appeared floppy. Her eyes were dilated, rolling back in her head, I thought, she's been drugged."' She put the paper back down. 'Did you give Calinda anything, Josh?'

'No. I don't do that stuff. I can't get a record, I want to be an astronaut.' He looked at the ground. 'Wanted to.'

Mrs Chapman's bottom lip was shaking.

'Did you see Benedict give anything to Calinda?' she asked.

'He wouldn't. I told you.' Josh shook his head. But he didn't look so sure this time.

The more time Nasreen spent with Josh, the more she saw he was frightened, scared. In denial about what had happened. They needed him to face up to it. Give them something concrete they could question Benedict with. 'We have found Calinda's body, Josh,' she said.

'You have?' he exhaled. His shoulders relaxed for the first time. 'I never wanted this to happen. I never thought…' He trailed off again. His pupils were dilated. His hands trembled. They were losing him to shock.

'We will run tests for substances in her bloodstream,' she said.

His eyes darted about. He shifted. An uncomfortable look

307

on his face. There was something else. Something he wasn't saying. About the drugs? Or the body?

'Whose idea was it to move the body to the attic, Josh?'

'I knew I'd be in trouble. That Mum would be upset,' he added. Mrs Chapman gave his hand a squeeze. He was getting smaller, younger, as if he were regressing before their eyes. 'It happened so fast. Like I couldn't get it straight in my head. B helped me. He knew what to do. But…' He trailed off again. Bit his lip.

'It's okay, Josh, you won't get him in trouble,' she lied.

He shifted again. Frowned. 'It's just it wasn't until after that I thought it wasn't right. B said she didn't have no family, that no one would be looking for her. But I saw them – her mum and dad, on the news?'

'Was the party in Tower A, is that why you put her there?' she said. They still didn't know where the crime scene was. She knew Saunders was listening outside, and would have checked out Benedict on the system by now. There would already be officers on the way to pick him up.

'No.' He shook his head. 'I didn't realise it was our block until it was too late. B knew what to do. He knew a back route, he said she was safer there.'

A back route? Nasreen's minded whirred through the plans she'd seen online. 'Did you take her underground?' Using the tunnels.

He nodded. Looked at his mum. 'I swear I didn't know we were in our block, I wouldn't have… she was so close.'

Did Benedict deliberately get Josh to hide the body there: a reminder to keep him in check?

'I went to visit her,' Josh said quietly.

'Calinda? You mean her body – after you put her in the water tank?'

He flinched. 'Yeah. Before I saw her parents. I just thought it wasn't right, like she was nice. Funny. I didn't like her being up there alone.'

She thought of the chrysanthemums in the attic. 'Did you take her flowers, Josh?'

He nodded. He looked painfully young now. Lost. Eyes wide. She wondered when he'd last slept. 'I was going to lay them on the water. They do that for burials at sea. But I couldn't. I was too scared. I'm a coward.'

Mrs Chapman's face folded in distress and she squeezed his hand.

'So B told you where to put Calinda's body,' she said. 'What did you do after that? Where are the clothes you were wearing that night?'

'He took my clothes. He knew what to do with them. No one would believe that it was an accident. I knew I'd be in trouble, but I don't care any more. I'm so sorry, Mum.' He collapsed into her, rocking gently. Mrs Chapman pulled her son close, tears streaming from her eyes.

'Okay,' Nasreen said. Josh had done some terrible things in first filming and covering up a crime. But he hadn't known Calinda was drugged, hadn't realised she was being assaulted until it was too late, and had been manipulated by Benedict into disposing of the body, incriminating himself further. 'Let's take a break.' She switched off the recorder.

Saunders was waiting for her and Chips outside. She pulled the door to gently, and they stepped away, so they wouldn't be overheard.

'I've been looking into Benedict Petrosyan,' Saunders said grimly. 'Seventeen years old. He's a known associate of the Dogberry Boys, though so far nothing on his record.'

'That explains how he knew his way around the tunnels,' Chips said.

'Is there another staircase?' Nasreen asked. 'One of the SOCOs said they hadn't found any blood drops in the stairwell.'

'I'll see if Green can get hold of proper blueprints for the estate,' Chips said.

'The preliminary pathology report is in – they've put a rush on it. There are traces of sedative in her bloodstream,' Saunders said.

'He seemed genuinely surprised when I suggested she'd been drugged,' Nas said.

'He could be faking it,' Saunders suggested.

She thought of the panic and fear in Josh's eyes. And the relief when they said they'd found the body. 'I think he wanted to come forward earlier.'

'And Benedict stopped him?' Saunders suggested. 'There's more.' He handed over his paperwork. Chips pulled his reading glasses from his pocket. Nasreen held the sheet so they could both see it. She tensed as she read the words.

Chips blew air through his teeth, voicing what they were all thinking. 'I reckon our laddie's been taken for a ride.'

Freddie

There was someone crying far away. No, not far away: here. Here, now. Freddie forced her eyes open. Light poured in. Everything was white. Blotted out. Blotted by the light. *Tibbsy?*

'Freddie? Freddie? Can you hear me?' There was a shape in front of her. The shape was crying.

Where was she? Pain seared through her head. Had she been drinking? No, though her mouth felt dry. Kate's face comes into focus, she looks worried. Cheeks streaked by tears.

'You...' She swallowed, tried to get more moisture. 'You okay?'

Kate glanced anxiously at the door. Away from her. They were in a room. A bedroom. The wall was painted a deep maroon. The double bed was neatly made. There was a window. It was light outside. Sunny. It was still daytime. Why couldn't she feel the heat? There was a door. Why weren't they going out the door? Why wasn't Kate getting help? Freddie

311

touched her head. Her hand was wet. Sticky. Blood. It took a moment:

There was a man. A pretty man. He'd hit her. Hard. Hit her with a gun. A gun.

Her mind stuttered. They had to get out of here. She thought of Nas. She needed to get Kate out. Freddie tried to push herself up onto her elbows. Tried to move. Her body felt heavy, weighted. The room wobbled. Why did she feel so cold? She could hear footsteps. Heavy footsteps. They were coming closer. Closer to the door.

'It's him!' Kate's face was close to hers. Desperate. Frantic. Freddie's head hurt so much. Kate was shaking her now, trying to move her. Half dragging, half pushing. They must get away from the door. They must hide.

'It's the boy in the film. It's the killer!'

Nasreen

Green was on her way to Benedict's home address. They'd given Josh another sugary tea, brought him back down from the precipice again. Soothed him, for now.

'Tell me about this back route you took Calinda along?' Nasreen said.

'Benedict knows all of them,' Josh said. 'I know you said I shouldn't use them, Mum. I'm sorry.' He looked as though he was threatening to cry again.

She needed to keep him focused. 'Did you take her up the main stairs?'

'No,' he said, shaking his head. 'I would have known it was our block then.'

'So there are other stairs?' They could search them for forensic evidence.

'Benedict said they were supposed to be for rubbish removal and stuff, but now only the Boys use them,' he said.

Did they even know about these other routes? She tried to remember a door, anything that looked like it might have led to another set of stairs. If each tower had one, no wonder officers chasing Boys lost them.

'Josh, here's what I think happened. I think B drugged Calinda and raped her,' she said.

'No.' Josh shook his head. 'I told you it was an accident.'

She saw Mrs Chapman's eyes widen. *You know,* she thought: *you know.* 'He raped her, and when she fought back he killed her. And then he used you to help cover it up. He made you complicit. He told you it was your fault.'

He was shaking his head. Faster and faster, as if it might work itself loose.

'Josh: this isn't the first time he's done something like this.' The paperwork from Saunders was in her hands. 'He was reported for sexually assaulting a classmate at his school. It's why he was suspended.'

There was a silence. Josh stared at her. His chest heaved up and down. A young boy, a kid. He shouldn't be here.

'If you tell me what Benedict did we can stop him from hurting anyone else.'

He started. 'I need my phone!'

What? 'I'm afraid I can't let you have your phone, Josh, it's been taken for evidence.'

He thrust his chair back. His mum reached for him. 'I need my phone! Please!'

'Calm down, Josh!' his mother said. 'This isn't helping!'

'But I told him, Mum! I told him!'

314

'Told who?' Chips says.

Oh, no. When he was in the bathroom. No, no, no. She should have followed him in. Shouldn't have left him alone. They need to warn Green. 'Did you send a message to Benedict?'

'I didn't know! I didn't know about the other girl. You've got to stop him!'

Chips jumped up as the boy's arms flailed.

'I didn't know what he meant. I thought he was angry.'

'Stop him doing what, Josh?' They needed to contain this. Put the alert out. If he'd contacted Benedict he'd have had at least an hour's head start.

'He messaged me. He said: it's that bitch on the telly's fault: I'll teach her. And, and…'

Her throat was dry. 'And what, Josh?'

'And he has a gun.'

He was going for Kate. They were up on their feet immediately. Running from the room. Saunders there. Car keys ready. Chips shouted for a PC to stay with Josh. They needed armed response. Saunders was on the phone. Nasreen shouted into her radio.

'All officers assist. I need immediate response. We believe there is a credible threat to a witness. One potential hostage. Suspect is potentially armed. Repeat, suspect is armed.' They should have taken him in as soon as they had a name. They should've known he'd go for Kate. She's been all over the news. He knows who she is. He knows she's the one that fought to have him found.

Chips was on his radio. The call handler crackling between them. 'Two hostages. Repeat. This is DI McCain. The suspect may have two hostages.'

'Two?' Nasreen stared at him. Her heart in her mouth. *No*. Chips's face bounced, pale, as he ran. Nasreen felt something snap inside her, like overstretched elastic. She knew what he was going to say before the words were out.

'Freddie texted me. She was on her way to see Kate.'

Nasreen

They had to wait for the armed unit to arrive. Nasreen paced at the end of Kate Adiyiah's road. Her stab vest as heavy as her guilt, her shirt stuck to her with sweat. Freddie's phone had gone straight to voicemail. Kate hadn't answered hers either. They had eyes on the house, watching, waiting. But they couldn't go in until the armed team was ready. Burgone was on his way. She wished he were here already.

'They won't be long, lass,' Chips said next to her. Green had reported that Benedict's address was clear. His mother hadn't seen him since earlier. No one had seen him. Why did Josh send that message? She should have stopped him. It was her fault.

'I want to go in,' she said.

Chips ignored her. Gave her the dignity of not patronising her. This was procedure, she thought with a laugh; the very thing Freddie hated. Why hadn't she called her when they found the body? She'd been pushing as hard as anyone. Harder. She deserved to hear it from her. Instead she was angry with her. And now she might not get to talk to her… She cut her own thoughts off. She needed to get control. Panicking wouldn't help Freddie.

Saunders walked back, briefing Ingham, the ex-army team leader of the armed response unit. 'Okay, two of us can go in at the rear. We're to give them a good couple of metres. Stand clear until they give the go-ahead. You in, Cudmore?'

She stepped forward. 'Thank you, sir.'

'Just don't get yourself shot,' he said.

None of them laughed. Chips looked worried; he was fond of Freddie. None of them wanted this. *Please, let her and Kate be okay.*

They advanced behind the armed team, running along the edge of the walls, crouching at intervals. All residents had been secured inside, told to stay away from windows. They moved swiftly. Ingham, a tank of a man, gave the signal and his team moved with choreographed precision. They waited. She could hear only the distant hum of the traffic and her own breathing.

Five.

Four.

Three.

Two.

One.

Go, go, go!

The lead guy smashed the door of Kate's house with the big red key and they poured in. Guns up.

318

'This is the police! Get down on the ground!'

Her heart raced.

'Clear!' The shout came. She and Saunders followed swiftly. Kate Adiyiah's hallway was shaded, cool. The curtains drawn, so it took a second for her eyes to adjust to the dimness. Blood pumped in her ears. She could smell freshly baked bread, and something behind that: cigarette smoke, maybe.

'Kitchen clear!' shouted Ingham.

Men thundered up the stairs, their boots ricocheting round the building. They must be up there.

'Cudmore!' Saunders shouted as she followed them. Taking the stairs two at a time. Her legs pumping. She'd been here before: running to save Freddie. It wasn't supposed to happen again. She might not be so lucky this time.

'Cudmore!' Saunders grabbed her arm and pulled her back into him as the two men in front kicked into the bedroom. Light poured onto them.

'Clear!' they shouted. Behind them another two shouted from the bathroom. 'Clear!'

'Where are they?'

'You're supposed to stay back.'

'All clear! Stand down. Property is empty. Repeat, property is empty.' Ingham was in stereo on her radio. Where were they? The armed unit were coming back out. Arms down. Some were loosening their helmets.

'In here,' Ingham shouted.

She shook Saunders off. Ran. Where were they? The bedroom was in full sunlight. There were photos on the floor. Broken glass. She picked one up: a smiling woman on a beach, with her someone who could be Kate, a bright blue floral kaftan on, pink sandals clutched in her hand, but she couldn't tell because a cigarette butt had been burnt through her face. Christ. The stench of the burned photo wove around her, smelling like melted plastic: beware. This man was angry. He was trying to stub Kate out. Nasreen took in the single pine wardrobe, the pine dressing table and mirror, the bed, the maroon-painted wall Ingham, his helmet in his hand, stared at his feet. Blood. Pooled on the wooden floor, disappearing into the cracks of the wood. A smear where something, or someone, had been dragged through it.

Her heart stopped. Restarted. Her training finally won the fight it'd been having internally. She gained control of her limbs. Her voice. Her hand. She reached for the radio and lifted it to her lips to speak.

'We need forensics in here. There's blood in the bedroom upstairs.' She stood back, searched the room with her eyes, started at the door, inch by inch, like she'd been trained. The edge of the duvet was crooked, just slightly. Apart from the smashed photo frame, it was the only non-straight edge in the room. Pulling on a plastic glove, she crouched next to the bed. Carefully lifted the duvet. Underneath was a small folded card, white, but for the smudge of blood. It was Freddie's business card, one of the ones she'd been so proud of earlier. Nasreen's eyes were misted with sweat. What she'd thought was a random smear she now saw was a letter N. N for Nas. It was a message. Freddie was here. And when she left, she was still alive.

Freddie

Freddie could smell petrol. They went over another bump. She tried to brace herself in the dark. Tried to think what those stupid Internet memes said to do if you got locked in a boot. She'd never read them, thinking it would never actually happen. Did you run out of air? She could hear Kate crying, muffled. The man was shouting instructions at her; she was driving. Freddie was nauseous. The cut above her eye was bad. Saliva pooled in her mouth, vomit clawed its way up her throat. She couldn't spew. She'd choke.

The car turned again. She'd tried to keep count at the beginning, but she'd lost track. She didn't know where they were, didn't know where he was taking them. She could feel his weight in the back seat. An angry pulsing seat. She thought about kicking and shouting, but the thought of the gun stopped her. It wouldn't take much for him to turn, shoot backwards, the seat acting as a silencer, and she'd be gone. The bullet would rip through her like it would the seat.

Wincing, she curled into a ball. Her limbs ached. She ached. She closed her eyes and tried to think of what her therapist said about keeping calm. About fighting anxiety. She recited the alphabet. Counted to one hundred, then started in French, getting stuck at *dix*.

He'd got her phone. He made her switch it off before she handed it over. She'd tried to press *call*, but he was quick. Quick and vicious. The gun caught her hard on the side of the head, a smear of bright white then nothing. She and Kate were in Kate's house, she knew that. Chips knew she was going there. Nas would be coming for her. He was smart to move them. That was what worried her; none of this felt spontaneous, it was more like he'd thought it through. Like he'd been planning this. Except she wasn't supposed to be here, was she? So she was the variable. The trouble. And what do you do with trouble if you're smart? You eliminate it.

Une, deux, trois, quatre.

They turned again; she could hear the car's indicator: tick tick, tick tick, tick tick, tick tick. And then they were slowing. Stopping. The engine cut, and she could hear Kate more clearly now, hear the sound of her crying. She could hear a deep voice – his – but couldn't make out the words. Two car doors opened; the car rocked. This is it, she thought. This is it. And she thought of Tibbsy trying to take her hand. *I think I'm falling for you too.* She heard the key in the lock, the boot opened and everything went white.

Nasreen

'What do you think you're playing at?' Saunders stormed after her as she stepped out of Kate's house.

She walked away from him, looked at the cars lining both sides of the street.

'Sergeant, I'm talking to you!' he snapped. He was red in the face, pissed off. His solid shoulders rocking back and forth as he strode after her. Turning it into an indignant strut.

She stopped. 'Kate has a Y reg red Corsa. I can't see one out here.'

'You were under orders to stay two steps behind the team until the building had been declared clear. You don't go running in after them. If the suspect had got hold of you, he could have used that against the team. You could have endangered the lives of other officers. You could have been injured or worse. I do not want to be known as an officer who gets one of his team killed.'

'Sir –' she whirled around '– with all due respect, that is not my main focus right now. Freddie and Kate are missing, and until we get them back I don't give a damn about what anyone else thinks.'

His face darkened, his eyes narrowed. She tilted her chin defiantly.

Saunders stared at her. Then looked away. 'The two roads either side of this will be on the same car parking system, we'll need to check those too. You take the left, I'll take the right.'

She jogged to the next street, her head snapping back and forth to take in each car parked down it. There were multiple red cars, but no red Corsas. By the time she was back outside Kate's her shirt was soaked through and she was panting in the heat.

'Nothing, you?' Saunders said. She shook her head.

Chips came down the steps, his hair plastered to his face. 'There's traces of blood in the hallway. It looks like they came out the front.' Nasreen looked on the ground, to see if she could see any more blood specks, but the grime of London, multiplied by the heat, formed a collage of splashes around her. It would take the SOCOs to piece this together.

'What about their phones?' she asked.

'I've put a trace on both Freddie's and Kate Adiyiah's, but both are switched off. Same with our lad's.'

'If he's got the kind of friends that can get him a gun, then chances are he'll know we can track him if the phone is on,' Saunders said, rolling his shirt sleeves up in neat stiff folds.

'We need eyes in the sky for Kate's car. I couldn't see any car keys with the others on her wall. He must have taken them in that,' Nasreen said.

'I'll radio it through,' Chips said.

'He could be making a break for the airport or port,' Saunders said.

'Then why detour to collect passengers?' Nasreen asked. She thought of the photo upstairs. A sick feeling twisted up her gullet.

'How did he know where to find Kate?' Saunders said. 'Josh texted him when he was in the bathroom, he'd have had minutes to run, we were all over the building.'

He could have run at any point in the last week. 'He knew already,' she said. 'We didn't know who he was. We had no name, and until this morning we had no body. Only five people knew what Benedict looked like. And only two of those have gone on television. He doesn't know about the others.'

'Do you think the MP is in danger?' Saunders said.

'Perhaps,' she said.

'I'll have uniform check in on him,' said Chips.

Had Benedict calmly got on the tube? Did he know Kate drove, that she'd have a car? 'He knew exactly where to come. He's been here before.'

'Okay,' Saunders said. 'So this is his plan. Now what? Where's he taken them?'

'Home?' Chips asked.

'Green's there – no sign of him.' Saunders nodded.

'That photo upstairs – that says he's angry. He wants to punish Kate for what she did,' Nasreen said, her stomach churning.

'Somewhere he knows: his school, that'd be empty in August.'

Nasreen was thinking about everything Benedict had done. He'd kept Calinda close. Not just to Josh, but to him. He hadn't fled when he had the chance, he'd come here. He'd probably been here before. Circling, returning home, returning to the scene of the crime. 'I think he'll take them back to where this started. To where Kate saw him that first time.'

'Here?' Chips seemed confused. 'But there's no one here.'

'No,' she said. 'Where the attack happened. He's taking them to Dogberry estate.'

Freddie

'Get out,' the man said.

Freddie's eyes adjusted to the blazing sunlight. She took in three big gulps of air, and placed her hands on the edge of the car boot to try and lever herself out. Kate stood next to the man, who had hold of her arm. She was shaking. Without obviously tilting her head, Freddie tried to work out where they were. A dusty car park? She pretended her arm had buckled so that she could dip her head and look to the side. They were in some kind of industrial park, abandoned by the looks of it. Grey-painted lock-ups bordered the scruffy square of land they'd stopped on. Was this a brownfield site? An abandoned construction site? Seagulls called and swooped to peck at the litter that sat festering around them.

'Where are we?' she said.

'Get out,' he repeated.

She looked the other way. More buildings. And beyond that towers. Beyond that further, she could see the twinkling glass of Canary Wharf. A faraway Emerald City. They must be east. Not that she knew what to do with this information. She should try and get a message out. An SOS. What would Nas do?

The man's patience had dwindled; he grabbed her arm and hauled her from the trunk. She wouldn't be able to overpower him. Could they both do it? If they worked together? Kate was still crying, silently now. Freddie winced as the bright sunlight bit into her head. The blood near her eye was drying, sticky and tight on her face.

The man had the gun in his right hand; low, tight to his body, almost out of sight. Not that anyone was around.

'That way,' he said, gesturing to the other side of the exposed land.

Freddie swallowed. There really wasn't anyone around. No witnesses. 'Who are you?' she said.

'That way,' he said again, pushing her with his hand. Her foot skidded across the sandy concrete under her feet.

'Where are we going?'

'Shut it,' he said.

'Not feeling chatty?' she said as they scrabbled over the wasteland, tied together by threat and fear. Her mind was running at a hundred miles per hour. Could they shout for help?

'Stop here,' he said. 'Open it.' He pointed down with the gun. Freddie's eyes followed the barrel.

She felt panic snake up her spine. At her feet was a large brown rusted metal covering. Was it a pit? Was he going to shoot them and leave them here? Was this their grave?

'Do it.' He pushed her again and she fell forward with a clang onto the metal. It had two square-edged handles, rough and hot in the sun. Swallowing, she tugged at them. The cover slid across revealing the top of a spindly metal ladder which went down into the darkness. Freddie knew where they were. She gulped down her breath, tried not to scream.

'Down,' the man said. 'You first.' He pushed Kate forward.

'Where are you taking us?' Kate's voice wavered between the authoritative head teacher and the terrified captive. Terror won.

'Do it, or I'll hit her again.' He raised the gun.

Freddie braced herself.

'Okay, okay. Please don't,' Kate said, hurriedly lowering her feet onto the rungs.

Freddie looked at her. Tried to smile. What would Nas do? 'It's okay,' she mouthed. But it wasn't.

As the top of Kate's head disappeared, the man pushed Freddie forward. 'You too,' he said. 'And no funny business at the bottom, or I shoot you both. Fish in a barrel.' He pointed the gun at the opening.

Freddie took a breath. Stay calm. The rungs were damp and cool to the touch, spreading like ice crystals through her as the sun disappeared and she descended into the darkness.

Nasreen

The Dogberry estate still had a heavy police presence, though most of the officers were outside, keeping people away from Tower A, which was roped off for forensic work. Could he really have bought them here? Nasreen began to question herself.

Her phone rang, and Green's name flashed up on her screen. 'Yup?' she answered, not taking her eyes off Saunders, who was jogging back to the car, a rolled paper under his arm. Chips had got hold of the official blueprints of the estate.

'I've been through his room and his flat with a fine-toothed comb,' Green said.

'Find anything?'

'Kate Adiyiah's name and address written in a notebook.'

'We guessed he must have been planning this,' she said. 'Anything that might suggest where he'd take her?'

'Under his mattress is a hand-drawn map: it ain't new, but I think it's for the tunnels underneath,' she said. 'There was also half an ounce of hash, three fake IDs and what looks like a bag of ecstasy pills.'

Nasreen thought of the sedative found in Calinda's bloodstream. It could be more of the same. 'Anything marked on the map?'

'Nope. But it's been folded several times, like it's been put in a pocket or similar,' she said. 'But he hasn't taken it with him, so?'

'Was it under the other stuff?'

'Yeah, actually,' she said. 'How'd you know that?'

'My guessing is he hasn't needed the map for a while: I think he knows his way around. Can you get down here – bring it with you?'

'On the way.' Green hung up.

'Green's found a map of the estate tunnels and Kate's full name and address,' Nasreen said as Saunders arrived.

'Let's see what we're looking at.' He spread the blueprints over the bonnet of the car.

'What's that?' She pointed at a segment that run up inside each tower.

'That's our missing staircase,' he said. 'That's where he brought the body in.'

The internal staircase ran sharper than the main one, seeming to stop at every other floor only. It connected straight down into the tunnels, which criss-crossed between the towers.

'Jesus,' Saunders muttered.

Two thousand six hundred and four flats. Five miles of underground tunnels. Which way had he taken her? Nasreen stared at the towers spreading away from them like concrete trees. *Tell me where you are, Freddie. Give me another sign.*

Chips had been on the phone to the station where Josh was still being held. 'Not good news,' he said as he hung up. Nasreen felt her stomach contract. 'His mum has lawyered up. Won't let us speak to the lad unless his solicitor is present. They're waiting for the duty solicitor, but it's going to be a couple of hours yet.' It'd been four hours since they'd found Calinda's body. Between two and three since Benedict had taken Freddie and Kate.

'Dammit,' Saunders said.

They couldn't wait any longer. 'They could be anywhere,' Nasreen said. 'He could have them underground.'

'If the gang are using that for drops, that'd increase his chances of being disturbed. We'll send some officers down to check, but I reckon more likely he's returning to the scene of the crime, like you say,' Saunders said.

The muscles in her legs tensed. Stay focused. Think. Your best chance to help Kate and Freddie is to stay calm. 'Josh said they moved the body – from the tower the party had been in to his tower. He lives in Tower A, so that can't be where the crime scene was. We can discount that one. And Benedict lives in Tower E, and he wouldn't have made Josh put Calinda's body in his water tank. Which leaves us with ten towers.'

'And two thousand, one hundred and seventy flats,' Saunders said.

Green jogged up to them. Her ginger hair was dark with sweat. 'We going in?' She passed Nasreen the papery map she'd found.

Nasreen took it, still looking at the plans. Even if they called in as many officers as they could, it'd take hours to search each of the flats. They had to narrow it down. 'Green, can you get onto the council? Josh said the party took place where there were a few empty flats. See if you can get a list of unoccupied flats – we might be looking for a cluster of them,' Nasreen said.

Green nodded and stepped away with her phone.

'Good thinking,' Saunders said.

'We've got twenty officers here,' Chips said. 'In the meantime, let's split them up to search.'

'Right, split into twos. Each pair will take a tower.' Saunders turned and shouted to the assembled officers. There was a murmur as they took in the daunting task.

'Stab vests on,' Saunders commanded. 'If we find them, no one is to go in without backup. Armed response go in first.' He looked directly at Nasreen. 'Do I make myself clear?'

'Sir!' said the crowd as they started to suit up. Six of Ingham's men were parked up behind them. Awaiting the call. Nasreen nodded.

Chips handed her her stab vest from the back of the car. It felt heavier, and when she pulled it over her head she could smell her own sweat, still damp from before. She pushed up her shirt sleeves, checked her radio, her phone and her ASP. All correct.

She turned Benedict's map over in her hand. It was overfolded, weak. Presumably handed to all Dogberry Boys members. Smart of them not to have digital copies. She opened it next to the blueprints. The snaking lines, a seemingly random pattern marked with X's, mirrored the tunnels. The enormity of the space they had to search yawned in front of them.

Green jogged back over to them, wiping the sweat from her top lip. 'They're getting someone to call me back.'

Saunders nodded. 'We'll start anyway.' They all knew time was running out. 'Cudmore, you and Green take Tower L. Chips, you take F. I'll take B, and that way we're spread across the site. I'll split the other partners across the remainders.' Saunders divvied up the plans. They all nodded. 'Green, as soon as you've heard anything from the council, radio it through.'

Nasreen and Green started for the furthest tower, as Saunders directed the other officers. Nasreen's heart was in her mouth. She willed the council to ring back: to narrow the odds. 'You've got signal, yes?'

'Yeah,' Green said.

The residents of Dogberry estate knew something was wrong. Nasreen had seen the small boys on bikes eyeing them as they drove up. They'd vanished now, the lookouts for the gangs, spreading the word that yet more police were here. CID. Plain clothes. The armed response unit. The usual groups of youths you expected to see loitering between the towers, smoking, shouting at passing girls or cops, had disappeared. The threadbare playground between the buildings was deserted. The swings empty. You could smell the concrete, warmed from the sun, sticky underfoot. Feel the eyes from above. The air felt expectant. Heavy. As if the whole place were holding its breath. Once they'd located Benedict, they'd clear the surrounding area, tell residents to keep inside, away from windows and doors. But on an estate like Dogberry,

334

where residents feared guns and were wary of being marked out as a police grass, it was a done deal. No one would come near.

'Just like Dodge City,' Green said. They were vulnerable down here, an easy target.

'Let's stick to the edges. I don't want anyone taking pot shots from above.' Her heart was thumping. A tinder-dry twig snapped under her foot.

They walked quickly and with purpose. Best not to look scared, no matter what you really felt. Through the first square of towers, on through the similarly deserted second square. Wet clothes were hung from the high windows and the metal gates that shielded the doors above them. Flapping trousers looked like hanging bodies in the corner of Nasreen's eye. The flickering colours of shorts and T-shirts played tricks on her mind, making her think she was constantly seeing people. Constantly seeing him.

'This place gives me the creeps,' Green said.

Turning back she could see the rest of the group advancing, pairing off into towers, ready to look for something, anything that might show where Benedict had Kate and Freddie. His map crinkled in her hand. They were ready. Primed. Freddie was here. But would they find her in time?

Freddie

Kate made a small yelping sound and pushed open the heavy door. Freddie stumbled after her. Inside, it took a moment for her eyes to adjust, the sudden black momentarily making her panic that she was back in the trunk. It smelt of rotting rubbish. Her eyes adjusted, and she saw they were at the bottom of a metal staircase. It must be the fire escape.

'Get going – up!' the man said. The door sealed shut behind them. There was a change in air pressure and Freddie felt her ears pop. 'Get on with it!' he commanded.

'Where are we going?' The metal banister was cool to touch; she wished she could lay her aching head against it. Kate's shoes gave off a metallic echo as they climbed. The steps were lumpy with safety bumps, which she guessed were designed for the blind, or anyone unfortunate enough to be caught in thick black smoke. The thought of fire made her panic again. 'Why are we here?' she repeated.

'Shut up and keep walking.' His voice was as cold as the metal under her palm. Keep going. Buy time. He kept looking behind them, and at the doors they passed. Could she make a run for it? They looked like they opened inwards only. The type with metal push bars on the other side. Were they alarmed? If she could trigger an alarm, then surely the stairs would fill with people. It smelt vaguely of piss now. She kept her eyes on the wall, searching for a little red fire alarm box.

Kate was huffing next to her. Freddie's legs were burning. She felt dizzy. How many flights had they climbed? She should've been counting. She didn't know what floor they were on; there were no markings on the walls near the doors. Looking over the banister, she saw a geometric swirl of steps going down, down, down. Her head swam. The higher they got, the more the heat returned. The air was thinning.

Kate caught her toe on a metal ring on the step next to her, stumbled and grabbed for Freddie. Freddie lurched and they fell forward. She clawed at the metal steps as her knee came into contact with the sharp edge of the steel.

Kate sprawled so her arm went through the gap between two stairs, her face close to the step edge. Freddie grabbed for her, yanking her back in time. Her face contorted.

'My ankle,' she gasped.

'Get up!' the guy growled.

'We need a rest!' Freddie snapped. 'Can't you see she's hurt?' She braced against the step with her foot and tried to lever Kate up. Her arms were hot to the touch. They were both slick with sweat. Freddie could smell the fear on her.

'Get the hell up!' The man's face, once beautiful, had contorted into a look of disgust and hatred. A stone gargoyle of fury. Would Nas know they were missing now? She would come, Freddie told herself. And again: Nas will come. But panic had taken residence inside her.

Kate was shaking. They had to keep it together. 'It's okay, it's going to be okay,' she whispered. Kate nodded, squeezed Freddie's hand in comfort and started to heave herself up the stairs again. 'The police will be looking for us. You won't get away with this,' she said. Freddie froze as the hard butt of the gun pressed into her shoulder. She could feel his breath on her neck, and she fought the urge to shudder. Her skin prickled with fear. She tried not to think of bullets. Of him pressing the trigger. Of her falling forwards, her blood dripping between the gaps in the stairs.

He was pressing so hard with the gun she had to arch her back: he was hurting her. His mouth was millimetres from her ear. She could feel his heat. His voice gruff, delighted.

'No one is going to find you until it's too late.'

Nasreen

Green's phone rang, making them both jump as they reached the final trio of towers. Nasreen held her hand up to indicate that they should stop. She didn't want to lose signal now.

'Hello?' Green said into the handset. Nasreen looked around them. 'Mr Singh, thank you for getting back to me so quickly. Right, I see.' Green made a thumbs-down sign with her free hand.

What did that mean? Nasreen couldn't hear the other end. Behind her she could see officers disappearing into the other towers. 'Come on,' she stage whispered.

'Let me just get a pencil,' Green said, pulling her pad from her back pocket. Nasreen passed her her pencil and tried not to scream at her to hurry up. Green scribbled onto the pad. 'Thank you, Mr Singh. No, that's very helpful. But if you do get hold of Mrs Hales, please call me as soon as possible.'

'What did he say?' Nasreen said as soon as she'd hung up.

'Shit,' Green said. 'The woman in charge of the residents' records in this locale only works mornings and they can't get hold of her.' They didn't have time for a full employment history. Green looked flustered. 'Apparently they can't get into her computer and they can't get hold of her – anyway – they've done the best they can. We've got a list of the number of flats that are unoccupied in each tower, but not the flat numbers.'

'Fuck. Better than nothing.' Nasreen took the pad from Green and activated her radio. 'Sir, this is Cudmore. We know which towers have empty flats, but not which flats are empty, over.'

The radio crackled in reply. 'Okay, over.'

'Three in alpha, seven in foxtrot, two in lima, five in Juliet, over.' Chips was in Tower F already. The next highest potential cluster of empty flats was Tower J.

'Received, over,' crackled her radio.

'Green and I are switching to Tower Juliet, over,' she said.

'Received, over,' came Saunders reply.

'Ready?' she said to Green. Green nodded. They had to pick up their pace.

The entry doors of Tower J were supposed to be locked and only accessible by intercom, but the latch didn't catch. The intercom had been ripped from the wall. Discolouration where the keypad had once been showed it wasn't a recent separation. The building wasn't secure. How many of the towers were like this? Looking up, she could see the bent chewed arm where a CCTV camera had once been trained on the door. They'd get nothing from surveillance. She swallowed. The tunnels underneath, and the lack of security, meant anyone could come and go. There were multiple routes someone could take to hide, escape or move a body.

'I think we should go down first, check out the tunnels,' she said to Green.

'Great. I love dark enclosed spaces full of gang drug runners.' Green took her torch from her belt. Nasreen hoped Kate wasn't claustrophobic. Freddie hadn't been frightened of the dark when they were growing up, but a lot had happened since then. 'How do we get down?' Green said.

She looked at the blueprint photo on her phone, and at Benedict's map. 'That way. I think.' Red tiles ran three quarters of the way up the walls of the Dogberry Tower J entrance hall, presumably once a playful pop art design. Now they were scratched and dull, and gave the place the air of a faded butcher's. Nice. Dark wooden doors robbed the room of any natural light, and their panels of blue shatterproof glass made it feel cold despite the trapped humidity. Pushing a door open, Nasreen saw a dirty white corridor, with blue-painted flat doors stretching away from them. Doormats, presumably assigned to certain homes, had dislodged and floated like teabags in the milky tan of the floor. She glanced up at the ceiling, like an upside-down ice-cube tray resting on top of them. There was nothing that looked like it corresponded to their map. 'It's not this way – try that one.' She pointed at the identical heavy wooden door behind Green.

Green pushed it, and it opened onto a grey concrete stairwell. The scent of rubbish floated up from below. Rotten eggs.

'Looks promising,' Nasreen said.

'Oh, goodie.'

It was cooler inside the stairwell. Nasreen ran her fingers over the rough concrete as they descended quickly. They needed to cover as much ground as possible. She reminded herself that her colleagues and the armed response unit were only a radio call away.

'So how do we get into these tunnels then?' Green's voice echoed.

Flies buzzed around them. Nasreen held the back of her hand to her nose to block out the smell that was growing stronger. 'I'm guessing this is the evacuation staircase. It leads to the bins outside, and then there should be another door off there.'

The concrete stairs stopped, and pooled into the lower ground floor. One door led to the bins. The doorway to the lifts was at the other end of the room. She spun round again. 'It must be off here somewhere.' She took in the dark stained walls, the stray takeaway cartons and congealing milk bottles that trailed the edges. On the far wall was what looked like a panel, the same shape as a door. Scuffed faintly down one side. 'That has to be it.'

She and Green ran their fingers round the seam, pushing at every point. She could feel air with her fingers. But it didn't give.

'Perhaps it opens from the other side?' Green had given it a firm shove with her body, and was brushing grime from the shoulder of her shirt.

Nasreen bent down; there were sweeps in the dust on the floor, curving outwards. Fresh. 'Someone's been here recently.'

'Coming out? I can't see how they could get in.'

Nasreen looked along from them. 'There's a brick there – could have been a wedge.'

'So how do we get in?' Green puffed her fringe away from her forehead. 'Does it say anything on the plans?'

Nasreen looked at the photo again. Zooming in to the measurements and unintelligible architect markings. There was nothing on Benedict's map. They needed to get this door open. Freddie could be in there. She rested her ear against it: listened. Nothing. 'We need something to lever it open with?'

'Credit card?' Green said.

'Not sure it'll be long enough.' The air coming from the other side blew softly against her face. Could Freddie and Kate feel that breeze too? Were they in there in the tunnel, awaiting help? 'We need something else.' They kicked over rubbish, looking for an implement. Nasreen turned over a polystyrene takeaway box, and a plastic knife and fork fell out. 'Ah!'

She rammed the fork prongs into the gap of the panel; it wobbled and moved toward them.

Snap!

The prongs broke off and fired toward her, landing disconcertingly near her mouth. She spat, not wanting to think about what might have been the last thing to touch them. A rat scuttled across the back wall.

'Urgh,' Green said.

'If Freddie were here, she'd be doing her Roland Rat impression.' It was comforting to think of Freddie making jokes. Nasreen slid the knife in further, further; it caught on the underside of the door and she levered it. Her nail bent back as she caught hold of it and tugged.

The panel swung out like a door. They pinned themselves to the sides in case there was anyone there, but all they could see was the entrance to the tunnel, rectangular, with pipe work running along the ceiling away from them into the darkness. Like peering into the mouth of a snake.

'This is it then,' Green said.

Nasreen held up her hand to shush her, straining to hear. Disturbing a gang drug run wouldn't be a good move, but it was silent. How much noise had they made getting the door open? Was Benedict hiding in the dark, his hand over Freddie's mouth? Or were they in one of the other tunnels? This was just one. They were just two people. They had to keep going at it methodically. One centimetre at a time.

She used the brick to prop the door open. The dark closed round them like a damp blanket. Nasreen thought of the waterlogged hoodie that clung to Calinda's body. Flicking on her torch, her heartbeat rocketed. Her skin prickled. She bent down and placed a finger on the dark splash; it came away wet and dark. 'Blood: they've come this way.' She clicked her radio, but nothing but static played. 'You got any signal down here?' The bars on her phone were empty.

'No.' Green tried her own radio. 'We must be too low for the signal. Should we go back? Raise the alarm?'

Nasreen spotted another glisten. A bigger splash this time. A few steps away. Freddie was still losing blood. Too much. She imagined her lying unconscious in this dark. Another rat scurried past, its tail a sickening swish in the gloom. Water dripped from the pipes above. 'No. This is fresh. We keep going. If we find them, we'll go for backup.'

Green angled her flashlight at the ground. Between them they swept it like a carpet, eyes down, ears pricked, looking. The torch flicked in time with Nasreen's heartbeat as they walked into the black heart of the tunnel.

Freddie

'Where are we going?' Freddie repeated the question as the man waved them through. He signalled for Kate to go first, presumably because if Freddie had stuck her blood-covered head round the door anyone in the corridor might have freaked out. She looked at the blood on her hands. Quite rightly so.

'In there.' He pointed at a flat door opposite. 'Hurry the fuck up.' He shoved her out after Kate. The hallway was long and empty. She could cry out – but would anyone come? She remembered reading some stupid internet meme about shouting 'Fire! Fire!' if you were being attacked, but from the scorch marks on the walls she thought the residents probably wouldn't flinch at all. Besides, shouting once had already seen her get pistol-whipped. She couldn't tell if it had split open her old scar or opened a new one. She touched her forehead. Would she be alive to care?

Kate was struggling with the flat door in front of her.

'Kick it!' the man commanded.

Kate pushed it.

'Hurry the fuck up.' He was getting agitated.

Freddie moved alongside Kate, thought about how she'd seen Nas do this. Turned, barged her shoulder into it. The door gave.

A smell hit them straight away, something rotten, and bleach, a lot of bleach. Kate staggered back. 'No, no. Please no!'

He shoved Freddie again, so she saw the hallway and the room beyond it at a twist. She slammed into Kate. Her fear was contagious. Whatever she could see, Freddie didn't want to. The hallway was deserted. Silent. If she was going to scream it had to be now.

The man stepped forward, waving the gun up. 'In there.' *Now. She had to do it now.* 'Help!' she yelled.

His elbow smacked into her head. Kate screamed. Freddie flew backwards, slammed into the doorframe. They fell. The side of his foot connected with Freddie's ribs and she felt them concertina, snap. Sharp. Burning. Stabs. A net of agony shimmered over her skin. Her vision shook.

'Please!' Kate screamed. She didn't know if it was at him or her.

She felt Kate's hands close over her arms and pull her backwards. Away from him. Black mist appeared, like wet watercolour paint in her sight. She fought to stay conscious.

The man stepped over the threshold and pulled the door shut behind him. Blocking them from the outside world. Blocking them from help. No one had heard her. No one had come.

It was then that Freddie saw what had frightened Kate. Spray-painted on the wall were two symbols that looked like an animal and a circle. A single bulb hung from the Artex ceiling. A discoloured duvet lay on the floor. This was the room the photofit artist had drawn. Someone had tried to scrub it out, wash it off with bleach, but everything was covered in smears of brown-red. Dried blood. This was where he did it. This was where he'd raped and murdered Calinda. Freddie's jagged breath quickened, burning over her trampled ribs. Her eyes scanned the room, taking in the one new addition. In a neat pile in the corner, like they'd just been unpacked. A roll of masking tape. A roll of black bin bags. New bottles of bleach. A small pile of knives. Kate was crying softly behind her.

Oh, Tibbsy, I'm so sorry I never got to tell you.

Nasreen

The blood dots had grown further apart. Nasreen tried to recall everything she knew about forensics. Had the bleeding slowed? Or was the victim running? The word 'victim' jarred in her head. She'd been counting her steps. Measuring a metre with her stride. It'd been nineteen steps since the last blood dot. They'd passed discarded cans. Cigarette butts. Syringes. Working in concentrated silence. Fast. She should have radioed where they were going. They were alone down here. Alone apart from Freddie, Kate and Benedict. And possibly half of the Dogberry Boys. What if the blood wasn't from Freddie or Kate? What if it was some random junkie who was stumbling around down here? No. There was too much for that. It was too fresh. Could be a knife wound. Or a bullet wound.

She checked her phone again. No signal. How deep had

they gone? Were they under the original tower or had they reached the next? The silence worried her. The pipes rumbled and echoed towards them, like a train. The first time it had happened they'd frozen. But it must just be water, or waste, or whatever else might be dripping down on them from above. If there was anyone else down here they'd have heard them, surely. Forty, forty-one, forty-two. This was the biggest gap between dots so far. 'It's stopped.'

'Did we miss a door?' Green's face was puckered with concentration, her eyes working across the ground in front of them. 'Perhaps she stopped bleeding? Or only started here?'

A fresh injury? A fresh attack? They hadn't found a body, she reminded herself. Freddie was still moving. That meant there was still time. 'Let's go back over the way we came. Maybe they went into one of the other towers – maybe we passed another panel?'

The tunnel looked identical in both directions. The photo of the plan was beginning to look like a map she couldn't read.

They must have missed something. She was letting the fear win. She was getting distracted. She tried to ignore the rising panic in her chest. Forget it's Freddie, she told herself. You're just doing your job. Do your job. You can do this. The pipes clattered and roared towards them, rattling fear in her ears.

They moved quicker this time. The necessity raw between them. They both knew that the longer Benedict had them, the less chance there was of finding them alive. He had killed before. Instead of running, he'd chosen to do this. He must know they were going to come for him. He was going to exact his revenge.

'Here.' Green stopped. 'This was the last bit I saw.' The blood splatter was tiny, tear-shaped.

'Me too,' Nasreen said. 'Okay. Check the walls, see if there's another panel. We might have missed it.'

She took the left hand side, running her hand up and along the wall, moving away from where they were, radiating outwards. They needed more light. The torch beam was strong, but too diluted over large areas.

'Sarg!' Green shouted. She was on the other side of the tunnel, further along than Nasreen. Looking up. 'Got it!'

It was only when she reached Green's side that Nasreen saw the rungs embedded in the concrete. They'd been looking down, studying the floor.

'There are hand marks – look.' Green shone her torch at the ladder. It was coated in dust, a dull grey-green like everything else down here, but there were smudges in the dirt. Fresh smudges, overlapping and covering each other. They would obscure some of the forensics if they climbed it but there was no choice.

'Gloves on,' Nasreen said. 'Let's go.'

'What if they're up there?' Green's torchlight stretched above them. The ceiling was high.

Nasreen checked along the tunnel. 'I'll go first.'

She put her torch in her mouth, gripped the bars. They were cool to the touch under the rustle of her plastic gloves, and she soon hauled herself up. Her breathing was magnified by the position of the torch; she tried to swallow the saliva pooling round it. She could feel air. Warm air. At the top there was a hatch. Metal, round, with a handle sculpted from metal.

'You okay?' Green whispered.

'Yeah,' she said through the torch. 'Handle. Get ready.'

She saw Green's torch beam wobble as she stepped back, heard her flick open her ASP with a snap. He could be the other side of this. He was armed. She should call for backup. She should go back and get the armed response unit. But he had Freddie.

One, two, three. She pushed open the hatch with all her might, ducking down as the sunlight poured onto her. She hurled herself up, wielding her torch. It took a moment for her to orientate herself. It was a patch of wasteland. Concrete pockmarked with weeds opened in a slab around her; turning back, she could see the Dogberry estate in the distance. They were behind it. They'd walked a long way. Maybe a mile. She couldn't see the police vehicles, but she knew they were on the other side. Turning, she took in the car. Red. Corsa. Y reg number plate. And her heart lurched. Green shouted her name, echoing up out of the tunnel behind her as she sprinted to the car.

The driver's door was open. Empty. No one was inside. Oh God. Oh God. The boot. Her heart thumped in her chest. Overhead she heard a gull calling. The air was thick as she walked toward the boot. It was open. Like the lid of a display box. Steeling herself, Nasreen stepped towards it. Her relief at finding it empty was fleeting. It was stained with blood, soaked. Inside, tucked just under a pair of wellies, she saw what she'd been dreading. Another of Freddie's business cards: Freddie was the one who was hurt. Scratched into it in shaky, crusty red were two letters: K and F. Freddie was the one bleeding. She was the one in the boot.

Green had appeared out the top of the manhole. 'Kate's car!'

The blood in the tunnel. The spots. The ladder. The car.

'It's hers, right, Sarg?' Green, was next to her, red-faced.

Shit. 'We've been following the trail the wrong way. They were going the other way.' Nasreen's pulse raced. One mile. She sprinted back to the ladder. Pressed her radio into life. 'Vehicle found approximately one mile from the Dogberry estate. Officers are in pursuit of suspect and two hostages. Reason to believe he entered the estate through the tunnel system underground. There's a blood trail underground. Going to follow it back. Request backup. Will radio when above ground.'

She clipped the radio onto her belt. Lowered herself down the ladder, two rungs at a time. 'Move it!' she shouted to Green. Stupid. Stupid. There'd been no sightings of the car at the estate: of course they came in another way. Green obscured the sun above her. They jumped the last few rungs. Nasreen took her torch out and ran. They were here. They must be. She ticked off the blood dots as she went, the torch-light bouncing. She could hear Green behind her. Her own torch bouncing up and into her vision. They came this way. They came this way and Freddie was bleeding. Bleeding badly.

Freddie

Freddie's head was thumping. She stared at the pile of goodies he'd prepared in the corner. 'You don't want to do this. If you let us go now it'll be better for you.'

'Shut up,' he snarled. 'You,' he said to Kate, 'sit.' He pointed at a dining chair with its wooden top snapped off, so that two prongs stuck up like fangs at the back.

Kate was pale-faced; she was breathing fast, whispering to herself as she half crawled, half stumbled to the chair. There was a cut on her face. A bruise on her cheek. Her top was torn.

Freddie clutched her side, still on the floor where she'd been dragged. She rolled herself up. Winced as she put weight on her arm.

'You: tape her up!' He kicked the roll of masking tape at Freddie.

Her own breathing was quick. Sore. The tape was heavy in

353

her hand, but not heavy enough to use as a weapon. Not that she thought she could swing it. Cupping her ribs helped.

His eyes followed her as she moved across the floor. She could hear Kate praying.

'*Our father who art in heaven, hallowed be they name...*'

'I work with the police. They'll know we're missing by now,' she said, her voice ripped at the edges. But it helped to talk. 'There are two of us. I know you didn't plan that.' Freddie squeezed Kate's hand trying to reassure her. 'They'll be looking for us. They'll be coming for you.'

'*...forgive us our debts, as we forgive our debtors...*'

He smiled. Kicked the duvet out from the corner. It was caked with blood: brown in places rather than red. She could hear the panic in Kate's breath. Freddie bent down with the tape. As she did so, she slid her ring off and put it between the fingers of Kate's right hand. Bought from Brick Lane Market, it was a stone wrapped in metal. Weighty. The stone made a point. An edge. *You can use this to get free.* Kate's fingers closed over the ring.

'What are you doing?' he snarled.

'Couldn't get the edge.' Freddie pulled off a length of tape and bit it with her teeth. The tape snagged on her lip and she thought: DNA. *My DNA will be on this when they find us.*

He walked towards them, and she quickly wrapped the tape around Kate's hand so that he wouldn't see the ring.

'Tighter,' he instructed. Freddie hesitated. If she wound it around again, would Kate be able to get out? The ring could get through one bit of tape, but maybe not two. He sensed her reluctance. 'Again.' She'd wound the tape three times now.

She tried not to press the edges: tried to give Kate a fighting chance. 'Over there.' He indicated for her to move.

Her nose whistled when she breathed. Blood clogged in it. He seemed remarkably untouched. As if he'd just popped to the shops, rather than kidnapped two women. She had to try again.

'We know things got out of hand that night.'

'You don't know anything,' he said.

'Please,' Kate said, her voice cracking. 'Let us go, please.'

'You're young, what, eighteen? Nineteen?' He smiled again. 'Don't make it worse.' If she could make him understand, if she could reach him, then there was still a chance. What would Nas do? She glanced at the bleach and black bin bags in the corner.

She looked back at him. The smile on his face had spread. She swallowed. It was a leer. His eyes were cold. Void. How did she not see that back at the house? When she'd knocked on the door? Why did she not realise he was a threat? Nas would have known. Slowly, deliberately he raised the gun. Freddie froze. Every cell of her body screamed, but she made no sound. If she could just make him understand… But what he said next told her that there was no hope. No understanding. There was no good side to reach.

The smile played on his lips. 'Take off your shorts.'

Nasreen

Nasreen burst back into the concrete stairwell, the stench freshly assaulting her senses. Which way did they go? Which way? She fell onto her knees, looking, looking: she had to find a blood drop. Find a card. Something.

Green was behind her.

'There must be a way to the other stairs, the back ones Josh took the body up.' She combed the floor with her fingers, looked around and around. How could they not see it?

Green's radio crackled. 'Shit. Still no signal, I'm going up. I'll request search in here,' she said.

When Green pulled the door into the staircase Nasreen heard it. Suction. The door to the tunnel was still propped open with the brick. But she heard it. There was a vacuum. She ran across and tugged at the door again. Listened. Tried to quiet her heartbeat. That was it. She heard it. Behind her.

Shit. Of course. The door wasn't in this room, it was in the entrance to the tunnel. That was how they'd passed unseen: they hadn't even come into the bin area. She looked at the bins, big, blue, industrial, lined up against the wall at the back. Was that the original wall? There was no time to think.

She raced back into the tunnel, turned, looked. Felt the breeze. Another panel. Pushed. Hard. It opened into a small foyer, dark and damp. Bingo. A metal staircase stretched up before her. Nasreen shone her torch along the steps. Blood. There. And in the corner, as if it had fallen, or been dropped, a white card. This was it. She tried her radio again as she climbed. Fast. It crackled with static. And again. Her steps echoed up above her. She kept her eyes on the floor. Come on, Freddie, one more, one more. Her breathing came fast. Her leg muscles pumped. Clang, clang, clang went her steps. There! Another card! Jammed down the side of the step.

'Sarg!' She heard Green shout, muffled below her.

She tried her radio again. This time the static stretched, grew, held. 'This is DS Cudmore, I am in pursuit of target. There is a back staircase. Repeat: there is a back staircase. It's behind the bins in the cellar. Request immediate backup.'

The radio crackled back, echoed up from below. 'I'm coming!' Green's voice burst through the vacuum.

Clang, clang, clang went Nasreen's boots. Hang on, Freddie. Hang on, I'm coming.

Freddie

'No.' The word was panicked. She was panicked. She knew that. Couldn't calm down.

He took a step backwards; his eyes raked over her body. Freddie felt sick. Without looking away he picked a glass bottle from the floor.

'No!' Kate shouted.

Thunder crashed through Freddie's ears. Blood pumped hard and fast round her head. 'No.' She shook her head. Looked at the door. It was six metres at most – could she make it out? Could she shout? No one was coming.

Kate screamed as he raised the bottle. Freddie ran at him as he brought it down, shattering it against the side of the chair. Shards skimmed Kate's body. A dark curve sprang onto her arm.

He whirled back to Freddie, gun in one hand, wielding the jagged edges of the bottle at her. 'I told you to strip.'

She stepped backwards. Her feet caught the duvet. She fell. Her hands hit dried blood, scrabbled against the fabric like Calinda's hands had done. He laughed.

'Please, don't!' Kate begged. 'Please.'

'But you like to watch, don't you?' he snarled.

Freddie shook her head. Tried to speak. Tried to shout. Panic had her around the throat.

He lifted the gun, pointed it at Kate. He was calm, enjoying her terror. 'Do it, or I kill her.'

Freddie shook her head. Pushed back, the duvet slid on the floor under her. He'd done it here before. On this. He was going to do it again. In two quick strides he reached her. Freddie looked up. Saw nothing but him. His eyes. His smile. He kicked her feet away.

No. No. No.

He fell onto her, dropped the bottle, grabbed her hip. Pulled her toward him. Her head slammed into the floor.

She tried to open her mouth to scream but no sound came. He dug his knees into her legs. The pain. Pinned her shoulder with his elbow. Pulled at her waistband. She kicked her legs. Bucked. Rage found its way through her; hot, white, raw. She would not go quietly. 'No!' Freddie punched up with two fists into his shoulders.

'Stop fighting!' The back of his hand cracked against her cheekbone. She saw her own blood splatter against the wall. Mixing with Calinda's. The black mist surged. He yanked her shorts, ripping them over her hips. She couldn't stop him. Felt his breath on her cheek.

Kate roared. Pushed up onto her feet, the chair still attached to her back and ran at them. 'No!'

He looked away, just for a second. Freddie slammed her elbow into his face, as the tape that had bound Kate to the chair snapped. The chair came hurtling towards them. Wood splintered.

The gunshot slashed through the room.

Freddie watched flecks of wood rain like stars in slow motion.

The bullet ripped into Kate's body, hurling her backwards. Freddie watched her thud and shudder onto the ground.

The screaming came rushing back into her ears. Her screaming. She had to help Kate. Freddie reached for the bottle. Slammed it into his side.

'Fuck!' he screamed. The gun was aimed at her. 'You fucking bitch, die!'

Freddie closed her eyes.

A crack sounded loudly behind them. She looked up to see him turn. Nas! Nas was through the door.

'Drop your weapon!' Nas bellowed as she swung her baton at him. Green was behind her.

Both of the officers were on him. Freddie scrambled back, away from them all. Into the corner. Pulled at her shorts. Held them to her, shaking. Hugging her knees tight.

Green had the gun. Freddie could hear shouts from outside. Footsteps.

'Benedict Petrosyan, I am arresting you for the rape and murder of Calinda…'

As armed police burst into the room, Freddie saw her. Kate Adiyiah, lying on her side, still where she'd fallen. Tiny flecks of blood on her eyelashes.

Nasreen

'Stay with me, Kate, stay with me!' Nasreen had Kate on her back. The beads in her hair splayed across the floor. Her eyelashes quivered. 'We need a paramedic up here now!'

'She should have stayed out of it! Minded her business,' Benedict shouted as one of the armed unit dragged him from the room. 'You've got the wrong guy! It was Josh! Josh did it!'

Like hell he did. Nasreen took in the devastation in the room. 'Freddie, you shot? Cut?' she shouted.

'You've got to help Kate!' Freddie screamed; she heard her scrabble towards them. Fall.

Behind Nasreen, one of the armed unit ran to help her. 'Don't try to move, honey.'

'Stay calm, Freddie,' she said, trying to sound reassuring.

'This is DC Green, we need immediate paramedic assistance

361

in Tower L...' Green was next to Nasreen, applying pressure to Kate's shoulder wound. Blood pulsed up through her fingers.

Nasreen felt Kate exhale. No pulse. 'No pulse,' she shouted. Green met her eyes. How long before they got help up here? Nasreen tilted Kate's head back, pinched her nose and breathed twice into her mouth. Kate's chest rose. She interlocked her fingers and pumped down onto her breastbone, fast. 'One, two, three, four, five, six, seven...'

She could hear Freddie crying behind her.

'Twelve, thirteen, fourteen, fifteen... Come on, Kate! Come on! Breathe!'

Everything around Nasreen fell away. It was just her and Green, fighting. Time became fluid, floated around them. *Twenty-seven, twenty-eight, twenty-nine, thirty. Breathe two. One, two, three, four...*

In a neon-yellow blur the paramedics arrived, and Nasreen was pulled back as they took over. Kate's face was covered with an oxygen mask.

Nasreen reached out for Freddie as she was taken past, wrapped in a blanket. Her fingers brushed her friend's hand. *Oh God, she'd almost lost her.*

One of the paramedics ripped Kate's shirt open as they prepared the defibrillator.

'Clear!' shouted the other. Kate's body jolted. Nothing.

Nasreen tried to speak. She should have got here sooner. Should have run faster. Should have tried harder. Green sobbed.

'Clear!' Kate's body jolted. Nothing.

Nasreen turned to see Saunders standing by the door, his face ashen. She blundered past him out into the corridor.

Uniformed officers were running to and from the room. Radios crackled.

'Are you okay, Sarg?' someone called, but she kept going.

Pushing into the stairwell she found Burgone, breathless from running up the stairs, looking up at her from two steps down, panic in his eyes.

'Oh my God, Nas, are you hurt?' He ran toward her and took hold of her hands. It was only then that she saw they were covered in Kate's blood. She shook her head. Tried to speak. *I'm sorry. I'm so sorry.*

As Burgone folded her into him and stroked her hair, Nasreen let the tears come. Outside it started to rain.

Freddie

Five Weeks Later

Freddie got off the tube and came out opposite a Chicken Cottage. Orientating herself, she saw a newsagent next to a florist, the front full of artfully stacked expensive flowers. She crossed the road and walked under the overpass, checking Google Maps on her phone.

Her ribs made her walking slower than usual, but that wasn't a bad thing. She'd been back at work a few days now, Burgone joking that he'd send her on hand-to-hand combat training. Chips bringing her coffee the morning. Nas seemed to be doing okay. They'd spent a lot of time together, talking about what had happened. Both of them reassuring the other it wasn't their fault. Chance had brought Calinda to a party on the Dogberry estate. And chance had meant Kate witnessed what happened to her. But Benedict Petrosyan was responsible for both their deaths. His actions on that awful afternoon would strengthen Josh Chapman's case that he had been manipulated and coerced by the older boy. Saunders had apparently, off record, recommended a good lawyer to Mrs Chapman. Calinda Gallo's parents would see the right man held to account for the death of their daughter.

Which just left the ongoing investigation into the Spice Road drugs website. Freddie had read up on Paul Robertson, the hardened criminal who'd handed himself in to save another parent the heartache of not knowing what had happened to their daughter. Trident were delighted to get their hands on the wanted man, and were pushing ahead with charges of drug dealing, possession and supplying an illegal firearm. Paul Robertson had resolutely refused to cooperate with all police staff. Except one.

Descending the concrete steps past pots of fading red flowers, Freddie felt the cool of the shade. The temperature was pleasant for what felt like the first time in weeks. She knocked at the door. A dark shape approached, distorted through the patterned glass in the door. It opened to reveal Lex Riley.

'What do you want?' His face was set in a sneer. Designed to be threatening, no doubt.

Freddie fingered her business card in her pocket. 'I want to speak to Amber,' she said.

'Not this again,' Lex growled. 'You pigs stupid or something? I told you I don't know no Amber.'

Freddie didn't move. 'I've got a message for her from her dad.'

Lex's face shifted. There was movement behind him, and

365

a girl with cropped blonde hair stepped into view from the bedroom. 'It's all right, let her in, Lex.'

His shoulders sagged, but he stepped back, holding the door for Freddie. 'Hello, Amber,' she said.

*

'How did you know?' They were sat round the kitchen table, a glass of water in front of each of them.

Amber seemed older than in the photo they had of her, and it wasn't just the hair. She looked well. Happy. Freddie recognised something in the relaxed way she held herself: *love*. If it wasn't totally saccharine, she might have mused on how Paul's love for his daughter had changed more than just the lives in this room.

'When we came before, Lex was drinking a protein shake made with milk, but the fridge was full of soya products,' she said. 'I knew there must be someone else living here. But I didn't put two and two together until I realised you were playing the album you guys had discussed on Facebook. Plus that Alpro stuff's minging – no one would eat it unless they had to.'

Amber smiled. 'That's what C. always says.'

'Corey?' Freddie remembered the name the old lady had called Lex on the first day.

'It was my dad's name,' he said. 'We thought it was best to change a couple of things. Go incognito, like?'

Freddie nodded. 'Was it always for real? You two?'

Amber took Corey's hand and smiled at him. He grinned back like a loon. 'It was a trap to begin with. Corey wanted to get to my dad through me…' She said it as if it was a joke.

366

'But then I met her and everything changed.' He smiled. It was ridiculous: hard man as soppy love interest. But then this was the same young woman who had inspired Paul Robertson to hand himself in. *Love*. 'She's like no one else I've ever known. It just sorta grew from there.'

'Does your father know?' Freddie asked Amber.

'No.' Amber shook her head. 'He'd never allow it. Dad saw me leaving the Dogberry estate once – I told him I'd been meeting a friend but he still hit the roof.' Freddie wondered if that was the fight in the street Tibbsy had interrupted. 'He'd never understand, you see? Corey – Lex – was one of the Dogberrys.'

'Not by choice. It was my fam,' Lex added. 'It was what you did. But I'm out now.' His face shifted when he spoke to her: it became harder, more guarded.

'We saw you with your cousin,' Freddie said. She had to make sure he was for real.

Amber shifted in her seat.

'He asked me to do one last job, but I'm not interested,' he said.

'Uber?' Freddie said, remembering he'd said he was a driver.

'Yeah. I'm gonna set up my own car company. Proper mint, you know, for airport trips and stuff. Amber's helping me with my business proposal. I'm gonna get a Merc. Real nice. Do it properly,' he said.

The tattoo on his arm had been changed; the dragon head was gone, a Celtic symbol extended over it instead. 'You covered up your tattoo?'

He rubbed at it. 'Part of the deal. Jay said I had to disappear. Totally. No mates. Never go near the estate again.'

Freddie nodded. 'Hence the driving – you can control which areas you work.'

Lex nodded. 'Lex is dead. It's Corey now. Corey and Amber.' He pulled Amber's hand towards him and kissed it.

Amber basked in his love, unconsciously stroking her own stomach. *A tell.* Freddie had read about them in her Civilian Investigator training notes.

'I think your dad might surprise you, Amber.'

'Have you seen him? Is he okay? He's not…' Her words trailed off. A worried daughter.

'He turned himself in,' Freddie said.

'What?' Amber looked shocked.

'He had some information pertaining to another case. Information about someone else's missing daughter.' Amber's eyes grew wide. Freddie continued. 'He said he would want to know if it was him. If it was you. He thought you were dead. Taken by the Dogberrys.'

Amber blinked and a tear fell down her cheek, tracing a faint path in her foundation.

'He's being held at Thameside until his trial.' Freddie put the visitors' leaflet down on the table. 'I know he'd like to see you.' She paused. 'To know your news.'

Amber's hand flew back to her stomach. She looked at Lex, anxious, questioning. He nodded. 'You should go, babe. I'll drive you.'

'You're still at college?' Freddie said. It must be daunting.

'It wasn't planned. I'm not stupid. But my IBS must have upset my pill: hence the soya stuff now. I was so scared about telling Corey when I knew I was five days late, but he's been brilliant.' She smiled. 'I'm going to take a year off,' she said.

'I've cleared it already with my teachers. Corey is going to babysit during the day when I go back. I'll only be a year late to uni, and I've already rung my first choice: they've got a crèche we'll be able to use.'

'My girl's going to be a doctor.' Lex kissed the side of her head.

Freddie hoped it all came true for her. They'd sacrificed everything they'd ever known to get here. She thought of Tibbsy.

'You said you had a message from Dad?' Amber said.

'He says he loves you very much. And he's sorry,' Freddie stood to go.

Lex walked her to the door, his built frame no longer threatening, but a safe harbour for Amber and their new family. 'Thank you,' he said quietly. 'It's the only thing she gets down about.'

'No worries. Everyone deserves a second chance,' she said.

Outside she checked her emails. Saunders had sent over some stats requests: a new lead in the hunt for the Spice Road owners. A forwarded joke from Chips. And an email thanking her for her donation to the Kate Adiyiah Memorial Foundation for Young Women. Freddie swallowed the lump in her throat. *Without you, Kate, we wouldn't have found Amber Robertson either. Another child reunited with their parent.*

A taxi drove by and she looked up. Pulled herself together. She had to get a move on if she wanted to get to M&S in time to pick up a chocolate pud on the way home. Nas, Green and her Mrs were coming over to Tibbsy's for paella tonight. *To theirs.* No more sofa surfing, no more commuting in from her parents', no more begging to borrow a bit of a mate's floor to kip on. She'd done it. Moved in with Tibbsy. She was no longer homeless. *Love,* she thought with a smile. It was a funny thing.

Kate

Her ears rang but there was no pain.

She felt no fear.

Kate blinked.

The sun dipped and shone, filling the room. Obliterated everything. A shape in the yellow light was stepping over the cans.

Tegbee? But she hadn't taken a pill today. Had she?

Her daughter's bare feet lifted up over the rubbish, then the flowers. There was grass all around them. She could feel it, cool and soft under her face and fingers.

'What are you doing down there, mama?'

She'd been sunbathing. Must have dozed off. That was it. 'Just your old ma having a rest,' she said.

Tegbee laughed, her eyes shining like black amber. Her beautiful daughter. 'You're not old!' she said.

Kate pushed herself up. There was a palm tree above, bathing her in cool shade. A light breeze blew. Was it off the sea? 'I think I've forgotten something.'

Tegbee laughed again. 'No, you haven't. You did everything before we left. You went through your list twice, like usual.'

Kate smiled. She could smell the fresh fish frying from the street stalls. They'd have kenkey sourdough dumplings for supper. But there was something, she was sure, something she should have done. Something to do with a girl with long dark hair.

'You did it all, mama,' Tegbee said. 'Everything's okay now.'

And it must be then. Standing up she could see that the grass edged onto the beach. There was a man playing the guitar. And she could hear the waves and laughter coming from the water's edge. Tegbee was already ahead of her, singing along. 'Come on, hurry up,' she said with a giggle.

Kate had never felt so happy. 'Hang on, baby girl, mama's coming,' she called.

And she stepped into the sunlight.

The End

Acknowledgements

This book, and indeed my career, would never had happened if it weren't for the force of nature, and goddess of goodness that is my agent Diana Beaumont at Marjacq. I'd also like to thank all at Marjacq and United Talent Agency for their help and ongoing support.

Thank you to my effervescent editor Phoebe Morgan for all her skill, time, and patience in helping me make this the best book it could be; and to the badass super star team at Avon, including Helena Sheffield, Helen Huthwaite, Hannah Welsh, Louis Patel, Rosie Foubister, Natasha Harding, Vicky Gilder, Tony Russell, and Oli Malcolm; and to Eli Dryden for believing in Freddie from day one.

Thank you to Elizabeth Haynes for her invaluable insight, advice and help with Freddie's role of Criminal Intelligence Analyst. Similarly, thank you to Merilyn Davies for Criminal

Intelligence Analyst information. Freddie definitely bends the rules of what she's allowed to do, so all inaccuracies are hers, or, indeed, mine; and to Nick Ramage and Neil White for answering what were probably very silly questions about criminal law. Thanks to @ScotlandYardCSI for CSI and DNA input. Any errors are my own. And thank you to Steve Kirby for water tank and plumbing advice, and generally allowing me to ask you weird questions while you tried to fix our toilet.

The crime scene is an incredibly warm, supportive, and sweary world and I'd like to offer blanket thanks to every one of the cocks out there.

To Wendy, Paul, Julie, Beth, and all at Orchard Physio for keeping me writing.

To all the book bloggers, book groups, reviewers, sharers, borrowers and readers who have supported the Social Media Murders Series: thank you.

Thank you also to Jenny Jarvis, Hayley King, Li Wania, Rosemary Harvey, James Harvey, Fleur Sinclair, Kate McNaughton, Lucy Peden, Amy Jones, Lauren Bravo, Erica Williams, and all my mates who go above and beyond; and to mum, dad, Chris, Guy, Hannah, Ani, Bertie, all the Clarkes, and all the Williams (and variations thereof).

Sarah Day and Claire McGowan always have my back, and most of my moaning, and are a core part of my 'when the apocalypse comes' plan, and I love them and thank them both. But I realised when I was copy editing Trust Me, that Claire had not only read this book before it went to print, but every single one of my four books before they went to print. She has given her time, her advice and her considerable skill to all of my works, and so I have dedicated this book to her. Thank you for always being there, mate.

And finally, to my wonderful Sammy, who I forgot to thank at the Watch Me launch, and who is still talking to me. If I let him get a word in edgeways.

To receive a free short story by Angela Clarke and other exclusive content, subscribe to the Pen Knife Readers and Writers Club here: http://angelaclarke.co.uk/free/

Reading Group Questions

1. *Trust Me* centres around the idea of a woman not being believed and being made to doubt herself. Why do you think this happens and how do you think it makes her feel?

2. Do you think Kate would have been treated differently if she was male rather than female? In what way?

3. The premise of this book is about teenagers filming brutal attacks and uploading them for all to see. What do you think attracts people to doing this sort of thing?

4. Why do you think people might want to watch violent videos? What can be done to counteract this?

5. Freddie and Nas both have complicated feelings around romance and relationships. Why do you think they are so different in this respect?

6. How do you think Freddie and Nas' friendship changes throughout the book? And if you've read *Follow Me* and *Watch Me*, how do you think their friendship has progressed in the series?

7. There are several guilty people in this book. Who do you think is the most at fault?

8. How much sympathy did you feel towards Josh in this book?

9. Kate deals with a lot of grief over losing her daughter. Do you feel sorry for her in the end, or are you happy for her despite her fate?

10. What do you think the future holds for Freddie and Nas?

Q&A with Angela Clarke

1. *Trust Me* is the third of your brilliant Social Media Murders series, following your debut, *Follow Me*, and your second book *Watch Me*. Which has been your favourite of the three books to write? Why?

   That's such a difficult question – it's like you're asking me to pick between my children! Argh, no, every time I go to answer it I feel like I'm rejecting the others. I loved writing them all, though I do feel bad that so many awful things keep happening to Freddie and Nas. They just can't catch a break. Maybe I'll write a book where they just go on sunny beach holiday, drink too many dodgy cocktails and dance to Beyoncé and Salt n' Pepa. Though I guess that'll be less fun for the reader, and I reckon both Nas and Freddie would be bored after one day.

2. Your second novel, *Watch Me*, hit the Sunday Times best-seller list at number 15. How did you feel when you got the news?

I didn't believe it! I kept asking for photos to prove it. When I saw the book and my name in the official chart it was a staggering moment. I was speechless for a good five minutes (much to Mr Ange's delight!). Then I made this high-pitched noise, somewhere between a yelp and an excited snort. A yort! Then I had a celebratory glass (or several) of champagne.

3. Tell us a bit about your writing life now – how has it changed since being a debut author?

When I first started writing, like most authors, I was off contract, so I had all the time in the world. Nowadays, I have much stricter deadlines to stick to, so I try to be more structured. I try to get up early and write first thing in the day. But as soon as any pressure is applied I revert to type and work through the night, and don't get up until 9.30/10ish. I wish I kept more normal hours, but it doesn't seem to suit me or my work.

4. *Trust Me* deals with some fairly dark subjects – from rape to a mother's grief over losing her daughter. Did these topics affect you emotionally as you were writing?

I hate saying it, because I think it sounds a bit wanky, but yes, I did get very emotional writing certain scenes in *Trust*

Me. You grow so attached to characters, you're inside their heads, and that means you feel their pain and sadness too. As a writer, you have a duty of care to ensure you handle certain subjects properly. I wouldn't want to write about a rape in a titillating or sensationalist way. That scene was partially inspired by a real-life case. And I wanted to write about it because I think it's an important conversation to have: this has already happened once in real life, let's try and stop it from happening again. When you write crime, you explore the darker sides of human nature and interaction, in a way that is safe for the reader. But you have a responsibility to do that in a careful and considered way, while still giving a great story. After I wrote the rape scene I had to take a break. I spent time with my loved ones, and I reminded myself that for every person out there who hurts someone, there is a Kate, a Nas and a Freddie doing the best they can to help people.

5. How much research do you do for your novels? How long does it take you?

I tend to do a bit at the beginning, usually talking to someone who has a relevant job. For example, for this book I spoke to a Criminal Analyst, who'd worked with the police for a number of years. I keep it casual – usually over drinks or dinner – asking specific questions, but also letting the chat naturally go where it wants to. It lets me get a feel for their work, and how they would go about their working day, in a way that reading a job spec wouldn't. From there I tend to write the first draft. Once I've finished, I go back and fact check any bits I need to: forensic detail, for example. That way I'm not tempted to put in huge lumps of unnecessary detail, because I've learnt it specially. It feels more natural to include only the bits relevant to the story.

6. What has been the most difficult part of your writing career so far?

There is never enough time to get everything done. It always makes me laugh that so many people ask 'how do you come up with your ideas?' Coming up with ideas isn't the hard part, the hard part is finding enough time to write them all down!

7. What has been the best part of your writing career so far?

Having loved books and reading since being a kid, there really is little that beats holding your new book, box fresh, for that first time. It's like magic. All those words, all that story, that just came out of your mind, and now it's paper and ink and real. And new books smell so good too.

8. What advice would you give to an aspiring crime writer?

Read as much as you can. I always think it's a good idea to read the charting crime thrillers, as that tells you what is being bought by both publishers and readers right now. There's no substitution for getting to grips with your market.

9. What do you see yourself writing in the future?

So many things. I have so many ideas, it's hard to see what I wouldn't write. I'm currently working on a couple of independent feature films and that's a new and exciting thing for me. It's much more collaborative than book writing, which is both challenging and rewarding in different ways. But, then, I have ten thousand words of my next book down and some killer plans for what happens next, so it won't be long before I'm back on that.

10. How do you come up with new ideas for your books? Does your story have to be fully-formed in your head before you begin writing?

Once I have an idea, I spend some time plotting it roughly out. I tend to have about six key points in the book in mind before I start writing. But when I do start writing things can change. I may have decided those key plot points on what *I* would do in that situation, but my characters are different people, and once we get to those key crossroads they have been known to go off in different directions! There comes a point where you have to trust the characters and the story, and from there it just flows

LIKE. SHARE. FOLLOW . . . DIE.

FROM THE DEBUT CRIME BESTSELLER.

YOU'RE NOT ALONE.

FOLLOW ME

'Compelling'
EMERALD ST

'Chilling'
HELLO

ANGELA CLARKE

'Impossible to resist...Clarke is one to watch'
DAILY MAIL

Discover book one in the
Social Media Murder series,
an Amazon Debut of the Month.

Freddie and Nas are back!

YOU SHARE EVERYTHING. YOU'RE ALWAYS AT RISK.

WATCH ME

'Disturbing'
INDEPENDENT

'Slick and clever'
SUN

'Chilling'
HELLO

ANGELA CLARKE

'A fast-paced, unpredictable ride'
KATERINA DIAMOND, author of *THE TEACHER*

**But they're not safe.
And they're not the only
ones in danger.**

You can only run from the past for so long . . .

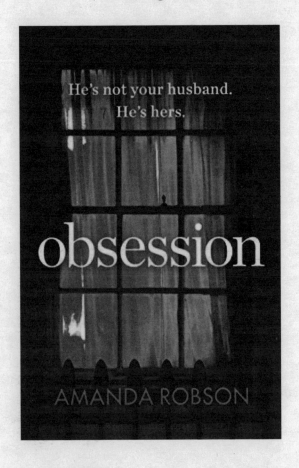

It will always catch up to you.

Looking for your next obsession?
Look no further . . .

'All hail the new Queen of Crime' *Heat*

The
Angel

Some things can't be forgiven...

THE *SUNDAY TIMES* BESTSELLER
KATERINA DIAMOND

A shocking psychological thriller where love affairs turn deadly.

For more heart-pounding suspense, try
the 'Queen of Crime' Katerina Diamond

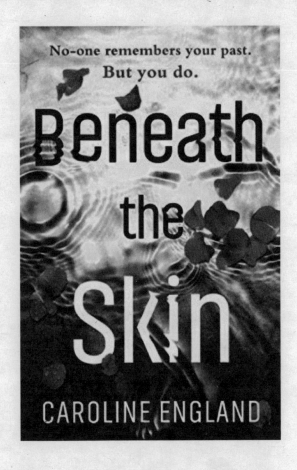

No-one remembers your past.
But you do.

Beneath
the
Skin

CAROLINE ENGLAND

Beware – not everything is as it seems . . .